Praise for

VINTAGE

"A wonderful, intelligent blockbuster ... I lapped it up!"
—Sophie Kinsella, *New York Times* bestselling author of
Remember Me?

"A dazzling tale following three women and their insatiable need for glamour, power and survival. Prepare for lust, betrayal and strictly no moral fibre."
—*Heat*, Top Ten Chart (UK)

"A return ... ie Collins is ... his book's a l ... en though I ... n-pagne I stil ... enjoyable read.
—Paper Cuts

"With three super-bitches slugging it out in the world of champagne ... a gro ...

"A ... bus ... ma ... and ... Gre ...

"We ... yard ... wind ... grov ...

The Urbana Free Library

DISCARDED BY THE
URBANA FREE LIBRARY

To renew materials call
217-367-4057

DATE DUE		6-09
JUL 13 2009	OCT 19 2009	
AUG 02 2009		
AUG 11 2009		

"As bubbly as a glass of champers."

—*Closer Magazine* (UK)

"I was thoroughly gripped by the book ... A very sexy fun read ... I really enjoyed it and I was actually quite sad to turn the final page!"

—TheBookbag.co.uk

"Champagne, shenanigans, skullduggery and grand cru sex ... *Vintage* has three heroines you genuinely care about, love-to-hate villains, and a parade of gossipy detail. Don't wait for the beach to enjoy this fantastic beach read; open up a chilled bottle of sparkling wine and enjoy it now!"

—Hester Browne, *New York Times* bestselling author of *The Little Lady Agency*

"A terrific debut from Olivia Darling. The sex pops like champagne corks, the action races along. Pure vintage fantasy. I loved it."

—Tilly Bagshawe, *New York Times* bestselling author of *Adored* and *Showdown*

Olivia Darling

A DELL BOOK

VINTAGE

A Dell Book / June 2009

Published by
Bantam Dell
A Division of Random House, Inc.
New York, New York

This is a work of fiction. Names, characters, places, and incidents either
are the product of the author's imagination or are used fictitiously.
Any resemblance to actual persons, living or dead, events, or
locales is entirely coincidental.

All rights reserved
Copyright © 2008 by Olivia Darling
Cover design: Yook Louie
Cover illustration: Alan Ayers

Book design by Ellen Cipriano

If you purchased this book without a cover, you should be aware that this
book is stolen property. It was reported as "unsold and destroyed" to the
publisher, and neither the author nor the publisher has received any
payment for this "stripped book."

Dell is a registered trademark of Random House, Inc., and the colophon is a
trademark of Random House, Inc.

ISBN 978-0-440-24514-8

Printed in the United States of America
Published simultaneously in Canada

www.bantamdell.com

OPM 10 9 8 7 6 5 4 3 2 1

To the man who inspired all my love scenes . . .

No, not you, dear. Him.

AUTHOR'S NOTE

In Champagne the term *"grand cru,"* French for "great growth," designates those vineyards considered to have the greatest potential for producing the very best wine. There are seventeen grand cru villages in the Champagne region. Le Vezy is my imaginary eighteenth.

VINTAGE

PROLOGUE

Champagne, France, twenty years ago...

Without dirt, there would be no champagne. As you hold your glass to the light and admire the pale golden fizz inside, consider this: a perfectly clean flute and your bubbly would not bubble. There would be no sparkle to your sparkling wine. Each glittering chain that rises to the surface originates from an imperfection, a minute blemish on the crystal, a fiber from a tea towel or a tiny speck of dust...

One last long string of bubbles escaped the girl's mouth as she drifted gently to the bottom of the river. Her silky brown hair shimmered around her face like waterweed, veiling those lips whose last kiss still lingered in Chanel rouge on the rim of a tulip-shaped glass. Her eyes were closed; her lashes perfect as they rested upon her smooth white cheeks. As she settled onto the riverbed, the current moved the girl's bare arms across her body, covering her beautiful breasts. Now she was a nymph, lulled to sleep by the waters of the Marne as it flowed south through the night toward Paris, opaque with the famous chalky sediment that made wine critics rave when they tasted it in a glass.

Nobody missed her yet. At the party in the house by the river, the wine was still flowing. The music was still playing. Young girls in tight dresses still laughed at jokes they didn't entirely understand, to please older guys who might find them the rent on an apartment in the sixteenth arrondissement. A waiter opened a bottle of vintage champagne—Salon—the proper way, turning the bottle and not the cork. Not a pop. Just a sigh and a wisp of vapor. No drop wasted. With one hand behind his back and the thumb of his other hand in the punt—the dimple at the bottom of the bottle—he poured out two glasses for a pair of expensively dressed revelers. One glassful barely effervesced.

"Oh," said the woman. "No bubbles. Is there something wrong with it?"

"Your glass must be too clean," her companion informed her. "You need dust to trap the tiny pockets of air that catalyze the fizzing action."

"I have no idea what you're talking about." She really did have no idea. This was her sixth glass of champagne that night and her schoolgirl French was somewhat rusty. Though her accent improved with alcohol, her comprehension didn't.

Her handsome companion looked deep into his own glass, considering the liquid inside as though examining the facets of a diamond.

"What are you thinking about?" the woman asked him.

She hoped that he was thinking about her naked. She wanted him to touch her. She wanted to run her fingers through his silver hair as he made love to her. Violently.

"I'm thinking that people are like champagne," he said eventually. "Our flaws are what make us sparkle."

"I think I know what you mean," she said.

She touched the rim of her glass to his. He raised it in a toast.

"*À nos imperfections,*" he said. "To our flaws."

PART ONE

CHAPTER 1

Room 512, The Gloria Hotel, Hyde Park, London

An empty champagne bottle lay on the floor. A half-eaten box of Belgian chocolates scattered its contents to the left of the wastebasket. A dozen red roses dripped dying petals onto the dressing table.

"That...was...brilliant..." Daniel sighed as he rolled onto his side in the big double bed.

Kelly Elson grimaced, then jumped up from the bed and went in search of a tissue, straightening her uniform along the way.

"Want me to do anything for you?" Daniel asked as she returned from the bathroom with a fistful of toilet paper.

"You don't need to," said Kelly.

"Good." Daniel lay back against the pillows looking smug. He reached out and gave one of her nipples a tweak.

Kelly fought the urge to punch him.

Oblivious to her annoyance, Daniel nodded toward the bottle on the floor. "I'll bring you some of that next time I see you. If you're a good girl."

"Thanks," she said flatly.

Champagne.

Again.

"I don't think anyone will notice if one little bottle goes missing." He smiled.

Daniel Weston sold booze for a national wholesaler. He visited the Gloria Hotel once a month to sell his plonk to Montrachet, the hotel's Michelin-starred restaurant. He liked to see Kelly after his appointments, if she could find an empty room. And he always brought along a little present. But it was never a bottle of vodka and some Diet Coke—something Kelly actually liked to drink. It always had to be some fancy wine with a name she couldn't pronounce. Daniel was pretentious about wine. Always spouting on about it. Nose? Legs? What the fuck did that mean? Most of what he said went over Kelly's head. Except for the words *"methode champenoise,"* which came to mind whenever she held Daniel's cock in her hand and went at it like a Formula One racing driver shaking a bottle of Mumm Cordon Rouge. That thought passed through Kelly's head again as Daniel squinted at the label on the empty champagne bottle. "Very nice," he said. "This house used to be legend."

"Uh-huh," said Kelly.

"Bugger." Daniel suddenly looked at his watch and jumped out of bed. "I should be at the Intercontinental in fifteen minutes."

He gave his penis a perfunctory wipe and pulled his trousers up.

"See you next month?" he asked.

"Sure."

He left the soggy wad of tissue on the bedside table like a tip. Next to the envelope he'd so neatly labeled with Kelly's name.

"Thanks a lot," said Kelly, counting out the five crisp tenners once he'd gone. She tucked the envelope into her pocket and surveyed the damage around her.

A patch of something unmentionable had dried into a patch the shape of America on the headboard. She would have to scrape that off. She got up, tugged her streaked brown hair back into a ponytail and pulled the dirty sheets off the bed. She threw the dying flowers that had been bought for someone else into the waste bin. She had just ten minutes to finish cleaning the room and get it ready for the next check-in.

Last of all, she picked up the champagne bottle that Daniel had so admired.

Champagne Arsenault declared the label.

"Champagne My Arse, more like," she muttered.

Then, not knowing quite why she did it, Kelly tipped the bottle upside down and caught the last drip of golden nectar on her tongue.

Actually, that's not bad, she thought. Not so bad at all.

CHAPTER 2

Nine o'clock on a Friday night. Madeleine Arsenault could think of far better places to be than sitting in a restaurant in London, no matter how many Michelin stars the chef had garnered with his nine-course tasting menu. It wasn't that the restaurant itself was so bad. The space was wonderful. It had been decorated impeccably with the kind of clever lighting that took twenty years off the clientele. And situated as it was on the fifteenth floor of the newly refurbished Gloria Hotel on the edge of Hyde Park, Montrachet had an absolutely breathtaking view of the city. But Madeleine had her back to the view that evening. The privilege of having something beautiful to look at was reserved for her esteemed guests.

"The good news," said her boss, Geoff, when he'd presented that evening's date to her, "is that I've secured a table at Montrachet. The bad news..."

The bad news was that Madeleine would be spending the evening across the table from Adam Freeman, of the investment banking division of the Ingerlander Bank. Quite the most unpleasant man in banking, if not a candidate for the most unpleasant man on earth.

"But I'm booked on the seven o'clock Eurostar," Madeleine protested. She was supposed to be heading back to her family home in France for the weekend. "My father is unwell."

"He'll last another night," Geoff insisted. "Tough as old boots, I thought you said. Get Tina to book you on the first train tomorrow. I want you at Montrachet with me, Madeleine. With the Ingerlander bid in place, Freeman's arse is the one we should be licking."

Madeleine winced.

"It's OK," said Geoff. "I don't think he's into that. But if he is..."

Madeleine shook her head. "I pray," she said to Geoff, "that it's merely the language barrier between us that makes me think you're saying something offensive."

Geoff smiled. "Good girl, Maddy. Wherever I end up, I'm taking you with me, I promise."

"That's what I'm afraid of," said Madeleine.

Geoff gave her a wink.

The news that Ingerlander Bank was launching a takeover bid had sent shock waves throughout the tiny Bank of Maine. Geoff feared for his job and well he might. He was closing on fifty. He had an expensive ex-wife, and two incredibly ungrateful daughters to finish putting through private school. Recently, he had been coloring his hair in an attempt to fool the Ingerlanders that he still had years before his sell-by date. Madeleine suspected he might even have had a shot of Botox in the crevasse between his eyebrows. It was going to take more than that, she thought sadly as she looked at him now.

Madeleine's situation was altogether different. She didn't have so much as a goldfish in the cool, white-painted Notting Hill apartment that had been her home for the past ten years. There were no other signatories on her credit cards. If she lost her job in the big takeover, would it be such a bad thing?

Possibly not, if remaining in her position meant that she would be working with Adam Freeman. He leered across the table at her as she settled into her seat. He was the kind of man you saw all over the City: tall and broad-shouldered but running to fat. Middle age wasn't doing him any favors. His hair loss highlighted the softness of his facial contours. Chin blurring into neck. His personality didn't make up for it.

Geoff was studying the wine list like a student looking for easy questions on a finals paper. He scratched the side of his face absentmindedly as he did so. Madeleine knew her boss well enough to know that meant he was having a terrible time too. Panicking.

"Better pick something good, Geoff," said Freeman. "Could be the last time you get to wield the company credit card."

Freeman's cronies guffawed.

"Some champagne to start with?" Geoff suggested bravely.

"If you think you've got something to celebrate..." said Freeman.

"Madeleine knows all about champagne," Geoff added. Madeleine sighed inwardly.

"Is that so?" Freeman turned to face her.

"I grew up there," she told him simply.

"Are your family in wine?"

"They have a place in Le Vezy."

"That's a grand cru village," said Geoff.

"I know that. Worth a lot of money, land in Champagne," Freeman observed. "I was thinking I might buy myself a château when I get my bonus."

Madeleine nodded politely.

"I reckon I could make a pretty good wine."

"It's hard work," said Madeleine.

"Madeleine got out as quickly as she could," said Geoff. "For the easy life in the City."

"At least you've got something to go back to," Freeman told her.

A thinly veiled threat. Had Freeman already determined their fate? Geoff looked shaken. Madeleine merely raised her eyebrows.

Freeman plucked the wine list from Geoff's hands and passed it to Madeleine. "You better choose," he said. "Then we know who to blame if it's shit."

Madeleine took the wine list and began to read.

Beneath the table, Freeman's hand crept onto her knee. Pitying his wife and three small children, Madeleine picked his hand up and let it fall back into his own lap without betraying the slightest hint that it bothered her. It didn't do to show your emotions in this world.

However, Madeleine couldn't help but blink when she saw the name of the bottle at the bottom of the list. "Clos Des Larmes." It wouldn't mean a lot to even the most passionate wine buff but to Madeleine...

"Excellent structure and finish," claimed the sommelier's notes. "Champagne Arsenault produced this single vineyard champagne only in the most exceptional years."

Madeleine knew that. It was a bottle from her own family's estate.

The Arsenault family had several hectares of vines on the hills above Le Vezy, near Bouzy and Ay, where they made a well-regarded Blanc de Noirs. But the Clos Des Larmes was particularly special. It was the wine produced from the pinot noir in the eponymous walled vineyard right next to the house where Madeleine had grown up. A tiny vineyard, it produced just a few hundred bottles and only in the very best years.

Unbelievable. Madeleine had never seen Clos Des Larmes on an English wine list before. This was a bottle from 1985. A vintage made by her father.

Anyone else would have pointed it out to their dining companions, hoping to impress them. Geoff would have wanted Madeleine to flag it up, she knew. But the sight of that name just made Madeleine sad.

That year, 1985, was a great year for champagne but a very bad year for *Famille* Arsenault. It was the year Madeleine's brother died in an accident and the year that Madeleine left France for the first time. She hadn't properly been back since. Her mother swore that she and Madeleine's father always intended to send their only daughter to boarding school in England but how could Madeleine have seen it as anything but a consequence of their grief? A punishment even?

With those three words, "Clos Des Larmes," Madeleine was momentarily back home. She could see the Arsenault house, square and solid inside its white-walled courtyard. The dark green painted shutters. The bright red geraniums in her mother's cherished window boxes. The gates high and wide enough to drive a coach and horses through, painted with the words "Champagne Arsenault" in extravagant curlicued letters. Proud letters. The roses in the garden. The scrawny black cat sunning itself on the steps. Then the Clos itself. The wild strawberries that grew beneath the vines in the summer. She saw herself as a young girl, playing in the Clos with her older brother. The single apple tree right in the middle...

"Made your mind up yet?" Freeman interrupted. "I need people who can make quick decisions on my team."

"I'm sure Madeleine just wants to make sure she makes the *perfect* decision," said Geoff, rushing to her defense. This business of defending her was a fairly new development in their relationship. She knew it was only because he thought his job depended on the impression that if he went, his entire team went too.

"We'll have a bottle of the Jacquesson '96," she said to the sommelier as she snapped the wine list shut.

Freeman nodded as though impressed by her decisiveness. "Bring two bottles," he added.

Madeleine had hoped for an early night so that she might be up in time to catch the seven o'clock train to Paris the next morning, but four hours later they were still at the table.

They had moved from the champagne to a fine Bordeaux. Now the men were finishing off a bottle of port. Madeleine tried to disguise the fact that she had stopped drinking hours before by occasionally raising her glass to her lips and pretending to take a sip.

In Madeleine's handbag, her mobile phone vibrated like a dying bee. When she got the chance to slip away to the bathroom to check her voicemail, she recognized her father's number in the list of missed calls. At almost midnight—one o'clock in the morning in France—it was much too late to call him back. In any case, she was too tired to face the telling-off she probably deserved. She'd been promising to visit for months. She swore she would make it that weekend. The last thing she needed to hear right then was how she had let him down. Again. She would telephone him first thing in the morning.

"You haven't been keeping up with us," Freeman bellowed when Madeleine got back to the table. He filled her small glass to the brim, slopping port all over the pristine white tablecloth. "On my team, we work hard. We play hard. We're the Tartars!"

"That's the name of our cricket team," said Freeman's henchman helpfully.

"Fascinating," said Madeleine.

"Come on, girl," said Freeman. "Drink up."

Madeleine gamely clinked her glass against his.

Beneath the table, hidden in Madeleine's gray snakeskin-trimmed Fendi, Constant Arsenault's name illuminated the screen of his daughter's mobile phone one last time.

CHAPTER 3

Mathieu Randon, head of the eponymous Domaine Randon, was an impressive man. As soon as he walked into a room it was clear he was a force to be reckoned with. His bearing was the very definition of patrician. Though in his mid-fifties, he had the physical strength, grace and agility of a man half his age. He had a full head of silver-white hair, swept back presidentially in style. Naturally, as a Frenchman, he knew how to dress. Everything he wore was bespoke. Handmade shoes, handmade suit, handmade shirts. His ties were the only items he ever got off the rack. But then again, he did own the racks...

Mathieu Randon had inherited Maison Randon, the family champagne house with vineyards in the grand cru villages of Le Vezy, Avize and Verzenay, when he was just twenty-one years old. The upkeep of the champagne business alone would have been enough to occupy most people his age. And the results young Mathieu achieved in his first year at the helm would have formed a big enough pile of laurels for most older, more experienced men to rest upon indefinitely. But even in his early twenties Mathieu Randon was not a man who liked to laze about.

In his second year at the head of the family business Randon bought out two of the small houses with vineyards neighboring his family's land, enabling the expansion of the Maison Randon brand. Ignoring the thought of his father turning in the grave, Randon concentrated on promoting the Maison's non-vintage champagne. It sold spectacularly well overseas. It was the height of the eighties, when City bonuses were big and everyone felt like celebrating. Randon embarked on an aggressive sales push in the United States and Great Britain.

Prior to his time at the helm, Maison Randon had never advertised. That had to change. Randon employed an advertising agency to help him position the brand just so. An up-and-coming French actress was chosen to head up the campaign. She was pictured in bed, her modesty barely protected by a champagne-colored silk sheet. In her hand, a glass of Maison Randon's non-vintage Brut. On the bedside, the bottle and another glass. The actress looked toward the camera as though her lover were behind the lens. The sexy image sent sales skyrocketing.

Meanwhile, Randon was still eager for more. He didn't need the money but if there was one thing Mathieu

Randon needed more than oxygen, it was power. And so Domaine Randon was born.

During the late eighties, it became increasingly difficult to buy more land suitable for champagne. The Champenois knew the value of their property and there was always someone to pass it on to, rather than let it fall into a stranger's hands. Frustrated, Randon bought in the Loire and branched into quality still wines. Brandy too. All came into the Domaine. After that he turned his sights on a different kind of luxury.

It was easy to convince the bankers that his expertise would work just as well in jewelry or fashion. And so Randon bought up Martin et Fils, a family-owned jewelry business with outlets in Paris, Nice and Monaco. The Martin family business had a reputation for quality but had been resisting expansion for years. Randon changed all that. He took some of the Martin family's classic designs and mass-produced them. The advertising agency that had taken Maison Randon from a relatively little-known marque to one everyone asked for, ran a similar campaign for the jewelry. It was seen on an Oscar-winning actress. Soon fashion magazines were clamoring to feature Martin et Fils jewelry. Randon bought another small jewelry house and amalgamated it into Martin et Fils to help meet the demand.

Next he took a side step into clothing. Once again he swooped in on small family-led companies: brands with reputations for quality but little real presence in the market. He took an Italian brand renowned for its cashmere and moved production to China. The goods were shipped back to Italy for hand-finishing, thus benefiting from the best of both nations: the cachet and quality of Italian design combined with cheap labor. Randon copied the formula with six other labels.

Three decades after his father's death and his rise to the head of the family business, Mathieu Randon had taken his family name global. His was the company behind almost any quality luxury goods brand you cared to mention.

"You must be about ready to retire," said the journalist who interviewed him on his fiftieth birthday for *Forbes,* the business magazine.

"Only when I'm dead," said Mathieu Randon.

That Monday afternoon, Randon was in his office on the Avenue Des Champs-Élysées. Back when the building was a private house the room had been the ballroom and the setting for scenes of legendary debauch, according to the real estate agent. Randon had kept the space largely empty, as though he were the kind of man who might leap to his feet and waltz the full length of the beautiful hardwood floor at any moment. He wasn't that kind of man.

Randon was studying an article in one of the British Sunday papers (naturally, he was fluent in English, German and Italian as well as French). The article reported on the "most expensive champagne in the world." It named one of Maison Randon's rivals: Champagne Brice. They had produced, they claimed, a fabulous single vineyard grand cru. It was available in such small quantities that its retail price would be $645 per bottle.

Randon snarled. The idea that anyone else could produce something worth more than the best bottle at Maison Randon irked him. He pulled out a map of the Randon vineyards in the Champagne region and leaned over it on his desk, studying closely where his land lay in relation to that belonging to Brice. So close. Bordering in many instances. Why did they think they had so much better results? As he studied the extent of the Brice vineyards, Randon kept his right hand over a part of the map he'd outlined in black (a few hectares in Le Vezy), as though to spare his eyes that other horror right then.

Having somewhat neglected the maison during the late nineties, lately he had been concentrating on the champagne house at the heart of his empire again. The fashion and jewelry departments of DR were pretty much running themselves, but Maison Randon had seen the first small slip in its market dominance in twenty-nine years. It didn't make Randon happy.

Randon approached the problem like a true dictator. He sacked all the high-level staff at Maison Randon and replaced them with younger, keener men and women. People who had reputations to make. Hungry people who worked harder and had better ideas. He'd promoted Stefan Urban to head up the new team. Stefan had worked at Randon's operation in Napa for the previous decade. He brought his young protégé, Axel Delaflote, from California with him. The two men were full of enthusiasm and energy. Still, Randon was not comforted by knowing that he had the best team possible on the case.

He would have to do something about that very soon. But first he had other business to attend to. He picked up the phone and barked at his assistant, "Get me my coat."

"Yes, Mathieu," said Bertille.

Randon's sigh said it all.

"I mean, yes, Monsieur Randon. At once."

Randon put down the phone and looked out of one of the five floor-to-ceiling windows onto the street.

He saw a van pass by with the legend Ruinart painted on its side. The reminder of yet another champagne brand didn't improve his mood.

Moments later, there was a gentle knock at the door and Bertille appeared. She was a petite brunette with a tiny waist who, nonetheless, was well endowed enough to make the buttons on her shirt look endangered when she took a deep breath. As the first point of contact most business associates had with Domaine Randon, Bertille was an excellent ambassadress for the brand. Now she leaned against the door frame in a manner she probably assumed looked coquettish. She had Randon's coat draped over her arm.

"Your car is here," she told him.

"Thank you."

Randon strode across the room. He took his coat from Bertille. He didn't let her help him into it as he usually did. She looked a little affronted at that. Hurt.

"Bertille," he said softly.

"Yes," she murmured back.

Bertille would have to go. It was a pity. She was an excellent assistant but lately she had become far too familiar. Randon knew he shouldn't have slept with her. It had been an unfortunate case of his loins getting the better of him and now, of course, Bertille thought things were different. Randon cursed his lack of discretion. He was normally very careful about these matters.

She looked up at him with soft, loving eyes. Dark brown. Doe-like. Or cow-like, thought Randon, less generously. He knew that she, like him, was remembering their single night together. But he also knew that, unlike him, she was remembering it with a pleasure that went beyond the physical. Hers was a look of love.

"I think it's time you took a vacation, my dear. In fact, I think you need to take a permanent vacation from Domaine Randon. I'd like you to clear your desk before I come back to the office tomorrow morning. I will have the personnel department arrange for a proper settlement."

"But..." Bertille began to protest.

"Sweet girl, one shouldn't mix business and pleasure," he reminded her. He reached out and touched her cheek lightly with the back of his hand. Bertille suddenly beamed.

Randon knew she'd misunderstood him, that she thought he wanted her to leave the company so they could see more of each other privately. When she realized her mistake, Bertille would protest against her dismissal, of course, but he didn't let that worry him. There was nothing that couldn't be sorted out if you threw enough money at it. Even French employment law.

CHAPTER 4

That afternoon's appointment was at a film studio on the outskirts of Paris where they were shooting the new cinema commercial for Maison Randon's finest grand cru vintage champagne: Éclat.

From the outside, the sound studio looked like a hangar on any industrial lot, but inside, it had been transformed into a slice of another world. Randon was greeted at the door by the advertising agency representative, Solange. She was a pretty girl, he noted. She looked intelligent too.

"Monsieur Randon. You've arrived at the perfect time. Everyone is just coming back after their afternoon break," Solange explained. "Mr. Tarrant and Ms. Morgan are in makeup. They'll be back on set any moment. Can I get you a coffee?"

Randon shook his head. He had little doubt that the catering on this job would leave everything to be wished for. Instead he accepted a glass of water—Aqua Blue, Domaine Randon's very own bottled brand "filtered by the Alps"—and took a seat beside the director's chair. The director for this little segment was Frank Wylie, a young Angeleno. Following three Oscar nominations for his first movie, Wylie's stock was on the rise. Even Randon had been impressed by his debut, a surreal extravaganza in the style of Baz Luhrmann's *Moulin Rouge*. And thus Wylie was the obvious choice to bring an injection of high glamour to Domaine Randon's Éclat.

"Mr. Wylie has asked not to be disturbed by visitors until the shoot is over," said Solange.

"Fine," said Randon. He was gratified to see that Wylie was taking this commission seriously.

The soundstage had been dressed to resemble Parisian rooftops. Randon allowed himself a little smile as the electricians fired up the lights and a glittering Eiffel Tower appeared on the backdrop.

"It looks a bit ropey from here," said Solange. "But if you'd like to look through the monitor, you'll get a better sense of how realistic it will look post-production."

Just then, while Randon watched via the monitor, a vision of a woman stepped out onto one of the make-believe rooftops. Her long blond hair hung straight and shiny almost to her waist. Her perfect apricot-pink skin was positively luminous beneath the studio lights. She moved with the grace of a dancer as she walked to the center of the stage.

Christina Morgan, the supermodel. She needed no introduction.

Solange explained the rest. "Christina is wearing a dress by Estrella..."

Estrella was the most recent of four new fashion houses to be absorbed into Randon's empire. Randon recognized the cut straightaway. The bodice fit like a second skin. The skirt was a waterfall of expensive black lace.

Meanwhile, Christina's earlobes, neck and wrists glittered with half a million Euros' worth of diamonds.

"And jewelry by Martin et Fils, of course."

Randon watched closely as the stunt manager unzipped the back of Christina's dress and checked the harness hidden beneath it. The stunt manager attached a couple of wires to the harness and zipped Christina back up. She turned and thanked him.

On the other side of the stage, while a makeup artist powdered his all-American action-hero jaw, Bill Tarrant was also being fitted up to fly. It was quite a coup having persuaded an actor with Tarrant's box office clout to appear in a commercial. He was the housewife's choice, commanding fees per movie that rivaled Cruise's and Clooney's.

Tarrant was wearing a suit by Trianon, the men's outfitter that Randon had shaped into a major contender for Gucci and Armani's role as the male star's tailor of choice for those red-carpet moments and *Vanity Fair* covers.

"Who made his shoes?" Randon asked.

"Patrick Cox for Trianon," Solange confirmed. Randon nodded at her attention to detail.

Fully harnessed, the two main players in Frank Wylie's scene smiled at each other across the gap between their two fake rooftops. Bill took out his chewing gum and handed it to an overeager production assistant. Then he gave Frank Wylie the thumbs-up. They were ready.

"In the ad itself we'll look down into the gap between the two houses to see the metaphorical gulf between them," Solange murmured into Randon's ear. "The power of computer imagery. We've already shot the moment when the bottle is opened. We used a hand model, since Bill still has quite a nasty scar on his right hand."

Randon had heard about the accident Bill Tarrant suffered on the set of his latest film—a science-fiction epic in which Bill bravely saved the world from an enormous blancmange (as it said in one of the kinder reviews).

"We've also done the pack shot," Solange continued. "That's the shot at the very end of the ad. The close-up on the bottle itself."

"I know what a pack shot is," said Randon.

"Of course." Solange was chastised. "I forget—"

"Silence everybody!" called the director's assistant. "Places."

The clapper loader dashed out in front of the camera with his clapper board, neatly annotated with the job, director and take number.

"And action!"

The ad's story was fairly simple. Morgan and Tarrant were guests at two separate New Year's Eve parties. Footage shot earlier in the day showed them as wallflowers at their respective gatherings, looking bored as hell while the other guests swirled around them, laughing, dancing and generally having a gay old time. Next, the hero and heroine were both seen climbing the stairs to the rooftops. Tarrant's character actually had to squeeze out through a tiny attic window. Both of them were carrying champagne glasses. Tarrant also had a bottle of Éclat.

Catching sight of each other across the fake divide, which would look like a giddying five-story drop once the CGI department had finished, Morgan and Tarrant raised their glasses to toast each other. And then, by the power of movie magic, the beautiful pair were lifted into the air by the bubbles in their champagne, through a sudden flurry of glittering snowflakes, to meet each other halfway across the rooftops and indulge in a magical mid-air dance to a lesser-known piece by Wagner (Wylie's choice). It wasn't exactly cheery music but somehow it worked, adding to the atmosphere of slightly edgy decadence.

On cue, both Tarrant and Morgan floated up into studio sky, looking suitably surprised and delighted by their sudden ability to fly. They met in mid-air, clinking their glasses before falling into a passionate embrace. They whirled around and around until the stunt master got nervous about the harnesses tangling and tapped the director on the arm.

"Cut!" shouted Wylie.

The camera stopped rolling.

Tarrant and Morgan broke apart and dangled in mid-air like a pair of masterless puppets.

"I think that's the one," said Wylie, conferring with his lighting cameraman.

"Great," shouted Bill. "Now can someone get me down? This freakin' harness is cutting into my balls."

Freed from her own uncomfortable harness, Christina Morgan joined her co-star and Mathieu Randon by the monitors.

"Matt Randon!" Bill clapped the Frenchman on the back. "Good to see ya, old man."

Randon winced.

"Bill, you have no idea of your own strength," Christina told him, assuming Randon was smarting from the smack. "Monsieur Randon. Hello." Christina extended her perfectly manicured hand. Randon lifted it to his lips and kissed it.

"So European," Christina laughed, as she affected a swoon. "Bill, you should try it."

"In the United States?" said Bill. "Forget it, sweetheart. If I went around kissing hands, I'd get punched. What did you think of the ad, Matt?"

"I liked it very much," said Randon. "The chemistry between you is very obvious."

"So it should be," said Christina. "We've only been married eleven months!"

She planted a kiss on her husband's cheek. She hoped it looked full of affection and warmth.

"It's like we're still on honeymoon," she said. "Isn't it, darling?"

"Do you know when the ad will begin showing?" asked Bill.

"The ad company rep has assured me that we have slots booked to coincide with the release of your new movie around Thanksgiving."

Bill nodded.

"That's good news," Christina concurred.

"I'm glad you think so. Now we should all go out to dinner and celebrate a very successful shoot," Randon suggested. "I understand Frank has chosen a restaurant."

"I'm up for that," said Bill.

"I'll join you boys but not for too long," said Christina. "I'm flying back to Los Angeles first thing. And unfortunately, I really mean first thing."

"I hope you're being well compensated for missing a night out in Paris," said Randon.

"Not this time," said Christina. "I'm heading back to shoot an infomercial for a non-profit. Battered women."

"Always doing charity work. She never turns down a request," her husband added.

"How could I?" Christina exclaimed. "Just a few moments of my time to change so many sorry lives?"

"And of course it keeps her name in the news," said Bill.

Christina glared at him.

"I'm joking, sweetheart. See what an angel I married?"

"She is definitely a heavenly vision," said Randon, kissing her hand again.

"Oh, Monsieur Randon," Christina's hand fluttered to her heart. "You are such a charmer! Later, boys."

She left them with a wink and crossed the floor to her dressing room as though she were walking the catwalk. She might as well have been on a catwalk, she thought to herself. She knew everybody would be watching. Well, she'd give them all a show.

"Your tongue is dragging on the floor," Christina heard Solange tell her young male assistant.

CHAPTER 5

That Thursday morning at the Gloria Hotel was the stuff of every chambermaid's nightmares. The previous night the hotel restaurant had hosted wine magazine *Vinifera*'s annual awards. The hotel was packed with people who had attended the ceremony (and the grand tasting) and none of them was likely to be checking out before mid-day, which meant that the chambermaids would have just two hours to change three hundred beds before the next lot of guests arrived.

Hilarian Jackson didn't even wake up until ten to twelve. His right arm felt dead. He panicked. He thought he'd had a stroke. It took a moment to register that it was just that he'd been sleeping so heavily, thanks to the booze, that he'd hardly moved during the night. Relieved to feel the pins and needles that heralded the return of blood to his arm, he rolled over onto his left side and closed his eyes again. And then he remembered.

"Arse," he said to himself.

He had a lunch date. Ronald Ginsburg and Odile Levert would be waiting for him downstairs in the hotel bar at that very moment.

He could have used another hour in bed. Maybe he should stand them up, he thought. It wasn't such a big deal, though he knew that to the cognoscenti, it was quite a gathering. Arguably the three most important wine critics in the world at the same table. Breaking bread and disagreeing about the booze. As usual.

Hilarian dragged himself to the bathroom and surveyed the damage from the night before. His memories of the *Vinifera* awards were vague to say the least. His head pounded. A lattice of bright red vessels patterned his ordinarily yellow eyes.

"I'm never drinking again," said Hilarian, as he always did. "Starting tomorrow."

When Hilarian finally got to the hotel bar, half an hour late, Odile and Ronald were already at the table. Ronald didn't look as though he'd slept much. He never did. He was seventy years old. He could have started a luggage concession with the bags under his eyes and there was always a dribble of something expensive on the front of his Brooks Brothers' shirt. Odile was entirely different. The Parisian was dressed from head to toe in cream. Probably Chanel. Always immaculate. Hilarian reflected that he had never seen her spill so much as a drop of wine in their long acquaintance. He'd never seen her drunk either. Not even slightly tipsy.

"Stallion's Leap worthy of a gold medal? Ronald, you must have a head cold," Odile was saying.

"Darling," Ronald retorted. "Are you absolutely sure it's not your time of the month? A woman's cycle affects her judgment of everything."

Hilarian saw Odile stiffen. He had arrived just in time. There was nothing guaranteed to put Odile Levert in a rage more quickly than Ronald Ginsburg's theory that women simply were not biologically suited to evaluating wine.

"At last! 'Ilarian!" When Odile said his name, Hilarian almost liked it. Odile was colder than a witch's tit, but her accent was pure aural sex. She kissed him on both cheeks.

Ronald tipped an imaginary hat. "Ah, the Noble Rotter."

Hilarian rolled his eyes, but in fact he rather liked his nickname, which reflected not only his supposed incorrigibility but also the fact that he was an hon and an expert on botrytis (the real "noble rot" so important to the production of sweet wine). "The Noble Rotter" was the name of his regular column in one of the Sundays.

"And who was the lucky lady last night?" Ronald asked pruriently. "I saw you go upstairs with that girl with the . . ." He mimed a pair of substantial breasts. Odile tutted.

"A gentleman never tells," said Hilarian.

"But you're no gentleman," purred Odile.

"Good point," said Hilarian. They didn't have to know that he'd simply helped the extraordinarily drunken subeditor from *Vinifera* to her room and kissed her good night at the door. "Who's choosing the wine?" Hilarian changed the subject. He picked up the list and started to scan it. These three always took more trouble over choosing the wine than they did the food. "And whose expense account are we on today?" he added.

"I'll pick this up," said Ronald. Ronald had *Vinifera*'s most important column. It was said that winemakers the world over tweaked their wine to Ronald's taste in search of his approval. His annual guides shifted millions of copies.

"In that case..." Hilarian suggested Chassagne Montrachet at three hundred pounds a bottle. Would have been rude not to.

Over lunch, the three critics discussed the previous evening's award ceremony. They agreed that the overall quality of that year's competitors was patchy, the result of very strange summer weather. Unusually heavy rain in Northern Europe led to much of the grape harvest there rotting in the sodden vineyards. Meanwhile, Southern Europe roasted and the grapes in that part of the continent had a cooked jammy taste. Ronald and Odile also agreed that *Vinifera* had been "dumbing down."

"I blame *Sideways*," said Ronald. "Now that everyone is getting into wine they keep telling me to make my columns more goddamn accessible."

"That's a good thing, surely?" said Hilarian.

Ronald and Odile looked at him as though he were mad; they actually prided themselves on producing impenetrable columns. They were elitists. Wine intellectuals. Snobs. Since his own main money-spinner was a guide to supermarket wines retailing at less than a tenner a pop, Hilarian often wondered why they bothered with him.

"So," said Ronald when the last of the wine had been drunk and the three were sipping espressos, "you ready to pay up, Hilarian?"

"Pay up?"

"Your bet," said Odile helpfully. A slightly cruel smile twisted her perfectly made-up mouth. Somehow she had managed to eat an entire meal without displacing any of her signature red lipstick.

"I made a bet? Who with?" Hilarian asked. "And," he added with a groan, "how much did I lose?"

He felt a chill travel the length of his body as Odile and Ronald looked at each other conspiratorially. Ronald's old eyes crinkled with pleasure. Hilarian tried to retain some semblance of composure but his mind was traveling back to the previous year's *Vinifera* awards, when he bet Ronald ten thousand pounds that Maison Randon's Éclat would take the highest prize in the champagne section. It didn't. Ronald had insisted that the bet be paid though Hilarian couldn't even remember having made it.

"You haven't lost anything," said Odile at last.

Hilarian was flooded with relief.

"Yet!"

Both she and Ronald laughed.

"By the look on both your faces," said Hilarian, "I'm guessing that I made a silly wager."

"Very silly," said Odile.

Ronald agreed.

"Well, for goodness' sake, tell me what it was."

"That an English sparkling wine would carry off wine of the year at the *Vinifera* awards within the next five years."

Hilarian didn't put his head in his hands but that was what he felt like doing.

"Oh dear," he said. "How much?"

"Fifty thousand dollars," said Odile, clapping her hands in glee.

"Sweet Jesus."

"Don't blaspheme," said Ronald.

"I must have been very drunk," Hilarian groaned.

"Of course," said Odile. "You always are."

"Neither of you took me up on it," said Hilarian hopefully.

Odile grinned wickedly as she reached into her handbag and pulled out a tattered paper napkin. She flourished it at Hilarian.

"Ta-daa! We wrote it down," she said.

Hilarian looked at his signature in blurry felt pen with horror.

" 'Fifty thousand dollars. English sparkling wine to win Wine of the Year within the next five years.' Signed Hilarian Jackson." Odile read it out as though she were trying to be helpful.

"And you're going to hold me to that?" Hilarian asked. He knew that shit-bag Ronald would. Fifty grand was nothing to that decrepit bastard. Odile came from money and Ronald's books had made him a mint but Hilarian didn't have that kind of cash. Nowhere near. He certainly had no "old money" as Ronald had often implied. Hilarian may have had a title but, as was the case with so many British aristocratic families, all the accompanying dosh had gone to repairing the drafty family pile in Northumberland.

"No," said Odile. "That would be cruel."

Hilarian was so relieved he thought he might lose control of his bowels.

"But when we had finished choking in horror at the very thought of a world-beating English sparkler, Ronald and I agreed that it would be a bit of fun to take you up on your challenge in another way. So, in five years' time, we're going to have our own private Judgment of Paris."

Hilarian raised an eyebrow. The Judgment of Paris was the name given to the infamous Paris wine tasting of 1976. Prior to that date, it was taken as gospel that French wines were the best in the world and, to prove it conclusively, a wine merchant named Steven Spurrier organized a blind tasting comparing French wines to their American equivalents. The idea was to put the upstart Yanks in their place. Eight of the nine tasting judges were French. And they judged the best wines to be American. When the competition was reprised several years later, some of the French houses tactfully refused to take part.

"Weren't there three competitors in the original judgment?" Hilarian mused. "I mean in the myth, of course."

"Exactly," said Odile. "You're not the only one who had a classical education. Aphrodite, Athena and Hera."

Hilarian gave Odile a small round of applause.

"And so we will judge wines from three different nations. All made from this year's harvest. Champagne for my country. 'Champagne' from the United States for Ronald here." Odile made little quotation marks in the air to remind her companions that she fully subscribed to the French view that no sparkling wine produced outside the Champagne region should ever be called by that name. "And from your country, Hilarian, a sparkling white wine. Whatever you want to call it." She flicked her hand dismissively. "Or if you prefer, we can make you an honorary Italian and you could champion Asti Spumante instead. Might give you a better chance."

"Ha ha ha," said Hilarian.

"What do you think?"

"It's not what I wagered," said Hilarian.

"No," said Ronald. "It gives you better odds. You only have to beat two other wines with your chosen vintage."

"How much?" Hilarian ventured.

"Let's stick with your original stake," said Odile. "Fifty thousand dollars each."

Hilarian tried not to wince. Fifty thousand dollars. What was that in pounds?

"Don't be ridiculous," said Ronald to Odile.

Thank goodness, thought Hilarian.

"It's got to be fifty thousand sterling!"

"Even better," Odile laughed.

"Are you serious?" Hilarian asked her.

"Of course," said Odile. "Winner takes all. Agreed? I'm going to buy myself a nice little Mercedes with your cash, boys."

"I wouldn't be too cocky, Odile," said Ronald. "You remember 1976."

"Not as well as you, old man," said Odile. "Are you in, Hilarian?"

He couldn't afford to be. He had an ex-wife, two teenage sons to put through university and a telephone-number overdraft. But the moment of reckoning was five whole years away. Maybe he would have fifty grand to spare by then. He didn't want to look a party pooper. Or give Ginsburg a reason to think he wasn't doing quite as well as him. And perhaps...a tiny flicker of optimism tickled the back of Hilarian's brain. His wasn't a *totally* impossible position. Some of the finest palates in the world had mistaken the Sussex sparkler Nyetimber for vintage champagne. And if he did win, what he could do with a hundred thousand pounds...

"I'm in," he said as confidently as he could. "You know I think East Sussex has a terroir that easily rivals that of the Marne. And if there's one good thing about global warming, it's that it has been fabulous for the Great Britain grape. We've had a couple of outstanding years. I'd be happy to put a hundred thousand pounds on an English sparkler."

"Then let's raise the bet!" said Ginsburg.

"No," said Hilarian quickly. "Really, fifty grand is fine. I wouldn't want you to have to raid your retirement fund, Ronald."

"Then it's settled," said Odile. "I love a competition. Fifty thousand each. We'll declare our chosen vineyards at the London wine fair in June. These are the parameters. No bigger than fifty hectares. Must never have won an award before."

Bugger, thought Hilarian. That ruled out Nyetimber and Ridgeview.

"May the best wine win," said Ronald.

They raised a toast to that.

"OK. Let's make this official." Ronald got out his pen and started to draw up a contract on another napkin.

"Will you please rip that up?" said Hilarian, nodding at the original wager from the night before.

"Don't you want to keep it as a souvenir of your overarching optimism?" Odile teased.

After lunch, Hilarian felt the beginnings of a headache as he climbed into a taxi and it wasn't the Chassagne Montrachet that had brought it on. Had he really just bet fifty thousand pounds that he could find a hitherto unknown sparkling wine from England that would beat a vintage champagne? He ran through the possibilities in his mind. And decided that there were no possibilities.

If the other two didn't let him wriggle out of this bet, he was stuffed.

CHAPTER 6

Kelly was smoking the remains of a cigar someone had left behind in room 506 when her supervisor caught her. In her hurry to put the cigar out, she missed the ashtray balanced on the bed beside her and stubbed the glowing butt straight into a pillow instead. The smell of singed feathers instantly filled the room.

Kelly fanned the smoke ineffectively.

"Kelly!"

She waited to be told she could collect her wages on the way out.

"You know you shouldn't be smoking," said Geraldine. But the expression on her boss's face told Kelly that her illicit puff on a Monte Cristo was the least of Geraldine's concerns that morning.

"We need to talk," said Geraldine ominously. "What I've got to say is very unpleasant, so I want you to sit down."

Kelly's heart flapped against her rib cage as she sat back down on the bed. Geraldine shook her head. This is it, thought Kelly. She's found out. Just that morning, one of the Polish chambermaids had caught Kelly buttoning up her overall as she followed Daniel Weston out of an empty room where they'd spent their usual half hour. Alicia must have said something to Geraldine. And now the jig was up. She'd definitely get the sack. It was a shitty job but Kelly couldn't afford to lose it.

"Sorry, I . . ." Kelly began. "I can explain. You see, I was feeling faint and I had to lie down and this bloke . . ."

Geraldine put up her hand to stop Kelly's excuses. "It's OK. Forget about it."

"Really?"

"Yes. Kelly, sweetheart . . ."

Sweetheart? Kelly was even more on her guard.

"Your mum's been on the phone. Said she's been trying to get you on your mobile but you've not been answering. Is your phone working?"

Of course Kelly's phone wasn't working. As usual, she was out of credit.

"It's urgent," Geraldine continued. "You better get home right away. Now."

"Right now?" Kelly had another three hours left on her shift.

"Yes," said Geraldine. "Oh, you poor girl! Come here."

Geraldine threw her arms around the younger woman and squeezed her tightly.

"Is Mum OK?" Kelly asked, suddenly really worried. "Has something happened?"

"Your mum's fine," said Geraldine.

Then what was the problem, Kelly wondered. What was all this friendliness about?

"Your dad's dead."

Kelly took up Geraldine's kind offer of an afternoon off.

"You look after yourself," Geraldine told her. "Get a taxi straight home, you hear?" She handed Kelly a twenty-pound note. "Call me and let me know you're OK."

"It'll probably cost twenty-five to get to Tooting from here," said Kelly, folding the twenty into her wallet.

Geraldine and the other chambermaids scraped together five more pound coins to cover the rest of the fare.

And now Kelly was spending their money in Topshop, Oxford Circus. There was, you see, absolutely no need to hurry home as far as Kelly was concerned. Her dad was dead. So what? She'd never met him. In fact, her mother had always refused to tell Kelly his name, leading Kelly to conclude that her mother didn't actually know who he was either. The slag.

With five pounds left after she had bought herself a couple of T-shirts, Kelly bought a top-up card for her phone. An hour later, she finally called her mum.

"Where the hell are you? I want you back home," said Marina. "Now."

"What for?" asked Kelly.

"What do you mean, what for? Your father's died."

"So? I'm not going to get upset about somebody I never even knew."

"Get yourself home now or you'll find your bags on the doorstep when you do, you stupid little cow."

.   .   .

The reason for that outburst of love from Kelly's mother was that the Elson family had a visitor. When Kelly finally got home, it was to find a tall, worried-looking man in a suit sitting on the very edge of the sofa, as though he were afraid it might swallow him up if he leaned too far back. Actually, that wasn't such a ridiculous concern. The sofa was old and had several dodgy patches where the springs had given up. It was the furnishing equivalent of quicksand.

"Kelly, this is Mr. Harper," said Marina in her "best" voice as she led her daughter into the "lounge." Marina never did remember that really posh people had "sitting rooms."

"Hello," said Kelly, ignoring the man's outstretched hand.

"Mr. Harper is from the firm of solicitors who look after your father's estate."

"Great. Are you going to tell me who my father is, then?" Kelly asked belligerently. She remained standing, arms folded across her chest.

"Of course," Tim Harper obliged. "Your father was Graeme Dougal Mollison."

"Dougal what?"

"Graeme Dougal Mollison," Harper repeated. "Though nobody ever called him Graeme. Went by Dougal to his friends."

Kelly wrinkled her nose. It meant nothing to her.

"You remember where we lived when you were very little, pet?" Marina elaborated. "Out in Norfolk? In that cottage near the big house with the horses?"

"Where you worked as a housekeeper? Yeah," said Kelly, "just about."

"And you remember the man the big house belonged to? Who used to come and visit us sometimes?"

"The one who used to bring me sweets and pinch my cheeks? That old creep?"

"Well..."

"Oh my God." The penny dropped. "You're telling me *that* man was my father?"

Marina nodded. She looked a little ashamed.

"He was about a hundred years old, Mum!"

"Only in his eighties, he would have been then," Marina corrected her. "And he looked young for his age. He had a young outlook too."

"Oh God." Kelly sank down onto a chair. "You had sex with him. An eighty-year-old man! You were only twenty. That's disgusting."

"He had a nice personality."

"Don't tell me it was love."

"Kelly..."

"Well, why do I care?" Kelly shrugged. "Some old bloke is dead. He never cared about me."

"On the contrary," Mr. Harper interrupted. "Dougal, your father, was very concerned with your welfare. He sent your mother five hundred pounds a month."

"What?"

"That's right. Every month for the first eighteen years of your life."

"But I never saw any of it!" Kelly protested.

"I spent every penny on you, love," said Marina. "I promise. Raising a child is so expensive," she added, addressing the remark to Mr. Harper as though he might sympathize.

"Bollocks. You spent it all on booze and fags!" said Kelly.

"I didn't," Marina said to Mr. Harper.

"You let me go to school in secondhand clothes, you bitch. You told me I had to pay rent as soon as I turned sixteen—"

"Kelly!" Marina pleaded. "We can talk about this later." She reached for her daughter's hand.

"Don't touch me," Kelly hissed. "You're worse than a prostitute."

"I can explain," Marina insisted.

"Don't bother. I don't want to know any more," said Kelly. "I'm going out."

She turned toward the door.

"Ms. Elson," said Mr. Harper, standing up. "Don't go yet."

"Fuck off." Kelly raised her hand, palm out in the "talk to the hand" gesture and carried on her way.

Mr. Harper caught her by the arm. "Please wait. There's something else you need to know."

"What more can I possibly need to know? My mum's a slag and my dad was some crummy old pervert."

"This is important. I've traveled all the way up from Sussex to let you know that you've inherited Froggy Bottom."

"What's that?" Kelly scoffed. "Now you're going to tell me I've got some kind of genetic disorder as well?"

"No, Ms. Elson," said Mr. Harper patiently. "Froggy Bottom is a *vineyard.*"

CHAPTER 7

'm so sorry for your loss."

"Thank you." Madeleine Arsenault nodded serenely at the platitudes of her father's mourners. She'd been surprised at the number of people who thronged the tiny village church in Le Vezy for Constant Arsenault's funeral. But of course she quickly realized that it wasn't love for her father that made the local vignerons dress up and turn out. It was curiosity. And self-interest. When they asked her "How are you coping?" they didn't mean "How are you coping with the loss of your beloved father?" but "How are you coping with Champagne Arsenault?"

Vultures. The lot of them. It was clear they assumed that now that Constant Arsenault was dead, the maison would be up for grabs. After all, Madeleine was a woman. She had no father, no brother, no husband. She couldn't cope with running a champagne house alone (they conveniently forgot about Veuve Clicquot and Madame Bollinger). The best thing for her would be to put the whole place up for sale, take the cash and go back to London, where she had spent the last ten years.

Well, they were right about one thing. Financially, it would be better to sell Champagne Arsenault. Madeleine knew that her father hadn't had the killer instinct of some of the local businessmen, but until recently she'd had no idea just how far into the red the maison had gone. Champagne Arsenault's debts were enormous. Simply vast. Madeleine was certain that worrying about those debts had been a factor in her father's demise, but she was perplexed. It was quite something to achieve such huge losses in the champagne business. It would have required an almost suicidal determination.

"My dear child . . . let me hold you."

Madeleine extricated herself from the too-close embrace of Monsieur Mulfort and headed for the one friendly face in the room. Axel Delaflote.

Madeleine had known Axel Delaflote since childhood. Axel's father had worked as a cellar master for Madeleine's family at Champagne Arsenault. They had grown up within a couple streets of each other. Now Axel took both Madeleine's hands in his own and kissed them.

"Ma pauvre chérie," he said.

"Look at all these people," Madeleine whispered. "None of them cared about my father when he was alive. Paying their respects? They've got no respect. They're only interested in getting hold of his land."

Axel nodded sympathetically.

"I can't stand it." Tears lent a glitter to Madeleine's eyes.

"You know," said Axel, "you don't have to put up with this any longer. Why don't you just go upstairs and take a rest? I'll get rid of this lot for you."

"Would you?" asked Madeleine.

Axel fixed her with his soft brown eyes. "Of course." He ran his hand over her cheek. "You need someone to take care of you for a change."

Madeleine squeezed his hand. "Thank you."

They hadn't always been such good friends, Madeleine and Axel. As children, they were perpetually at war. As one of the heirs to Champagne Arsenault, Madeleine must be a snob, assumed Axel, while young Madeleine subscribed to her brother Georges' view that Axel Delaflote was a pleb (though she had no idea what "pleb" meant). But pleb or not, Axel and Georges were inseparable, so Madeleine and Axel had plenty of opportunities to engage in battle. Axel launched countless water bombs over the walls of the Arsenault Clos at Madeleine. Madeleine and her friends demolished Axel's den in the woods. One day Axel actually cut off Madeleine's plaits with a pair of pruning shears. Madeleine retaliated by exploding a stink bomb in his schoolbag. The smell followed him around for months.

Of course, all that changed when Georges had his accident and Madeleine was sent away to school in England. Suddenly, the easy hate-hate relationship of Madeleine and Axel's childhood was reduced to the odd nod when they passed in the street during the school holidays.

After school, they found themselves on different continents. Madeleine studied English at Oxford. Axel studied viticulture in Montpellier before he flew to the United States and joined the graduate program at the University of California, Davis. Again they saw each other only at holidays. Easter. Christmas Eve, at Midnight Mass. Sometimes in January on patron saint of Champagne, St. Vincent's Day. And then Madeleine got her job at the bank and for almost ten years they hadn't seen each other at all.

Lately, Axel had been spending more time in Champagne. After graduating with top honors from UC Davis, Axel had been recruited by a big American wine producer in the Napa Valley. He'd moved from there to Domaine Randon's Napa operation. Now he had returned to France, with his boss, to work for DR at the jewel in the conglomerate's crown: Maison Randon Champagne. Madeleine had heard the news from her father during one of the rare phone conversations that didn't turn into a fight about when Madeleine would also return to her roots, her people, *her* Champagne...

Madeleine knew her father liked Axel. As far as Madeleine knew, Axel was the only person from the village who had visited her father while he was ill. Not like the vultures he was shooing out of the house right now.

"I'll come and see you tomorrow, Madeleine," Monsieur Mulfort called up the stairs. "Make sure you're doing all right."

"Thank you," Madeleine called back down. "Bastard," she added under her breath.

A knock at the sitting room door.

"Come in."

It was Axel.

"They're all gone," he said. "For now."

"At last. Thank you so much," said Madeleine.

"You need to watch out. I think old Monsieur Mulfort is planning to propose marriage. Quickest way to get his hands on your land."

"Oh God!" said Madeleine. But the idea brought a smile to her face. Jean Mulfort was at least ten years older than her father had been.

"I told him being a newlywed again would kill him," said Axel. "But that it would probably be a nice way to go."

"You sod." Madeleine threw a small cushion at Axel's head. "Sit down. Drink?"

Axel nodded. "Yes, please."

"Papa's marc?" she suggested, holding up a bottle of the deadly local spirit.

Though he tried to prevent it, Axel couldn't stop a slight grimace from flitting across his face.

"Wise choice," said Madeleine as she poured them both a glass of brandy instead.

Axel raised a toast. "To your father."

"And the mess he's left me with," said Madeleine.

Axel gave Madeleine's hand a squeeze. She smiled gratefully. She hadn't told him quite everything about the state of the maison's accounts but it must have been obvious that all was not well. Apart from Madeleine and the undertakers, Axel was the only person who had seen the state of the place as it had been when her father breathed his last.

Madeleine hadn't known what to do when she let herself into the house and found her father stiff and cold in his bed. She'd run out into the street and narrowly missed meeting her own demise beneath the wheels of Axel's car. He'd scooped her up from the road, ascertained the reason for her tears and took over from that moment on.

So, Axel had seen the truth behind the grand gates of Champagne Arsenault. The dirt and the disarray. The dishes piled high in the kitchen sink. The rotten food in the fridge. The filthy sheets on the bed. The tattered pajamas that were her father's shroud. Her father had died in conditions that would have made the average tramp turn up his nose. And Axel had seen it all. Madeleine shuddered at the thought.

As if he sensed that she needed distraction, Axel broke the silence. "We'll take a proper look at the vines tomorrow," he said.

Like the house, with its peeling paint, Madeleine suspected that the Arsenault vineyards had suffered badly from some seasons of neglect. There was no doubting that was true of the Clos. Once her father's pride and joy, the tiny walled vineyard at the back of the house was choked with weeds. Brambles held the rusted gates shut.

"Do you have time for that?" Madeleine asked.

"I've got plenty of time," Axel assured her.

She wondered if he knew how grateful she was.

They sat companionably side by side looking at the fire. As Axel held up his glass to look at the flames through the amber liquid, Madeleine studied his profile.

Like the Le Vezy Rouge his father had once produced for Champagne Arsenault, Axel Delaflote was aging very well. He had a fine, aquiline nose. Noble. His dark hair flopped over expressive eyebrows and dark chocolate eyes. His mouth was a strong, straight line. His skin was perfectly tan from years spent working outdoors in Napa, checking the progress of Domaine Randon's grapes. He had taken off his jacket and rolled up his sleeves. Madeleine looked at his well-muscled forearms and felt a flicker deep inside.

Axel Delaflote had always been the most interesting boy in Le Vezy.

She wasn't the least bit surprised when they ended up in bed...

It began, as these things do, with a kiss. Without saying a word, Axel placed his glass on the floor and turned toward her. He cupped her face in his hands and pulled her close. Automatically, Madeleine closed her eyes and parted her lips in anticipation of the touch of his.

What started softly soon became more passionate. They devoured each other's mouths. Meanwhile, Axel's hands roamed the exquisite curves of Madeleine's body. She sighed happily as they moved slowly from her waist toward her bottom. They moved to the bedroom and soon he was undoing the buttons at the back of her plain black mourning dress. Madeleine lifted her arms obediently so that he could pull the dress off over her head. Axel gave a murmur of appreciation as he took in Madeleine's expensive pewter-colored silk and lace underwear. His fingers traced the edge of the balconette bra that lifted the perfect white orbs of her bosom. Her nipples were already tight and hard.

While Axel dipped his head to kiss the soft skin of Madeleine's décolletage from the notch at her throat to the bow between her breasts, she worked at undoing the buttons on his shirt, eager to feel his bare chest against hers. Soon they were both completely naked. Chest to chest. Skin on skin.

Axel briefly caught Madeleine's eye and grinned before he parted her long slim legs and dipped his head down between them. The touch of his tongue on her clitoris sent an electric shock right through her. She was already aroused. Kissing Axel was enough to have done that.

When it became too much to bear, Madeleine pulled him up to lie down on top of her. She parted her legs around his body and felt his penis resting hard against her pubic bone.

She slid her hand down between them and sought out his erection. Meanwhile, Axel's fingers had moved to the silken tuft of her pubic hair. Madeleine couldn't help gasping as she felt him make contact with her clitoris again, sending more shivers of arousal up and down her spine like sparks.

Now all Madeleine wanted was to have him all the way inside her. Not just his fingers. She wrapped her hand around his penis, gently moving the soft sheath of his foreskin backwards and forwards while her other hand massaged his balls. It wasn't long before he was hard enough for Madeleine to tilt her pelvis toward him and slowly guide him in.

She had never felt such pleasure as she did in that moment when her body relaxed around Axel's penis and he began to move. Madeleine wrapped her arms and legs around him and held him so close it was as though she had started to melt into him. She loved the way he kept kissing her or buried his face in her neck. She loved the taste of the sweat on his skin when she kissed him back.

He moved slowly at first. She moved in time with him, rising up to meet each of his thrusts. Their breathing grew heavier as the pace quickened. Madeleine dug her fingers into Axel's buttocks, pulling him still deeper inside.

After a while he flipped her over so that she was on top. Her hair shaded his face like a veil. She balanced above him so that they were touching only where he entered her, teasing him until he had to roll her over again.

She came right before he did. Her orgasm electrified her. Her entire body seemed to dissolve as she started to come. He came quickly afterward; the sound of her ecstasy tipping him over the edge.

"I have waited for that for a very long time," Axel sighed as they lay in each other's arms.

"Me too," said Madeleine, realizing in that moment that it was true. "Me too."

When Geoff, Madeleine's boss, called from London the following morning to tell her that they were definitely going to lose their jobs in the takeover, Madeleine wasn't half as disappointed as she expected to be.

"Don't worry, Mads. I'm not going to take this lying down," Geoff assured her.

I will, thought Madeleine, placing her mobile phone on the bedside table and sinking back into the pillows with an expression that was approaching beatific.

"Good news?" asked Axel, as he snuggled against her side.

"Lost my job," she said simply.

"If it means we're going to see more of you out here in Champagne," he said, "then I'm glad."

Madeleine certainly didn't feel bereft as, later that day, Axel helped her chop through the brambles into the Clos and assured her that, though her father hadn't been properly tending the vines for quite a while, all was not lost.

"Buds," he said, beckoning her closer to one of the sticks she had assumed was dead. "A new beginning."

CHAPTER 8

The fifteenth of April was a very special day in the Morgan-Tarrant household. Exactly a year ago Christina and Bill had celebrated their marriage in the artfully wild garden of their luxuriously appointed Malibu beach home.

Given the bride and groom's status, the wedding was a hotly anticipated affair. To put the press off the scent, caterers and wedding planners set the scene for three identical wedding parties at three venues in the Greater Los Angeles area: a hotel, the beach house and the Bel Air estate belonging to the director of Bill's most recent movie. Celebrity guests were informed of the actual location just hours before the ceremony began, whence they were whisked from a rendezvous point at the Beverly Hills Peninsula Hotel to the beach in a fleet of blacked-out limousines.

When they reached the beach house, the guests were disgorged from their cars beneath a pink ribbon-trimmed gazebo that shielded their identities from the press helicopters that were somehow already circling overhead. Since the couple had done an exclusive deal with *Hello!* magazine for the photographs of their nuptials, cameras and even mobile phones were banned. A few days later, one of the papers carried a small gossip piece in which a grande dame of Hollywood "anonymously" objected to the way she had been frisked by the security staff. "I don't even know how to use the camera function on my

Motorola!" she complained. An ad campaign for the phone company, in which the actress did learn to use her picture function properly, swiftly followed.

Just one prettily impromptu shot sneaked out; taken on a phone that had somehow made it through the X-ray machine provided by the security company that provided machines to international airports, it was a photo of Christina and Bill at the altar, having just exchanged rings. They were leaning together over their joined hands, foreheads touching, smiling deep into each other's eyes. This was the photograph that would appear every time a magazine ran an article that mentioned the couple as an example of a successful celebrity marriage. Christina loved that photograph. It was taken from her best side.

A year later, Christina Morgan and Bill Tarrant woke up in separate bedrooms in the three-thousand-square-foot penthouse suite of the Mark Hopkins Hotel in San Francisco. Christina took a couple of calls on her mobile and answered a few e-mails while sipping Earl Grey from a bone china cup. She stood at her window and looked out at the view. Ocean mist. There was nothing to see. She heard the sound of the Cartoon Network drifting out from Bill's room and considered going in there. It was their anniversary after all. But she decided against it. She needed to wash her hair. It was especially important to look good that day. That was what she'd told Bill the night before when he started making advances.

"I need my beauty sleep, darling."

Bill had no idea how much work went into being one of the world's most beautiful people.

It was another hour or so before the anniversary couple greeted each other in the shared sitting room. Christina held out her cheek for a kiss. Bill responded perfunctorily.

"Are you wearing that?" was the first thing Christina said to her husband of precisely twelve months. She was wearing a dress by Zac Posen, her current favorite. Bill was wearing ripped jeans and a khaki T-shirt that had definitely seen better days.

"What's wrong with what I'm wearing?" Bill asked. "You want to tell me what I should wear?"

"No. But..." Christina felt the rising frustration as yet another mundane exchange threatened to grow into a fight. Why did he always have to be so difficult? This was not what she'd signed up for.

"Don't worry. The magazine is bringing the clothes," interrupted Bill's towheaded personal assistant, Teak, who had just stepped out of the private elevator that went directly from lobby to penthouse. "Car's waiting," he said.

The happy couple boarded the elevator back downstairs.

Their silence continued all the way across the Golden Gate Bridge and up the 101 toward Napa Valley. Well, not silence exactly. Both Bill and Christina took calls from other people. Christina's agent, Marisa, had news of an advertising campaign for a Japanese sportswear line. Bill's manager, Justin, gave him an update on box-office figures for his latest film. They were good, though he had been knocked off the top spot by the sequel to the previous year's surprise hit: a wholesome teen movie about two kids who befriend a drug-addled prostitute and keep her in the basement of their parents' chichi townhouse. If they weren't taking calls, the famous couple simply stared through the dark-tinted windows at the scenery passing by. When they arrived at their destination, however...

Bill leaped out of the car first and raced around to open Christina's door before the driver could get there. Christina stepped from the car sporting an enormous smile, wrapped her arms around her husband and planted a lingering kiss on his cheek. Bill grinned back at her: "still crazy in love after all these months," their expressions said. The camera caught it all.

"Could you put your hand on his face so we can see your engagement ring?" the photographer asked.

Christina's engagement ring—an enormous canary yellow diamond set in white gold—was legendary. It was said that it had originally belonged to Mumtaz, wife of Shah Jahan and inspiration for the Taj Mahal. Teak had done some research that seemed to confirm the diamond's provenance.

A year after the Morgan/Tarrant wedding (a.k.a., Hollywood wedding of the year!), *Hello!* had commissioned a new photo shoot of the couple, which would be accompanied by a nice big piece sharing their views on the secrets of a happy marriage. The setting was inspired.

"The first anniversary of a wedding is traditionally celebrated as the 'paper' anniversary and Bill Tarrant certainly honored that tradition when he handed his exquisite supermodel wife, Christina Morgan, ownership papers on his anniversary gift to her: the Villa Bacchante," the article would report.

"Situated in the Carneros region of California's famous Napa Valley, the Villa Bacchante is twelve thousand square feet of Tuscan-style home set in forty acres of vineyards. As you can see from our pictures, Christina was certainly surprised by her husband's extravagant present. But she was definitely delighted."

"To own a vineyard has long been one of my fantasies," Christina told *Hello!* magazine. "As you know, I was raised on a farm in Iowa and I always dreamed that one day I would get back to the land. I can't wait to get my hands dirty!"

For the benefit of the magazine's readers, Christina

and Bill spent the rest of the day posing all over the Villa Bacchante and throughout its gardens in clothes by Armani, Zac Posen and Michael Kors. They posed in the vineyard. They posed by the huge "living flame" fireplace in the "family" room (which was fired up for the shoot though it was seventy degrees outside). They posed in the kitchen and the living room. They even managed a coy pose by the Jacuzzi bath in the master en suite, wrapped in matching white bathrobes, each of them toting a flute of champagne.

Bill took a slug from his.

"It's just a prop, Bill," said Christina.

The crew from *Hello!* magazine laughed at the friendly married banter.

The photographs looked great. The natural beauty of the vineyards really set off the designer clothes, even if it was too early for grapes. (The stylist taped a couple of bunches of black table grapes bought at Whole Foods to one of the vines for the purposes of a more impressive close-up.) Despite that, everyone agreed it would make a wonderful spread. At the end of the shoot, Bill and Christina sat down with the journalist in the garden of this, the newest of their four "palatial" homes.

"What are you going to grow here?" the journalist asked.

"Grapes, I guess," said Christina. "It is a vineyard."

"I mean, what kind of grapes," the journalist persisted.

Teak, Bill's PA, flicked through a folder and announced. "Most of the vineyards here are given over to pinot noir. The Carneros region is particularly suited to the grape and the Villa Bacchante has long been renowned for its sparkling wine, modeled on the famous Blanc de Noirs champagnes of France in Europe."

The journalist nodded approvingly.

"There are production facilities to make a hundred and fifty thousand bottles per year," Teak concluded his spiel.

"One hundred and fifty thousand bottles?" Now the journalist was really impressed. "And you'll be involved in the winemaking process yourselves?" she asked.

"Of course," Bill and Christina assured her.

"Though I wouldn't want to drink any wine made from grapes pressed with Bill's gnarly feet!" said Christina, to add a bit of authentic teasing color to the piece.

The interview then moved from wine to the couple's more urbane projects. Bill talked about his new movies; he had three blockbusters coming up that year, filmed back-to-back in Romania. Christina talked about the clothing line that she had been asked to design for H&M.

"I mean, I'm not actually going to design it but I am coming up with the overall concept."

"You're quite the Renaissance woman," said the journalist.

Christina looked at her blankly.

"Modeling, wine, fashion design . . ."

"Oh, yes. I love all that stuff."

"Well, I think that about covers it." The journalist turned off her digital recorder. "Thanks, guys. I should be able to pull something really good out of this."

"We'll be sent the copy for approval, of course," said Christina.

"Of course."

Half an hour after the last of the *Hello!* crew had gone, Bill and Christina got into their limousine and were driven to San Francisco International Airport. Bill went with Teak to New York and Christina returned to LA.

·   ·   ·

Christina was furious. What kind of anniversary present was a vineyard? It was Bill's dream, not Christina's, to get back to the land. In the many articles that had been written about her enormous success, Christina had often romanticized her childhood in Iowa, but the truth was she couldn't wait to get out of there. She thanked God on a daily basis for the looks that had brought her the crown of Miss Teen Dairy which gave her the courage to move to New York, where she got a nose job that slimmed her little bobbed snout into something more suitable for the pages of *Vogue*. After that, she never looked back. She'd certainly never been back to Des Moines.

But she had to admit the Villa Bacchante had made a fabulous backdrop for the anniversary photo shoot and Bill's super-geek PA had assured her it was a wonderful investment. When the estate came onto the market, fifteen buyers put in a bid for it, Teak said, which was why Bill had to pay so much over the asking price. One of those fifteen other buyers would almost certainly pay even more than that to wrestle it back from Bill, especially with the *Hello!* spread as a marketing tool.

"You better be right," Christina told the little smart-ass. Teak had a literature degree from Harvard and she was convinced he was only working for Bill so that he could write a warts-and-all exposé when his contract ran out.

Back in the Beverly Hills house, Christina prepared for bed. It was a long process involving three different kinds of dermatologist-prescribed night cream for the different "zones" of her face. The ritual was very important to Christina. She knew she was lucky to still be doing so well at the age of thirty-four. As one of her fellow models had pointed out, the only models who continued to get covers after that age were usually subtitled "fabulous at thirty-five" like it was some kind of miracle they hadn't gotten moldy. Just a few days earlier she had heard a British fashion photographer describe Gisele as "aging like a fine wine. That's been left too close to a radiator."

And so Christina kept up the nightly routine that supplemented six-weekly visits to her dermatologist for Botox, micro-dermabrasion and intense pulsed light laser therapy. You name it, she was having it. There had been just one night in the past ten years when she hadn't taken off her makeup and applied some kind of anti-aging serum before her head hit the pillow. It was the first night she ever spent with the man who would become her husband...

Bill and Christina were introduced by Christina's agent, Marisa. Marisa was a superficially abrasive but ultimately kindhearted New Yorker who took the pastoral care of her models so seriously that she often went so far as to find them suitable husbands and wives.

What Christina didn't know was that Bill had flicked through Marisa's modeling agency book as though it were a mail order catalog and requested introductions to three girls who caught his eye. Christina also didn't know that she was actually Bill's third choice. The two girls he chose ahead of her were both attached.

Still, Marisa set up a dinner party in Los Angeles and invited both Bill and Christina to attend. Christina hadn't been single for all that long. She'd recently broken up with a New York finance guy. And so, Bill would later tell her, when Christina walked into the party that night, she was looking a little wistful. "Like that pre-Raphaelite painting of the lady in the boat," he said. They could neither of them remember the painting's name or that of the artist but it didn't matter. Though Bill's status as a huge movie star meant Christina was automatically on the alert for a charm offensive, she was flattered to be compared to a classic work of art and by the end of the evening, Bill had almost convinced her that losing the "love of her life" was actually a lucky escape.

Having spent the previous month panicking that she would never find another man of the right caliber, Christina was delightedly surprised to feel that familiar tingle of arousal when Bill brushed her arm to draw her attention to something on the other side of the room. She didn't even mind when he used one of the oldest tricks in the book on her.

"I can read palms," he said, taking her right hand between his and stroking it gently. "And the lines on your hand tell me that you're coming home with me tonight."

"Bill Tarrant, I hardly know you," she said, channeling a Southern belle.

"So you'll be glad of the opportunity to get to know me better."

They quit the party ten minutes later. She followed him in her little silver Mercedes SLK convertible up through the winding roads above Sunset Plaza to his bachelor pad—an enormous Frank Lloyd Wright–style house with glass walls and panoramic views. He made them nightcaps, which they drank by the pool, looking out over the glittering city below. By the time she had finished her drink, Christina knew for sure she would be staying the night. The cognac had put her way over the limit for driving home. Bill had almost certainly planned it that way. But she didn't mind. She'd already decided she was going to sleep with him. Even if she never saw Bill Tarrant again, she didn't care. When her ex found out that she had ended her post-break-up run of celibacy by sleeping with a movie star . . .

Bill got to his feet and started to take off his clothes.

"It's hot out here. I'm going for a swim," he announced.

He wore nothing beneath his well-cut black linen pants.

Christina followed Bill's lead, discarding her pale blue silk dress on the poolside lounger. She kept her bra and panties on and jumped into the pool. Bill swam across to her as she surfaced and when she opened her mouth for air, he covered it with a kiss. Moments after that, he divested her of her underwear. He plunged his penis into her and the deal was sealed.

Afterward, catching sight of her reflection in the mirror in Bill's en-suite bathroom, Christina thought she hadn't looked that good since the first time she had Botox (it had never worked quite so well again; she'd simply found other ways to frown).

"You are the most beautiful woman I have ever met," Bill told her as she climbed back into bed. "And I've met most of *FHM*'s top hundred," he added with a smirk. Christina swatted him with a pillow but for some reason it didn't bother her. She knew that the first part of his assertion was true. There was something in his eyes as he said it.

Christina never went home. They had the traditional Hollywood whirlwind romance. The very next morning, Christina was photographed outside Bill's home in a baseball cap and one of his big blue shirts. A week later, they were pictured looking cozy in front row seats at a Lakers game. They were seen leaving The Ivy on Robertson Boulevard in Bill's Hummer. Just a month later, they were snapped "window-shopping" at Harry Winston (in fact, they were just strolling past). They ended the leases on his bachelor house in the Hollywood Hills and her pokey place in Santa Monica and bought somewhere together in Beverly Hills. Bill's big payday for *Maverick* funded the beach house in Malibu. He already had an apartment in New York.

Bill wasn't the kind of man Christina thought she would end up with. Actors were notoriously unfaithful and had the kind of career paths that made professional poker players look like a sensible option. But Bill seemed to be on an unstoppable upward trajectory. He had a lot of big toys. He had been signed for five new movies. Christina started to wonder if she should take him seriously.

Two months after she met Bill, Christina was on a shoot for *Vogue*'s fall collections issue when she overheard a stylist gossiping about Victoria Beckham. "She'll never leave him," the stylist said. "She knows that a celebrity couple is worth way more than the sum of its parts. How else is a thirty-something from a nineties girl band going to make a living?" Later on the same shoot, far worse, Christina heard the photographer say to his assistant of her, "We need to do something about the lines around her eyes. How old is Christina these days anyway?"

The following day Bill proposed, as he often did when he was drunk. This time, Christina accepted. She wasn't sure she'd made the right decision, but then a month after her wedding, Christina bumped into her ex at a cocktail party. She introduced her new husband to him.

"Bill Tarrant. The movie star."

The old boyfriend went green. Christina was thrilled. It took a lot to impress her extraordinarily wealthy ex. She'd obviously made a very good match indeed.

And yet she found herself alone on their first wedding anniversary.

Beauty routine finished, Christina peered at her face in the bathroom mirror. Could Bill really not have waited until the morning after their anniversary to fly to New York? How did that look? What would people think if they knew he would rather be on a plane than have dinner with his wife of one year?

She'd asked him to stay. He'd asked her to fly to New York with him. She'd explained that she *had* to stay in Los Angeles because she'd been invited to a fund-raiser sponsored by *InStyle*.

"It's going to get four pages in the August issue," she said.

"Well, if that's more important to you..." Bill concluded.

It was important, Christina told herself. She needed to be seen at that fund-raiser. Her public profile mattered just as much as Bill's did. In any case, he was only going to New York for some cheesy award ceremony where he wouldn't win a thing. It would have been a far better idea for them both to go to the *InStyle* party. To present a united front. Remind people they were a double act.

Just as she was about to fall asleep, her mobile started to ring. Christina made a grab for it. Bill's plane should have landed in New York about fifteen minutes earlier. Perhaps...

"Happy wedding anniversary, my darling. I hope you're having a fantastic day," said her mother.

Christina assured her parents that life as Mrs. Tarrant was absolutely wonderful, but she couldn't convince herself. When her mother hung up, Christina lay back on the pillows and nibbled absently at a cuticle as she looked at the framed black-and-white photos on the bedroom wall. She had been photographed by all the greats: Meisel, Bailey, Testino. The Bailey photo was her favorite. She was just twenty-one when he took it. She was running down a beach, her long hair flying out behind her. Physically perfect and full of optimism that shone from her laughing face.

Christina hadn't been booked by Bailey in five years.

She hadn't had a cover in almost as long. Turning her face away from the haunting images of her past perfection, she felt a tear spring to her eye.

CHAPTER 9

The news that she had inherited a farmhouse and a vineyard in Sussex did a great deal to improve Kelly's mood on the day she learned of her father's death. She immediately started fantasizing about the money she would get when she sold the place and the smart London flat she would buy for herself with the proceeds.

Unfortunately, the fantasy didn't last long.

"Oh dear. I'm afraid you can't actually sell the farmhouse," said Mr. Harper. "At least, not yet. The conditions of the will are that the house cannot be sold for at least the next five years."

"What?" Kelly was furious. "But you said it was my house."

"Not quite. It's in trust," Mr. Harper repeated.

Kelly was not glad to hear that. Five years was for-fucking-ever in her world.

"Your father explains in this letter, which he asked me to give to you. I think the idea is that you should produce a 'vintage' of your own before you make a decision whether or not to pass the farm on to someone else."

Kelly looked confused.

"Vintage?" said Mr. Harper. "It's a wine term. Five years is roughly how long it takes to make a bottle of good sparkling wine, which is what Dougal was producing at Froggy Bottom."

Kelly looked at Marina. Marina shrugged in response.

"So, basically, what you're saying is I can't get my hands on any money until I'm twenty-three?"

"But it's an exciting opportunity for you to learn about wine ..." Mr. Harper tried.

"Oh, for fuck's sake," said Kelly. "Forget it. I don't know fuck about wine and I'm not bloody living on a farm. Just call me when the five years are up."

"I'm afraid I can't do that. The conditions of the will are that you have to get your hands dirty, as it were, to get any money at all."

"But I don't know anything about wine! I told you."

Mr. Harper explained that Kelly wouldn't be expected the run the vineyard on her own. There was already a vineyard manager in place at Froggy Bottom and there were three trustees to take care of the financial arrangements: Dougal's former accountant, Reginald Bryden; his former bank manager, Georgina Nuttall, and Hilarian Jackson, Dougal's great friend. Overall responsibility would remain with Mr. Jackson until the five years had passed.

"He'll steer you right. He's a noted wine critic," said Mr. Harper.

"I've never heard of him," said Kelly.

Still Mr. Harper persisted. He pulled a map out of his briefcase and showed Kelly exactly where Froggy Bottom lay. It was pretty close to London, he pointed out. Between Brighton and Lewes on the South Downs.

"Brighton?"

Kelly perked up a little. She had been to Brighton often as a child, and later she and her friends would sometimes catch a train down there to go clubbing. A big house near Brighton was much more appealing than a vineyard in the middle of nowhere.

"I suppose I ought to have a look at it," said Kelly. "It sounds a bit better now."

The day came for her to visit Froggy Bottom for the first time.

Mr. Harper picked her up for the drive down to Sussex.

"You must be very excited," he said.

"Sure," said Kelly. But she was soon feeling uncomfortable about the whole thing again. This place was nowhere near Brighton. At least not within cabbing distance. As they drove through a couple of tiny villages that didn't even have their own pubs, Kelly could already feel the boredom that would eat into her bones if she actually had to live there. And then it got worse.

Mr. Harper asked Kelly to navigate for the last part of the journey.

"Turn up the farm track," was the first instruction Kelly read aloud.

Within three minutes they were out of sight of any human habitation. It was as though they had driven back in time. Kelly felt oddly apprehensive. The downs rolled before them like a quilt freshly shaken out, rain-forest-frog green against the gunmetal gray of a stormy May sky. It had rained solidly for the past fortnight and now it looked as though it was about to start again. Mr. Harper's brand-new Audi A8 didn't seem quite such a smart choice of transport anymore. This really was a track, two deep channels worn by years of tractor traffic. As they drove on, Kelly stared out of the car window in horror. If Mr. Harper feared for his Audi, Kelly feared for her boots.

A large puddle loomed across the track ahead of them. It was as wide as the child's paddling pool in the park near

Kelly's house and the muddy water made it impossible to tell how deep it was.

"I guess we'll just have to chance it," said Mr. Harper, manfully.

It was a bad mistake. The Audi got just halfway across the mini-lake before it was stuck. The channels were too deep, impossible to navigate in anything less than a Land Rover. Mr. Harper revved the engine but the car was going nowhere. Not forwards; not backwards. Just nowhere.

"I'll have to get out and push," he said. "You steer."

"You are fucking kidding me," said Kelly.

"I'll steer if you push?" Mr. Harper attempted a joke that failed to elicit a smile from either of them.

"Fuck off."

Mr. Harper opened the car door and looked at the puddle that swirled around the car as dark as chocolate milk. Wisely, he took off his shoes and rolled up his trousers before getting out. Kelly moved across into the driver's seat.

It was hopeless. After three more minutes of wheel-spinning, Mr. Harper reappeared from behind the car. He was absolutely drenched from the water that the tires had kicked up. He opened the driver's door and leaned inside.

"I don't seem to be making much progress," he admitted. "Perhaps if we push together?"

Kelly stared at him in horror. "I'm not getting out of here," she said. "Send someone to fetch me."

Mr. Harper nodded with resignation. He got out his mobile to call the farmhouse. There was no signal.

"What now?" Kelly asked him, her voice getting shrill with panic.

"Just stay here," said Mr. Harper bravely. "I'll walk down there. It can't be far."

"It better not be. I'm cold and hungry."

"And I'm soaking wet," said Mr. Harper. He waded to the other side of the puddle, put on his shoes and followed the path until he was out of sight.

"Great."

Kelly remained frozen behind the steering wheel, staring in the direction Mr. Harper had disappeared. Forgetting his experience, she pulled her mobile out of her handbag. She could at least call one of her mates and moan until she was out of this hellhole. But her phone could find no signal either.

"Fuck, fuck, fuck!" she swore at the screen. "For fuck's sake! I didn't even want to be here. I just want to go home!"

Then all was quiet again. Nothing but the sound of the wind rustling through the wheat in the fields on either side. Nothing at all. Until a frog jumped from the puddle through the open driver's door and straight into her lap.

It was more than three quarters of an hour before Mr. Harper returned. By that time, Kelly had almost given up hope. As it was, she had completely lost the will to be polite or friendly to her father's solicitor and the man who made up the rescue party in the Land Rover.

"Hilarian Jackson," said the man, extending his hand. Kelly could tell at once that he was posh. He was properly equipped with Wellington boots and had the red face of a bon viveur. "I'm representing the trustees today," he explained to Kelly. "Piggyback?"

"Anything. Just get me out of here. A frog left slime on my skirt."

Hilarian just laughed. "They don't call this Froggy Bottom for nothing. Let's get you in my car." He hauled her out of there and gave her a fireman's lift.

The view from that final bit of road was breathtaking,

but Kelly didn't notice. She was almost crying as the Land Rover crested the last hill that hid the vale of Froggy Bottom. She didn't see the chalk cliffs stretching into the distance or notice the seabirds wheeling overhead, brilliant bright white flashes of flight against the blackening clouds. She certainly didn't notice the neatly planted vines, marching up the south-facing slopes like regiments of thin, green soldiers.

All Kelly could see was the mud that lay between her and the house.

"I want to go back to London," she said.

There was one person at Froggy Bottom who really did hope that Kelly went back to London. Guy Harcourt had been running the vineyard for the past three years. He couldn't believe the girl's luck. In Guy's opinion, she had inherited one of the best vineyards in Europe.

Guy had come to England from South Africa. He was passionate about grapes. At just twenty-three he had far more knowledge than many men twice his age. It was largely because he was so young that old man Dougal had taken Guy on, thinking he would be able to pay him half the wages of someone more experienced. Guy didn't mind. It was worth the pay cut to be able to run the vineyard his way, without any interference.

And so, as far as Guy was concerned, the best-case scenario (after the old man leaving the vineyard to him) was that it should go to someone fairly disinterested, so that he could continue to experiment without having to justify himself.

He was hugely relieved when he discovered that old Dougal Mollison had not left the vineyard to his legitimate children (they had to make do with the enormous house in Norfolk and the Scottish shooting lodge with its associated fishing rights). But he didn't expect the illegitimate child to be any more exciting. He certainly didn't expect her to be beautiful.

It took a rare vision to notice that Kelly Elson was beautiful behind the cheap makeup and tight ponytail that showed off her thrice-pierced ears to perfection. The ring through her nose distracted from its snub prettiness, and as for her attitude...it was very hard to notice the elegance of Kelly's heart-shaped face when she jutted her chin out so belligerently.

"I'm your new boss," she said to Guy when Hilarian introduced them. "You better impress me."

They were off to a very bad start.

"There is no way this is going to work," Kelly said to herself as Hilarian led her into the farmhouse that he referred to as her "new home." For a start it was far from new.

"The original building dates from the sixteenth century," Hilarian explained. "The outhouses were built in the eighteenth. It's been in your father's family all that time."

The place was disgusting. The ceilings were low. The windows were tiny. It was dark and smelled of mildew. The furniture was ancient too. Kelly saw no point to antiques. The three-piece suite in the sitting room made her mother's settee look positively smart. Neither did the inglenook fireplace impress her.

"You mean like you have to light a proper fire if you want to sit in here in the winter?"

"Yes," said Hilarian. "Or in the summer. It does get chilly out here. But I think it's rather romantic."

"Filthy," Kelly said. Not to mention labor intensive. The rest of the tour confirmed her worst fears. There wasn't a radiator in the place. There was no dishwasher in the kitchen. The washing machine was on its last legs. Hilarian merely laughed when she asked about a tumble dryer. There was no shower in the single bathroom. Kelly turned on a tap full blast and was rewarded with a trickle of cold brown water. How could anyone live like this? Kelly certainly didn't intend to.

Guy was in charge of the tour of the winery.

"Let's start with the vineyard itself," he said.

"You've got to be fucking joking," said Kelly. "In these boots?" She indicated the dagger-sharp heels. "It ain't happening."

"We must have a pair of wellies around here somewhere," said Hilarian. He went back into the farmhouse and returned with a pair of green Hunters. "Bit big," he said. "But we're not going to walk far. These must have been your father's," he added.

"What? You want me to wear a dead person's shoes?" Kelly was incredulous. "You are having a laugh. Fuck off!"

So they didn't go up to the vineyard. Instead they stayed on the relatively safe concrete outside the winery while Guy pointed to the vines they could see from that vantage point and let Kelly know what varietal was planted where with the help of a drawing he'd taken hours to prepare.

"Doesn't mean anything to me," she told him when he had finished a fairly impassioned speech about the suitability of the terroir at Froggy Bottom for creating sparkling wine. Guy said he could explain it all again if she wanted, but Kelly told him the only thing she wanted right then was to get inside and out of the drizzle.

And so they went into the winery. It was the newest of the ugly-looking sheds that flanked the courtyard, and inside it was like any other factory—all piping and concrete floors. Kelly stared up at the enormous stainless steel vats and started to zone out while Guy explained the whole process of making sparkling wine from grape to bottle. The occasional word—familiar from Daniel Weston's wine monologues—drifted into her consciousness but seeing the tools of the craft laid before her didn't make things any clearer or more interesting. Meanwhile Guy's strong Afrikaans accent began to grate on her. He sounded as arrogant as he looked.

Kelly glanced from Guy to Hilarian and caught him looking back at her. He'd seemed happy enough when he came to her rescue in the Land Rover, but now she decided that he'd taken a dislike to her too. His eyes were narrowed as he regarded her. He probably thought she was stupid and common, Kelly decided. People like him always did. Well, it didn't matter what he thought. She'd never have to see him again. She wasn't coming back to this place until the time came to sell it. Kelly had talked to one of the girls at work: a law student at the London School of Economics. She said she thought Kelly would be able to get around the whole trust thing if she wanted to. "Circumvent" was the word she'd used.

"OK," said Hilarian suddenly. "I can see that our guest of honor is flagging in the face of all your jargon, Guy. Shall we cut to the chase?"

Guy had already prepared a little tasting area in the corner of the winery. He'd covered a small folding table with a white tablecloth and arrayed eight glasses in front of two different vintages of Froggy Bottom's finest. He poured out tasting measures. Hilarian and Mr. Harper examined the color of the wine against the background of the tablecloth. Kelly listened to Hilarian's pretentious description of what looked like bubbling piss to her.

"I'm very proud that Froggy Bottom has produced a wine this good," said Hilarian. "Which is lucky because in five years' time, I'm going to need your first vintage to be a world-beater, Kelly."

"Eh?" said Kelly.

"I made a little bet," Hilarian told her, "with a couple

of other wine critics, that your wine would be better than their favorite sparklers. Actually, it was quite a big bet. So if you don't produce a great first vintage . . ." Hilarian pulled his forefinger across his throat in a slashing motion.

Kelly frowned.

"Don't worry. You won't be doing it on your own. Guy and I will be with you every step of the way. Now, tell me what you think. Slight hint of grass on the nose," he suggested. "Biscuity overtones."

Kelly took a small sniff and a big gulp. She swallowed. She knew the men were waiting for her verdict.

To her surprise, Kelly tasted the grass Hilarian spoke of at once. She also tasted fresh green apples, and the fizz lingered longer than she had expected when she looked at the bubbles in the glass. What word was it that Daniel Weston had used to describe fizziness? Mousse? No, that didn't sound right.

She didn't want to make a fool of herself.

"I'd prefer a Bacardi Breezer," she said at last.

The visit ended fairly shortly after that. Guy and Hilarian helped Mr. Harper get his Audi out of the mud and waved him and Kelly back off to London. With relief.

Visitors gone, Hilarian and Guy retired to the farmhouse for a debrief over what remained of the bottles they had opened for the tasting.

"Thanks for coming today," said Guy. "I don't think I could have handled that without you."

"I think it went particularly well," said Hilarian.

"English sarcasm, I presume," said Guy.

"I suppose the one good thing is that you now know for certain you don't have to worry about someone moving into Froggy Bottom and sweeping all your hard work on the vines aside in favor of planting GM tomatoes or some such nonsense."

"I'll raise a glass to that," said Guy.

They clinked their glasses together.

"So, Hilarian," Guy asked then, "just how big is this bet you keep talking about?"

Hilarian swallowed. "I suppose you should know the whole story. Fifty."

"Pounds?"

"Times a thousand."

Guy, who had been taking another sip of wine, suddenly snorted it all over the table. "That we can make a wine better than a champagne chosen by Odile Levert? Or better than Ronald Ginsburg's favorite California Blanc de Noirs? Are you crazy?"

"No. I don't think so," Hilarian lied. "I have absolute faith in you. And the new chatelaine of Froggy Bottom."

"Do you think she's actually going to come here and get involved?"

"I don't know," said Hilarian. "I really don't know. She prefers Bacardi Breezers." He shook his head with a mixture of amusement and bewilderment. "Poor old Dougie must be spinning in his grave."

CHAPTER 10

Almost a month had passed since Madeleine's father's death. Realizing just how big a mess the maison's affairs were in, Madeleine had resigned herself to the fact that she would be spending some time in Champagne. Two days after the funeral, she returned to London to pick up her car and the clothes and other bits and bobs she would need for a couple of weeks in the country. But a fortnight had turned into four weeks and still no return to London was in sight. Trust her father to force her to stay in Champagne from beyond the grave. Madeleine's grief was mixed with large portions of anger and annoyance.

Madeleine spent hours every day sitting in her father's dusty office going through his papers, trying to work out how the maison's bank account was quite so far in the red while all his neighbors—even those who made wine that tasted like cat's pee—swanned around in Mercedes Benz. It became clear that while her father had sent out lots of champagne—the maison was represented in some surprisingly good restaurants and hotels—he hadn't been quite so good at chasing up payment for it. There were simply dozens of unpaid invoices.

And dozens of gambling chits.

Madeleine groaned as she saw how much money her father had spent on the horses. It would never have happened while her mother was alive, but since she'd died, seven years before, it was clear that Constant Arsenault had done whatever he wanted. And he obviously wanted to gamble. Pity he didn't have Lady Luck on his side.

Meanwhile, the vines still had to be tended. On arriving in France to bury her father, Madeleine had learned from Monsieur Mulfort (who recounted the tale with some glee, she thought) that Constant Arsenault had been tending his grapes up on the hill alone for the few months before his death. The Clos had been pretty much left to go wild. It transpired that Madeleine's father had argued with his vineyard manager over unpaid wages. The manager had walked and the maison's three full-time workers had walked with him. Champagne Arsenault had subsequently fallen behind on every aspect of that year's production.

Madeleine discussed the situation with Axel, who told Madeleine that as far as he knew, Henri Mason, the former manager, was a good man who would not have deserted her father lightly. Having left Arsenault, Mason tried to find work at Maison Randon. There were no vacancies and thus he was still unemployed. Axel suggested that Madeleine contact the man and ask him to come back. Beg if she had to. Fortunately, she didn't have to beg. Henri Mason was only too happy to return to his former position once Madeleine had made good the shortfall in his wages with money from her own pocket. It was worth it. She had yet to decide what to do with the maison and, as Axel pointed out, a champagne house without its vines was...well, it was just a house.

"The vines are the maison's biggest asset," said Axel. "Especially the Clos. You need to get that into shape right away."

"You're taking such an interest in all this," said Madeleine. "I'm very grateful for that."

"Anything for an old friend," said Axel.

"You've forgotten the stink bomb, then?" Madeleine asked.

"I'll never forget the stink bomb."

"What are you going to do about the old place when you've sorted it out?" Geoff, her former boss, asked every time he called with news of the job hunt, which was daily. She could hear the desperation in his voice. Poor Geoff. His ex-wife was snapping at his heels like a Hermès-clad hellhound. "You can't be planning to stay out there forever, Mads. I mean, you're not...are you?"

Geoff wanted Madeleine to tell him she was coming back to London to be part of the killer team that would get him a position at another, better bank. But Madeleine couldn't give him that answer. At least, not yet.

"You should make the most of this time off," Madeleine suggested instead. "Enjoy your children."

"Yeah, right. Have you met my lovely daughters? Take after their mother."

One afternoon, tired of calling the maison's debtors to claw back what little she could of the money her father was owed, Madeleine drove up to the Arsenault vineyards above the village. She sat down on a picnic table erected for the tourists who flooded the region each summer. Looking down over the valley, she remembered sitting in that same spot with her father and her brother, Georges, while Constant pointed out features in the vineyards below and explained why they were the luckiest children in France because they stood to inherit the best patch of land on earth.

Well, Constant was wrong. A year later, Georges was dead and Madeleine came to see the vineyards as cursed. Could she ever feel any differently? Could she have a life in Champagne?

There were bright spots. Definitely. Well, at least one bright spot. She'd been seeing a lot of Axel Delaflote. He was often in the village, attending to Maison Randon business; Randon had several hectares in Le Vezy. After that first night, when they made love in front of the fire, Madeleine had told herself not to expect too much, but despite her reservations—including the peculiar fleeting thought that at any moment, Axel might revert to calling her names over the wall of the Clos—something seemed to be growing between them. If she didn't actually see Axel, then she spoke to him every day. Was he interested in something serious?

Madeleine's phone shattered the peace of her moment on the hill with a tinny rendition of "The Ride of the Valkyries." Geoff had changed her ringtone for her back when they were still fighting for their jobs. It was a battle cry. She had rather liked it, but now it just made her dread the sound of Geoff's voice.

Thankfully, it was Axel's number that appeared on caller ID.

Madeleine relaxed.

"Do you have plans for dinner this evening?"

"Well, as you know, my diary is absolutely packed these days," Madeleine laughed. "But perhaps I can squeeze you in."

CHAPTER 11

Unfortunately, Axel's plan for a romantic dinner with Madeleine was scuppered by a call from his boss. Mathieu Randon had been in the United States, visiting the Manhattan headquarters of Fast Life, a sportswear firm he'd had his eye on for some time. It was a relatively small company but it was ripe for dramatic expansion, having recently become deeply cool thanks to the endorsement by a popular rap star who claimed that she never wore anything else.

The owner of Fast Life was keen to sell to fund an ugly divorce. Randon was keen to buy, sensing an opportunity to profit from the other man's misery. And so he called a meeting of the main board of Domaine Randon to expedite the process. His flight landed at Charles de Gaulle at 7 P.M. The meeting in the Paris boardroom was called for eight o'clock—clashing exactly with Axel's dinner reservation in Champagne.

And so, when he should have been sipping champagne with Madeleine, Axel was pouring himself a glass of still iced water while Randon's new personal assistant (who bore an uncanny resemblance to the unfortunate Bertille) passed out folders containing everything the team needed to know about Fast Life.

Axel wasn't quite sure what he was doing there, sitting at a table with the most important players at Domaine Randon. He could only imagine it was because his direct boss at Maison Randon, the champagne house's Managing Director, Stefan Urban, was holidaying in the Maldives. Axel tried to convey the impression that he wasn't fazed, however. He was just glad he was wearing his best suit, pulled out specially for dinner with Madeleine.

Axel Delaflote had always been ambitious, but unlike Mathieu Randon, his ambition had not been instilled in him as a means of living up to the family name. On the contrary, Axel had grown up thinking that his family name meant *merde*. He wanted to succeed in spite of it.

It was true that like the Randons, Axel's family had been in the champagne business for several generations. But his family name had never been on a bottle. The Delaflotes had always been employees. In fact, his great-grandfather had briefly worked for Maison Randon. His grandfather and father had both worked as cellar masters for Champagne Arsenault.

Axel remembered quite clearly the night when his father Alain had announced proudly that Champagne Arsenault might as well be called Champagne Delaflote, since it was his nose that made the maison's wine as good as it was. Axel's entire family had applauded Alain Delaflote that night, but the following day, when eight-year-old Axel repeated his father's assertion to young Georges Arsenault, he got a kick in the head for his trouble.

"What are you talking about? The Delaflote family are Arsenault's slaves!" Georges had announced with the kind of cruelty that only a child could show.

From that moment on, Axel was ashamed of his father. It was true. His father was an employee, not a freeman like Georges's father. Though he attended the same local state-run school as Georges and Madeleine Arsenault, from that day forward Axel no longer felt their equal. He was a serf. The Delaflotes lived in a house that was rented from Champagne Arsenault.

Even when Madeleine was chosen to play Marianne, symbol of the French Revolution and personification of *la liberté et l'égalité,* in their school pageant, Axel saw it as confirmation that she had been marked for better things than him from birth. Her beauty was just another in a long list of privileges Axel would never have.

Stefan Urban, head of Randon's Napa operation, had recognized Axel's talent and nurtured it further. Axel had felt his heart swell with pride when Mathieu Randon told Urban that he wanted Stefan to head up the champagne operation and Urban responded, while Axel stood in front of his desk and listened in on the call, via speakerphone. "I'm moving nowhere without Delaflote. Axel is my right-hand man. Damn it, Mathieu. He is my right hand!"

Randon agreed to bring Axel back to Champagne too.

"Would you really have turned down the job if he'd refused to transfer me?" Axel asked his boss later.

"Of course," said Stefan. "You make me look good."

Such unequivocal support meant a great deal to Axel and so he was determined to be a good representative of Stefan Urban's team when he joined the rest of Domaine Randon's board at the huge oval table in the office on the Champs-Élysées.

The meeting continued until midnight. It was tiring but exciting too. Axel had always wanted to be a part of this world in which he found himself now, where people bandied about seven- and even eight-figure numbers without batting an eyelid, though he found it slightly nerve-racking when Randon went around the table asking each person present to give their opinion.

"What about you, Delaflote? Will Fast Life be a worthy addition to the DR stable? Would you wear Fast Life?"

"I'm wearing their underwear right now," said Axel, regretting the words even as they came out of his mouth. But, thank goodness, everybody laughed. Mathieu Randon laughed hardest.

"Then it's done," he said.

Finally Randon called the meeting to a close. Like obedient schoolchildren, the attendees stood up almost as one and began to gather together their belongings.

"Not you, Monsieur Delaflote," Randon said to Axel.

Axel paused in packing his briefcase, empty but for his phone and a pen. Randon beckoned him to the head of the table. Axel was aware that every gaze in the room was following him.

"I need a dining companion," said Randon. "And you're today's lucky winner. Bertille, call Le Cochon D'Inde and tell them I'll be there in twenty minutes."

"I'm not Bertille..." the girl began. A smile from Randon quickly silenced her.

Le Cochon D'Inde was one of the best new restaurants in Paris. Ordinarily, its kitchen closed at midnight, but a call on behalf of Mathieu Randon could persuade most Parisian chefs to stay after hours, even if they knew that the great man would order nothing more than an omelet when he did arrive. Randon had recently invested heavily in a couple of restaurants and every eager young chef courted his patronage.

Axel's mouth watered as he studied the menu. He was ravenous. He fancied a steak. But even as he was reading it, Randon plucked the menu from Axel's hand and ordered for him too.

"The usual. Two omelets. Much too late at night for anything heavier, don't you think?"

Axel demurred.

There was to be no wine either. The waiter poured two glasses of sparkling water. Axel prayed that his stomach wouldn't growl as Randon began to speak.

"I've heard good reports about you, Monsieur Delaflote."

Axel nodded. He wanted to say "thank you" but he had a mouth full of bread.

"You may have wondered why you were invited to join our meeting this evening," Randon continued.

"It had crossed my mind," said Axel. He had definitely been the most junior person present at the boardroom table that night. "I suppose you wanted someone to represent Stefan."

"I've decided that I want to give you more responsibility."

Axel raised an eyebrow. He tried to look cool. As though such an honor were inevitable.

"As you know, Domaine Randon began with, and still very much revolves around, my family business in Champagne. Maison Randon dates back to the eighteenth century. It was a favorite of Napoléon. It is the seat of my family and the heart of my empire. So you can imagine how much it concerned me when that heart began to ail."

Axel nodded.

"That's why I asked Stefan to bring you across from Napa Valley."

"Thank you for the opportunity," said Axel.

"You've proved yourself to be worthy of it."

Randon paused for a moment while the waiter placed their omelets in front of them.

"You're a Champagne man yourself, Delaflote. You know how proud the Champenois are. You understand the meaning of family pride. Well, I want to reinvigorate my family name. I want to grow Maison Randon. Here is a list of the land I would like to acquire over the next three to five years."

He passed the list on monogrammed paper across the table to Axel, who read the names written thereon with a sense of rising panic.

"I want you to do due diligence on each of these houses. I want to know how much you think they're worth. I trust you, Monsieur Delaflote. I know you won't disappoint me. And people who serve me well are always rewarded."

Dinner over, Randon offered Axel a ride to the Gare de L'Est in the back of his chauffeured car.

"Damn nuisance to have to catch a train at this time of night. We should get you an apartment in Paris," Randon commented, peering out of the car window. "I'll have the personnel department find you something in town."

"I'm happy in Épernay. It suits me just fine," said Axel.

"Not with your new job title, it won't. You'll need a place here, as well as in Champagne."

"I'm sorry . . . ?" Axel began.

"Kill the engine for a moment," Randon instructed his driver. "Stefan Urban takes a lot of holidays," he continued. "I'm not entirely sure of his dedication to the cause. Since he seems to enjoy his time off so much, I think it may be time for him to take a proper sabbatical. And for you to take a promotion. How do the initials 'MD' sound to you, Monsieur Delaflote?"

Axel's mouth dropped open. "Are you serious?"

"We'll talk about it further in the morning. My office. Nine o'clock sharp. Now get some sleep. By the way," Randon said, almost as an afterthought, "I do hope you didn't have to cancel an important assignation on my behalf."

Axel shook his head automatically. He was absolutely in a daze.

"Of course not."

"Good," said Randon, nodding approvingly. "Because as every man should know, love is the enemy of success."

CHAPTER 12

Christina and Bill hadn't seen each other in almost a month. Since their anniversary, Bill had been spending most of his time in New Mexico filming an action movie called *Kings of the Stone Age*. It was about a paleontologist who foolishly believes the modern scientific community's view that the dinosaurs were made extinct before humankind evolved, but is suddenly transported back in time to a world where dinosaurs and man co-existed. And all the girls wore fur bikinis...

"This shoot is pure hell," Bill assured Christina whenever they spoke on the phone.

"Are you lonely, honey?" Christina asked.

"Very."

Christina didn't know that Bill was so lonely that he had generously agreed to share his Winnebago with model/actress twins Misty and Lisa from Dallas.

Each phone conversation would end in exactly the same way.

"I miss you, baby," Bill would tell Christina.

"I miss you too," she'd tell him back.

But the truth was, Christina didn't have all that much time to miss her husband. The *Hello!* magazine anniversary spread and the gorgeous publicity stills released from the Maison Randon commercial shoot seemed to have reminded the fashion world that Christina still existed. She was on a small roll. Marisa had her fully booked for a month: editorials and commercials back-to-back, culminating in her own swimsuit calendar shoot in Baja. Every supermodel had to have her own swimsuit calendar.

It was while she was in Baja that Christina caught up with a very old friend...

Christina was kneeling in the sand, having Evian water sprayed on her thighs and décolletage to make her skin glisten for the camera, when the commotion began.

"Hey!" one of the shoot's bouncers shouted at a couple who were trying to walk by. "You can't come through here. The beach is closed."

"You're shitting me. You can't close the fucking beach," the man shouted. "This is public property."

"Not today it's not," said the bouncer.

"Says who, asshole?"

The makeup artist who had been making Christina glitter paused to watch the fight. The stylist and the hairdresser craned over Christina's head to see what was happening. The photographer's assistant let the reflector he had been holding aloft droop to the sand. Even the photographer was distracted.

Christina was furious. How had members of the public gotten so close to her in the first place? She stood up and pulled on a dressing gown. The shoot team seemed to have forgotten that she was topless. Not that she would be showing any nipple in the calendar. She would have her arms folded tastefully across her chest.

Christina strode over to the water's edge, where the bouncer and a small, skinny white guy in voluminous board shorts were scuffling while the entire team watched. Christina addressed the shrieking girlfriend.

"Will you please take your boyfriend and go back to whichever skanky low-rent all-inclusive resort you came from? We are trying to work."

"Fuck you," said the girl. "Who do you think you are anyway?"

Christina's mouth dropped open. The girl squared up to her. The circle that had formed around the men fighting shifted their attention to the altogether more exciting possibility of a bitch fight.

Christina stood firm but felt her legs turn to jelly. The last thing she needed was a single scratch on her perfect form.

Meanwhile, the bouncer finally subdued the girl's boyfriend, trapping him in a neck-lock and knocking off his sunglasses to reveal his famously mismatched eyes.

"Oh my God!" the stylist shrieked. "Oh my God. Oh my God."

Rock god, to be precise.

Christina Morgan's chin dropped farther still when she recognized her ex-boyfriend, Rocky Neel.

"Christina Morgan!" Rocky shook his head affectionately inside the bouncer's armlock when he saw her. "My oh my, haven't you grown."

Christina quickly ensured Rocky's release and he spent a jolly half hour signing autographs for the shoot team, including the bouncer, who was suitably mortified at not having recognized his victim. Together with his band, Cold Steel, Rocky Neel had been one of the biggest-selling rock artists in the late nineties. His star was somewhat out of the ascendant these days but Cold Steel could still sell out an international stadium tour. They'd just released their second "greatest hits" album in five years.

That night, Rocky and Christina dined together on the private terrace of his oceanfront suite at the exclusive Santa Maria spa and resort. The girl Rocky had been promenading with on the beach that afternoon was nowhere to be seen.

"Oh her? She's just a friend," Rocky claimed. "I sent her back to Los Angeles. And you?"

"Happily married," Christina assured him. She fluttered the fingers of her left hand and Rocky gamely pretended to be blinded by the bling.

"Ah yes. To the film star. I saw the eight-page spread in *Hello!* How come I didn't get an invite to the wedding, eh?"

"Didn't want to walk down the aisle in front of *all* my ex-boyfriends." Christina smiled.

"Not even me?"

"*Especially* not you," said Christina as he turned on that old Rocky twinkle. "Are you kidding? Bill would have had a seizure."

"That's good to know."

Rocky went to pour more chilled white wine into her glass. Christina put her hand over the rim to stop him.

"Uh-uh. I'm working tomorrow," she told him. "Can't risk having puffy eyes."

"As I remember," said Rocky, "you look rather lovely even when your eyes are puffy and bloodshot..."

"My eyes are never bloodshot!" Christina swatted him on the hand. "Rocky Neel, you haven't changed at all."

"Oh no, I've definitely changed," Rocky assured her. "After I had that near-death experience I realized that there's more to life than material success. I'd been living like a maniac. You know how it gets, Chrissy babe. I had six houses, twenty-four cars—OK, twenty-three, after the crash. But while I was in hospital, I realized that none of it matters. A man's got to have some spiritual fulfillment too."

"Spiritual fulfillment?" Christina rolled the words around her mouth as though she'd never heard them before. "Has the real Rocky Neel been abducted by aliens?"

"Let me finish."

As he explained to Christina just how important this "spiritual fulfillment" was, Rocky illustrated his speech by waving his hands in the air. On his left wrist was a solid-gold Rolex. On his right pinkie finger, a diamond as big as an almond. Around that wrist, he wore four thick gold bangles. There were more diamonds in his ear and a gold hoop through his left eyebrow. Still, he seemed quite sincere as he introduced Christina to his latest project.

"None of the material stuff matters. It's all about icicle now," he said.

"Icicle? Rocky"—Christina leaned forward and put her hand on his arm—"are you talking about some kind of drug?"

Rocky let out a laugh.

"God, no. That's funny. I am completely clean these days. I swear. Almost...Actually, it's ISACL: the International Society for the Abolition of Child Labor. Stay there. I want to show you something amazing."

He jumped up.

Christina couldn't help remembering the first time Rocky had uttered those words: "I want to show you something amazing." It was the night she discovered he had a gold bar through the tip of his cock. But this time, Rocky slipped into the suite and returned with his trousers still safely done up. He was carrying a black MacBook. He logged into the hotel's wireless network and opened up a connection to ISACL's website.

"I'm telling you, this is such bad stuff," he said, as he clicked on the photo of a small, sad-eyed orphan. "I knew I had to do something after I met these kids in India. They have no choice but to work for a pittance wherever they can. It's that or begging, prostitution. They have to work or starve. You can't believe the conditions they live in, Chrissy. It'd break your heart. Look at that. That's not a pile of rubbish I'm showing you. It's this poor child's home."

Christina felt her eyes begin to tear up.

"This is just awful," she said, as Rocky flicked through the pictures, each more shocking than the last. "I will write you a check at once."

"I'd like you to do more than that," said Rocky, laying his hand over hers. "You and I meeting on the beach this afternoon, that's destiny. I've been thinking about how I can get the message out to a broader audience. You could be the perfect spokesperson for ISACL. Will you help me make an infomercial?"

Christina put her hand to her throat in surprise.

"Me?"

"Yes. Of course. Not only one of the most beautiful women in the world, but an incredibly caring one too."

"Are you serious?"

Rocky nodded. "It was your caring heart that made me love you."

"Wow, Rocky, that's . . . of course I'll do it."

Christina was delighted to be asked. And her delight only grew when Rocky told her about the other celebrities who had already agreed to take part. The list was like a Who's Who of Hollywood (her husband excluded). Christina would be in incredible company. To be associated with such a cause could only be good for her profile. She couldn't wait to tell Marisa.

Rocky proposed a toast to their new association. Christina toasted in water. She'd already had that night's glass of wine. And then he proposed a walk along the shoreline in the moonlight. Christina agreed. It was a beautiful night. The sky was clear. The moon was nearly full and its cool white light made it almost as bright as day. As they walked, Rocky reached for Christina's hand. She held his happily. It seemed appropriate. As did allowing him to slip his arm around her waist and pull her close. Friendly. It was lovely to be back in Rocky's company, as his friend, so many years after they dated and broke up. And she felt so very honored that he had asked her to be in his campaign . . .

After walking for an hour, they were back at the gates of the hotel.

"Nightcap?" Rocky suggested.

"I can't," said Christina. "I told you I have to be up at six."

"Decaf coffee?" he tried again.

Christina shook her head.

"You're right," said Rocky. "Decaf coffee is horrible."

They were standing face-to-face. Suddenly, Rocky tucked his fingers through the belt loops on her jeans and pulled her closer.

"How about we just go to bed?"

"Rocky!"

"Just a kiss? For old times' sake."

"Rocky . . ."

He didn't wait for permission. Instead he leaned in and placed his warm lips upon hers. He wrapped his arms tightly around her so that their bodies were pressed together and she felt his hardness against her. Taken by surprise, Christina found herself returning the embrace. But, seconds later, reality overtook her and she pushed Rocky away.

"I'm a married woman," she said, brushing herself down.

"Worth a try," said Rocky ruefully.

Christina shook her head.

"I hope this doesn't mean you won't be in my infomercial."

He gave her the cheeky, English schoolboy smile that had first attacted her to him more than a decade before. It was such an innocent look that Christina didn't consider for a moment that he might only have asked her to support his cause in an attempt to flatter her back into bed.

"I'll do your infomercial," Christina told him. "For the sake of the kids." Then she grinned and planted a good-bye kiss on Rocky's cheek. Quite chastely. "Have your people call mine."

"The minute I get back to NYC."

As Christina sashayed away, Rocky sang a few bars of "Super-Sexy Lady," the hit song he had composed especially for her—and the two other women he had been seeing at the time.

CHAPTER 13

☙

At the Elson household in South London, an affectionate mother-daughter exchange was taking place. A man walking his dog in the alley behind the scruffy terraced house bent to fasten the dog's lead just in time to avoid being decapitated by a plate flung from the open kitchen window. He straightened up just in time to see a couple of mugs fly past, also at head height, and smash against a wall.

"You're an ungrateful little cow," Marina screamed at her only daughter. "I gave up all my hopes and dreams to have you. I could have had an abortion."

"I wish you *had* had an abortion," Kelly spat at her. "I didn't ask to be born into this shit-fest of a life."

Marina paused in throwing the contents of her crockery cupboard into the street to light another cigarette. "You are breaking my heart," she said, between anguished drags. "Why do you have to be so nasty to me all the time? Your own mother?"

"Oh, boo hoo," said Kelly. "Here we go. Here come the waterworks. You expect me to feel sorry for you, you old slag? You stole my last fiver to buy those fags."

"I'd have paid you back," said Marina, affronted.

"Like you paid me back all the money my father sent you for me? For my upkeep? Five hundred pounds a month for the past eighteen years! And you spent it all on yourself!"

"Not all of it. But it's fucking hard being a single mother. You'd begrudge me some happiness?"

"You begrudged me a fucking school uniform."

"Whaddya mean? I put a roof over your head!"

"Maybe it wouldn't have been such a crappy one if you'd spent my money on rent instead of fags and brandy."

"Well," said Marina, stubbing out her cigarette on a dirty plate and stiffening up for a fight again. "You don't have to stay under my crappy roof now, do you? I've had enough of this. Go on. Go upstairs and pack your bags. Get out of here. Go on. Fuck off."

"If that's how you want it," said Kelly, "I will."

Kelly slammed her way out of the kitchen and ran upstairs to her bedroom. She opened her wardrobe and flung every item of clothing she owned onto the sagging single bed. It didn't take long; there wasn't much to fling. Then she took the one proper piece of luggage in the house and stuffed as much as she could inside. The rest, she stuffed into a trash bag. Which promptly split open.

"Fuck. Fuck. Fuck."

Kelly started again.

Marina watched from the doorway, puffing on three more cigarettes in quick succession and occasionally shouting encouragement.

"I'll be glad to get rid of you, I will. I'll rent your room out and spend all the money on fags!" she roared.

"You do that." Kelly set her jaw and carried on packing.

"You can't take that," said Marina, when Kelly tried to pack a ratty old towel. "That's linen, that is. It belongs to the house. That stays here." She snatched it from Kelly's hand.

"Fine," said Kelly. "I'll dry myself on this."

She brandished a tea towel in her mother's face.

"Take it," said Marina, failing to register that the tea towel her daughter stuffed into her bag was the one Kelly had brought home from primary school, aged six. One of the teachers tried to raise funds for new books by printing up tea towels with the children's drawings and selling them to proud mums and dads. Kelly had drawn a picture of her mother. A pretty good one. Written beneath it, in her childish handwriting, were the words "My butifull mummy."

Marina didn't look too beautiful now. Her face was twisted with anger as she followed her daughter downstairs to the front door, spewing out expletives all the way.

"So you're really going, then? Good. I'll call you a fucking taxi."

"I can't wait that long," said Kelly. She stepped out into the night and started off down the path, dragging her luggage behind her.

"Wait!" Marina came after her.

Kelly paused. Was her mother about to attempt reconciliation?

"I want your bloody keys!" screamed Marina. "I'm not having you coming back here and stealing all my stuff while I'm out, you little slut."

Kelly pulled her keys out of her pocket and dropped them into her mother's open palm.

"You're welcome to them. I don't want anything more from you. I don't even want to know if you're alive or dead. Forget you ever had a daughter," she added dramatically.

"And you can forget you ever had a mother and all!"

Marina slammed the door hard behind her.

And so Kelly found herself standing in the street with a wheelie case, a dangerously flimsy trash bag and nowhere to go. She tried calling Gina Busiri—her best friend and fellow chambermaid at the hotel—but Gina didn't answer.

At ten to midnight, Guy Harcourt was woken by the insistent ringing of the telephone. The ancient answering machine was on the fritz so the phone simply rang and rang until it was answered or the caller gave up. This caller wasn't giving up. Guy hauled himself out of bed and followed the sound of the ringing downstairs.

"I'm at the station," said a girl's voice.

"Who is this?" Guy asked. "You must have the wrong number."

"It's Kelly Elson," said the caller. "I've decided I want to come to Froggy Bottom after all."

Perhaps it was because he was too tired to argue. Perhaps he thought he was dreaming. In any case, Guy didn't protest. He merely told Kelly to wait in front of the station until he could get to her.

"Don't get into anyone else's car," he warned her.

"I won't," said Kelly. "I'm not twelve years old, you know."

She may not have been twelve years old but she didn't look much older when Guy found her. She was smaller than he remembered. Possibly because her thin brittle hair was flattened against her head. The orange glow from the single street lamp also stripped away the years. And the hardness.

In the brief moment before Kelly spotted the car, Guy watched her standing under the street amp with the reverence of a museum visitor admiring a Renaissance Madonna. Her face was so open and innocent. Her eyes were far away. You could have projected a thousand different thoughts onto a face like that.

Kelly's gaze turned toward the car.

"Hello," he said.

"Hi," she said. "Thanks for picking me up."

"No problem at all," he managed sincerely.

He loaded her wheelie case and the bursting trash bag

into the back of the Land Rover and cleared the passenger seat of maps and random paperwork so that she could sit down. She'd clearly been crying.

"So, what made you change your mind?" Guy asked, regretting the question almost as soon as he'd asked it. She would probably unleash the waterworks again, he thought. But she didn't.

"I dunno," she said. "Just got fed up of London, I suppose. Thought it might be a laugh to come to the country for a bit."

"Well, I'm sure your father would have been very glad to welcome you to Froggy Bottom so I will do my best to make you feel at home on his behalf."

"Thanks," said Kelly. She stared out of the window at the blackness passing by. Guy had a feeling she was still trying very hard not to cry.

"It might be a bit cold in the farmhouse," Guy continued. "The place has been pretty much shut up since your dad died. I stay in the flat above the barn. Smaller and easier to heat. You could have my room tonight. I'll sleep on the sofa."

"The farmhouse will be OK," said Kelly.

Guy let Kelly into the old place and showed her where the ancient boiler was hidden and what she should do to reignite the pilot light when it blew out, as it often did. He turned on the equally antique immersion heater so that she could have hot water for a bath. There was linen in the airing cupboard, but since the house had been empty for so long, it smelled distinctly musty. Guy nipped across the courtyard to his own home and returned with a set of bedding and two towels from his own collection. He made another trip and came back with half a pint of milk and the remains of a loaf of bread that he had been saving for his breakfast the following day.

"We'll go into town tomorrow," he said. "I'll show you where the supermarket is. You can get yourself properly set up."

"Thanks," Kelly managed.

But Kelly didn't bother to dress the bed with the sheets that Guy had provided for her. Neither did she bother to run a bath with the hot water from the boiler that had valiantly spluttered into life. Instead, keeping all her clothes on—taking off only her boots—she climbed under the bare duvet and the scratchy blankets. She lay in bed, looking up at the beams that made frightening shadows on the peeling paintwork and wondered what she had just done.

On the other side of the courtyard, Guy fell asleep pretty quickly. He felt sorry for Kelly but also optimistic. She was a sweet girl, he decided. He'd soon instill in her some enthusiasm for Froggy Bottom and what he hoped to create there. He'd long since decided that Froggy Bottom was a magical place. No one who came there for any length of time could possibly remain unchanged.

CHAPTER 14

Two months after her father's death Madeleine was still in Champagne. Geoff had stopped calling daily with news from London. For her part, Madeleine's time in the City was slowly receding and becoming more and more like a dream. She found herself considering letting her

London flat out to tenants. Only in the short term, of course. But her life in Champagne was definitely taking on something of a routine.

Henri Mason was only too pleased to remind Madeleine of the way the vines needed to be cared for. He had known Madeleine since she was a little girl and Henri was, as Axel had promised, a very reliable worker. But he was almost as old as Madeleine's father had been and he was starting to show his age as he moved around the vineyard. Likewise the three other guys Henri referred to as "the youngsters" were a bunch of emphysematic fifty-somethings, who spent more time complaining about their backs than pruning. Madeleine soon found herself picking up the slack.

That morning, Madeleine left Henri alone in the Clos while she went up to the Arsenault vineyards on the hill above the village. When she began work, thankful that her years in the City had made her used to early starts, it was quite cool, but by midday she had stripped down to a T-shirt and a pair of cutoff jeans she'd found stuffed in a drawer in her old room.

Pausing for a drink from a battered canteen that had belonged to her father, she looked down over the valley and spotted Axel's car. He was quite a way off. It was un-usually hot for the time of year and he'd taken down the soft top of his BMW. The music he was playing drifted toward her across the vines. Some heavy rock band. Madeleine smiled to herself. Axel might dress like a grown-up these days but his musical taste was that of a teenager.

Seeing Axel's car turn onto the track that led to her vines, Madeleine set down her canteen and her pruning shears. She took off her gloves and gave herself a quick once-over in the rearview mirror of her father's old Twingo. By the time Axel got to her, the big smudge of dirt on one cheek was gone and her lips glistened with Blistex, the only thing approaching makeup she had to hand.

But Axel didn't seem to care whether Madeleine was perfectly groomed. He skidded his car to a halt on the dusty track and sprang out. When he opened his arms Madeleine practically skipped into them. They kissed. Deliciously.

"You didn't tell me you were coming out here today," she said.

"I didn't expect to be. But Randon wanted me to show some Americans around the house. I just put them on a train back to Paris and decided I would take the rest of the day off."

"Good. I'm glad you did. You work much too hard."

"It suits you," said Axel, smoothing Madeleine's hair out of her face.

"What does?"

"Outdoor work. You look more fantastic every time I see you. Do you have time for lunch?"

"Sure. I've just about finished up here for the day," said Madeleine. "I'll follow you down into the village. I've got nothing in the house but if we hurry we should be able to catch the brasserie."

"Not necessary," said Axel. "I've brought lunch to you."

He took Madeleine by the hand and led her to the BMW. On the back seat was a wicker basket covered with a bright red and white gingham cloth.

"Oh, how lovely," said Madeleine. "Where shall we have it?"

"Not here," said Axel. "Too much like having lunch at your desk. How about at Les Faux?"

Madeleine grinned. The Faux De Verzy—a forest of beech trees that had somehow grown so twisted that they were more like domes than trees—was a well-known courting spot. Or, rather, it had been. These days the trees were fenced off and the tourists could only troop past on prescribed paths.

Axel opened the passenger door to the BMW and Madeleine slid gracefully onto the seat. She might have been wearing the clothes of a farmworker, but she put her knees together and swung her legs into the car in one smooth movement like a finishing-school graduate. As Axel whipped along the road toward Reims, Madeleine untied her long dark hair and let it flow behind her.

En route to the forest, he amused her with his impressions of the American visitors. One of them had asked for some Perrier to mix with a glass of Éclat.

"Can you imagine?" Axel asked. "She's lucky Randon wasn't there. He'd have gutted her with his Mont Blanc pen." Taking one hand off the wheel, Axel mimed the action. Slash, slash, stab. Madeleine shivered.

A couple of minutes later, Axel pulled the car off the road into the tourist car park but he and Madeleine were soon well away from the crowds who stopped to marvel at nature's diversity from behind the barriers.

"There's a particularly good tree over here," he said, taking Madeleine by the hand and leading her farther into the woods.

"How do you know? Don't tell me you've brought another woman out here?" Madeleine teased.

"Of course not," Axel teased back.

There weren't many people who'd grown up in Champagne who hadn't taken someone to Les Faux. It was the perfect trysting place for anyone who didn't have a home of their own or, for other reasons, couldn't go home with the one they wanted to make love to.

Axel parted the branches so that Madeleine could step inside this particular domed beech. He took the red and white checked cloth from the top of the basket and spread it out on the forest floor. It was wonderfully cool beneath the tree. And private.

"Like our own little house," said Axel.

Madeleine was surprised to feel a little frisson of pleasure at the words "our own."

Axel had packed a wonderful picnic, cobbled together from the lunch the Maison Randon chef had prepared for the American visitors. They'd hardly touched a thing, he explained. Too many dietary complications that the Randon chef—like most French chefs—refused to pander to. And there was champagne, of course.

"Maison Randon?" Madeleine observed.

"What can I say?" Axel shrugged. "It was free. And in any case," he added, "I think the '96 Éclat tastes perfectly good. If you mix it with Perrier."

Madeleine laughed. Axel removed the cork from the Maison Randon with a pop.

"I'm feeling exuberant," he explained.

Madeleine held out two tulip-shaped glasses, also lifted from the Maison Randon tasting room, and Axel filled them halfway.

"We should have a toast. To you," he said, raising his glass. Simple but perfect.

"And to you," said Madeleine.

They both took a sip. And pulled suitable faces of disgust though in fact the Éclat was excellent by anyone's standard. Even that of a rival champagne grower.

"It's OK," joked Madeleine afterward. "I have had worse. Pass me that egg to take away the taste."

"How are you really finding it?" Axel asked later. "Being back here in Champagne."

Madeleine lay back on the gingham cloth and gazed up into the canopy of leaves.

"It has its moments. Lunch breaks weren't like this when I worked at the bank."

"But it can get quite dull, can't it? Hitting the town in Reims can't be like going out in London. You must be bored."

"Hitting the town in London with a bunch of bankers was getting pretty boring too."

"Fair enough. But you're not itching to go back."

"Not right now, I'm not. I could stay here forever."

Madeleine closed her eyes and stretched luxuriously.

Axel plucked a blade of grass from the ground. He rolled over onto his front, supported on his elbows, and used the grass to tickle the end of her nose. With her eyes shut, Madeleine assumed she was being attacked by some kind of insect. She batted the blade away. Eventually she opened her eyes.

"Axel," she said.

He placed a kiss on the end of her nose.

"Stop teasing me."

"With the grass?"

"Yes."

"Can I tease you some other way instead?" A slow smile spread over his lips.

Madeleine felt the blade of grass on her knee this time.

"Axel..."

Then she felt his lips touch her knee where the grass had been. Meanwhile, Axel was using the blade of grass to trace a path all the way up the inside of her thigh. Madeleine's inner thigh tensed in anticipation and, sure enough, Axel followed the blade with his lips. Soft short kisses like the footsteps of a butterfly on her silky skin. Both Madeleine and Axel sighed with disappointment as he reached the hem of her tiny denim shorts.

"Foiled," said Axel.

"Wait there," said Madeleine. She unfastened her belt

and wriggled out of the denims. Beneath them she was wearing a pair of simple white cotton knickers.

"Shouldn't you take those trousers off?" she asked Axel. "Don't want to get them creased."

Axel had put on a smart linen suit for the Americans' visit. He happily took Madeleine's advice and soon they were both completely naked, rolling around on the picnic rug, sending the half-full glasses of Éclat flying.

"Joey!" called a Canadian-accented voice. "There's another one over here. Bring your camera."

Madeleine sat up abruptly, pulling the picnic blanket around her just in time. Axel was still naked to the world when Joey's companion parted the branches of the gnarled old beech and peered into the gloom.

"A glass of champagne perhaps?" asked Axel, offering the poor shocked woman a flute.

That evening, Axel took Madeleine to dinner at Château Les Crayères in Reims. This time, Randon would not call him away.

Madeleine hadn't been to Les Crayères in almost ten years. The occasion had been her parents' wedding anniversary—the last anniversary they shared before her mother died. It had been a relatively solemn event. But her evening with Axel was to be very different.

It began with drinks on the terrace overlooking the perfect lawn that swept down toward the trees. Les Crayères was the kind of place that demanded a certain level of effort from its clientele. Madeleine's lacy black dress suited the occasion perfectly. As did her black satin Chanel evening bag.

The elegant dining room was busy yet somehow still perfectly intimate. The wonderful acoustics kept the place quiet as a cathedral. The last of the sunlight bouncing off the soft cream-painted walls bathed the room and its occupants in a veil of beauty.

It was so easy to be with Axel, Madeleine reflected as he bantered with the sommelier. He had the kind of manner that fit well anywhere. Even the poor Canadian woman who had disturbed them at Les Faux had left the scene relatively charmed.

Wine chosen, Axel raised another toast.

"To my beautiful Madeleine. I truly cannot think of anywhere in the world I would rather be right now," Axel said.

"Me neither," Madeleine agreed.

Madeleine felt almost grateful to her father in that moment. Coming back to the house had brought Axel back into her life. It was astonishing. She had never felt so much excitement at the thought of seeing someone as she did every time she thought of Axel Delaflote. Everything in her life she wanted to share with him. She couldn't look at him without wanting to reach out and touch his gorgeous face. She hoped he felt the same way; it seemed he felt the same way. As she thought it, Axel reached out and stroked her cheek.

"You're so beautiful," he said.

Madeleine felt herself actually welling up with happiness.

"I've got something to show you," said Axel when the waiters had cleared away everything but the coffee cups.

"Oh yes?" Madeleine leaned forward.

"Don't get too excited," he warned.

She leaned back again.

"Tonight is a double celebration for me," said Axel. "Firstly because, at long last, I get to take the woman of my dreams to Les Crayères."

Madeleine smiled and shook her head. "Delaflote, you are so smooth."

"Secondly, because . . ."

Axel reached into his jacket pocket and brought out a little silver card case. Madeleine raised an eyebrow. It wasn't the kind of executive accessory she would have expected Axel to have. He flipped the case open and pulled out one of the neat cream-colored cards inside. Madeleine immediately recognized the color of the Maison Randon label. And there indeed was the Maison Randon crest. Beneath it, in the same script used on a bottle of Éclat, were the words: "Axel Delaflote, Managing Director."

"Axel!" Madeleine exclaimed. "What is this?"

"I got a promotion. Bit of a surprise."

"You're telling me!"

"Actually, I feel quite bad about it. Stefan was away in the Maldives when it happened. He went crazy when he heard, of course. But apparently he's been thinking about doing something else for a while. Randon said he knew Stefan had been taking interviews elsewhere. And Stefan had talked to me about how unhappy his wife is in Champagne. She wants to move back to the south and he's quite keen on Montpellier—"

"Axel," Madeleine interrupted the litany of justification. "This is incredible. Managing director. You are officially one big swinging dick, as they say in the City."

"I'll take that as a compliment," he laughed.

"Can I keep this?" Madeleine asked.

"Of course."

"Autograph it," she said.

"What?"

"Write something on the back of this card so that when you're too big to talk to the little people like me, I can tell everyone that I knew you."

"You're nuts," said Axel, taking the card back and pulling out a Mont Blanc.

"I knew it!" Madeleine laughed. "You've even got rid of your old Biro."

"Signing-on gift from Randon," Axel explained as he put a smiley face and three kisses on the back of the card.

"Kisses! Thank you," said Madeleine.

"The formal announcement will be made on Monday."

"But we should start celebrating now. What would you like?"

"I suppose it should be a glass of Éclat."

Axel summoned a waiter. Meanwhile Madeleine tucked the business card into a tiny pocket inside her evening bag.

"I want to keep this safe," she said. "Axel Delaflote, head of Maison Randon. I ask you . . ."

In the taxi back to Le Vezy, Madeleine found herself falling into a snooze against Axel's shoulder. He planted a kiss on top of her head. She felt so perfectly relaxed in his company. Safe.

Axel reached for Madeleine's hand as they walked across the courtyard at Champagne Arsenault, dropping it only when she had to look in her bag for the key. While she opened the door, he kept his arm around her waist. It was as though he didn't want to lose physical contact with her for a second. Madeleine was happy with that.

They started to kiss as they were taking their coats off in the hall. Still kissing, they ascended the stairs and stumbled into the bedroom.

"Your dress is beautiful," Axel murmured, as he searched for the zip. "But I'd far rather see it on the floor."

Madeleine was happy to oblige. Meanwhile she loosened Axel's tie and slipped it off over his head. She undid the buttons on his cool blue shirt. He unfastened his own belt and stepped out of his trousers. Madeleine delighted in the feeling of his bare chest as he wrapped his arms tightly around her and pulled her close. He kissed her tenderly.

They lay down on the bed. Axel kissed Madeleine's breastbone and pulled one lacy cup of her bra out of the way so that he could find a nipple. Madeleine gave a small groan of delight as she felt his tongue make contact with the small pink bud. She tipped her head back, exposing her long throat. Axel kissed his way up it until he found her lips again.

"I want you so much," he said.

"Me too," she assured him.

Soon they were entirely naked. Madeleine slid her hand between their bodies and felt the hardness of Axel's penis with great anticipation. Hard as he was, Axel slid easily inside her. Madeleine immediately wrapped her long legs around his back, feeling him thrust as deep as he could. She rocked her pelvis up to meet his and soon they were moving in the fast frantic rhythm of two people who couldn't get enough of each other. Again.

Madeleine's hands moved all over Axel's body. Across his back, through his hair. He raised himself above her just a little and stared right into her eyes. She stared back at him. Every part of them was joined. Bodies and minds.

"I'm coming!" Axel's voice was ragged with excitement when at last he found he could hold back no longer.

Madeleine squeezed her thighs more tightly against his waist. But she didn't try to slow him down. She loved it when he lost control. She felt him lose his rhythm as he pushed hard against her and his orgasm ripped through them both.

Afterward came the best bit. Axel wrapped his body around hers protectively. Spooning. Madeleine felt perfectly content, listening to the sound of his breathing in her ear. Feeling the warmth of his breath on her neck. She would happily have stayed like that all night. Every night. Because suddenly the three little words were on the tip of Madeleine's tongue. She wanted to whisper them in Axel's ear. She wanted to shout them out loud. She wanted everyone to know that this was it. She was in love.

"I love you, Axel," her mind rehearsed. "I love you, I love you, I love you."

Madeleine rolled over to face him. She looked deep into his eyes. She was going to say it. Now was the moment. It wasn't as if he couldn't tell from the way she gazed at him anyway...

Without warning, Axel suddenly sat up against the pillows and announced, "I've got to get up."

"Are you leaving?" Madeleine sat up too. Panicked.

"No. Of course not," Axel stroked her cheek. "It's just that I've got to make a couple of phone calls before I can fall asleep in your loving arms." He was already standing up. "The boss is in New York this week. I said I'd check in before close of play his time."

"What time is it over there?" Madeleine asked.

Axel glanced at his watch. "Six in the evening. I should have called earlier. He'll have me skinned."

"Is he really so awful?"

"Yep." Axel smiled. "He's a complete tyrant. And now I'm even more at his beck and call than ever."

"Price of success, Monsieur Managing Director."

"I'm sorry, sweetheart. I will be right back."

"You better be."

While Axel left to make his calls, Madeleine drifted into the bathroom, the romance of that perfect day making her feel lighter in spirit than she had in a very long while. She floated from her bathroom into the bedroom and began to pick up the clothes scattered across the floor. She folded Axel's suit carefully over a chair. She hung her simple black dress on the wardrobe door, catching sight of herself in the mirror as she did so.

She was still flushed. Her hair was prettily loose and disheveled. A month working on the vineyard had left her looking much better than six years with a personal trainer in London. Muscles tight and sexy. She gave herself a wink.

Axel was still on the phone—Madeleine could hear the murmur of his voice drifting up the stairs—so she took a shower. Afterward she anointed herself with Chanel No. 5—the first perfume she had ever worn. She wondered if it would take Axel back to being a teenager too. She arranged herself on the clean white sheets and waited for his return.

But Axel's boss kept him on the phone for far longer than Madeleine had expected. After an hour had passed, she decided she would see what was going on, using the pretext of fetching a water glass from the kitchen. Not quite knowing why she felt the need to be sneaky in her own home, she crept down the stairs as quietly as possible. It wasn't hard. She'd had plenty of practice as a teenager at getting out of the house without alerting her parents to the fact that she was leaving.

Madeleine glimpsed her lover as she passed the study door. He was sitting at her desk, doodling on a notepad as he made the transatlantic call. He looked bored, she decided, and hoped that meant he would try to wind up the call soon. She walked on by to the kitchen and fetched the water glass. On her way back she paused in the door frame, letting her elegant dressing gown fall open to reveal the shimmering oyster-white silk negligee beneath. She expected Axel to turn around, sensing her presence. But he didn't. He carried on talking.

"She grew up here," said Axel. "So she knows what she's doing to a certain extent. And she's got the old boy Henri Mason helping out. I fixed that myself. The vines are in perfect condition."

The person Axel was calling—Randon, Madeleine assumed—spoke back. Axel nodded. "I haven't broached the subject yet but I will do. I think the right time is almost upon us. Tomorrow. Monday at the latest."

Randon spoke again.

"Of course she'll sell," Axel replied. "She's enjoying it now, sure, while the weather's fine and being away from London seems like a nice break. It's a novelty. But it won't be long before she's begging us to take Clos Des Larmes off her hands. Madeleine Arsenault is no vigneronne."

Madeleine stiffened.

"I'd better go. She's waiting for me upstairs right now."

Axel laughed in response to his boss's doubtless lewd comment.

"Actually," said Madeleine, mustering all her resources to address Axel without bursting into tears, "I'm waiting right behind you."

"You heard me wrong," insisted Axel.

"I heard you say that Madeleine Arsenault is no vigneronne."

Axel reached out and rubbed the tops of her arms placatingly. "Well, darling, let's face it. You're not. You never wanted to be. Even when we were kids you used to talk about escaping. You got out of Champagne as soon as you could. You only came back for your father's funeral and you wouldn't be here now if you didn't feel guilty for not having seen him before he died."

"That's not true." Madeleine shut her eyes and tried to oust the memory of the last time she heard her father's voice in the message he left while she was having dinner at Montrachet to try to save a job she hated. It was impossible. The message replayed as though the answering machine were inside her head.

"Fine," said Axel. "Maybe it isn't. But I don't think it would be such a bad idea. Randon would look after this place. You know he would. And he'd give you a good price."

Madeleine looked deep into Axel's eyes. He smiled at her, as though he was certain that she was going to see sense. He even leaned forward to kiss her nose.

"Get off." She pushed him away. "I can't believe you're saying this to me. Is this what you've been building up to? Everything that's happened since my father's funeral? All that talk about how much you've always wanted to be with me. The flowers. The phone calls. The picnic this afternoon. Dinner at Les Crayères? It was all sponsored by bloody Mathieu Randon! Did you get it on expenses?"

"No," Axel insisted. "I swear to you. I came to your father's funeral because I respected him. I've been spending time with you because I enjoy doing that. I went to bed with you because I wanted it more than anything in the world."

Axel tried to take Madeleine's hands again. She pulled away.

"It's too late," she said. "I want you to go."

"Just hear me out. Randon's not trying to rip you off. I wouldn't let him. I'm only putting his offer to you because I think you might subconsciously want the opportunity to be rid of this place. It wouldn't be an ordinary deal to Randon," Axel continued. "He wants Arsenault because it used to be part of his own family's estate. Did you know that?"

"I did not."

"Long before your family moved out here. So you can trust that Randon won't mess you around. This land is important to him in more than a financial sense. It's an emotional deal. A good proposition. I've had my land agent look over the vines and . . ."

"What? How did you? When?"

"While you were in London picking up your car."

"You came onto my land without my permission?"

"Madeleine, we're friends. It was right after the funeral. I didn't want to disturb you while you were grieving."

"You mean, you didn't want me to say no. Axel, I can't believe you would do that to me."

"Well, I'm sorry." Axel stiffened. "I suppose I did think you might find the idea distasteful, but I wanted to be able to offer you a proper price and that meant I had to know what state the place was in."

"Champagne Arsenault is not for sale."

"Think about it. Randon will offer you at least five percent over the face value. A premium because it means so much to him to reunite his ancestral lands."

"It's not for sale."

"Just look at the figures. I've had the contract drawn up. You would have enough money to do whatever you wanted. You could get a bigger place in London. You could go to the States."

Neither of the options he mentioned included the possibility that Madeleine might have wanted to remain near him. Or that he wanted to keep her nearby. That was what finally brought the truth of the situation home to her. Madeleine couldn't even pretend that Axel had wanted what was best for her. This was a business deal.

"Get out."

"Madeleine, think about it properly."

"I have thought about it. I have thought about it every day since I was born. And I am telling you one more time that Champagne Arsenault will never be for sale."

"You're an idiot," said Axel flatly. "You've told me what a mess this place is in. What use is all this family pride you talk about when you can't even afford to harvest your grapes?"

"If I have to pick every bunch myself, I will do it."

"Madeleine, you might be able to organize a dinner for a few bankers but you don't have a clue when it comes to making champagne."

"I'm a fast learner."

"You better be."

"Just go."

Axel was already looking around for his car keys. Madeleine pulled her robe more tightly around her. She was suddenly very, very cold.

"In a year's time you will be begging me to take this wreck of a maison off your hands. I promise you. And I will buy it from you. But at half the price I am offering you today. And I will plough up your father's precious vines and turn your home into a bed-and-breakfast. In ten years' time, no one will have heard of Champagne Arsenault."

"Fuck you," said Madeleine. "Fuck you, Axel Delaflote."

Axel blew her a kiss. There was nothing affectionate about it.

He slammed the door as he left the room. And as if on cue, a chunk of plaster fell from the ceiling and landed on the tiles in the hallway, smashing into dust.

CHAPTER 15

Early mornings were not Christina's thing, but you didn't become a successful supermodel by demanding to sleep in on a commercial shoot and so she had forced herself to get used to it. Besides, in this case, the pain of being up at five to catch a flight from Buenos Aires, where she was shooting a spread for *Elle,* to New York was offset by the warm feeling inside that Christina got when she thought about what she was flying there for. The final list of participants for the ISACL campaign was stunning. To be in their company would really put Christina on the map.

Rocky Neel was true to his word. As soon as he got back to the States, he had the team at ISACL call Christina's agent and make arrangements for the filming of her infomercial on the charity's behalf.

One of Rocky's assistants had drafted the short speech Christina would deliver to camera and faxed it through to the hotel in Argentina. Christina read the speech on the plane, made a couple of minor adjustments, and was word perfect by the time her flight touched down twelve hours later. A car met her at the airport and whisked her straight to the studio, where two dozen assorted supermodels, rock stars and actors were all waiting to do their bit.

"This must be what it was like to do *Live 8,*" Christina commented to Rocky.

Rocky nodded, though the words "Live 8" always

made his hackles rise. He hadn't been invited to join that particular bandwagon.

Christina was gratified to learn that, of all the people present, she had clocked up the most air miles to be there. It gave her instant status in the celebrity generosity stakes. And made the whinings of some other models, just flown in from London or Paris, seem rather pathetic.

Thankfully, Rocky had hired one of the best makeup artists in the United States to knock everyone into shape before filming started. The makeup guru quickly put the rose back into Christina's flight-dehydrated cheeks. Meanwhile, the set hairdresser gave Christina a fabulous blowout that made her look like she had twice as much hair. And she was extremely pleased to discover that the T-shirts the stars would be wearing had been printed up in hot pink. Christina looked fabulous in hot pink. Unlike some of the other girls.

"Rocky? Do I have to wear this?" asked Koko, a hot new model from Finland. "Pink just makes me look sick."

"You could go nude," Rocky suggested.

"Rocky, you are as awful as you ever were," said Christina, sticking up for Koko while simultaneously reminding the younger girl that Christina had known Rocky for years.

"My name is Christina Morgan," she began. "I'm a model. You probably know my face. You probably know I'm from Iowa. You probably know that I'm married to Bill Tarrant, the movie star. But what you probably don't know about me is that I'm absolutely passionate about the rights of children worldwide."

Significant pause. Eyes to camera. Lids slightly lowered. "Think Princess Di," the director had suggested.

"As people born in the West, you and I have already won first prize in the lottery of life. For most of us, a roof over our heads and enough food to fill our bellies can be taken as a given. For children in the Third World, however, the reality is very different. No wonder so many of them are tempted to abandon their education—if they ever had access to education in the first place—and get to work as soon as they are able. But we're not talking about the kind of jobs our children have here in America. These aren't newspaper delivery rounds or weekend jobs at the local supermarket. Children in the Third World are forced to do the kind of dangerous work we've outlawed in the United States."

There followed a segment of film showing children working in a textile factory, sad-eyed and skinny, like little ghosts. Then a close-up on a small girl, probably less than seven years old, who had lost an eye in an accident at that same factory. She was, nonetheless—the voice-over explained—back at work just a few days later because her family needed any financial contribution she could make.

"It's a sad picture, isn't it?" said Christina as the film cut back to her.

Serious face. She thought about her childhood pet dog being hit by a tractor, until her eyes glittered with tears.

"If, like me, you're asking how you can help these children to a more dignified way of life, the International Society for the Abolition of Child Labor can offer you some pointers. You can give money, of course. You can find details of how to contribute tax-efficiently on our website. Or you could give your time. But even if you have neither time nor money to spare, there is a very simple way you can make a difference. You can help these poor children by showing those Western companies who are prepared to profit from child labor that you aren't buying it. *I Don't Buy It*. That's the name of the ISACL's new campaign. Boycott the big names who are prepared to exploit the small workers."

Behind Christina was a montage of the labels on the hit list.

"Refuse to fund these dreadful conditions. Force these companies"—she gestured to the names scrolling down the screen behind her—"to examine their business practices and add ethics into the mix. I've already made a stand. I've told my agent I won't be modeling for any company that can't show a completely clean record where child labor is concerned. I may not be a mother but I've decided that these children are my responsibility. They're your responsibility too. Don't shut your eyes to their plight. And when you see injustice, don't buy into it. Say 'I don't buy it' to the results of exploitation. It's as simple as that."

Christina finished her final, perfect take to applause from the production team.

Rocky raced onto the set and enfolded her in his arms.

"You were magnificent, my darling."

Then he opened his arms and whirled around as if to embrace everyone in the room. "You've all been magnificent. I can't thank you enough. The children of the Third World can't thank you enough!"

Everyone whooped and cheered in an orgy of self-congratulation.

The day ended with a magnificent dinner at a fabulous new Japanese restaurant in the meatpacking district. All evening long the great and the good discussed the fabulous, glittering fund-raising events they could stage for ISACL's cause. Meanwhile, in the kitchen downstairs, two new illegal immigrants on less than the minimum wage struggled to keep the sushi coming.

The high-profile supporters of ISACL meant that every newspaper in the States and many in Europe picked up news of the campaign too. It was shocking. Fortunately the professional team at ISACL had plenty of evidence to back up their claims, so there were no libel suits. Instead, one by one, the companies on the blacklist began issuing carefully worded statements, claiming they had been unaware of the conditions in their overseas suppliers' factories and would implement changes at once. The infomercial ran all over the world. Christina did several interviews on TV and in the papers regarding her involvement. Oprah ran a special item on supermodel philanthropists in which Christina featured heavily.

As she was a model, no one particularly expected Christina Morgan to have a firm grasp on all the facts she spouted as spokesperson for the "I Don't Buy It" campaign. But as a spokesmodel for Maison Randon champagne, Christina might have hoped that someone, somewhere in the vast entourage of people who made a pretty decent living around the fringes of her life would have noticed that one of the labels to be boycotted was Fast Life. And further, to have noticed that the high-end sports gear line was the most recent addition to the Domaine Randon luxury goods empire.

Mathieu Randon watched an extract from Christina's interview with Oprah while flicking through the channels in his suite at a London hotel. He was unimpressed.

Randon called Bill Tarrant right away. He knew the actor was currently filming in Romania and was probably still awake.

"Do you have no control over that wife of yours?" he demanded as soon as Tarrant came on the line.

"Hey, Randon. What are you talking about now? Tell me you haven't seen a photo in some tabloid of that pretty wife of mine going wild with my credit card? Again."

"I've just seen her on *Oprah,*" said Randon flatly.

"You did? Plugging that ISACL campaign? It's quite something, eh? My wife the activist? Standing up to all those evil designer brands. Who would have thought it?"

"Indeed. Who would have thought it? You obviously didn't think about it, did you, Bill?"

"I'm sorry?" Randon was obviously disgruntled but Bill didn't understand.

"This 'I Don't Buy It' campaign. Claiming that Western brands are profiteering from child labor. Specifically, claiming that one of *my* brands, a Domaine Randon brand, Fast Life, is involved!"

Bill cleared his throat.

"Fast Life is one of your brands?"

"As of last month. You might have noticed the name at the bottom of the headed notepaper that accompanied the new contracts you and your wife received last week."

"Our agents look our contracts," Bill said by way of an excuse.

"Then you need a new agent."

"But I wasn't involved in the ISACL thing," said Bill. "Christina did that all on her own."

"Silly girl. What we have here," said Randon, "is a conflict of interests."

CHAPTER 16

June was a busy time in the vineyard at Froggy Bottom. Not that anyone would have known that by peeking behind the curtains of the main farmhouse.

The curtains of the farmhouse had been perpetually drawn since Kelly moved in. They were closed when Guy left his tidy flat above the shed at six in the morning to get some work done before the sun came up. They were closed when he headed back to his flat to grab something to eat at nine o'clock. And they were still closed when Guy came back from a second morning shift in the vineyard for his lunch.

In fairness, Kelly hadn't actually been asleep for the whole of that time. She'd had to get up to use the bathroom and then she made herself a cup of coffee and smoked a couple of cigarettes. Then she got back into bed. It was cold in the bedroom and she needed to warm up again to give herself the energy to get dressed. The farmhouse had such thick stone walls, Kelly had no idea whether it was four or twenty-four degrees outside. And, of course, while she was warming up beneath the duvet, she couldn't help drifting back to sleep. She was finally awoken by a call at five in the afternoon.

"Hey, babes."

It was Gina Busiri, her best friend and former colleague from the Gloria Hotel. "I've come to see you, like I said I would. I'm at the station."

"What? Now?"

"Yes. Like we agreed."

"Shit," said Kelly. "I forgot."

"Charming!" Gina laughed. "Just come and get me, will you?"

Truthfully, there was no one that Kelly would be happier to see than Gina. They'd clicked the very first day they met, two years earlier, when they sat side by side at the Gloria Hotel's induction day for new staff. At sixteen, they were the youngest girls in a room full of older women, but they couldn't have infiltrated the Polish and Romanian cliques if they'd wanted to. So they gravitated toward each other. They shared a fag and a moan during the first coffee break and had been firm friends ever since.

They did their best to work the same shifts and they covered for each other. If one of them had a heavy night and would rather take a nap on an unmade bed than make it, then the other would keep a lookout and warn of a supervisor's approach. And while chambermaids were meant to pool what paltry tips they found, Gina and Kelly shared them only with each other. Soon they were spending most of their time outside work together too.

Plenty of Kelly's former colleagues were consumed by jealousy when they heard that Kelly had moved to Sussex. Only Gina understood the pain Kelly felt at having left London behind. Gina sympathized with Kelly about her relationship with her mother. Her own upbringing had been hell in a different way. Gina's father had been a violent man. Together with her older brother, Gina had spent her childhood following her mother through a variety of women's shelters.

The girls talked about their families sometimes but most of the time they just tried to have fun. Clubbing at the weekends. Hitting Topshop on payday. These were the things that made them feel better about life.

"You're the sister I never had," Kelly often told her dear friend.

Which was why it was particularly embarrassing that Kelly had forgotten about the visit. Thank goodness Gina was so easygoing she wouldn't hold it against her.

Kelly dressed as quickly as she could but the Land Rover was nowhere to be seen. Guy had taken it into town to pick up parts for the rotavator. So Gina had to get a taxi from the station to Froggy Bottom. Only she didn't have the cash to pay her fare. She banked on Kelly having some money at the farmhouse but Kelly didn't have a penny either, so she let herself into Guy's flat and took a twenty out of the ginger jar on his mantelpiece. A very obvious place to hide your money, she thought. Guy was the trusting type. She'd pay it back. One day. If he noticed it was missing.

"Give me the tour!" Gina said excitedly.

Kelly led her friend through the house, desultorily pointing out its features. The five bedrooms, all with working fireplaces. The wood-paneled study. The inglenook fireplace in the kitchen. The old beams. The tiny door in the wall that had once led to a salt cellar. Kelly pointed them out as though she were noting the scratches on a rental car. Meanwhile, Gina walked around the farmhouse touching everything she could reach: the walls, the old furniture, the mullioned windows with their glass thickened at the bottom of the panes after centuries of slow dissolution. She gazed at it all with the reverence someone might have held for a proper stately home.

"Wow. Wow!" she said. "This is crazy. You could do so much with this place. You've even got an Aga."

"I don't know how to work it," said Kelly. "I can't turn it off."

"And a Welsh dresser! I've always wanted a Welsh dresser."

"You can have it."

"If I had somewhere to put it, you know I would take you up on that. How old is this table?" Gina murmured as she ran her hands over the oak, worn smooth with age. "Just think of how many people must have sat here over the years."

"Gina," said Kelly. "What are you wittering on about? It's all old crap."

Then the girls wandered out into the cottage garden that Guy tended as a hobby when he got in from the vines.

"Are those the grapes?" asked Gina, pointing at the rows marching up the hill.

"Yeah. Pinot noir from there to there. The rest are chardonnay and pinot murn-something." She had always struggled to say pinot meunier.

Still Gina seemed impressed.

"This is, like, amazing. And it's all yours."

Kelly shrugged.

"Kelly!" Gina reacted to Kelly's nonchalance. "This place is crazy. It's so beautiful. The view coming over the hill when the taxi brought me here was incredible!" Gina whirled around in the little cottage garden with its firework displays of delphiniums as though she were standing in the garden of Eden itself.

"You haven't seen it in the rain," said Kelly flatly. She dragged Gina out of the sunshine into the fuggy darkness of the farmhouse again. "Did you bring me any cigarettes?"

"How's life at the Gloria Hotel?" Kelly asked later.

Gina shook her head. "It's a lot less fun since you went." She paused and sighed. "I've got to get out of there."

"Well, duh," said Kelly.

"What else am I going to do? I've been trying to get some money together," she said. "I made about five hundred quid last week."

"Five?"

She didn't need to tell Kelly that she hadn't made that five hundred quid in tips from hotel customers grateful for the professional way she'd emptied the wastepaper basket and folded the ends of their toilet paper rolls into tidy triangles.

"Oh God," Gina sighed after a moment's silence. "There have got to be easier ways to make money. One of them got his wife's dress out."

"What's so bad about that? Was it made of a synthetic fabric? Too cheap for your delicate skin?"

"He didn't want *me* to wear it." Gina frowned. "I can't tell you how hard it was to keep a straight face. It's all right for you," she said. "You've got it made now. You've got all this. I'm stuck, Kels. I've got no money. I've got no qualifications to do anything different."

"What else would you do?"

"I could do my A levels. I always wanted to go to college. If I hadn't had to move school every term, I might have done it. I could have done a nursing course or something."

"And end up dealing with old men's bits for a fraction of the money you get for doing the same now? Forget nursing, Gina. Forget A levels. Aim higher."

"How?"

"I mean, aim higher with your class of punter. How many did you have to do for five hundred?"

"Five."

Kelly tutted. "You could have made that off one."

"You reckon? You haven't seen the competition. The

bar at Montrachet is crawling with girls fresh in from Moscow. That's what all the rich guys want now. They're more exotic."

"You're exotic," said Kelly.

It was true. Gina didn't look like the average pasty British girl. She was tall and slim with a neat, narrow waist and smooth long limbs. She'd inherited her Egyptian father's dark eyes, which combined with her mother's pale English skin to leave Gina looking more like a Spanish or Italian princess than a girl who had grown up in battered-women's homes in South London.

"You're gorgeous, Gina. You could be raking it in. You just need to make more of yourself."

"That's exactly what the careers teacher said when I left school. I don't think she meant I should scrub up to get a better class of John though." Gina managed a laugh but Kelly knew it was time to change the subject.

"I'd help you out," said Kelly. "You know I would. But it's not how it looks here. I can't get any money out of this place for five years. It's in a trust."

"I know," said Gina. "You told me already."

"After that, I'll sell this place like a shot, I swear. And I'll lend you the money to do whatever course you want and you can come and live with me in my new house. In London."

"You'd do that for me?" Gina started to sniffle. She dabbed at her eyes.

"Oh, don't get emotional on me, please," said Kelly. "It's the least I can do for my best friend."

Fortunately, at just that moment, Guy reappeared with the Land Rover, drawing Gina's attention away from Kelly to the window. He jumped down from the driver's seat and crunched across the courtyard.

"Who is that?" asked Gina, catching sight of him and

giving up on being miserable for a moment. She gave a low whistle.

Kelly rolled her eyes. "Oh, that's the bloke I've been telling you about. The one who's making my life a misery."

"The wine guy?"

"Yes, the wine guy. You'd think those bloody vines were his children."

"You never told me he was so fit."

"He's not."

"Have you gone blind? He's gorgeous!"

He certainly looked textbook good as he unloaded a box from the back of the car and carried it to his door. His thick blond hair, usually cut so short, was starting to curl over his collar. He could have been modeling his check shirt and jeans for a catalog. But Kelly couldn't separate the way Guy looked from the way she felt about him or the way he treated her, which she had decided was dismissive.

"You've got weird taste, Gina."

"I can't believe you're living next door to that and you slob around all day in your pajamas! Get him to come in and have a drink with us," Gina suggested. "Go on."

"No," said Kelly flatly. "He wouldn't want to anyway. I don't know how you can make booze and be so square. But now he's brought the car back, let's go down the pub and have a proper drink. Quick," Kelly grabbed her bag from the Welsh dresser. "Before he comes back down from his flat."

Guy reemerged just in time to see the taillights of the Land Rover disappearing through the farm gate as Kelly put her foot down and escaped from the "Valley of Doom" as she had come to call her new home.

Guy was furious. The parts he needed to fix the rota-vator were still in the back of the car. He'd planned to spend that evening getting the damn thing sorted out. He kicked the barrel full of flowers he had placed outside the farmhouse in an attempt to make nice with Kelly. He almost broke his toe.

"Bloody, bloody, bloody," he swore. The pain was so bad he only just managed not to use the F word.

The girls didn't get return until the pubs closed, which, this being the deepest darkest countryside, was much later than closing time in any city. In fact, the sky was already beginning to lighten again by the time the Land Rover crested the hill. Guy had intended to wait up and confront Kelly but he fell asleep in his armchair around midnight, a book about the pruning methods used in the Champagne region still open on his lap. He was so tired he didn't hear the girls tumble noisily from the Land Rover or Kelly's loud cursing as she tripped over the barrel that Guy had earlier kicked.

"That pub was all right," said Gina.

"Thank God. There's nothing else to do around here," said Kelly.

"Then you should make your own fun," Gina suggested.

"You sound like my gran."

"Seriously, you know what? You could hold an incredible all-nighter in this place. Your own mini-Glastonbury."

"What?"

"A festival. Right here in Froggy Bottom."

"Gina, you are a genius," Kelly exclaimed.

"A Gina-us," said Gina before she was stricken with an attack of the hiccups.

Kelly was suddenly energized with excitement. Gina's

idea was brilliant. Kelly insisted that they stay up and thrash out some of the details before they lost enthusiasm. She pulled out a bottle from Dougal's cellar—an extremely rare claret that tasted much better watered down with Diet Coke—to drink while they discussed how the first-ever Froggy Bottom Festival might happen.

"First of all we need music," said Kelly.

"That's easy."

Gina's brother, Antony, fancied himself a DJ. He was having some success in the clubs. He'd probably appear for free if he could headline, Gina suggested.

Kelly had Gina call him right away. They caught him between sets at a club in Clapham. He agreed that the idea was a brilliant one. They could definitely count him in and he'd ask his DJ mates to see if anyone else was up for it too. Less than half an hour later he'd recruited a couple of friends.

Kelly and Gina danced around the kitchen. Kelly put on a CD of garage tunes and cranked the volume up loud, not caring whether it woke Guy up as it drifted across the courtyard and in through his window.

"We need to make some proper plans," said Kelly after a while. She found some paper and they started to make notes.

"So we've got your brother and those two other guys. We can have camping on the field below the chardonnay. That's pretty level."

"You could stick a Portaloo in the car park."

"There's a load of old bricks behind the barn. We could build a massive barbecue. We could roast a pig!"

"That'd be crazy! What will we do for drinks?"

"Get a load of beers from the cash-and-carry," said Kelly.

"Beer? What about your wine?"

"Sure, we'll sell some of that too. If people really want it. And there's tons of the old stuff in the cellar. We could get rid of that. We'll just dust off the bottles. By the time people have had a few beers, they won't care what they're drinking."

"Speaking of which..." Gina gestured to her empty glass.

Kelly duly disappeared into the cellar and returned with a bottle of 1997 Amarone Classico from Quintarelli.

"This is Italian," she said. "Might be better than this French shit."

Kelly pulled the cork and poured out two glasses at a retail cost of approximately forty pounds a glass. The girls each took a couple of swigs and pulled identically disappointed faces.

"That is so nasty! You got any white?" Gina asked.

"I'll have a look."

The planning continued over a bottle of 1996 Corton-Charlemagne Domaine Jean-François Coche-Dury.

"That's better," said Gina, as she took a gulp that was worth more than her shoes. "Tastes a bit like Jacob's Creek. Got any ice cubes?"

Gina added a couple to her glass. Kelly hesitated and decided against it.

"I quite like this how it is," she said.

"How much do you reckon we can charge for this party, then?" Gina continued.

"Fifty quid a head. Easy," said Kelly as she spilled roughly the same amount's worth of wine down the front of her shirt.

CHAPTER 17

"Madeleine Arsenault is no vigneronne."

Axel Delaflote's words echoed in Madeleine's head. From the moment she awoke in the morning to the moment she finally managed to go to sleep—with the aid of the pills she'd persuaded her doctor she needed to cope with bereavement—she could hear his voice as he discussed the future of Clos Des Larmes with that idiot Mathieu Randon. Axel had turned out to be a big swinging dick indeed. She had never felt so humiliated. And hurt.

Well, she would show them both. Madeleine Arsenault had champagne in her blood. She may have chosen to leave Champagne as soon as she was able but that didn't mean she had forgotten the things she learned by her father's side. Her pride was at stake. She was going to make this work. The very morning after Axel's sudden departure from her life, Madeleine was back in the vineyard.

Madeleine knew that ninety-nine percent of good winemaking took place among the vines. Unraveling her father's financial affairs still took up plenty of time but Madeleine made sure she was in the vineyards on the hill and the Clos next to the house daily, inspecting progress with Henri.

For a few days after her fight with Axel, Madeleine worried that Henri might be in the employ of Randon too, hired to scupper that year's harvest so that Randon could get his hands on her land for even less. But eventually she came to realize that idea was ridiculous. She had known Henri since childhood. He had carried her to hospital when, aged seven, she fell off the wall of the Clos and broke her arm. She couldn't think of a more honest man. In fact, when she told him the reason why young Monsieur Delaflote was no longer welcome at Champagne Arsenault, Henri seemed genuinely shocked.

"You did the right thing, mademoiselle," he assured her. "You should never part with Arsenault. Your father would be proud."

Madeleine accepted Henri's compliment gracefully though she very much doubted he was right about her father. She couldn't think of a single time in her childhood when she felt that Constant Arsenault had truly been proud of her. After Georges's death it seemed he couldn't even be bothered to be exasperated with her anymore. The house, which had once been filled with the sound of children playing, was suddenly silent. A house so deep in mourning it was as though time had simply stopped. No one seemed to consider that Madeleine missed her brother too.

Madeleine preferred to think of her grandmother. *Grand-mère* Arsenault looked fierce but she'd always been soft for her granddaughter. When Madeleine was in trouble with her father, she would creep into her grandmother's room at the back of the house and cuddle up on her lap.

"You're as good as the boys, Madeleine. Always remember that."

Well, she was going to prove her *grand-mère* right.

A month after her fight with Axel, Madeleine received a visit from one of her girlfriends from London, Lizzy Parker. Madeleine and Lizzy first met when Madeleine was sent to boarding school in Hampshire. Later, they shared a flat in London before Madeleine's career took off and she could afford a place of her own. Lizzy's career had also taken off—she was a well-respected magazine journalist—but her personal life was never quite so successful. She had drifted through a number of hopeless live-in relationships that always ended with her turning up on Madeleine's doorstep with her bags. That weekend was no exception. Like Madeleine, Lizzy was heartbroken. She'd just come out of a three-year affair with a dope-smoking physics teacher who'd claimed he was too damaged to love. Of course, just a couple of weeks after dumping Lizzy, he was seeing someone else. Thus Lizzy was only too happy to corroborate Madeleine's view that men were not to be trusted.

"I'm not in the least bit surprised to hear that Axel bloke turned out to be such a cast-iron arse," said Lizzy. "He was much too good to be true. Just like James! I can't believe I put up with his crap for three years! Three years, Maddy. All that bleating about how damaged he was. Making me feel sorry for him when he was really just being crap like the rest of them. Why didn't you tell me?"

"I did," said Madeleine. "We all did. Even he did," she observed.

"Well, we're better off without them."

Lizzy clinked her champagne glass against Madeleine's, spilling half its contents as she did so.

Over the next three hours Lizzy dissected James's character—or lack of it. Madeleine remained quiet except for the occasional psychiatrist-style "mmm-hmm." She knew that was all Lizzy wanted really, the sense that she was being listened to. She wasn't asking for answers or advice, which was lucky since Madeleine didn't have any to give.

Between them, the girls drank two bottles of wine.

Madeleine had cooked a fabulous dinner but Lizzy hardly touched the food laid before her.

"The only good thing about splitting up with James is that I can get into my old jeans again," she said ruefully. "I'm so miserable, I just keep forgetting to eat. You're looking very thin, Mads," Lizzy added with something approaching admiration.

"Working in the vineyards," she said.

"Oh yes," said Lizzy, forcing herself out of her solipsism at last. "How is that going?"

Madeleine was only too glad to change the subject. She told Lizzy in great detail about the state in which she had found the house and the vineyard when she returned for her father's funeral.

"Despite all that, this may actually turn out to be a good year. I may even make a Clos Des Larmes."

"What is a Clos Des Larmes?" Lizzy asked.

"It's the name of Champagne Arsenault's finest wine. A clos is a walled vineyard. Clos Des Larmes is the walled vineyard behind this house. It means 'Vineyard of Tears.'"

"Tears?"

"Yes. It got its name during the First World War. My great-grandmother had just been widowed. She was pregnant with my grandfather, about seven months gone. It was August. The fighting was within miles of the house but the grapes still had to be harvested. She was able to do it only with the help of two of her old schoolfriends, also widowed. They cried the whole way through. Hence Vineyard of Tears."

"That's so sad," said Lizzy. "Your great-grandmother must have been a brave woman. Can you imagine? I can barely get out of bed because of that stupid shit James. If I'd been widowed in the middle of a pregnancy, I think I would have left all the grapes to shrivel."

"Times of adversity bring out the best in the

Champenois. In fact, I think that's true of most people. You're only as feeble as you allow yourself to be," said Madeleine.

Lizzy pulled a doubtful face.

"You're better than this, Lizzy. You'll be over James in no time at all. I promise you. Perhaps you should come back here at harvesttime. The place will be crawling with young Australians on working holidays. Soon take your mind off James and his saggy jowls."

"He does have jowls, doesn't he?" Lizzy finally admitted.

"Terrible jowls. We all used to talk about them when you weren't around. That and his man-boobs."

"Oh God. The man-boobs!" Lizzy giggled properly for the first time that night. "You know he was actually considering breast-reduction surgery," she cackled. "If he started having tucks, I don't know where he'd finish!"

And so the evening ended on a slightly brighter note as Lizzy convinced herself—at least for the moment—that she'd had a lucky escape. What woman wanted to sleep with a man whose bra size was bigger than her own?

Madeleine couldn't comfort herself in quite the same way, alas. No jowls on Axel Delaflote.

The following morning she awoke halfway through a dream in which Axel was lying beside her. Their faces were turned to each other. He was looking deep into her eyes. She thought she could see love there.

And then she was awake and back to hearing him sneering about her ability to keep Champagne Arsenault afloat and plotting with Randon to absorb her family name into bloody Domaine Randon along with all those crappy brands.

Unable to get back to sleep, Madeleine got up and roused Lizzy too.

"What? Is it morning already? My head hurts."

"Have a glass of water," said Madeleine brusquely. "And put your boots on. We're going to get cracking with these."

She waved a pair of shears at her friend.

"On James?" was Lizzy's sleepy first reaction.

"On the vines, you nitwit. Need to take some leaves off to help the ripening."

Physical labor. That would keep those stupid men out of their heads.

CHAPTER 18

Christina's faux pas with regard to Domaine Randon's Fast Life and the ISACL "I Don't Buy It" campaign unleashed a flurry of legalese between Christina's agent and Randon's lawyers. Marisa was terrified, but didn't show it; Bill was mortified—he did show that; Christina was unrepentant. After all, Domaine Randon wasn't actually able to quash the accusation that Fast Life products were made using cheap child labor.

"But Bill," Christina said when they finally found themselves in the same house for more than a couple of hours and were able to discuss the matter face-to-face. "Since Domaine Randon *does* profit from child labor, then we ought not to be involved in their advertising anyway."

"What?" Bill stared at his wife.

"I mean, never mind Mathieu Randon being upset about the association. How is it going to *look* for me that I took his dime in the first place? I have to be *so* careful about my image. Either he has to make an announcement saying that he's willing to ensure his companies don't use child labor or I will have to resign from the champagne campaign and pay Randon's fee back."

"Christina, have you gone completely out of your mind? Do you know how much we got for that campaign?"

"We don't need his money."

"Oh, but we do," Bill murmured half to himself. He cast an eye around the living room of their Malibu beach house, with its unobstructed view of the Pacific Ocean. The mortgage was astronomical. Not to mention the cost of everything in it. Even the ashtrays, in which Bill had stubbed out an alarming number of Marlboro Lights in the last hour, cost five hundred bucks apiece. Christina had been responsible for decorating the house and she had expensive taste. While Bill would have been happy with a shack on the sand and a table made of driftwood, she had to have Italian furniture, French china and antiques on every surface. And Bill had indulged her; it seemed to make her happy.

Bill walked out onto the balcony and lit another cigarette to calm the rising panic. He was sure Christina had no clue how much they needed the next Éclat campaign.

"Billy." Christina followed him outside.

Bill stared out at the sea as she wrapped her arms around him and rested her chin on his shoulder.

"Please don't be angry with me, sweetheart. It's not the end of the world if Randon won't do the decent thing. If we stand down from this campaign there will be others. I know there will. Much better ones. There has to be a brand out there that will actually appreciate our stance on child labor."

"Our stance?" said Bill. "You think I give a shit who sews my socks?"

"I know you don't mean that," said Christina

Bill snorted in response. He unpeeled Christina's arms from his waist.

"Trust me," she persisted. "Ultimately this will turn out to have been a fantastic move for both of us. Think of how this could look. The public wants their stars to have integrity as well as glamour. There is a great brand out there that will be very, very happy to be associated with doing the right thing. As we are."

"Christina, there isn't a luxury brand left in the Western world that you haven't just told your fans to boycott! The only thing you approve of is sackcloth. You don't think the news has got out about this foul-up? Nobody gives a shit about integrity. Everyone is laughing at you. As far as advertisers are concerned, you're trouble. You're a fucking liability. You've just shot yourself in the foot. And me too."

Christina sighed audibly and shook her head at Bill. He felt as though he were a difficult child being told off by his mother.

"Well, I'm not asking you to step down. You go ahead, Bill. Go where your conscience leads you, if you've actually got one. You can keep your half of the blood money."

"Believe me," said Bill. "I would. But without you the champagne ad can't go ahead. The whole point is that it's you and me. Bill Tarrant and Christina Morgan. The most fabulous couple in Hollywood. Ha ha ha."

He went back into the house and snatched up his leather jacket from the back of the sofa.

Christina found herself alone on the balcony. She heard Bill slam his way out of the house. She heard the engine of his stupid Hummer roar to life and growl its way down the PCH toward Santa Monica. They would have to have a talk about more eco-friendly transportation soon, she reminded herself. Such conspicuous consumption of fossil fuels did not look good. When she was sure that he had gone, Christina flipped open her mobile and dialed Rocky Neel. He was sympathetic. "It's tough for you, sweetheart, but the kids can't thank you enough for raising the charity's profile. You look great in the new brochure," he added. It was exactly what she needed to hear.

Marisa, likewise, promised that she was devoting herself to fire-fighting the whole Randon thing. In fact, less than an hour after Bill stormed out of the house, Marisa was on the phone again.

"They're in no position to sue," said Marisa. "They have to prove what the campaign claims is untrue to win and, thank God, they can't. I've just had a long chat with their top lawyer. He says that Domaine Randon is willing to investigate and put right this terrible child labor business, if you continue to promote their champagne and promise that Fast Life's name will be dropped from the ISACL list."

"I'll think about it," said Christina haughtily, though in that very moment she finally realized just how much the prospect of having to put her own money where her mouth was had rattled her. Thank goodness it looked like they were coming to an amicable solution. Perhaps Bill would stop freaking out.

Marisa had some other good news. Guilty Secrets, the lingerie company, wanted Christina to take part in their annual fashion show. It was a big deal. Guilty Secrets wasn't La Perla. In fact, their underwear was rather cheap and tacky. But the Guilty Secrets fashion show had taken on a life of its own and become something more than a simple fashion fixture. It was an annual event on a par with the release of the *Sports Illustrated* swimsuit edition or the

Pirelli Calendar. Being chosen to be in the Guilty Secrets show was an acknowledgment that you had one of the best bodies in the business.

"I'll only do it if I get to be the last girl on the catwalk," said Christina. The last spot was the most important. The final girl got to wear the showstopper outfit—the jewel-encrusted bikini—and make the picture that would appear on the front pages of just about every newspaper in the world.

"Would I have agreed to anything else for my favorite client?" Marisa asked.

Christina snapped her phone shut with a smile. Forget Bill and his stupid tantrums. Forget that sleazeball Mathieu Randon. Everything was all right in her world.

CHAPTER 19

A couple of days later, Bill Tarrant flew to Paris to promote his latest movie. He was slightly surprised but very gratified when his agent called to say that Mathieu Randon had requested an opportunity to meet. He was absolutely delighted when Randon suggested dinner. That was a good sign, Bill decided. If Randon just wanted to vent, he would have done so in his office over a bottle of mineral water. Dinner proved Bill was not on the shit list.

Bill met Randon at Eponine—one of the best new restaurants in the sixteenth arrondissement. Bill wasn't surprised they got a table. The big business guy and the film star. Still, he was excited as he got ready that evening.

Though he was at the top of his game as an actor, giving Brad Pitt a run for his money, lately Bill had been craving a different kind of recognition. He was secretly in awe of guys like Randon who juggled millions of dollars on a daily basis. Bill had only played—quite literally—at being powerful in that very tangible way. But he had ambition. He wanted Randon to recognize that he had the potential too.

Randon was already at the restaurant when Bill arrived. Bill took that as another good sign. Randon wasn't going to keep Bill waiting. It was a fairly clear indicator of the balance of their relationship.

"My dear friend," said Randon. He stood up and greeted Bill with a friendly clap on the back.

"Matt. I'm glad we got the chance to meet like this," said Bill. "Good table," he commented as he sat down. "Perfect view of the room."

"And of the lovely young ladies of Paris," Randon added just as Bill's attention was drawn to a girl in a very short skirt who was doing her best to climb onto a bar stool without flashing her underwear. She didn't succeed.

Bill nodded approvingly. Randon laughed. He seemed to be very relaxed. Bill allowed himself to think that everything was going to be fine.

But of course, Christina's faux pas had to be the first topic on the agenda. Bill brought it up as soon as he could. He thought that pre-empting Randon on the subject might help him control the conversation's outcome.

"What can I say?" said Bill. "I did my best to convince her that she's talking rubbish, but she won't back down. You know what it's like. The more I argue with her, the more entrenched she gets. She's a very headstrong woman."

"I understand," said Randon. "The world has changed since men could tell their wives what to do."

"Could they ever?" Bill sighed. "I think in the old days, women were just more sensitive about letting us guys believe we were in charge."

Randon gave a little snort of amusement. "That's why I've never married. But let's not allow this little problem to spoil a wonderful evening. I understand that our people have been negotiating a compromise that will suit us all," Randon said as he summoned the waiter and ordered, of course, a bottle of his own champagne.

And that was it. Bill was astonished at how quickly the subject of Christina's boycott seemed to have been forgotten. Dealt with in a couple of minutes. Instead, Randon wanted to talk about Hollywood. About Bill's movie career.

"I saw your new movie," Randon said. "I had your agent send me a DVD."

"You did?" said Bill. He was surprised. His agent hadn't mentioned it.

"Yes. It was quite a revelation. I enjoyed your performance very much. You have great range."

Bill nodded enthusiastically. He did have great range. Not many people acknowledged that. The critics certainly didn't understand.

"Very convincing," Randon continued.

"Thank you. You know," said Bill, getting braver, "I think it's important to diversify. Lately I've been thinking I want to have a go at directing."

"Really?" asked Randon.

"It's the natural step for me to take. When you get to my position as an actor, you're practically directing yourself anyway. For example, in the movie you just saw—*Do or Die Trying*—about half of that stuff was scripted but the rest was me ad-libbing. Deciding how the character should be on the fly. You know what I mean?"

Randon nodded.

"I helped my co-stars with their character development too. They seemed to appreciate that. And one of my great strengths is that I have a natural eye for the composition of a scene. I've always had that eye, but when you're just starting out as an actor, no one takes any notice if you pipe up and say, 'Hey guys, don't you think this scene would look better shot from this angle?' "

"That must be difficult," said Randon.

"It sucks," said Bill, sensing sympathy. "And when you get to our stage in life, Randon, you don't want some spotty kid straight out of film school telling you what to do. It really gets my goat. I'm a professional. I know film. I *am* film."

Bill emphasized his point by waving a forkful of rare steak in the air.

"So what exactly do you want to do?" Randon asked.

"I want to do a western," Bill announced. "But not like the old-style westerns. This one is going to be real. There's an appetite out there to know what really happened when the West was won. The historical point of view."

"And you'd like to star and direct?"

"You got it. I've been thinking about it for years. I picked up this book a few months ago by this historian out of Princeton. It's amazing stuff. And so relevant to the way we live today. The parallels between the Wild West and what goes on in the House of Representatives right now...well, it made my hair stand on end. That's how I know a good idea when I've found one. My hair, quite literally, stands on end."

"Fascinating. It sounds like a project I could be very interested in."

Bill put his fork down and looked at Randon intently.

He allowed himself to believe that Randon was serious. Why wouldn't he be?

"You could?"

"Absolutely. Doesn't everyone want to get into movies at some point?" said Randon.

"Then come out to the States," said Bill, leaning back in his chair and throwing his arms out magnanimously. "I'll fix up some meetings. Matt, let me tell you, I would be more than happy to have a guy like you on board."

"Thank you," said Randon. "I would like that."

"Consider it done."

"More wine?" Randon topped up Bill's glass.

Another bottle later and Bill felt truly relaxed in Randon's company again. He regaled Randon with tales from his life in the limelight. Discretion flew out of the window. He impressed Randon with a long list of sexual conquests that sounded like a roll call of every Academy Award Best Actress nominee since 1985. Then he moved on to the people he *hadn't* slept with, a short list comprised of two actors well known for defending their heterosexuality.

"That baby? Turkey baster, I'm telling you. He is not interested in girls at all . . . Unlike my lady wife."

Randon leaned forward. "Really?"

"Oh yeah. Behind the scenes at some of those catwalk shows. The girls are all over one another. Sodom and Gomorrah. You could make a fortune if you released a video."

"Quite. That's very interesting. But it's getting late, and right now, I've got someone I would like you to meet."

"Oh yes?" Bill asked.

"*Oh yes.* Someone I think you'll appreciate very much." Randon flipped open his mobile and sent a text.

An hour later, in a sumptuous suite at the Hotel Crillon, Randon took the petite dark-eyed girl by her shoulders and led her towards Bill as though he were offering the actor her hand in marriage.

"I think you'll find an evening in Amelie's company quite relaxing," he said with a smile.

"Relaxing" wasn't the word for it.

Like the little wrap of cocaine Bill found in the top drawer of the bedside cabinet, exactly where Randon had said it would be, Amelie's attentions were complimentary. And absolutely exhilarating.

She had naughty brown eyes and a mouth as red and wide as a British postbox. How could Bill resist? Why should he?

Bill hadn't had sex in a month. Sometimes it made him want to laugh out loud when he thought of the men who envied his sham of a marriage to Christina Morgan, the supermodel. There were whole websites dedicated to their envy. Some jerk was so worked up about it he even sent Bill death threats. But the truth was, since Bill had put a ring on Christina's finger just over twelve months earlier, he'd been getting less sex than the average eighth-grade pupil. Not that he even wanted it so much anymore; not with Christina anyway. Who was it that said "Show me a beautiful woman and I'll show you a man who's tired of fucking her?" Bill now knew exactly what that guy meant. How quickly he'd become immune to the way Christina looked and started to focus on her uglier aspects.

And jeez, there were plenty of ugly aspects to that woman. Bill should have handed that stalker guy a list. She was bitchy. She put him down the whole time. She was sanctimonious. She was ignorant. She was stupid. Really, really stupid.

It was her stupidity that had brought him to this, he told himself as Amelie began to prance around the room, shedding her clothes like a burlesque dancer. If Christina had been a bit more careful what she proselytized about on national television, if she'd just done a little basic research, Bill wouldn't have had to suck up to Randon. And if he hadn't sucked up to Randon, then Randon wouldn't have paid this rather pretty little whore to suck Bill's dick. Excellent logic. Flawless, Bill would have said, if Amelie's talents hadn't already rendered him speechless.

Bill Tarrant closed his eyes and forgot about everything else.

The following day, the legal team at Domaine Randon and the lawyers representing Christina Morgan signed an official agreement regarding the ISACL debacle. Randon had asked that Christina remain as the face of Maison Randon provided she refrain from denouncing Fast Life in public. Domaine Randon would, of course, fully investigate the allegations of child labor and put them right.

"I knew that ad was just too good to waste," said Marisa. More to the point, it was just too expensive. Frank Wylie's services had bumped the budget of a single thirty-second commercial up to that of the average TV movie.

Regardless of the real story behind Domaine Randon's decision to step down, Christina was satisfied that she had won a moral victory. She agreed to keep her mouth shut.

Hearing the news in Paris, Bill gave an enormous sigh of relief. Pushing an image of Amelie to the back of his mind, he called Christina and told her that he couldn't wait to see her. He loved her. Everything would be all right.

CHAPTER 20

The business of being a small-scale winemaker doesn't stop at making the wine. It needs to be sold. Guy had discussed with Hilarian the possibility of Froggy Bottom taking a stand at the London International Wine and Spirits Fair at the ExCeL center that year. The cost of a stand was a big outlay for the vineyard at a time when there wasn't a great deal of money to spare but Hilarian persuaded his fellow trustees that it would be a good way to introduce Froggy Bottom to lots of potential new customers.

"And to see if we can change their minds about us," he said.

Hilarian was only too aware that like most English wine, Froggy Bottom was seen as something of a novelty by the general public. Not to be taken seriously. But that was before Guy arrived. Two years after it was harvested, Guy's first vintage for the vineyard was looking—and, more importantly, tasting—very good. It was time to show the rest of the world.

The day before the fair opened, Hilarian drove down to Sussex to help Guy load up the wine and other promotional materials they would need for the Froggy Bottom stand. He found Guy in a grumpy sort of mood.

"How are you getting along with Kelly?" he asked, when they paused in stacking boxes for a restorative cup of tea.

The news wasn't good.

"Hardly ever see her. She doesn't get up before noon. Ever. She's like a vampire. I've never managed to persuade her to come out to the vines. I don't think she'd know what a grape looks like if she slipped on one and broke her stupid neck."

Hilarian shook his head.

"No need to be so nasty, dear Guy," he said. "I can't imagine it's quite that bad. Perhaps she's bored. Maybe she needs a trip up to London to cheer her up?" he suggested. "Have you asked her?"

Guy looked panicked. "I haven't even mentioned I'm going. Don't tell me you want me to take her to the wine fair?"

"Why not? It might spark some enthusiasm in the dear girl. I'll suggest it."

"Please, no," said Guy. But it was too late. Hilarian had made up his mind.

Hilarian did his best to humor both Guy and Kelly. Guy was a very hard worker. He had enormous talent as a winemaker—managing to turn the acidic piss that Dougal used to make into something almost drinkable was a feat worthy of Jesus Christ himself. But, unusually for the wine trade, Guy could be a bit stuffy. He took his winemaking very, very seriously. It didn't take an enormous leap of imagination for Hilarian to imagine how Guy might have wound Kelly up.

On the other hand...

The first thing Hilarian spotted as he neared the old farmhouse was the row of empty bottles on the step.

While he waited for Kelly to open the door, Hilarian couldn't help but pick a couple of the empties up. He expected to see a few bottles of Jacob's Creek. Maybe some of Froggy Bottom's finest. And indeed, there were a couple. But he did not expect to see three bottles that had once contained Petrus.

"What? For goodness' sake!" Hilarian goggled at the vintage and made a quick and horrible calculation in his head. At a Michelin-starred restaurant those three bottles alone would have set you back the cost of a small car. Kelly must have got into Dougal's cellar. Suddenly feeling a little less indulgent and avuncular, Hilarian hammered for attention.

Kelly eventually opened the door. "Hey, Hilarian." She looked sleepy. Possibly because she was still wearing her pajamas. "I wasn't expecting you."

"Clearly. I hope you enjoyed this," he said, brandishing an empty bottle from 1989. "Where did you find it?"

"Oh, that. There are loads of bottles under the stairs. I think it must have been past its sell-by date. It tasted a bit funny but it was all right when we added some Coke."

"Coke? You…" Hilarian decided to bite his tongue. "I'll tell you what," he said. "Why don't you stay out of the cellar from now on. I'll take those out-of-date bottles off your hands and bring you some Bacardi Breezers instead, how about that?"

"That'd be great," said Kelly, quite sincerely.

"Good," said Hilarian. "Can I come in?"

"Did you bring any fags?" she asked.

Over a cigarette and a cup of tea, Hilarian made his suggestion about the wine festival.

"Great," said Kelly, shocking him with her speedy and seemingly enthusiastic response. "Saves me having to get the train into town."

"We're not just going to drop you off in London," Hilarian warned her. "I'm inviting you to come with us to the festival, not offering you a lift to go shopping or whatever it is you girls do."

"Boring," said Kelly.

"It won't be," Hilarian assured her, "You're going to help set up the stand. Represent the winery."

Kelly groaned.

"And it will give me an opportunity to introduce you to some different sorts of wine."

After that morning's horrible shock with the Petrus, it was clear that an education was in order, and Hilarian intended to deliver it.

It was an hour and a half before Kelly emerged from the farmhouse carrying an enormous suitcase.

"We're only going for two nights," said Hilarian.

"Didn't know what to wear," said Kelly.

That much was clear.

Guy planned to dress up for the occasion and had packed a suit. He had just one. He'd bought it on sale. It cost a good deal more than he could really afford but he told himself it was important for a man to have at least one proper two-piece. Guy imagined himself walking into Berry Bros. and presenting his wine for their consideration. He was certain that one day soon, his wine itself would open doors all over the world, but until Froggy Bottom's reputation was established he needed to look the part to wow the old boys in St. James's.

Kelly was obviously wearing what she considered to be the best outfit for a day in the capital. Or a day as an extra in a rap video.

As he took in her short skirt and those stupid little white ankle boots, Guy subconsciously shook his head. He didn't even know he'd done it until Kelly spat out, "What?" in her usual dulcet tones.

"We're supposed to be ambassadors for Froggy Bottom," said Guy. "There are going to be important people there and you . . . you look like . . ."

"I think she looks rather lovely," said Hilarian, anxious to avert a disaster and hopeful that there was something better in her case. "Shall we get a move on?"

Guy climbed into the driver's seat, clenching his jaw with irritation. Hilarian offered Kelly the front seat next to him, but she declined, preferring instead to loll right across the backseat with the earphones to her iPod clamped firmly to her head. She glared out of the window like a teenager being driven to visit her grandmother.

Meanwhile, in Calais, Madeleine Arsenault made a last call to Henri Mason back in Le Vezy before she drove her car onto the train for the Eurotunnel trip to England and the onward journey to the London International Wine Fair.

"Don't worry about the vineyards," said Henri. "They're doing fine. You just get out there and sell your father's last vintage."

Madeleine assured Henri that she would do her best.

Having at last made some sense of the piles of receipts and bills her father had left behind and knowing that the vineyards were well cared for under Henri's watchful eye, Madeleine knew it was time to turn her own attention to promotion. The London wine fair seemed like a good place to start. Madeleine had missed the deadline for securing a stand at that year's Vinexpo in Bordeaux but London was a big market too. After all, the British were, after the French, the world's biggest consumers of champagne.

That said, Champagne Arsenault would not have its own stand that year. Madeleine had joined together with a couple of other negociants from Le Vezy. People she liked and trusted to promote her champagne as avidly as they promoted their own if she had to step away from the stand. And so Madeleine was quite excited as she boarded the train, not least because the trip would give her the excuse to catch up with a few of her old friends. Lizzy for sure. Perhaps even Geoff.

After a few wrong turns on her way into London from Dover, Madeleine arrived at her Docklands hotel just before midnight. She ate a disappointing room service sandwich and answered a couple of e-mails before settling down to sleep. One of the e-mails was from Odile Levert, the wine critic.

Madeleine had recently sent a couple of bottles of Champagne Arsenault's last release to Odile's office. The moment the bottles had left her hands, Madeleine regretted the move, fully expecting that Odile would at best ignore the offerings and at worst savage them in her column. And so Madeleine was surprised to read Odile's e-mail, which said, "I was quietly impressed by your father's last vintage but I would be even more interested to hear *your* plans for Champagne Arsenault. I notice your name in the program for the wine fair. I'd like to meet with you while you are in London."

Madeleine had long admired Odile Levert. Not just as a wine critic but as the kind of impeccably elegant woman that all young French girls aspired to be. Madeleine's father, who had little time for any wine critics, had had a surprisingly large amount of respect for Odile.

"For a woman, she has a remarkable nose," he said. It was high praise indeed from the old vigneron. Constant would have been pleased to know that Odile liked his last vintage.

Madeleine sent back her acceptance of the invitation at once.

CHAPTER 21

The London International Wine and Spirits Fair was one of Hilarian's favorite engagements. It was a wonderful social occasion for him. A chance to catch up with old friends and gossip. And, of course, being one of the most recognizable, and affable, wine critics in town, he was treated like a VIP. Hilarian's column was written with such skill and genuine enthusiasm that even those winemakers he had savaged somehow took his criticism in their stride and continued to send him their bottles. Within five minutes of walking into the ExCeL center, Hilarian had four invitations to lunch.

But before the partying could begin, the Froggy Bottom stand had to be set up. They'd paid for the smallest booth available. They didn't have the money, or the time, to get proper posters produced, so Guy had painted the Froggy Bottom logo onto a piece of driftwood. He was worried that it wouldn't look professional, but in the end, Hilarian assured him, it worked very well. There was something artisanal and original about it.

The exhibition organizers were providing glasses to each of the stands. When Froggy Bottom's box of ISO-standard tasting glasses was delivered, Guy immediately took them out and examined each one as though he were the sommelier in a top-class establishment. Hardly any of them met with his approval.

"These look like they haven't been cleaned since last year. We've got to wash them," he said.

"But nobody's drunk anything out of them yet," said Kelly.

"See?" Guy held a glass in front of her nose. "It's smeary."

Kelly shrugged. "Looks all right to me."

"Not to me. I want to make a good impression."

"You're doing a very good impression of a complete weirdo," Kelly said.

"Help him dry up the glasses, Kelly," said Hilarian. "There's a good girl."

"All right," said Kelly. "If it'll stop him freaking out."

They were still polishing glasses when the wine fair officially opened. The immediate and sudden rush of visitors into the hall surprised Guy. At nine in the morning, it seemed a little early to start drinking—even if you were going to be spitting most of it out.

Madeleine didn't have time to polish glasses before the fair opened. Odile Levert had responded to her e-mail of the night before immediately and suggested that they meet for breakfast. Odile chose the restaurant at her hotel as the venue. She welcomed Madeleine at eight o'clock precisely.

Madeleine was glad in some ways that she didn't have much time to prepare for her meeting with Odile. More time to prepare would have given her more time to be nervous. As it was, she was shaking ever so slightly when Odile extended her hand in greeting. Madeleine was used to holding her own in rooms full of powerful men but there was something about Odile that really unnerved her.

As she read the menu, she could tell that Odile's eyes were on her, cool and appraising. She was glad she'd worn her favorite suit, a neat little number in black by Paule Ka. She ordered as carefully as a girl on a date, working out what she could eat without getting in too much of a mess. She settled on toast. Odile just had coffee.

They talked about that year's crop in Champagne. They discussed some political wrangling within the CIVC. Odile said once more that she was very impressed by the champagne Madeleine had sent her, but Madeleine still wasn't sure why she merited this face-to-face meeting with a woman who was doubtless courted by the big names: Bollinger, Taittinger, Veuve Clicquot, Domaine Randon.

"I need to find a small vineyard to champion for the purposes of a bet," Odile said at last. "And I think that you're the one."

Madeleine was surprised and thrilled all at once. Was this an official endorsement?

"You think I could win the bet for you?" she asked.

"Don't get too excited," said Odile. "There's a lot of work to be done. And if you embarrass me, I'll ruin you."

Just before mid-day, Ronald Ginsburg stopped by the Froggy Bottom stand. Recognizing him at once, Guy bravely offered him a glass, which Ronald merely sniffed before he turned to Hilarian, who had hurried back from talking to a friend to lend Guy his support. He knew exactly what Ronald was about.

"Is this the wine you think will be a world-beater within five years?" Ginsburg raised a sceptical eyebrow.

"We're looking forward to seeing the *Vinifera* Wine Challenge results," said Guy.

"You mean you actually entered this?" Ronald feigned surprise.

"I think Froggy Bottom has a good chance of a respectable rating," said Hilarian, wishing he could punch Ronald square on his big red nose.

"I'll see you at the *Vinifera* luncheon, Hilarian," said Ronald, pouring his tasting measure of Froggy Bottom straight into the spittoon.

"Who was that old git?" Kelly asked.

"Alas," said Hilarian, "that old git is probably the most influential wine critic in the world."

"He'll be dead soon," said Guy.

"Hopefully," Hilarian concurred.

"This is boring," said Kelly.

Kelly had helped to set up the stand with relatively good grace but Hilarian's concession to Guy had been to agree that Kelly would not try to talk about Froggy Bottom to anyone, lest she deliver an erroneous or just plain unflattering message about the brand. And so Kelly was relegated to washing the used tasting glasses. And that didn't suit her at all.

"I'm going for a walk," she said.

Guy started to protest but Hilarian cut him short with a look. Kelly had been on washing-up duty for four solid hours. "Good idea," he said. "You could do with a lunch break. Why don't you go and get yourself a sandwich? Perhaps even taste some wine on your way back to us." He picked up a copy of the festival's brochure and underlined a couple of stands. "This is good. And this is very good. I think you'll like this."

"Sure. Thanks." She shuffled off.

Kelly didn't bother with a sandwich. And she didn't much feel like tasting wine. The stands Hilarian had chosen were manned and surrounded by besuited old duffers, who either looked at Kelly as though they wanted to lick her or closed ranks as she drew near like she was one of those Romanian women with a tightly swaddled baby you see rattling empty coffee cups on the Tube.

Kelly caught snippets of their conversation as she passed. "Great length. Medium body. Hint of asparagus." She knew what they meant but she was sure that if she said the same sort of thing, it would only make those wine snobs laugh. Wine was for snobs, she concluded. Someone from her background would never fit in.

Fortunately, wine was not the only thing available to the keen punters. Kelly discarded Hilarian's brochure with its careful underlining and made straight for the spirits section. It wasn't long before she found something that took her fancy. There were no Bacardi Breezers to be had but there were several similar beverages. And there was plenty of neat vodka.

Kelly could do neat vodka if she did it quickly enough. Which she did, downing three shots in five minutes. By a Finnish vodka stand, Kelly even made herself a couple of friends. Iain and Ryan from Johannesburg were saving up to travel around Europe by working at a Majestic Wine Warehouse in South London. Entrance to the strictly trade-only wine fair was the best perk of their job so far, they told Kelly.

"Man, this is crazy," said Ryan. "Can you believe all this alcohol is free?"

Ian and Ryan accomapnied Kelly on a tour of the best of the spirits section, quickly enlivening the experience further with their rugby players' drinking games.

"No one can drink more than a South African," Iain roared as he slammed an empty shot glass on a counter.

"Watch me," said Kelly, downing another shot of vodka and lining up her own glass for more. "London girls are invincible."

Iain and Ryan watched in awe as Kelly matched them drink for drink.

An hour later, the trio found themselves in front of a stand promoting absinthe: *la fée verte*. A green fairy fashioned in thin neon tubing buzzed and crackled on the canopy. By this stage, all three of the new friends were swaying. Several stand owners had pointedly ignored them when they tried to get served, but the guys in the absinthe stand were from South Africa too. They weren't about to curtail their fellow countrymen's fun and games.

"What is this shit made of?" asked Kelly, recoiling from her first sniff of the viscous green liquid.

She didn't bother to listen to the sales pitch; indeed, the guy in the stall didn't bother to give it. Instead, she followed Iain, pinched her nose and tried to tip the shot down her throat without letting it touch her tongue. She shuddered as it burned its way toward her stomach.

"That was disgusting," she said. "Who the hell drinks this stuff?"

"Like another?" asked the guy in the stand, melting a spoonful of sugar and letting the syrup drip into the glass.

"Yes, please."

Big mistake.

CHAPTER 22

While Kelly was drinking for England, Hilarian was also representing his country, at the *Vinifera* luncheon. It was quite an exclusive affair. Hilarian was there in his capacity as a sometime columnist for the magazine, as were Ronald and Odile. But they were all three expected to sing for their rather tasteless chicken. Each of the critics found themselves matched with a couple of *Vinifera*'s biggest advertisers. Hilarian made small talk with a chump from Galaxy, the world's biggest wine and spirit company, who admitted that he had come from a job selling white goods and preferred beer to chardonnay any day of the week.

The lunch was mercifully short. After an hour or so, Gerry Paine, *Vinifera*'s editor, announced that coffee would be served in an anteroom. Freed from their obligations, the three critics soon found themselves together in a corner.

"Ah, the unholy trinity!" Gerry Paine infiltrated their cozy huddle. "What do you three talk about when you're off in a corner like this? Not comparing fees, I hope?"

The three critics laughed politely. That was exactly what they had been talking about. Still, it wasn't worth complaining about that to Gerry Paine. Paine wasn't just the editor of *Vinifera,* he was the owner of the magazine and a good few others besides. He didn't need to turn up at the office every day to pay the mortgage. He did it because he liked to keep his hand in. Gerry was a true wine enthusiast and he'd bought *Vinifera* to give him exclusive access to the world he loved and the people who knew about it, like Hilarian, Ronald and Odile. Naturally, they all three despised him.

There was a moment of awkward silence. Odile jumped in to keep the conversation going.

"We were just talking about our little wager," she lied.

"A wager?" Gerry cocked his head to one side. "I'm interested," he said. "What's the bet?"

"Oh, just a small blind tasting we're planning for five years' time. You see, Hilarian here thinks that English wine is catching up with the rest of the world. Thanks to global warming. Ronald stupidly thinks that American sparkling wine has earned the right to be called champagne. And I, well I'm a traditionalist. I will always favor *la belle France.* So we're all going to pick a vineyard from our own country to champion and see which performs best with this year's vintage."

"Sparkling wine?" Gerry clarified.

"Yes."

"And have you chosen your vineyards?"

"Hilarian has rather romantically bet his shirt on his old friend's place, Froggy Bottom."

"Where you're trustee? To that girl?"

Hilarian nodded.

"I'm backing Champagne Arsenault," said Odile. "I met Madeleine Arsenault for breakfast this morning."

"Another girl," said Gerry. "How about you, Ronald?"

Ronald shrugged.

"We have to decide today," Odile reminded him.

"I can't make my mind up," said Ronald. "The United States is full of fantastic contenders."

"For sure," said Odile.

"I've got the perfect idea," interrupted Gerry. "If you'll allow me to interfere. A bet like this would be a great story for *Vinifera*. It could be the new Judgment of Paris."

The three critics shared a look. But it was best to let Gerry think he was coming up with something original.

"What would be even better is if all three of the vineyards you chose were run by women. We could have them on the cover of the mag dressed as goddesses."

"I wasn't necessarily going to choose a vineyard with a woman at the helm," said Ronald.

"You are now," Gerry told him. "Ginsburg, I'm putting you in touch with someone very special. I've got the perfect Californian vineyard for you."

Ronald looked to the other two in exasperation. Odile smiled slyly into her coffee cup. Hilarian too stifled a chuckle. They had no doubt that Gerry would choose a stinker of a vineyard.

"The supermodel"—beginning a sentence about a vineyard with the words "the supermodel" was warning enough—"Christina Morgan, has a vineyard. In Carneros. She makes sparkling wine."

"Perfect," said Odile before Ronald could protest.

"I am loving this," said Gerry. "Just the thought of Christina Morgan on the cover. A real coup for *Vinifera*. But I know I'm probably taking the fun out of your little bet, so I'll throw in an incentive. A hundred thousand pounds for the vineyard that takes the top prize. And fifty thousand for the critic who champions it."

Odile raised an eyebrow. Ronald coughed. Hilarian exclaimed, "Crikey, Gerry. Are you sure?"

"It's worth it," said Gerry. "I'd probably have to pay half that again to get Christina Morgan on the cover. The advertising revenue will double. And maybe we'll do it every year. Like the swimsuit issue of *Sports Illustrated*... perhaps the girls should wear swimsuits."

"I hardly think that's fitting—" Odile began.

"Great idea, Gerry," Hilarian spoke over her.

"Brilliant. Glad you all agree. Let's get the three girls together for a little photo shoot right now, shall we? Your girl at Froggy Bottom is still a teenager, isn't she, Hilarian? Jane," Gerry called his assistant over. "Would you go down to Champagne Arsenault and invite Madeleine Arsenault to join us by the Froggy Bottom stand in half an hour. I'll deal with Christina myself," he concluded. "She's here today too. Excuse me."

He went in search of his supermodel.

"Now things get interesting," said Odile. "I must tell my little protégée."

Ronald was furious. "I'm stuck with the novelty vineyard! A model, for heaven's sake. She'll have forgotten about the vineyard and be off adopting African babies before the harvest's in."

Hilarian just wondered whether Kelly had anything in her suitcase that didn't make her look like a stripper.

The girls in charge of PR for the wine festival had lobbied hard for ISACL to be the charity benefiting from the

Vinifera party on the festival's last night. It wasn't so much that they were particularly bothered about the terrible injustices of child labor than that they wanted to meet Rocky Neel, the charity's founder. Right up until the week before the festival, it looked as though their wish might be granted. Rocky's assistant said that the big star would not miss the festival for the world.

"For the world, I tell you! He's just so excited that you wine people are getting behind our cause."

Two days before the festival began, however, the ISACL PR called to announce that Rocky was undergoing some "personal difficulties" and would not be flying through London en route to the next leg of his world tour after all. The girls prayed for Cold Steel's drummer, Jimmy "The Thunder" Curtis, as a replacement. When they heard that what they got was Christina Morgan, who was already flying in for the festival as part of her promotional duties for Domaine Randon, a groan went up around the office.

Still, there was no doubt that Christina was giving value for money. She had committed herself to spending an entire day at the fair as well as appearing at the *Vinifera* party. She was giving an interview for the official wine fair podcast when Gerry Paine caught up with her and told her about the bet.

At first she was a little unsure about his proposition.

"You want me to take part in a wager? I don't know, Gerry. I'm not sure I want to get involved in something like that."

"But I thought of you right away," Gerry assured her. "When Odile Levert mentioned that she would be backing Champagne Arsenault, I knew that I would have to help Ronald out by suggesting a vineyard of true caliber."

"This will be the first year ever that Bill and I have made our own wine," Christina warned him.

"And I have no doubt that you will do it wonderfully. I was very impressed by the cellar notes you produced for *Vinifera*'s festival issue."

Gerry had already asked Christina to write a small article about her top five wines of all time in the hope of getting her on the cover that way.

"They confirmed to me that you're a woman of great taste," he added.

"Well . . ." Christina cast her eyes to the floor as she accepted the compliment. "Woman of great taste" was an epithet she aspired to—though, in truth, Marisa had written the notes for her. Marisa, freed from the constant dietary concerns that plagued her stick-thin clients, was a real foodie and wine fanatic.

Still, Christina was hooked in by the unearned compliment. If she'd had time, she would have written the notes herself. When Mathieu Randon took her and Bill on a guided tour of Maison Randon in Champagne, the winemaker had declared her tasting notes on his champagne "inspired." And since Bill had spent so much of their money on that white elephant of a vineyard, Christina had been reading up on viticulture in the Carneros region. How hard could it be?

Persuaded that Gerry genuinely thought the Villa Bacchante would produce great wine under her stewardship, Christina's only worry then was that Gerry's wager would clash with her obligations to Domaine Randon and ISACL, but a quick phone call to Marisa assured her that it would not.

"So you'll have your photograph taken with the other contestants?" Gerry asked her.

"Oh, I don't know," said Christina. "I have to be kinda careful about my image. I need to meet the other women first."

"Of course," said Gerry. "Though I don't think you need to worry about being outshone."

Christina laughed as though the thought had *never* crossed her mind.

Madeleine didn't need any persuading. When Odile told her that Gerry Paine had heard about the wager and insisted on covering it in his magazine, Madeleine was delighted. She was grateful for any kind of publicity. She happily left her stand in the care of her neighbor and followed Odile to the first meeting of the three competitors.

"Hilarian Jackson is championing an English vineyard called Froggy Bottom," Odile explained. "It belonged to a good friend of his and now he's a trustee of the place until its teenage chatelaine comes of age. Ronald Ginsburg has picked a supermodel." Odile rolled her eyes. Madeleine was confused.

"A supermodel's vineyard. Christina Morgan. Have you heard of her?"

"She's married to that movie star Bill Tarrant."

"Well, I certainly haven't deliberately watched any of his films," said Odile. "The man is idiotic. I don't suppose he knows the first thing about wine. They'll be no competition."

Madeleine had gone slightly quiet, but she wasn't thinking about how good a winemaker Bill Tarrant would be. She was thinking about being presented to one of the world's most beautiful women.

"How do I look?" she asked Odile.

"Stand still," said Odile. She reached out and smoothed a thumb over one of Madeleine's eyebrows. "Now you look perfect."

"Thank you."

"We're meeting by the Froggy Bottom stand," Odile explained. "By all accounts it looks rather homemade and

Gerry thinks that's the kind of fun image we need to launch the competition. Alas," Odile sighed, "Gerry Paine is an utter fool."

At the Froggy Bottom stand, Ronald Ginsburg awaited the arrival of Christina Morgan like a Labrador waiting to be allowed to run amok in a butcher's shop. It hadn't taken him long to get over his horror that Gerry had chosen his vineyard for him once Gerry's assistant had shown Ronald a picture of Christina on her iPhone.

"Christina, this is Ronald." Gerry introduced them.

"I am honored," said Ronald, practically genuflecting.

Christina, used to being drooled over, gave him a weak smile.

"I said to Gerry that I would be thrilled to back Villa Bacchante. I'm a big fan of Carneros. I'm sure you're going to make a fantastic wine."

"I'm just a beginner," said Christina.

"That's where I come in. I've been telling Hilarian here that I intend to keep a very close eye on you and your wine."

"Bill will like that," said Christina. "Who is that?" she asked Gerry, seeing him wave to Odile Levert.

"Odile Levert, the French critic, and Madeleine Arsenault of the eponymous champagne."

"She's one of my competitors?"

"Yes."

Christina couldn't disguise the coldness in her appraising look as Madeleine drew close. If Madeleine had never worked as a model then she could have. She was almost as tall as Christina, at least five feet nine. Her shiny dark hair had the kind of bounce to it that hairdressers spent hours trying to re-create in Christina's poker-straight locks. Her olive skin was clear and smooth. She walked with elegance even though she was wearing flat shoes. Christina did *not* want to be photographed next to her.

"Gerry," she said. "I really think I need to talk to Marisa again before your photographer does his thing. Perhaps it would be better if you photographed the other two girls today and I sent in a photo of Bill and me at the vineyard. Wouldn't that give any piece more variety? More glamour?"

Odile and Madeleine were upon them.

"May I introduce Madeleine Arsenault," Gerry began. Christina nodded at Madeleine.

"This is an amazing opportunity," said Madeleine to the assembled crowd. "Don't you think so?" she asked Christina. "Though it's terrifying to think that Odile has so much riding on my champagne."

Christina just nodded again. She was too busy checking Madeleine for a flaw to engage in conversation.

"How has the weather been in Napa this year?" Madeleine tried.

"I've not spent much time there," said Christina briefly. "I spend most of my time traveling. I have a pretty international career."

"Of course," said Madeleine, feeling slightly put down. As she was supposed to.

"I'm Odile Levert." Odile stepped forward and shook Christina's hand. "This really is a pleasure."

Christina gave Odile a lukewarm greeting in return. Odile was older than Christina but she too was surprisingly attractive. Like the French movie stars that Bill was always raving about, Odile had an aura about her. A confidence that shone through the direct way she met Christina's eyes.

Christina suddenly felt deeply uncomfortable. In her purse, her BlackBerry buzzed. She fished it out and took a look at the display. She didn't particularly want to talk to her mother right then but she decided to take the call anyway.

"I have to take this. It's my agent," she lied to Gerry. "I'll ask her to have her assistant send over some jpegs you can use in the magazine."

"But we might as well take a new picture. All three of you girls are here right now..."

Kelly Elson had arrived at last.

Kelly thought it would be a good idea for Iain and Ryan to visit the Froggy Bottom stand. It took them quite a while to find it, ricocheting their way down the aisles like three human pinballs, ignoring the disapproving looks of the people they bumped into on the way. When they reached the Froggy Bottom stand, they found it surrounded by a small group of people who were listening earnestly while Hilarian talked about Guy's revolutionary winemaking methods and his hope for the future of the brand. Kelly had no idea who the other people were. All she knew was they were in her way.

"I need two glasses of my wine for my friends," she slurred, lurching into the middle of the crowd and leaning on the stand as though it were a bar.

"Kelly," hissed Guy. "Where have you been?"

"Two glasses," Kelly repeated. "For my friends."

Guy didn't move to serve her. Instead, he tried to draw Hilarian's attention to the fact that Kelly had turned up.

"For fuck's sake, Guy. Do as you're told. This is my bloody vineyard," Kelly announced, before turning to the crowd, reeling as though she'd just been shot and vomiting absinthe green all over the shoes of Gerry Paine, Ronald Ginsburg and Madeleine Arsenault.

CHAPTER 23

News of Kelly's spectacular faux pas quickly spread its way around the wine fair, putting a smile even on the lips of Mathieu Randon. Randon had arrived that afternoon on the Eurostar to see how his own people were faring.

The Domaine Randon stand covered a whole block in the "wine village" at ExCeL, promoting as it was not only the house's champagne but its US sister brand, Randon Prestige, and Randon's latest wine baby, a New Zealand sauvignon blanc called Randon Symphony.

It was a slick operation. The Randon staff was all uniformed. They had been drilled in their elegant sales patter on a weeklong training course in Paris and warned that drinking on the job would lead to instant dismissal. It was a threat that everyone took seriously. There was no danger that Mathieu Randon would be embarrassed by one of his staff.

Not even Christina Morgan. Randon greeted Christina warmly when they met at the Domaine Randon stand for a quick photo shoot. It was as though the unpleasantness over Fast Life had not happened. In fact, Randon even asked Christina about ISACL's progress.

"I'll give you a full update when I'm onstage this evening," she told him.

Each year the London wine fair culminated in a grand charity event, and the charity that would benefit from the ticket sales that year was ISACL.

"I look forward to hearing your speech," said Randon. Of course, he had already seen it. Marisa had faxed Christina's script both to Christina and to the lawyers at Domaine Randon that morning.

Odile Levert had dressed very carefully for the *Vinifera* charity dinner. She was wearing a dress by Azzedine Alaia. Vintage, it might have been called. It was the dress she bought with her first ever paycheck from *Vinifera*. It was a matter of great pride to her that, almost two decades later, she could still fit into the tight black sheath with its little fishtail skirt. It was a matter of enormous pleasure to her that the look pioneered by the eighties' King of Cling was suddenly very much back in fashion. As she walked across the room, she knew she still turned heads.

Of course, plenty of people were keen to pay their respects to Odile Levert, including Mathieu Randon.

"Odile." Randon kissed her on both cheeks. "You're looking wonderful. As always."

"Thank you," she said, accepting the compliment as simple fact.

A waiter was circulating with a tray full of sparkling wine. Randon took two glasses and handed one to Odile. They each took a sip of Australian fizz (the wine fair's exhibitors fought for the opportunity to supply wine for the charity events) and, to the waiter's perturbation, replaced the glasses forthwith. It was the sixth time that had happened since the waiter first left the drinks station with his tray. The attendees at the *Vinifera* dinner were a difficult bunch to impress.

Instead Randon led Odile across to the Maison Randon table, where one of his employees was uncorking a bottle of Éclat, freshly smuggled into the room in a Domaine Randon cooler.

"A proper drink?" he suggested.

Odile gratefully accepted.

"And how is this year shaping up for Maison Randon?" she asked.

"Vintage," said Randon.

"Mathieu, you say that every year," teased Odile. "I heard through the grapevine that you're interested in expanding your operations in Le Vezy."

Randon nodded.

"Clos Des Larmes? The pride of Champagne Arsenault. Am I right to understand that Champagne Arsenault was once part of the Randon estate? Until your great-grandfather lost it in a bet."

Randon's right eye twitched. Odile was satisfied that she had hit her mark.

"It's a fabulous vineyard," she said. "I'm not surprised you want it. Shame it isn't for sale."

"Everything is for sale. You just have to guess the price."

"But you're still guessing."

"For the time being."

"I have to say I think you've underestimated her."

"Of course, she's your new protégée. I heard about the wager. She's quite a girl," Randon admitted.

"I'd have to agree with that," said Odile. "I fear it may be quite a battle to part her from her vineyards. Oh look. There she is. I'd better leave you. Wouldn't do any good at all for me to be seen fraternizing with her number one enemy."

Randon and Odile shared a knowing smile.

Madeleine paused at the entrance to the hall. It wasn't that she was trying to make an entrance, more that she was a little nervous. This was her first public event as the proprietor of Champagne Arsenault. She wanted to make the right impression. She scanned the room for friendly faces.

Her gaze was immediately drawn to Odile Levert, who was talking to Hilarian Jackson.

Madeleine felt herself transported back to her school days when she saw Odile. So elegant. Absolutely timeless. It was impossible to tell whether her fellow Frenchwoman was thirty or fifty. Looking at Odile made Madeleine very glad that she had dressed up. Especially when Odile caught her eye and nodded her approval.

She scanned the room for other familiar faces. Remi Brice of Champagne Brice was entertaining a crowd of women with, no doubt, his patter about each of his single vineyard wines representing a different aspect of femininity. Perhaps he was offering them a glass of "pleasure," his favorite line.

There was no one else she recognized.

"Madeleine."

A hand on her elbow made her turn around.

Her smile instantly disappeared. "Axel."

It was the first time she had seen him since that terrible weekend in Le Vezy. Although it wasn't so strange that he should be there, Madeleine was a little surprised. The really big players, like Domaine Randon, didn't always bother to send their best men to the London trade fair. Especially in a Vinexpo year. That Randon and Axel were both there was quite something.

"I didn't know you were going to be here," he said.

"I didn't tell you."

"Are you having a good time at the festival?"

"Wonderful," she said.

"Do you have a stand? I didn't see one."

"I'm sharing a stand. This year."

She tried not to meet Axel's gaze. Instead, she looked over his shoulder in search of someone, anyone, she could claim she needed to talk to instead. She prayed that Remi Brice might stop reading the palm of one of his pretty companions and beckon her over. He didn't. Madeleine could see no other escape route. An emergency toilet break would be much too obvious.

A waiter passed by. Axel took a glass of champagne and proffered it to Madeleine.

"I can get my own," she said sharply.

"Take it," said Axel. "You're empty-handed. And it's not as though I'm buying you the drink. It's free."

Madeleine snatched it from him.

"On second thought," said Axel, "perhaps I shouldn't have armed you with something you might throw at me if I say something wrong."

"You're very good at saying the wrong thing," Madeleine snapped back at him.

"I've been meaning to talk to you about—"

"Oh, watch out, Axel," Madeleine interrupted him. "Here comes your master. Better snap to heel."

Mathieu Randon was walking toward them, hand extended to shake Madeleine's. She didn't offer her own hand in return, merely dismissively flicked her eyes down toward Randon's. He withdrew it.

"Mademoiselle Arsenault. Allow me to introduce myself—"

"Monsieur Randon, you need no introduction."

Randon shrugged in what he obviously assumed was a charming manner.

"Well, it's nice to be known," he said.

"You certainly have a reputation."

"And so do you," said Randon. "I'd heard it said that you are the most beautiful woman in Champagne. Now I think that description can be widened to make you one of the most beautiful women in the world."

Madeleine raised an eyebrow to let him know that she was unmoved by his flattery. Unimpressed.

"I don't think we need to continue with this charade,

monsieur, I know you're only interested in my champagne house."

Randon shrugged his shoulders again and had the decency to look just a little embarrassed.

"Of course I am interested in Champagne Arsenault. Who wouldn't be? I was a great admirer of your father, Madeleine. He was a true artist. I have, in my cellar, a bottle of his Clos Des Larmes from 1975. I have yet to find an occasion special enough to warrant drinking such a masterpiece."

Madeleine said nothing. The Clos Des Larmes made in 1975 was her father's favorite vintage; the one he made in the year of her brother's birth. Her own birth year wasn't good enough to warrant a vintage at all.

A wine waiter hovered. Randon waved the man away and stepped a little closer to Madeleine as though he were about to impart a great secret.

"Madeleine, I understand your loyalty to your father's memory. You believe that he would want the Clos Des Larmes to stay in the family. Knowing your father as well as I did, I believe he actually had a slightly different plan."

"What do you mean?" asked Madeleine.

"I understand that you spent the last ten years working in London. Investment banking, wasn't it? The hours are very long, I know. It can be difficult to keep up with your family obligations when your career demands so much from you."

"What are you getting at, Randon?"

"In the ten years prior to his death, I believe I spent more time with your father than you did, dear girl. I presented myself to him as a disciple. I wanted to know everything your father could tell me about champagne. I revered him above all other vignerons. We became good friends."

"He didn't tell me you were such great friends."

"When would he have told you? You didn't see him at all in the year before he died, am I right?"

Madeleine looked sharply to Axel. Had he told Randon that? The possibility that Randon was actually telling the truth about his relationship with her father was just too horrible. Madeleine tried to picture Mathieu Randon sitting beside Constant Arsenault's deathbed. She imagined her father telling Randon that his daughter never visited anymore. Randon sympathizing. No. Randon *had* to be lying. If he'd felt such strong regard for old Arsenault then why hadn't Randon been at the funeral?

As though he were able to read Madeleine's thoughts, Randon continued, "I was terribly sad to miss your father's funeral. I was detained in New York by bad weather. I asked Axel to pass on my regards."

"I don't think my father missed you," said Madeleine.

"Your father confided in me that he wanted Clos Des Larmes to be cared for by someone with a passion for wine."

"Stop," said Madeleine. "Don't try to tell me that my father would want me to sell Champagne Arsenault to you?"

Randon gave a little nod.

"You're lying, Randon. Family was the most important thing to my father. I may have let him down in the ten years prior to his death but I'm damn well not going to let him down now. I will send you a bottle of my first vintage at Clos Des Larmes to drink when you open the '75. And I promise you, it will be a vintage that would have made my father proud."

"Or perhaps, as is more likely, you will finish the job your father began and send a once great marque into oblivion."

Randon leaned forward and took Madeleine by the elbow as though he were about to give her a friendly kiss good-bye. Instead, she felt his fingers digging hard into the bare flesh of her upper arm as he hissed into her ear, "You're a proud and stupid woman, Mademoiselle Arsenault."

And with that, Randon withdrew.

Axel remained. He looked nervously after Randon, finding himself between a rock and a hard place. "Madeleine, I'm sorry. He came on a bit strong there. I didn't know that stuff about your father. I mean, I knew that they knew each other. I didn't know they'd actually talked about the future of Clos Des Larmes."

"Just leave me alone," said Madeleine. "There's no point trying to mend bridges."

"Madeleine—"

"Fuck off. If I never see you again it will be too soon," she said. "You betrayed me, Axel. The only news I ever want to hear of you is that you are dead."

Madeleine exited the ExCeL building as though the devil himself were on her tail. She snatched her coat from the cloakroom attendant and threw a couple of pound coins into the tip dish. Then she made for the door, walking as fast as she could. Trying not to run. She didn't want anyone to see her running. She especially didn't want anyone to see that she was starting to cry. Though by the time she reached the big glass doors of the exhibition center, she was pretty much blinded with tears, which was how she came to run straight into the chest of someone heading in the opposite direction at equally high speed.

The man grasped Madeleine by the upper arms to stop her from falling.

"Steady on," he said as he set her upright again.

"I'm sorry."

"That's all right. Happens all the time," he said. "Women can't help throwing themselves at me."

Madeleine paused just long enough to thank him and to take in the scent of Creed Royal Water, and the teddy bears on his Hermès silk tie, before she was off again, into the night.

Odile Levert watched Madeleine leave. Madeleine was an intelligent girl but overly emotional, Odile decided. Such softness would be her undoing against an opponent like Mathieu Randon.

CHAPTER 24

Though she was nobody's first choice, none of the PR team could deny that Christina was making a real effort as the biggest celeb at the wine fair. For the *Vinifera* dinner supporting ISACL, she dressed in Armani Privé. A heavily sequinned dress in pale lemon with matching shoes by Manolo.

"Almost the color of champagne," Christina explained to Lauren, the PR girl charged with looking after her. "I thought that would be appropriate for the evening."

The evening opened with aperitifs, of course. Guided by Lauren, Christina mingled with the party guests. Except that Christina could never really mingle. As usual, the moment she walked into the room, she found herself surrounded by a knot of admirers, most of whom were too shy to actually talk to her as she made her way around the room like a whale shark followed by a shoal of remoras—

a very small whale shark, Christina assured herself, even as the thought popped into her head.

She spotted the French girl, the one who had been vomited on, in conversation with Mathieu Randon and hoped he wouldn't call her over for another introduction. The French girl's dress looked expensive, Christina observed from a distance. And it fit her well. She had a particularly small waist. Curvy. No matter how hard Christina worked out, she could never quite get that shape. She felt another pang of unease of the kind that she didn't often feel even in a room full of models. Somehow, she felt in competition with Madeleine over more than just their wine.

The English girl, the one who threw up (Christina couldn't remember her name), was nowhere to be seen, thank goodness. What a stupid little girl. She had a lot to learn about the art of making a good first impression. Mess up in the first few minutes and you could spend a lifetime trying to change someone's mind. Though her incredible vomiting stunt had saved Christina from having to get heavy with Gerry over the photo issue. Christina was grateful for that.

"Christina, can I introduce you to . . ."

Suddenly Ronald Ginsburg stood in front of her, blocking her view of Madeleine Arsenault. He had on his arm a blond woman in her late twenties or thereabouts who wouldn't be a challenge to Christina even if she spent two years on one of those plastic surgery cruises. Christina didn't catch her name and didn't bother to ask to hear it again. Instead she offered the girl her hand with about as much enthusiasm as a princess shaking hands with a stinking shepherdess. Then she turned her attention back to Ronald, who was saying something complimentary about her dress.

"You look sensational."

Christina couldn't hear it often enough.

For the dinner itself Christina was seated with Lauren, the PR person; Gerry Paine, the editor of *Vinifera;* Ronald Ginsburg; and his guest.

The chat largely revolved around wine, of course. Gerry and Ronald talked excitedly about the wager.

"The minute I heard about the Villa Bacchante, I knew that was the vineyard for me," said Ronald.

"We mostly grow pinot noir." Christina fed her dinner companions the spiel that she'd picked up from Bill's assistant, Teak. "The Carneros region is slightly cooler than other parts of Napa, perfect for pinot, which, as we all know from *Sideways,* is a very particular grape."

Ronald gave her a little round of applause. He was rapt.

"I can't wait to come and visit you guys and see exactly how that pinot is planted," said Ronald.

"You'll never get rid of him," Gerry warned.

Then the conversation moved on to wine-world gossip. Christina listened as attentively as she could but beyond a few big names that she recognized, the conversation started to go over her head. She began wondering how early she would be able to get away—her eyes were looking tired and she really didn't want that caught on camera—but then Ronald brought her back into the conversation.

"You're the face of Maison Randon, aren't you?" he said.

Christina nodded. "That's right. Éclat."

Ronald smiled. "Great champagne, Randon's Éclat. You know, I knew Mathieu Randon thirty years ago when he was just starting out, when the champagne house was the only business he had. Of course, it's two cents to talk to him these days, now that Domaine Randon's taking over the world."

The young blonde on Ronald's left—the one who Christina had assumed was an airhead colleague of Lauren's—suddenly sat up a little straighter.

"How does that sit with your views?" she asked.

"I'm sorry. What do you mean?" Christina responded.

"Being the face of Randon Champagne?"

"Maison Randon," Christina automatically corrected her.

"My apologies, Maison Randon."

"I'm very happy to be representing such a top-class wine."

"Really?" The girl raised an eyebrow. "I'm surprised. I mean, I read all about the campaign you did for ISACL. We covered it in some depth in my paper."

"You're a *journalist?*" said Christina.

"Jennifer Gardner. The *Sunday Herald.*"

"She's doing a profile on me for their Sunday supplement," said Ronald.

Christina hoped that Ronald would seize the opportunity to talk about himself again but he didn't.

Jennifer continued, "One of the brands you asked people to boycott is a Domaine Randon brand, right?"

Christina stiffened. "I'm not sure what you're talking about," she said. Of course she knew exactly what Jennifer was talking about but Marisa had assured her that the Fast Life episode was finished and that the only policy from now on was to pretend it never happened. "Fast Life is a really new Randon brand. People won't make the connection," Marisa had promised her most successful client.

But this Jennifer girl had made the connection.

"Fast Life *is* a Domaine Randon brand, isn't it?" she tried again.

Christina could only nod.

"And you're prepared to continue representing the company despite Fast Life's track record. Didn't they have three children actually die in an accident with a loom last year?"

"I..." Christina hesitated.

"Perhaps you already know what Domaine Randon plans to do about the ISACL accusations regarding Fast Life? Have you spoken to Mr. Randon personally about your concerns regarding the use of child labor to produce his luxury goods?"

Christina found herself blushing. She couldn't help it. Glancing across the table she saw that Lauren the PR and Gerry Paine had stopped talking and were watching Jennifer's inquisition with interest.

"It would seem to be the obvious thing to do," Jennifer continued. "I'm sure, being the face of his champagne, you must have Mathieu Randon's ear. And I'm equally sure he would want to keep you and your husband happy. A great many people are influenced by the ideals and actions of celebrities such as you. That's undoubtedly why Rocky Neel asked you to support ISACL in the first place. But maybe it doesn't really matter to you? Perhaps you thought no one would make the connection. Perhaps *you* didn't make the connection. I understand how these things work," said Jennifer, waving her hand dismissively. "Famous as you are, you must get asked to do all sorts of charity work. Your agent picks the best causes for you. The ones that fit your public image. You turn up. You put on the T-shirt. You read a script. It's just like any other job, right?"

"No. ISACL and its aims are very important to me," said Christina. "I have a personal connection with the charity. Rocky Neel and I have been friends for years—"

"But you need the Randon ad money to pay the mortgage. Hey, I'm not judging you. We've all been there.

Taking a job we know we shouldn't because we don't want the bank to take our house back. It's no different from me writing puff pieces on my editor's old cronies to pay the rent." Jennifer waved her hand in the direction of Ronald Ginsburg. "So, I perfectly understand your dilemma. It's morality versus necessity. Your husband's last film bombed, right? That must have hurt your bottom line."

Christina struggled to find an answer. Who did this girl think she was?

"I don't think I can speak for my husband," she began. "But this has been a tough summer for the movie business in general and—"

"What were the figures?" Jennifer persisted.

"You know, I really don't want to talk about this now," said Christina before Jennifer could come up with the numbers.

"But we're all interested to hear what you have to say."

"I just don't think that any of this has any relevance to—"

Just then, a young and nervous-looking waiter leaned in to refill everyone's wine. Jennifer frowned at the interruption, but for Christina it was a gift from God. She suddenly reached for her water glass, knocking the waiter's arm as she did so. Just as Christina had hoped he would, the waiter slopped red wine all over the table and onto her lap. She jumped up, knocking into the waiter again, thus ensuring that she was soaked.

"Why you clumsy…" Ronald got to his feet and rushed to Christina's assistance.

"It's OK, Ronald. I'm fine," she batted away his attempts to mop down her cleavage. "Really," she assured the waiter. "It's just a bit of wine. I'm OK. I've got a spare dress. Excuse me, everybody."

Christina fled from the table.

.   .   .

The second she was out of sight, Christina dove into her handbag for her mobile and called Marisa in New York to ask for her advice on how to deal with the journalist girl. Christina knew that after she presented the awards, Randon was expecting her to join him and his team at the Domaine Randon table for another photo op. Christina could already imagine what the journalist would make of that.

Marisa was not in the office. Christina got through to Marisa's assistant, Louis, instead.

"Darling, don't worry about it. You will be magnificent!" he said. It was the kind of advice that worked when Christina was feeling nervy about stepping out onto the catwalk in a swimsuit made of nothing but a couple of carefully folded dollar bills, but this was different. The journalist was questioning her integrity and so far Christina had not found the right answer.

"Are you all right in there?" Lauren called through the dressing room door. "Gerry has just gone up onstage to start the speeches. We don't want to leave him up there on his own for too long. He's so boring!"

"Just a minute," said Christina.

She could think of no way to buy herself more time. She stripped off the ruined dress and replaced it with the backup: a hot pink version of the same design. Then she touched up her makeup. Her reflection in the mirror frowned back at her. Christina pressed on the two worry creases between her eyes, hoping to make them disappear. If only she could make Jennifer the journalist disappear too.

"Miss Morgan?" Lauren knocked on the door again.

"I'm ready," Christina called back, feeling further from ready than she had ever been.

.   .   .

"Ladies and Gentlemen, Miss Christina Morgan."

Christina took to the stage and tapped on the mike. She wondered if the audience could hear her heart pounding against her rib cage as she prepared to make the speech of her life. She glanced back at the table where she had been sitting with Ronald Ginsburg and the others. Jennifer Gardner was leaning forward expectantly, pen poised over a pad of paper. Christina gave the woman who had been giving her such a hard time a nervous smile.

"Time to do the right thing," Christina said to herself.

"Ladies and gentlemen," she began. "I'm so glad to be here this evening. Not as a model but as a fellow winemaker. It's a real honor to be in such great company. You have welcomed me into your bosom and I'm truly grateful for that. But my passion for wine is eclipsed by my passion for the charity we're here to support this evening. It's an involvement that has changed my life. ISACL stands for the International Society for the Abolition of Child Labor.

"Now, you might wonder what child labor has to do with you, but glancing around this room tonight, I can see that many of you are unknowingly supporting the practice, wearing clothes and shoes produced by children who work sixteen hours for as little as a dollar a day."

Christina glanced down at those faces in the crowd she was able to see. She seemed to have their attention.

"It is up to all of us to make sure that the children in the Third World have the same opportunities our own children do. That is how we make a better future for everyone. So I'm here today to tell you that I'm standing by everything I said on behalf of ISACL when I made that infomercial two months ago. One of the brands I asked the general public to boycott was Fast Life, a sportswear brand that you may or may not know as a subsidiary of Domaine Randon, parent company of Maison Randon champagne, for whom I am ashamed to say I have made a commercial. Ladies and gentlemen, I have decided that I can no longer be the face of Maison Randon because I do not support child labor. It really is as simple as that. Monsieur Randon, change your working practices or accept my resignation!"

"Good God," said Odile.

"Bit of excitement," said Ronald.

"Now, that is what I call a resignation. Does Mathieu Randon have a history of having people assassinated?" asked Hilarian.

"If I were you," Ronald said to Gerry Paine, "I'd get out there and start the dancing."

Mathieu Randon merely shook his head as Christina finished her passionate speech to a round of raucous applause. He wasn't going to hang around and dignify the stupid woman's half-baked opinions with a response. Before the crowd even finished applauding the beatific supermodel, Randon was installed in the back of a black BMW that whisked him back to the Craven Hotel on Park Lane. The driver knew not to make small talk.

As the sole senior representative of Domaine Randon remaining at the wine fair's awards dinner, it was left to Axel Delaflote to issue a hasty rebuttal of Christina's claims in the manner he assumed his boss would have expected. Jennifer led the gaggle of journalists that gathered around his table and shot tough questions at him like a firing squad. There would be no opportunity for Axel to relax over port that night.

"Ladies and gentlemen," he began. "Miss Morgan's revelation is as much news to Monsieur Randon as it has been to you this evening. Of course, Domaine Randon will be investigating claims that child labor was involved in the production of the Fast Life sportswear range. But as far as Maison Randon is concerned—and I think that all of us gathered here today are rather more interested in wine than in trainers—I can assure you that no children were involved in the production of our world-class wines. Though perhaps you should ask one of the kind gentlemen from Bollinger about their Côte aux Enfants. Now, if you'll excuse me..."

The Bollinger rep shook his head and prepared to spin the old yarn for the journalists who hadn't yet heard it.

"It's just a legend," he promised them. "We do have one particularly steep vineyard at Bollinger called the Côte aux Enfants that was traditionally picked by children. Of course, these days..."

Axel took advantage of the moment to slip away.

CHAPTER 25

Gina had been thinking a great deal about her future since that weekend with Kelly at Froggy Bottom. There was no doubt she needed to escape. Living with her mother and slogging away as a chambermaid at the Gloria Hotel didn't work for her anymore. It was not where she wanted to be. She wanted her own place. She wanted a future that didn't involve more of the same until she got married to some dickhead who treated her like dirt until she divorced him and she ended up in a bedsit as had happened to her mum. Might as well make the most of her assets now.

And so Gina did as Kelly suggested and tried to make

the most of her looks. She had one real designer outfit in her wardrobe: a little black dress by Gucci that she had found left behind in a waste bin at the Gloria. Clearly somebody's mistress had dumped some very expensive gifts after a dirty weekend gone wrong. It was the luckiest shift Gina had ever worked. A brand-new set of silk-and-lace La Perla underwear—still bearing the tags—had also been left behind. Gina hid the lingerie and the dress in her trolley. The dress was ripped but it was easily repaired and, miracle of miracles, it fit Gina like a dream.

Gina wore that Gucci dress as she walked into the lobby of the Craven Hotel—a little farther down Park Lane from the Gloria—and made for the bar. She knew she looked as good as she ever would and that gave her a glow of confidence, even as her cheap leather-look stilettos pinched her feet. She'd pay for that in blood later on.

She took a high stool at the bar and ordered a glass of champagne. At fifteen pounds a pop, she couldn't afford it, but it was important to set the tone. To ooze "expensive." She also tipped the barman five pounds, knowing that he would suss her out soon enough and his collusion was vital to her being allowed to remain in the bar nursing that one glass for as long as she needed to while less savvy girls were discreetly escorted outside.

The bar at the Craven was perfect for Gina's purposes. The mirror behind the optics afforded her a fantastic view of the people coming in and out without her having to turn round. She could see who was alone. Who looked lonely. There were lots of groups of businessmen in that night but very few guys on their own. She kept an eye on two guys at a corner table. They were having an animated and sometimes angry conversation. Eventually one of the men got up and bid his companion good night. The other guy remained seated for a while, looking contemplative and slightly stressed-out, swirling the ice around in his glass. Then he got up and walked over to the bar. He asked the barman what kind of cigars they kept in-house. The barman offered him the pick of the humidor. While the barman went in search of the cigar cutter, which had not been returned to its proper place the last time it was used, the customer caught Gina's eye in the mirror.

"I've been watching you all evening," he said. "Hard to believe that a beautiful woman like you would have to spend her Friday night alone."

Gina took in the French accent, the elegant suit, the handsome face, and allowed herself the fantasy for a moment that she was being chatted up by a man who would take her out to dinner, whisk her away on a surprise weekend break and finally present her with a diamond solitaire. That he wasn't thinking about any of those things was obvious in the way he let his eyes travel the length of her body with no hint of embarrassment. To him she might have been a pair of shoes, a car, a horse ... He wanted to know exactly what was on offer. It was just another transaction.

"Perhaps you'd like another glass of champagne?" he suggested.

Gina nodded. Dutch courage.

"Not your house rubbish," he told the barman. "Randon Éclat."

Gina was impressed.

"Come and join me," he said, gesturing toward the table he had occupied with his colleague.

The man smoked his cigar, Gina drank her champagne and they went upstairs. The deal had been sealed at five hundred pounds for the night. While her new client was in the bathroom, Gina observed the man's expensive designer luggage and texted Kelly.

"I think I've moved into the premier league."

CHAPTER 26

The weather throughout Britain was spectacularly clement for the time of year but there were storm clouds over Froggy Bottom.

After the wine fair debacle, Guy and Kelly traveled back to Sussex in silence and they hadn't spoken since. Hilarian had tried to broker peace between them (his own disappointment in Kelly was tempered by the secret joy he felt at seeing Gerry and Ronald get covered) but a whole week later, Guy was still white-hot with rage. When he thought about the absinthe-induced vomiting disaster, Guy simply wanted to throttle the stupid, ignorant girl. He wished he had Hilarian's patience.

As Dougal grew older and frailer, Guy had worried endlessly about the fate of Froggy Bottom. He knew that Dougal had kids—a daughter and a son—but neither had ever visited the farm, not even when their father was on his last legs. Guy knew that Dougal had divorced his wife for a brief fling with the Croatian woman who cleaned their house in South Kensington. Dougal had lost touch with his children after that. But, as Hilarian explained, it wasn't as though Dougal's children had actually been children when he got divorced. They were in their thirties by then. Their mother had been shagging one of Dougal's schoolfriends for years. It seemed extreme that Dougal's children couldn't find it in their hearts to forgive him as he lay dying. As it was, they didn't even turn up at the funeral.

Guy and Hilarian were the only mourners at the service in the tiny parish church of St. Jude.

Still, Guy expected to meet Dougal's children soon enough. He had imagined them descending on Froggy Bottom the moment Dougal's death was announced, with an estate agent or three in tow. But the will soon changed that. It had seemed like the lesser of two evils when Kelly turned up. She had no interest in wine whatsoever and yet the trust meant she couldn't just sell the house and vineyard either. But now she was installed in the farmhouse like an overgrown teenager: sleeping till midday, smoking, drinking, stealing money—Guy knew exactly where the cash from his ginger jar had gone. He began to wonder whether he wouldn't have preferred to find himself in the employ of one of Dougal's legitimate children.

And so Guy seethed as he went about his business in the vineyard, carefully calibrating the amount of leaf cover so that the ripening grapes would get just the right amount of sun.

Guy had some radical ideas about growing vines. He pruned aggressively. Some might have thought too aggressively. But he had persuaded Dougal that they should not go for bulk at Froggy Bottom. There was no point, he argued, since the kind of person who bought cheap wine would always pick an Aussie chardonnay over an English wine anyway. They would assume that anything from England was a novelty. A joke. So Froggy Bottom had to focus on attracting the cognoscenti with a top-quality wine and that meant getting the very best grapes.

That was why Guy clipped whole bunches of unripened grapes and cast them aside so the grapes that remained would have a better chance to flourish. He stuck to organic methods of pest control. Roses were planted at the head of each row of vines to attract the hungry bugs that might otherwise make themselves at home on the grapes.

The metal stakes holding the vines up weren't pretty but they too were the ecological option. He explained to Dougal that wooden stakes required coats of distinctly inorganic preservative to keep them from having to be replaced year after year.

Guy was happy that his methods were paying off. But he was aware that if he didn't get Kelly on board soon, then at the end of her five years there, it might all be for nought.

Kelly was woken by her mobile phone ringing. It was Gina.

"Five hundred pounds," she said. "For one night's work."

Kelly sat up at once. "What was it like?" she asked.

"Same as usual. Only much better paid!" Gina laughed. "Actually, it was really all right. He was French."

"Ugh." Kelly pulled a face at the thought. "Did he smell of garlic?"

"Of course not. He was pretty good-looking," Gina continued. "Knew what he was doing. Seemed to enjoy himself. And he's asked me if I'd be willing to go and see him at home. In Paris!"

"Oh my God," said Kelly. "Are you going?"

"A thousand quid and a trip to France? Of course I am."

"When?" Kelly asked.

Gina named the weekend. "It's your birthday weekend, I know. And I said we'd go out in London but this is a big opportunity for me, Kels. My brother said he'd still hang out with you though."

"You've told him you're going to Paris?"

"Not who with, of course. I told him my new boyfriend is taking me," said Gina. She sounded a little sad, thought Kelly as she considered the rather less romantic truth. "This could be it, Kels. I've read about this sort of thing in magazines. There was this girl who got into this kind of circle and next thing you know she's on a yacht in the Med, entertaining some sheik. She came back from one weekend with enough money to pay off the mortgage on her flat. I just want to get enough money to go to college."

"I don't know why you want to go back to school," said Kelly.

"Not school, Kelly. College. It's because I want to make something of myself."

Kelly snorted.

"It's not funny," said Gina. "You've got to make the most of the opportunities you're given. And your gifts. I wish I'd known that when I was at school."

"Don't you start," said Kelly. "You're beginning to sound like Hilarian."

"How's it going down there in Sussex?"

"Badly. I got wasted at the wine fair. Threw up."

"So?"

"Over three people."

"Oh."

"Everyone was really pissed off with me. Hilarian's put a bet on Froggy Bottom in some competition. The people I threw up on were something to do with that. If we win, the vineyard gets a hundred grand."

Gina exhaled slowly.

"Wow."

"It's not for five years but Guy's already like a headless chicken about it."

"The hottie?"

"He's not hot."

"He is. How is he?"

"Still not talking to me."

As a matter of fact, at that exact moment, Guy decided that he would try to talk to Kelly again after all. She wasn't going anywhere. She had nowhere else to go. Since she was a resident evil, he would have to make the best of the situation. Perhaps he had been too harsh on her. Perhaps he should try a different approach, "nice" her into treating Froggy Bottom less like a flophouse and more like the cutting-edge business Guy wanted it to be. He resolved that when he'd finished tying the chardonnay vines to their new position on the stakes, he would invite Kelly to join him in his flat for a drink. Just a small one. And he would try to draw out of her how she envisaged her future in Sussex. If he could discover just one thing she was passionate about, then he was sure he could use that knowledge to fire up her enthusiasm for the farm. The wine business wasn't just about mud and vines. There was marketing to be done, for example. Perhaps Kelly could find a niche for herself there.

Guy had a very vivid flashback to the *Vinifera* vomit debacle.

Perhaps not.

When Guy came in from the vineyards, he found Kelly sitting on the step outside the farmhouse. Though it was almost four in the afternoon, she was wearing a dressing gown and fluffy slippers. She had a fag in one hand and her mobile phone in the other.

"Better signal out here," she said.

Guy's attempt at reestablishing friendly relations started badly.

"Got over your hangover?" he asked.

"Don't start," Kelly snapped. "I'm sorry, OK, I let you down, I let Froggy Bottom down, but most of all I let myself down," she paraphrased the traditional teacher's lament. "I'm a waste of space. I know."

She got up and turned as if to go back into the house.

"Hang on," said Guy. "Come out into the garden with me. It's a nice afternoon. Just right for drinking rosé."

Kelly frowned.

"You want to have a drink with me?"

"Yes. Toast the start of the weekend."

"I'll put my jeans on," she said.

Kelly's suspicion only increased when she joined Guy in the garden. He really was making an effort. Kelly discovered that he had got out the picnic table and laid it with a white cloth. A bottle of rosé—Froggy Bottom's own—was already chilling in the ice bucket. He even pulled out Kelly's chair.

"What are you up to?" Kelly asked him.

"Why do I have to be up to anything? I just thought it would be nice to share a bottle of wine with my nearest neighbor on this most beautiful of evenings."

It was indeed a beautiful evening. It was approaching what is sometimes known as the "magic hour" when the setting sun casts a gentle pink glow over everything and smoothes out any flaws like a soft-focus lens. There was hardly a breath of wind, so the sound of the swallows could be heard overhead though they were almost too high in the sky to be seen.

For a little while Guy and Kelly didn't talk and the silence seemed almost companionable, but pretty soon both of them realized that the silence wasn't companionable at all; it was awkward. Kelly had hardly touched her glass of wine.

"Don't you like it?" Guy asked.

"I don't feel like I can drink in front of you. What was it you called me at the wine fair? A drunken slut?"

Guy shifted awkwardly in his chair. He had indeed called Kelly a drunken slut and much worse too. He had been raised by a mother who had instilled great respect for women in her son and being reminded that he had used such a gender-specific slur didn't sit well with him at all.

"Well..." he hummed. It was on his lips to ask her if she didn't think he had a point. Thankfully he managed to keep it in. "I'm sorry," he said. "That wasn't what I wanted to talk about tonight. I really just wanted to have a friendly drink. Look"—he took a big gulp from his glass—"I'm not so uptight that I don't occasionally go over my weekly units myself."

Kelly managed a little smile. She picked up her glass and took a swig of her own.

"Do you like it?" Guy asked.

"It's OK. Tastes like strawberries," she added.

"That's what I was aiming for. Listen, we've started off badly," Guy admitted then. "You said that these vines were like my babies. Truth is, they are. Your father planted the first vineyard in the seventies but they were getting a bit tired. I saw my chance to put my mark on this place."

Kelly nodded. And helped herself to some more rosé. She noticed Guy watching her closely. Too closely, she thought. He threw up his hands when he noticed her reaction. "No, no. I mean, help yourself. I'm glad you like it."

"Thanks. What were you going on about?"

"I've wanted to be a winemaker for so long, Kelly. It's not the kind of ambition you'd expect the average kid from Jo'Burg to have. But my parents took me to Stellenbosch when I was about twelve and we visited the vineyards there. It was so beautiful. I decided there and then that I was going to study at the university of Stellenbosch and one day I would have a vineyard of my own. Well, I'm still a long way off owning a vineyard, but your father gave me the chance to be pretty much my own boss at Froggy Bottom."

"That's great," said Kelly.

"So, you can understand why I get so precious about it."

"I suppose."

"But I do realize that makes me blinkered. I mean, before your father died, you'd probably never even thought about where wine comes from."

"I knew where wine comes from," said Kelly. "I'm not that thick."

"That's not how I meant that comment to come out." Guy tried again. "What I meant was, while I went out to the vines this morning, I was feeling pretty angry, but as I worked it came to me that maybe I was being a little judgmental."

Kelly nodded. "Er, yeah."

"Wine isn't your passion. It's perfectly understandable that you don't want to get up at the crack of dawn and work outside all day."

Kelly nodded again.

"But that doesn't mean that you can't have anything to do with the future of Froggy Bottom. There are all sorts of aspects to the wine business."

"I'm not interested in anything about wine except drinking it," said Kelly flatly.

"But you're wasting an enormous opportunity here. There are people who would give their right arm to have the chance to make something of a place like this. It's a glamorous world. I could make the wine and you could be involved in marketing it. You could go round the wine merchants and restaurants and sell Froggy Bottom."

"I don't want to do marketing," said Kelly.

"But it's a glamorous career. Lots of girls want to do it."

"You think I should want to do marketing because I'm

a girl? I'd heard South Africans were racist. I didn't know they were sexist too."

"I'm sorry." Guy didn't know how to come back from that. "It was just a suggestion."

"I don't need you to suggest anything to me."

"Then what do you want to do, eh? Sit in the dark for the whole bloody summer?" Guy was finding it increasingly difficult to rein in his exasperation.

"What are you getting at?"

"I'm getting at the fact that you seem incapable of getting off your backside. Don't you want to do anything with your life? Are you happy to achieve absolutely nothing at all?"

Kelly bristled. "For your information," she said, sticking out her chin. "I am doing something. I'm organizing an all-nighter."

"A what?"

"I'm going to hold a rave here. I've already got a couple of DJs ready to do sets. I just have to set the date."

"You can't do that."

"We're going to set up decks in the barn and—"

"No way. The barn is full of winemaking equipment."

"We can party around it."

"Kelly, you're not holding a party on this farm."

"I don't seem to remember *your* name appearing in my father's will, Guy. I'm going to get some flyers done. Gina's brother will hand them out when he does his set at the Fridge next week. Gina reckons he might even be able to get a new band to do a set here. Five hundred people at fifty quid a head. I reckon we can charge at least that. Maybe more."

Guy didn't care how much they were willing to pay. Five hundred people? He had a horrifying image of all his hard work trampled underfoot as a bunch of kids, high on drugs, marauded through his vineyard. "You can't do this," he echoed hopelessly.

Kelly stood up. "It's already done. Second weekend in September," she announced.

Even worse. With the summer shaping up to be a hot one, there was a very real chance that Kelly's stupid rave would take place right in the middle of the harvest.

"Please don't do this to me," said Guy.

"Too late," said Kelly. "I am. Thanks for the drink."

As Guy slammed the empty wine bottle into the rubbish, Kelly strutted back across the farmyard puffed up with the knowledge that she had won that argument. Then she demonstrated the first bit of initiative in months. Back inside the farmhouse, she pulled out a pad of paper and began to design the flyer she would give to Gina's brother. Gazing around the kitchen while she hoped for inspiration, Kelly's eyes alighted on one of the empty champagne bottles that were lined up along the top of the Welsh dresser. She fetched it down.

The bottle, which had once contained Perrier-Jouët, was decorated with a beautiful hand-painted pattern of flowers that wound all the way up around the bottleneck. Kelly began to sketch a design that would incorporate this art deco–style motif. In the center, she drew a woman's face, looking off into the distance.

On the other side of the courtyard, Guy lay awake, racking his brains for some way to put a stop to Kelly's ridiculous plans for Froggy Bottom. How could he get her to leave? How could he persuade her to go back to the city? What would put her off staying in the farmhouse? He remembered one summer when the neighboring farmer had spread his fields with muck during one of the hottest weekends of the year, causing the local campsite to lose almost one hundred percent of its custom as previously happy campers succumbed to the smell and were pestered away by the flies. Guy didn't even have that option. He dare not risk putting anything on the soil that might taint the eventual flavor of his wine.

But there was no need to panic. September was a couple of months away. He'd get Hilarian and the trustees to talk to her. Or maybe he'd just call the police. Hadn't all that legislation in the nineties made it illegal to throw raves anyway?

Bloody Kelly. He punched the pillow.

CHAPTER 27

There were definitely moments over the first few weeks that followed the wine fair when Madeleine wondered whether she should have taken up Mathieu Randon's offer after all. Though the maison seemed to have made pretty much zero money for the last five years, somehow Champagne Arsenault still owed a vast amount of taxes. Even for a woman used to dealing in seven-figure sums in her career as a banker, the figure was frightening.

"Can this really be right?" she asked Champagne Arsenault's new accountant, Laurent Parisot.

Laurent promised to look into it but he warned her that her father had not paid taxes for several years and, in all probability, the horrifying figure he had come up with was conservative. Madeleine closed her eyes as she allowed the news to sink in.

Madeleine had used all her banking experience to draw up a new business plan for Champagne Arsenault. Of course she had built in contingencies for late payment of the outstanding debts of her father's customers, but for some reason it hadn't even crossed her mind that there might be an outstanding tax bill. Certainly not such a big one. She'd simply assumed that no income meant no taxes. The amount her accountant had whispered into the phone was five times Madeleine's emergency margin. There were other big costs coming up too. Picking was the most pressing but far from the least of them.

"Can you cover it?" her accountant asked.

"Yes," Madeleine murmured. "I think so."

But she was far from certain.

Madeleine called Geoff in London. He had promised when they last spoke that he would do anything he could to help Madeleine keep Champagne Arsenault afloat, but though he took her call, he didn't seem quite so sure anymore that he could help her. Somehow Geoff had found himself back at Ingerlander Bank and under Adam Freeman. And when Madeleine asked outright for a fast, low-interest loan, Geoff cleared his throat and said, "I'm not going to get this past him, Mads. I don't know what you did to him . . ."

Nothing, thought Madeleine ruefully. Absolutely nothing.

She didn't bother to press Geoff on the subject. There was no point. There may be loyalty among thieves but bankers . . .

Ironically, while the financial affairs of Champagne Arsenault seemed to worsen daily, the vines were doing well. Henri Mason kept Madeleine up-to-date on progress. The vineyards on the hill were flourishing. But there was still better news.

"I think we may be able to make a Clos Des Larmes this year," said Henri as they stood in the walled vineyard a couple of hours after Madeleine's conversation with Laurent Parisot.

"Really?" Madeleine asked.

He nodded. "Look at this," said Henri, cradling a bunch of pinot noir grapes in the palm of his hand. They were flawless. Each one looked as though it had been blown in glass. "Beautiful. This year is going to be vintage, Madeleine. *Your* first vintage."

Madeleine wrapped her arms around Henri and pressed her soft face against his stubbled cheek just as she had when she was a little girl. It had comforted her then but it didn't comfort her now. In fact, she held him closely so that he wouldn't see her tears of anxiety. Still, he must have sensed that something was wrong from her ragged breathing or the tightness of her embrace.

"Is everything OK?" he asked.

Madeleine nodded into his shoulder. He was so proud of the grapes. She didn't have the heart to tell him right then that he was wasting his time. If Madeleine were able to afford to pick Champagne Arsenault's grapes, she wouldn't be able to afford to press them. If she found the money to press the grapes, she wouldn't be able to keep the wine in Champagne Arsenault's caves until the time came to sell it.

Madeleine disentangled herself from Henri and went back into the house, claiming that she had a cold coming on and needed to blow her nose. Once inside, she gave way to the tears that had been building since Geoff announced that he was unable to help her clear Champagne Arsenault's tax bill.

Every day the tax bill went unpaid, the amount Champagne Arsenault owed crept higher. The revenue wouldn't wait to be paid. The grapes wouldn't wait to be picked. The wine in the vats wouldn't wait to be bottled. Madeleine sat on her bed with her head in her hands and wondered what price Mathieu Randon would give her.

CHAPTER 28

Mathieu Randon may have been furious about Christina's speech at the wine fair but it didn't seem to have done her any harm. The day after a little article about her surprise denunciation of Domaine Randon appeared in the *Times,* Christina's agent, Marisa, fielded a call from the editor of *Vanity Fair.* Their November issue was to be all about stars taking a stance against globalization. Would Christina consider giving a small interview regarding her decision to walk away from an extremely highly paid job and toward the moral high ground? She responded that she would be delighted.

"You see," she said to Bill when they passed briefly in the corridor at the Manhattan apartment. "My 'stupid stance,' as you call it, may yet turn out to be the best move I ever made. *Vanity Fair* wants to interview me, Bill. That's *Vanity Fair!*"

Christina knew the *Vanity Fair* article would drive Bill crazy. He had yet to make the pages of the magazine except the odd appearance in their film review section, wherein his work was invariably panned. Each February, when the

March edition of the magazine—the traditional pre-Oscars "Hollywood edition"—hit the shelves, Bill would spend days brooding over why he never made the cut when his box-office figures rivaled those of Tom Cruise and Brad Pitt. That the editor of the magazine himself had called Christina directly and assured her he would devote at least four pages to her and her stupid causes sent Bill into something approaching clinical depression. Well, served Bill right, thought Christina. He was her husband. He was supposed to support her.

A week later, Christina flew from NYC to Napa Valley where she was photographed for the article on the grounds of the Villa Bacchante. She was dressed like a goddess, all flowing drapes and Roman-style sandals. A wind machine blew her long blond hair back from her perfect face. She was like Botticelli's Venus in a vineyard instead of on the half shell.

Mathieu Randon heard all about Christina's forthcoming appearance in *Vanity Fair* via the journalist who had written his profile for the same magazine. Randon had an unusual talent of inspiring loyalty in the journalists who came into contact with him. The female ones at least. This woman, an unmarried forty-something from Manhattan, would have done anything for the chance to bask in the beam of Randon's Gallic smile for just a few more moments.

"Thank you," he said, when she passed on the message. "You are very kind to let me know. I look forward to seeing you next time you are in Paris," he added, not meaning a word. In Manhattan, the journalist immediately began searching the Internet for cheap flights to Europe.

Randon could just imagine how the article would be. Though just a couple of years previously he had been happy enough to pose for the magazine himself to illustrate an article on the new establishment, Randon had little time for *Vanity Fair*'s thinly disguised celebrity puffs. To him, the magazine was on a par with *Hello!* Would it have featured ISACL's campaign at all if someone altogether less photogenic had been fronting it? He was white-hot furious that, as yet, no one had called Domaine Randon's office to get his side of the child-labor story.

Still, Randon wasn't going to let some dozy supermodel and a lazy journalist undo years of hard work. It was time for a preemptive strike.

He dialed his assistant. "Bertille, will you get Jeremy Fraser on the phone?"

Fraser was a publicist specializing in "kiss and tell."

"There's someone I'd like you to meet," Randon told him.

Amelie's fifteen minutes of fame had come at last. While *Vanity Fair* was working photoshop magic on the results of the Christina Morgan shoot, Amelie the call girl was taking part in a photo shoot of her own in a warehouse on the outskirts of Paris. It wasn't the first time she'd been in front of the camera, but it was the first time she'd been in front of a camera with her clothes on. If you could call the scraps of fabric she was wearing clothes.

"Chin down, eyes to camera," said the photographer. "Give me a smile, sweetheart. That's great."

Amelie was a natural, running through a whole gamut of pouty, seductive faces, blowing kisses and cupping her own breasts in classic glamour-model mode.

Because of France's strict tabloid journalism laws (and because the French didn't really care about Bill Tarrant), the story would be broken in Britain's *News of the World*. Alongside the full-color shots of Amelie in a virginal white bra and knickers set, the paper would run a couple of grainy pictures lifted from the chip in her mobile phone:

Bill Tarrant, exhausted after a night of Parisian hospitality courtesy of Mathieu Randon...

"I hope that one day in the future Bill will look at this article and smile," said Randon to Fraser as they admired the finished piece in their respective offices on either side of *La Manche*. "Five times in one night. Without Viagra! He's quite a guy."

"If it were true." Fraser laughed. "It's a time-honored tradition," he explained to Randon. "Five times a night. What man is going to bring a libel suit if he has to gainsay an article that paints him in quite such a spectacular light?"

Randon allowed himself a rare burst of laughter.

Christina was in Napa Valley when the story broke. The previous night she had hosted a fund-raising event for ISACL at the Top of the Mark, the restaurant at the Mark Hopkins Hotel in San Francisco. And so, by the time she awoke—slightly later than usual because she was so exhausted from being on show the night before—the story of Bill's adventures in Paris had raced around the globe and was waiting in her in-box. When she turned on her mobile, she was momentarily gratified to hear she had fifteen messages on her voicemail. The first seven were from Bill.

"Baby," he said. "Pick up the phone. You've got to call me as soon as you get this message. Don't check your e-mail first. Promise me you won't. Call me right away. I need to speak to you the minute you get this. Please pick up the goddamn phone, my love. Don't check your e-mail first."

Christina checked her e-mail.

It took a moment before Christina connected the grainy photograph that popped up on the screen of her Mac with the man she had exchanged vows with. She felt a little sordid as she clicked on a link to YouTube that actually showed a video clip from the same evening. Her husband lying on a messed-up hotel bed. Spent. The girl holding the camera phone used her free hand, with its chipped red nails, to lift his flaccid penis from his washboard stomach and try to coax it back to life.

Bill woke up and looked into the camera.

"What are you doing?" he asked his companion.

"Taking a souvenir," said the girl in her heavy Parisian accent. "Smile."

"Don't show anyone, will you," said Bill, then he lay back against the pillows and closed his eyes.

"Oh, Bill." Christina put her head in her hands. "You stupid, stupid man."

She turned off her laptop and remained sitting at her desk with her own eyes closed for quite some time. The screen might be blank but now the scene played inside her head instead. She wondered if she would ever be able to see anything else.

Meanwhile, her mobile was vibrating intermittently—irritatingly—to tell her that she had messages. People were trying to get through. Not just Bill now but her agent, Marisa; her lawyer, Todd; her mother...eventually, she had to pick up.

"Hello," she said wearily.

"Christina?" It was Bill. "Are you OK?"

"What do you think, you fuck?" her voice cracked.

How on earth was this going to *look*?

Bill flew back to the States from London right away, missing the last day of the film junket he had flown to Europe for (he was, in any case, in no state to do TV interviews after a bout of very heavy drinking in anticipation of the shit hitting the fan). Christina arranged to meet her husband in New York, at an apartment belonging to Marisa's sister, since the paparazzi were staking out all their own properties. She was snapped rushing through SFO wearing a scarf and a beanie hat despite the eighty-degree heat.

God, she hated her husband for doing this to her. He better have a good excuse.

"I guess the honeymoon period is well and truly over," Christina sighed when she saw him. Her mood had not been helped by the fact that every newspaper she was offered in the first-class cabin of her United Airlines flight (where were your friends with private jets when you needed them?) carried pictures of Christina alongside a cheap headshot of the slut her husband had slept with. No matter that the headlines expressed their incredulity that Bill would cheat on a *supermodel* with a cheap French call girl by asking "Would you swap this for *that*?" The awful truth was he *had* swapped her for *that*. Christina was humiliated. Devastated. Crushed.

"That bastard Randon stitched me up," Bill launched into his defense right away. "He took me out to dinner and got me drunk."

"Bill," said Christina, full of faux patience. "You're not some sixteen-year-old girl. You're a grown man. No one gets a forty-year-old man drunk without his cooperation."

"Then maybe someone drugged me. Rohypnol or something. I'm telling you, my darling, all I remember after having dinner with Randon is going up to my hotel room and going to sleep. I'd had a hard day. I swear I left him and that girl in the bar. But when I woke up, she was there."

"Sitting on your cock," said Christina bluntly.

"No." Bill covered his eyes. "I swear I don't know how she even got into my room!"

"How about you let her in? Bill," sighed Christina, "I'm not an idiot. I don't want to hear any excuses. You're a jerk. You're a dickhead. You're the sorriest bastard I ever met and I wish I'd never laid eyes on you!"

When it was clear that Christina wasn't going to accept his assertion that he had been drugged and set up, Bill tried that other tactic. So maybe he had slept with a prostitute. It was, of course, Christina's own fault. They'd argued before he flew to Paris to try to rescue the Randon deal. *Their* deal. She'd made him so angry that he needed to let off steam. He deserved to.

"You deserved to let off steam by having some girl blow you? Why couldn't you have just gotten into a fistfight like you normally do?" Christina asked. "That way it's only you who has to face the humiliation the morning after. You have made me look an idiot, Bill. My face is in all the papers next to a mug shot of some girl who looks like she hasn't seen a dentist in ten years. People want to know what's so wrong with me that you'd choose to stick your cock in that thing, that slut, rather than in the world's most beautiful woman. Do you know how bad that is? I'm a laughingstock. They love it. That you would rather go with some ugly little French bitch than fuck me. It's so embarrassing."

"Is that all you care about? How you look in the papers?" Bill deftly turned Christina's argument back on her. "That's all that matters to you, isn't it? Not me. Not our marriage. Just how it looks in the news. Is that what's important?"

"Fuck you," said Christina. "It *is* important. I'm going to bed. On my own."

"Yeah," scoffed Bill. "Like that's a change."

After a night in separate bedrooms Bill convinced himself that Randon had been right. He didn't need Christina. She was holding him back with her holier-than-thou stance on globalization. She was a model and he was a film star. Their job was to entertain, not proselytize. Quite apart from that, Christina was colder than a penguin's backside. Not only did Bill never get laid anymore, he didn't get any appreciation either. He needed someone who understood how hard he worked. Someone who would be grateful for the flowers and the jewelry and not ask what he'd done that he needed to offset with a last-minute gift from duty-free.

Bill hated always being the bad guy. He screwed up sometimes but he wasn't a bad man. Fuck. Much to his chagrin, he didn't even really remember what that stupid French slut had done to him. Was he going to have to be punished for some forbidden pleasure he couldn't even recall? Every guy slipped up from time to time, didn't he? Anger swiftly morphed into self-pity.

All Bill wanted was to be forgiven, he told himself. To be loved unconditionally. He hugged a pillow tightly against his body like a little boy missing his mother. Christina was supposed to forgive him. Wasn't that in their marriage vows?

But Christina wasn't up for unconditional love. The following morning, she departed for the airport before Bill even woke up. She left a note on the kitchen counter explaining that Bill could stay in the Beverly Hills house if he needed to be back in California. She was going to the villa in Napa Valley to think about their future.

"Think about our future."

Bill read that single phrase as a rejection. If he knew anything about his wife, it was that she had done her thinking the second she saw the video clip, and her decision was already made. And so Bill didn't bother to call her. Instead, he called his lawyer and sued Christina for divorce. His lawyer suggested that the lack of sex in their marriage amounted to psychological cruelty.

"Well, Matthew," said Bill to Randon in a phone call on the day his divorce papers were served. "I took your advice and filed for divorce. You were right. Christina was just one big downer on my career. Now, you and I should get together and discuss that movie idea of yours. I think now would be a great time for me to look into the possibility of directing. Shall we meet in New York?"

"I don't think that will be necessary," said Randon, who knew that the time had come to let Tarrant know that his services were no longer required at Domaine Randon either.

"But I don't get it!" Bill protested.

"Bill, old buddy, you were photographed passed out drunk with a prostitute. People are saying you've got a drinking problem. Do you know how tough the advertising-standards people are these days? It doesn't look good. A drunkard advertising champagne? May I suggest you call your local branch of Alcoholics Anonymous. And, incidentally, my name is not Matt."

CHAPTER 29

That same evening Mathieu Randon sent word to Odile Levert that she should meet him at Bibliotek. When she received the message, Odile couldn't help smiling. Bibliotek was one of her favorite restaurants.

She arrived ten minutes late, as was her custom. She liked to ensure that her dining companion would be at the table before her. She wore black, as was usual in the evening: an elegant dress by Lanvin that hung beautifully from her mannequin-style bones. Her hair had been cut just that afternoon into an extra-sharp bob that emphasized her ageless cheekbones. Her heels finished the look of polished perfection that had the girl on the front desk standing to attention and promised good service all evening.

It gave Odile quite a kick, walking into Bibliotek and having the staff fawn over her.

Randon stood as she approached their table. He leaned to kiss the air on both sides of her face.

"I don't know how you do it," he said admiringly. "You look younger every time we meet. How long have we known each other now, Odile?"

"Almost fifteen years," she told him.

"Ah yes. Since you were just starting out as a critic. Vinexpo. I could tell you had something even then."

"Because I approved of Éclat?" Odile joked. "Thank you."

The waiter, who shook out Odile's napkin and placed it on her lap, hid the critic's mischievous smile. It tickled her enormously that Mathieu Randon still thought that day at Vinexpo was the first time he'd laid eyes on her.

Hilarian and Ronald had Odile Levert all wrong. She didn't come from some grand old French family at all. She'd had her introduction to wine in a rather more prosaic setting than the elegant dining hall of Champagne Arsenault, or the grand ballroom at Maison Randon. Like all French children, she'd been raised on *vin de table,* but she got her first taste of something good in the kitchen of the five-star restaurant where she was working as a waitress. The sommelier had taken her under his wing and the rest was history.

And history has a habit of repeating itself.

Odile Levert had joined the waiting staff at the new Parisian restaurant Bibliotek with her fraternal twin sister, Odette. They were named after the princesses in *Swan Lake*. Their mother, Erica, was obsessed with the ballet. She was convinced she could have been a star of the stage herself, if she had been born into a different family. And married a different man...

The twins' father was a charming but violent man. He was also a hugely talented chef. When he was in a good mood, there was no better place to be than in the family kitchen. When he wasn't Erica bore the brunt of his dissatisfaction with life. After that, Odile. For some reason Odette was untouchable in her father's eyes. Perhaps it was her beauty. He called her his little angel, of course.

Odile always saw the disappointment on people's faces when Odette introduced her twin sister. Odette had the timeless beauty of a Renaissance portrait, a movie star or a fashion model. Odile had similar features but they were just a little less well put together. Her big brown eyes were a little too close. Her nose just a little too big. The difference in the girls' looks was reflected in the tips they made as waitresses.

That night, almost twenty years ago now, Odette and Odile were assigned to look after a party of six businessmen. A very important party, the chief waiter informed them. "Don't fuck it up."

Odette distributed menus with the wide, white grin that guaranteed her at least fifteen percent from the start. From her place behind the bar, Odile watched the customers settling in. She noticed at once the man who would become so important to her. There was something about him that reminded her of their father. He was white-haired though probably only in his early thirties. He was well dressed, of course. This was the kind of restaurant that demanded a certain level of style—and income. From the way he was leaning back in his seat while his companions all leaned toward him, it was clear he was the one to impress. Odile didn't like the look of him.

"Your turn," said Odette, as they crossed paths in the middle of the restaurant.

Odile tried to mimic her sister's flourish as she presented the white-haired man with the wine list.

"An aperitif perhaps? May I suggest a glass of champagne?"

There was something cruel about the white-haired man's smile as he replied, "Yes. Why don't you suggest a glass of champagne to me."

"I'd like to recommend the Bollinger. In my opinion, this is an exceptional vintage . . ."

As Odile continued with her spiel, she became aware that her customers found something amusing in her delivery. She glanced down at the front of her blouse nervously. Had she come unbuttoned? Odette would have mentioned it, surely. The man to the left of the white-haired guy began to snigger. Soon the entire table was laughing with him.

"Are you some kind of moron?" the white-haired man asked her. "I said you could suggest a glass of champagne to me, not recite your dissertation on the origins of urine."

Odile stepped back at the force of his words.

"How long have you been working as a sommelier?"

"This is my first month."

"And your last. You just made a fatal mistake. You suggested Bollinger to the head of Maison Randon."

Odile blushed to the roots of her hair. She began to make her apology.

"Don't bother," said Randon. "Send me someone who knows how to do his job. A man. You see," he addressed his companions, "women know shit about wine. They're only good for fucking. And then only until they're twenty-five." He looked Odile up and down as though she were a horse. "What are you still doing here?" he asked her then.

Odile did her best to walk, not run, back to the kitchen.

It was a day that would remain imprinted on her memory as though it had been branded there with a hot iron. Clearly, it had not been quite so important for Randon.

"I hear via the jungle drums that Arsenault is in terrible trouble," Randon observed as they finished their coffee. "Unpaid tax bill? Enormous. Poor little Madeleine must be about ready to sell to big bad Domaine Randon now."

Odile shook her head. "Apparently not."

"Well, let her watch her grapes rot."

"But that's not good for you, is it? If Madeleine can't afford to look after her vineyards properly, then it makes more work for you when you finally come to take Champagne Arsenault over. It's one thing hoping that some disaster will force her to sell at a lower price than you anticipated, but the way I see it, you'd have to pick up the difference anyway. If she cuts corners now, you'll be paying for it for the next few vintages. Besides, Randon, you and I both know that this is going to be a particularly good year. You could miss out on putting out the first ever Maison Randon Clos Des Larmes."

"Don't you think I've thought of that?" asked Randon. "Odile, I didn't invite you to have dinner with me this evening so that you could insult me."

"I'm sorry. I do hate to see you so exercised. Perhaps you should talk to Madeleine again. Stress to her that the death of her marque would be a far greater disaster than for it to be brought under the caring umbrella of Domaine Randon."

"Stupid bitch won't listen to reason."

"Perhaps it's the medium rather than the message. Perhaps she needs to hear it from someone she trusts."

Randon narrowed his eyes.

"But you have a lot to lose too, Odile, if she doesn't hear the message. What about your bet?"

"What's it worth to me? A few thousand pounds? Hardly worth getting out of bed for, as your friend Christina Morgan the supermodel might say. I've got better things to do than babysit Champagne Arsenault."

"What would make it worth your while?"

They were interrupted by the maitre d', who wanted to be sure that Monsieur Randon was pleased with his meal.

"Wonderful," he said. "But I think we're ready to leave."

Odile, who was used to Randon's sudden lapses in sociability, was only too happy to agree.

The maitre d' of Bibliotek had been a waiter when Odile worked there. His memory was as faulty as Randon's. If only he knew, thought Odile as the stupid fool helped her into her coat.

Madeleine accepted Odile's invitation to the Women in Wine lunch in Paris at once, as Odile had known she would. She met Madeleine in the lobby of the Hyatt Vendôme and embraced her warmly.

"My lovely little protégée. What a pretty dress," she commented. She could tell from Madeleine's blushes that the girl was unduly flattered by her praise. "So, how have you been since I last saw you?"

"OK," said Madeleine.

"I can't stop thinking about how we're going to win that little bet with your first Clos Des Larmes," said Odile. "You will make one this year, of course?"

Madeleine's brow wrinkled. Odile immediately wound her arm through Madeleine's and said, "Darling, shall we take our drinks and go outside?"

Odile walked Madeleine out onto the little atrium in the middle of the hotel, whereupon Madeleine unleashed her frustration. She told Odile everything about the tax bill, the rising costs and her fear that she would have to sell. She even, feeling incredibly disloyal as she did so, told Odile about her father's gambling habit.

"I just feel so unsupported!"

"Ssssh," said Odile. "It's OK. You do have people behind you. There are so many people who want to see you succeed. I most certainly do. You know I have a lot of money riding on Clos Des Larmes to win that silly *Vinifera* challenge."

"I've got a feeling you're wasting your money," said Madeleine.

"Not at all. Madeleine, I think what is required here is a little of what the Americans call 'thinking outside the box.' You're justifiably worried that you don't have enough money in the Arsenault coffers to bring in the grapes from all your vineyards and get them processed this year, right?"

Madeleine nodded.

"Well, silly girl, the answer hits me between the eyes right away! You don't have to bring in all your grapes."

"I can't leave them unharvested."

"I'm not suggesting that either. I think you should sell them."

"What?"

"The Arsenault vineyards are all grand cru, yes? What's the CIVC set as the price for grand cru grapes this year? Pinot must be at five Euros per kilo. Chardonnay at five point three. Sell your grapes. Pay your tax bill."

"I can't! Champagne Arsenault has *never* sold its grapes."

"Times change."

"I can't let someone else have the pinot from the Clos Des Larmes."

"Ah, I'm not suggesting that. You keep the Clos Des Larmes. You must. I'm relying on you to make a spectacular vintage. But sell the rest. Keep Champagne Arsenault afloat. Just for this year, Madeleine. That's all that matters."

That afternoon, Odile helped Madeleine hone her plan. It would be easy to sell the grapes from the vineyards on the hill. The big houses such as Moët were always happy to buy from grand cru vineyards to press and bottle under their own labels to meet the demand their brand image created. Odile knew exactly whom Madeleine should talk to to get the best terms. Such a deal would provide Madeleine with enough cash to pay Henri and the guys and keep Arsenault afloat while the next part of the plan took shape.

The Clos Des Larmes was an entirely different prospect from the vineyards on the hill. The vines in the tiny walled vineyard had been grown using not just traditional but positively ancient methods. Unlike the strictly regimented vines on the hill, the Clos Des Larmes vines grew higgledy-piggledy, in an arrangement known as *en foule*. They were old vines. Their maturity was reflected in the complexity of flavor in the grapes.

As Odile suggested, Madeleine would keep all the grapes from the Clos Des Larmes for herself, to be pressed in-house for Champagne Arsenault. The vineyard was small. The yield would be tiny. But it would be *so* valuable. Madeleine remembered that fateful dinner at Montrachet the night her father had a heart attack. The price of the

Clos Des Larmes on Montrachet's wine list was astronomical. If they could make a Clos Des Larmes, then it could save Champagne Arsenault.

"Thank you." Madeleine kissed Odile. "For making me see sense."

Odile stroked Madeleine's cheek affectionately. "In a few years' time you'll be able to press all your own grapes again. You'll make Champagne Arsenault a force to be reckoned with. I believe in you."

Madeleine went back to Champagne and joined Henri in anxiously watching the weather. Throughout the village— as happened every year as harvesttime approached—there was talk of nothing else. *Véraison*—that moment when the grapes changed color from green to red—had taken place a little earlier than expected. Would this year's harvest beat the previous year's record for early ripeness? Madeleine found herself out in the Clos several times a day, checking the sugar levels of her grapes in degrees Baume with her refractometer. She couldn't help but be reminded of the days she had spent watching the fluctuating price of some stock or other with similar obsessive attention. The two things had a lot in common. If Madeleine and her banking friends miscalculated the sale price then heads would roll. Likewise in the vineyards grapes picked too early or too late would be worthless.

The harvest in Champagne is a closely regulated affair. The dates upon which harvesting may start are not set by the individual vigneron but by the CIVC—the body that regulates the making of champagne in the region. As the earliest possible date for that year's harvest drew closer, Madeleine swung into action. The big champagne house that was going to buy the grapes from the hill vineyards had agreed to provide its own team of pickers to ensure the harvest was done to its particular requirements. For the Clos Des Larmes, however, Madeleine had to call in some favors.

She e-mailed all her friends back in London.

"A week in Champagne," she suggested to each of them. "All expenses paid."

The offer was greeted with plenty of initial excitement but unfortunately the unusually early harvest fell right at the end of the British school holidays. Madeleine had forgotten how many of her friends were now the parents of school-age children, all of whom were just a little bit too young to roll up their sleeves and join in with the picking. No one was available to help out, except for Lizzy, Jane and Helena, who jumped at the chance to be doing something, anything, other than sitting in London.

For the first time in almost ninety years, it looked as though the Clos Des Larmes at Arsenault was to be harvested solely by women.

CHAPTER 30

Napa Valley was beautiful in the summer. The vines were resplendent with bright green foliage. The grapes were ripening. Birds were singing. It was blissfully warm. All of nature seemed to be rejoicing. But Christina Morgan shivered on the veranda of Villa Bacchante wrapped in an enormous dressing gown. One of the few things Bill had left behind.

How had it gone so wrong? They'd been married for only slightly more than a year and now they were getting divorced? They were the Hollywood couple of the century! This wasn't meant to happen.

Christina worried at a cuticle as she stared sightlessly out over the vineyards. In her head ran a continuous feed of headlines relating to the end of her marriage. The public speculation as to why it had imploded was unbearable. Bill was the one who had slept with a slut and yet somehow the blame had been laid firmly at Christina's feet. "Christina's beauty is only skin deep," claimed one magazine writer. "Bill's co-stars on *Kings of the Stone Age,* twins Misty and Lisa Legrand, claim that Bill felt lonely in his marriage. Christina was more interested in promoting her own brand image than supporting her man. While Bill was sick with pneumonia on set in New Mexico, Christina was cavorting in Baja with Rocky Neel."

All lies! Pneumonia? Bill had had a *cold.*

Christina saw the hand of Bill's manager in all this bad press. Christina had never liked Justin. She knew that Justin thought Bill should have stayed single for longer, like Clooney. The fans preferred it that way. And so Christina fought back, saying that Bill had refused to work on their marriage. She had been willing to forgive him, she told a weekly gossip magazine. When she flew to New York the day she got the news about the Parisian prostitute, she had been ready to listen to his explanation, accept an apology and try to move forward. She was prepared to let it go. But he'd been so unapologetic! He'd made it her fault! And all because she'd tried to do the right thing. Because she had stood up for her beliefs and supported ISACL. He called her stupid for choosing the moral high ground over Maison Randon. She couldn't sit there and take that. He was her husband. He was supposed to stand by her.

She may have flown back to California without saying

good-bye but she told him where she would be. He knew how to get hold of her.

Bill was supposed to follow her back to the West Coast. He was supposed to call Teak, his personal assistant, and ask him to book a ticket to Oakland or Sacramento, whichever was quicker, and have a car waiting at the airport. Bill was supposed to drive up to the villa in Napa and hammer on the locked door until Christina relented and let him inside to talk. He was supposed to prove that their marriage meant at least that much.

Instead, while Christina held her breath in Napa Valley, Bill hit the town in New York. He moved out of Marisa's sister's apartment and into the best suite at the new Ian Schrager Hotel. That very night he was pictured enjoying a cozy dinner *à deux* with his co-star from his last action movie. And later he was photographed again, lurching out of a nightclub with two girls who apparently accompanied him back to his room "to console him." Bill was the battered bad boy; Christina was a cold-hearted witch. And that despite her charity work! Marisa reminded all the journalists she spoke to that Christina was still very much involved in fighting for the rights of child workers.

But for whatever reason, the media didn't seem to care about Christina's point of view. They swung behind Bill. Even *Vanity Fair* called to say they weren't going to be running their piece on ISACL after all. They would be printing a hot new exposé about Bobby Kennedy instead.

"I'm sure they'll run your piece next year," said Marisa. Christina knew that wasn't going to happen.

And then there was the divorce itself...

Christina had hired a hotshot lawyer but the things he discovered as soon as he started digging offered her little hope of walking away with a decent settlement. Christina was absolutely stunned to learn that her husband, Bill Tarrant, the man once hailed by *Variety* as "box-office gold" had barely a nickel to his name. The apartment in Manhattan, the beach house, the fabulous home in Beverly Hills, all were heavily mortgaged on behalf of Bill's production company. He'd been hemorrhaging money as he tried to set up his stupid western.

"I would help you take your husband for everything," said Christina's lawyer, Todd, "but alas there is nothing to take him for."

Having expected to walk away with at least two of their four properties, Christina found herself negotiating to keep just one: the Villa Bacchante.

Christina's life was falling apart.

Two months after Bill's indiscretion, she forced herself to show up for a fitting for the Guilty Secrets lingerie fashion show, hoping that hanging out with so many familiar faces from the industry would help her break out of her funk. But once there she was shocked to find that her famous breasts no longer filled out the show-stopping diamond-encrusted bra she was supposed to model. She'd been neglecting to watch her diet. The bejeweled brassiere was given instead to Viviane Caine, a model from Texas who had been hailed as a Jerry Hall for the noughties. Caine got top billing in the show. Christina stalked down the catwalk ahead of her in a black basque made of fake leather and was rewarded with articles in all the gossip rags speculating about whether she had anorexia. The crisis deepened when Guilty Secrets regretfully informed Marisa that they would not be renewing Christina's contract for their catalog. They were going in a fresh direction, they said. With Viviane Caine.

After the humiliation of the lingerie show and being dropped as the face of Guilty Secrets, Christina became a hermit. While Bill was photographed out and about on a daily basis, "rebuilding his life," Christina all but disappeared. She holed up in Napa. She sat alone on the patio at Villa Bacchante for hours, just staring out over the vineyard. The only person she saw was Ernestina, the housekeeper.

She felt cold all the time. It was as though she had been kept warm only by the glow of public approval and now that the public had turned away from her, the sun no longer shone.

Christina cried herself to sleep night after night. It was all over. Her marriage was over. Her modeling career was over. There was nothing left. No family. No future. Nothing.

Marisa understood up to a point but after a month during which Christina had barely changed out of that horrible dressing gown (Marisa recognized the lapels of the hideous thing whenever she talked with Christina over Skype), she decided that it was time for some tough talk. She flew from New York to Napa for the weekend. She arrived at the villa with a basket full of bagels. Christina pushed them aside.

"Now, this isn't something I tell many of my girls," said Marisa, "but you really have to put on some weight. You have to eat. And not just because you've completely lost your tits and I couldn't get you a job modeling incontinence pants. I can't let you kill yourself slowly like this."

Christina looked up at her agent and friend with watery eyes.

"I feel like someone died," she said.

"You certainly look like someone died," said Marisa. "In fact, you look like you're going to follow suit. You're a walking skeleton."

"I'm grieving."

"What are you grieving, Christina?"

"My marriage, of course!" Christina looked at Marisa incredulously.

"Really?" Marisa paused significantly. "Only I didn't see that you were all that excited while you were in it."

"What?"

"I don't think it's Bill you miss at all."

Christina's mouth dropped open. She started to say something but Marisa interrupted her.

"You weren't in love with him. You were in love with being one half of the world's most recognizable couple. It was all about image. For both of you."

"How can you say that? We were going to spend the rest of our lives together. We were going to have a family. We had everything planned." Christina continued, "I'd been reading about adopting in Africa."

"Too much bother to have sex, eh?"

"I . . ." Now Christina was really upset. "What the hell is wrong with you?" she asked Marisa. "You're supposed to be on my side."

"And I am," said Marisa. "I'm just pointing out that you're pining away for something that didn't exist. This perfect marriage."

"We had a good marriage."

"You had an agreement. You don't love Bill. You never did. He was only supposed to be a quick fuck to help you get over that finance guy. I should never have let you two tie the knot. You're hiding out here like a kicked dog because you're worried about what people think of you. Well, let me tell you something. If you're going to carry on hiding, people will just carry on saying that you're finished."

"I am finished," said Christina, feeling suddenly even

smaller and more insignificant. "You see the way everyone has turned against me over this. You haven't had a call asking for me in weeks, right? It's like I lost my future. That's the truth. I mean, I always knew I couldn't be a model forever, but after that? What? What's next for me, Marisa? I can't act. I have never had a proper job in my life. I couldn't even be an agent."

Marisa smiled tightly.

"I didn't mean that to sound so bad."

"I understand," said Marisa.

"But it's true. I'm not actually qualified to do anything. I started modeling before I left high school. My mother told me it was a mistake. And maybe she was right. I've got nothing to fall back on. I couldn't even hang on to a husband."

"Stop thinking like that really matters. I'm doing perfectly fine without one. Don't you think?"

Marisa had never been married. Never had a boyfriend for longer than six months. In truth, Christina felt rather sorry for her. It never occurred to her that Marisa might be happy with her life the way it was.

"Did you think Bill would have supported you in his old age?" Marisa continued. "He wasn't your guarantee of security. You know what a mess he made of his finances."

"He can at least build them up again."

"I'm telling you, darling, the shelf life of an action movie hero is almost as short as a model's."

"I wish I could take more comfort from that."

"Indulging in *schadenfreude* is not such a good trait. Leave that nasty habit to me."

"What else do I have?"

"What else do you have?" Marisa parroted, sarcastically. "You know, you're never going to be destitute, you silly girl. In real terms, you've got plenty of money in the bank. And when you get something approaching boobs again, I'll be happy to keep sending you out on modeling jobs for as long as they come in. Which will be for years," she added. "And after that? Bill's pretty much agreed you can have this place, right?"

Christina nodded. Bill had been remarkably conciliatory in an effort to keep down his legal costs.

"Well, I think it's a pretty wonderful spot to hole up in while you're deciding your next move." Marisa took a thoughtful sip from her glass. "You could even become a winemaker for real. You like wine, don't you? You've got a great palate. I think you'd be a natural."

"Well, yes, but...so I know a bit about the finished product. I don't know anything much about making the stuff."

"You're living in Carneros, darling. This is great land. You can't go wrong. Get involved. Throw yourself into learning about viticulture. It will take your mind off things."

Christina automatically shook her head. "What's the point?"

Marisa leaned forward and took her former star model by the shoulders.

"It's time to get a grip, Christina. Of all the models I have ever represented, you were always the most driven. No one works like you did; no one takes more care of his or her image. And now you're really going to let it go because your sham of a marriage didn't work out? Yes, you're getting older. Everybody does. But you're not over yet. You will turn this terrible time to your advantage. One of the biggest difficulties some advertisers had with your image is that you were always too perfect. You had that wall of glitter around you at all times. The tide always turns in the media. Bill's little-boy-lost act will get old and then people will want to know what's happening with you. If you just get on with your life, quietly and with dignity, it will stand you in good stead for when that moment comes. Show people the humility and humanity I know you have inside."

Christina sniffed.

"There's a market for real," said Marisa with a wry smile. "I could get loads of work for an ice queen turned nice."

"Do you think I'm a nice person?" Christina asked Marisa suddenly.

"I know you are. Come here, you idiot."

And Christina practically threw herself into her agent's arms.

By the time Marisa left, Christina had to admit that she was feeling better than she had in a while.

During the time that she'd been living like an exile in the Villa Bacchante, life had been going on. The world had continued to turn. June became July became August. The grapevines didn't know that Villa Bacchante was a house in mourning for a shattered image. An hour after Marisa got in her hired car for the drive back to San Francisco, Christina finally took off the dressing gown, put on her boots and took a walk to the vineyard.

If the vineyard was all that she had, then Christina was going to make the most of it. She remembered her maternal grandmother uttering that famous saying "If God gives you lemons, make lemonade." Well, God had given Christina something better than lemons to play with at the Villa Bacchante.

She held a bunch of pinot noir grapes in her hand and marveled at their ripeness. She pulled off a single berry and crushed it, letting the juice ooze between her fingers. She licked them clean.

"Enrique!" she called to her vineyard manager, who

was tinkering with the irrigation system. "Will you come over here and explain to me exactly what needs to be done to turn these grapes into wine?"

CHAPTER 31

Madeleine's dear girlfriends, Lizzy, Jane and Helena, arrived in Champagne two days before the official start of the *vendange.* They drove down from London together in Jane's enormous Porsche Cayenne.

And so the all-female team to pick Clos Des Larmes was assembled. Not widows this time, but certainly all heartbroken. Lizzy was still pining for the physics teacher; Jane was desperate for something to do while her ex-husband took their children to Tuscany with his new girlfriend—"She's just two years older than our daughter!" Jane wailed; Helena was also in the throes of a horrible separation. From a divorce lawyer.

"Why the hell did I marry a divorce lawyer? I am stuffed," she admitted as she considered the fight to come.

"Do you think our bitterness will affect the taste of the grapes?" Lizzy asked, remembering Madeleine's father's theory that the 1914 Clos Des Larmes was magnificent because every grape was harvested with love and pride for the men who couldn't be there.

"In that case it's a shame you're not making vinegar," said Jane.

"Girls," said Madeleine, brushing aside their fears.

"Let's put some happy faces on. I promise this is going to be fun."

To be honest, it wasn't that much fun at all for the first two days that the women were holed up in Madeleine's house. There was nothing to do but wait for the CIVC's chosen date, smoke cigarettes and moan. Madeleine, meanwhile, spent all her time dashing in and out to the vines with Henri, taking measurements of the sugar levels in her grapes like a nurse tending her patients in intensive care.

"This must be what it's like waiting for a baby to be born," said Lizzy as she watched Madeleine take yet another reading. "Are we nearly there yet?"

Madeleine frowned as she read the meter. "I think we are."

Henri looked at the reading and nodded. The vines on the hill were already being picked. Only the Clos remained.

"We're off," said Madeleine at last.

There was something soothing about such heavy manual work; Madeleine had come to know that well. When you were moving through the Clos, concentrating on removing the bunches of grapes from the vine without damaging them, there was no time to think about hopeless boyfriends or ex-husbands and their new women. After a while Lizzy, whose misery didn't seem to have abated one bit since she was last in Champagne, actually started to sing. Even if it was "I Will Survive" rather than one of the traditional French songs that had filled the air during the harvests of her childhood, Madeleine was glad to hear it. She joined in on the chorus, laughing when Lizzy stopped harvesting for a moment to sing into the handles of her secateurs.

Gradually, the baskets filled with grapes. Madeleine

and Henri loaded them into the back of the Twingo and drove them down to the winery. There, the officials from the CIVC watched as the grapes were poured—whole bunches—into the press. The first pressing was carefully measured out according to the strict guidelines set by the board.

As the juice ran into the tank, Henri used a wine thief to draw some of it out for the women to taste. He poured each of the women a glass.

"*À vous,*" said Madeleine, toasting her friends.

"To a vintage year for all of us," said Lizzy.

Each pressing took four hours. The presses at Champagne Arsenault were running all night.

Eventually, four days later, all the grapes from the Clos Des Larmes were safely pressed and in the barrel. The juice that was left over after the carefully measured CIVC limits per kilo had been used was sent away to the distillery, as local law required. There it would be distilled into Marc De Champagne or Ratafia.

High on the excitement of having brought in the harvest (and possibly a little delirious from exhaustion), the girls hit the town in Reims, which was full of local vignerons in liberation mood.

The population of the relatively sedate town exploded during the harvest. The bars were suddenly as busy as the nightclub in Nicosia during high season, and just as rowdy. The air was full of laughter and chatter in accents from every corner of the world, adding to the holiday atmosphere.

Madeleine's picking crew hesitated at the door to one of the bars on the main street, the Place Drouet D'Erlon.

"Wow," said Lizzy, looking at the crowd that spilled out onto the pavement. "There is so much talent in here."

"Terrifying!" said Jane. "I need a drink!"

Inside the bar the jukebox, which lay silent most of the year, played non-stop. Unfortunately, the discs within it hadn't been changed for the past twenty years, so the music was a medley of the cheesy Europop that Lizzy had mocked so mercilessly when she and Madeleine shared a room in boarding school. That and the perennial Johnny Hallyday. Still, old as the music was, it was perfect to dance to. A couple of glasses of wine and Lizzy was on her feet, bumping hips with a blond guy from Brisbane. Soon she had dragged Madeleine and the others up to join her.

Madeleine gave a small squeak of protest as blondie from Brisbane's mate wrapped his arm around her waist and pulled her close. With his pelvis pressed against her buttocks, the Australian guy moved to the rhythm of the music. Madeleine was mortified to be dancing that way with a complete stranger but at the same time she felt excited. It was as though the sun in the vineyard had made her skin more sensitive. As the Australian leaned forward to shout his name—Dave—into Madeleine's ear, the feel of his breath on her skin made her shiver. In a good way.

"Want to get out of here?" he asked after a couple of dances.

"What?"

"Come on." Dave took Madeleine by the hand and led her out onto the street. They walked a little while and then found a dark shop doorway. Dave pulled Madeleine into the shadows and fastened his lips upon hers before she could protest. But why protest? she asked herself. As they'd danced in the bar, Madeleine had tried to guess Dave's age and put him in his early twenties, probably a decade her junior. But it didn't seem to bother him and she couldn't help but be thrilled by the firmness of his young body. Giving in to the moment, she let her hands stray beneath the hem of his T-shirt and up to his firm high pecs.

Meanwhile, Dave's tongue flickered inside Madeleine's mouth. There was no standing on ceremony with this guy. His hands roamed her body freely, squeezing her buttocks and then seeking out her breasts. He pushed her bra out of the way to better get at her nipples. Opening her shirt, he fell upon her nipples hungrily, using his tongue to great effect, then sucking hard until Madeleine moaned with desire. She pressed herself against him, loving the feeling of power she got from knowing that the erection in his pants was all because of her.

Who knew what might have happened had another student picker not interrupted them, lurching into their hideaway to vomit.

"Jeez, Pete. Your timing sucks, mate."

While Dave attended to his friend, Madeleine slipped away. The moment was definitely lost. But she returned to her friends in the bar with an unmistakable glow about her face. Her friends raised a bawdy toast.

"Where's Lizzy?" Madeleine asked.

Jane and Helena both looked in the direction of the jukebox. Lizzy leaned upon it, engaged in some tonsil hockey of her own.

Lizzy stayed out all night. When she rolled in as the others were having breakfast the following morning, her cheeks were pink with happiness.

"I broke my man drought," she said. The girls gave her a round of applause.

That evening, their last evening together, the women fell into a stupor around the dining table. Eventually Helena put her head on her folded arms and actually fell asleep with her half-eaten meal still in front of her. Madeleine raised a toast to her two conscious friends.

"Thank you. Thank you so much for being here for my first harvest. I'm so grateful you're all here today. I don't know what I would have done without you. Truly I am the luckiest woman in the world to have such wonderful friends."

"Oh, stop it," said Jane. "We only came to get a look at the Australian students with their tops off."

Lizzy dabbed at her eyes. "I came because I love you, Mads," she sniffed.

Madeleine gave her dearest friend a hug.

"Over-tired," Madeleine mouthed at Jane over the top of Lizzy's head.

"You're never coming back to London, are you?" asked Lizzy then.

"I don't think so," Madeleine admitted at last.

"Well, I miss you madly," Lizzy responded. "But I think you've made the right choice."

"Really?"

"Yes. I know you always used to say that you didn't care about this place, but it's obvious that you do. It matters to you that you make good champagne here, doesn't it?"

"I suppose it does," said Madeleine.

"And I don't think it's just about showing your father what you're capable of anymore."

"Of course not," said Madeleine. "He's dead."

"You know what I mean."

"I don't think he would have cared anyway."

"That's not true. He did love you, Mads. You know that too. Sometimes, when you and I were living together, when he called the flat and you weren't there, he and I would have a little chat. He wanted to know everything that was going on in your life. He was so proud of you. I know how it must have seemed after Georges died. Your father knew that was when things really went wrong. He wanted to bridge the gap between you but he didn't know how to begin. Lots of men are like that. I think my father only ever used the L word once in his life, but that didn't mean he didn't feel it."

Madeleine nodded.

"But anyway, it's not just about your father. This is your place now. You want to make great champagne for *you*. And I want to drink a bottle of it when I finally manage to drag some poor sucker down the aisle."

"I'll drink to that," said Madeleine.

As she went to bed that night, Madeleine recalled her conversation with Lizzy. Though she had said it with some authority—that she was going to be staying in Champagne—the strength of Madeleine's assertion had surprised even her. It was as though until that moment, she herself had not known she'd actually made her decision. But she had. Watching her grapes go into the press had felt so natural.

For the first time in a long while, Madeleine found that she was able to fall asleep quickly. She wasn't worrying about anything. The vendange had gone without a hitch and the second she tasted the raw juice, she knew that Henri was right: the grapes were more than good enough to make a Clos Des Larmes. Madeleine closed her eyes and for once she dreamed of opening a bottle of good champagne rather than drowning in it.

The following afternoon, Madeleine gave her friends a lift to the railway station in Épernay, whence they would catch a train to Paris. After waving them off, she parked her car and walked into the town to run some errands. She saw

Axel Delaflote coming out of a bank. She wasn't certain he had seen her. He was talking into his phone. For a moment, Madeleine thought about hiding. She looked about her for an open shop to dip into. But she changed her mind. Instead she walked straight by him with her head held high. She had done it. The grapes were harvested. The juice was pressed. And Henri Mason had confirmed that they would make a Clos Des Larmes.

Catching sight of Madeleine heading straight for him, Axel tried to wind up his phone conversation. He put his hand out as if to stop her. But the person on the other end of the call would not stop talking. In any case, Madeleine didn't even look at him. She kept on walking and thanked God that she'd washed her hair just that morning.

Madeleine Arsenault was a vigneronne. And this was going to be a vintage year.

CHAPTER 32

In Napa Valley, the harvest was a little later than expected. An unexpectedly cold and rainy spring had set the season back. But a warm August had made up for the slow start, and finally, in the second week of September, Enrique, the vineyard manager, was satisfied that the pinot noir had reached its peak.

The Villa Bacchante had its own pressing equipment of course. Brand-new stainless-steel vats. The very best on the market. And new French oak barrels in which to effect a first fermentation. And Christina Morgan had more than enough money to pay for a huge gang of the itinerant workers who drifted around California to bring the grapes home in a day. But Marisa had other ideas. She got out her BlackBerry and started to make calls.

A movie about a man who inherited a vineyard in France had instilled a somewhat romantic view of the grape harvest in the Hollywood mind-set. Add to that a promise of a party and soon the Villa Bacchante had no vacancies. The staff at the nearest private airport could not believe their luck as Marisa and Christina's glamorous pals booked slots to land their Gulfstreams and helicopters.

"Are you crazy?" Christina asked. "Why do they want to come up here?"

"Because they care about you," said Marisa. "And they want to help you. Let them help you, Christina. You don't have to be so self-sufficient all the time."

Enrique was only too pleased to have a bunch of actors and supermodels on his team, though he didn't expect them to last a day.

In the end, they did quite well. Only one of the models begged off mid-morning, fearing unsightly sun reddening that could be a problem for a lingerie shoot the following week. But even that girl continued to help out, assisting the housekeeper as she set up a picnic lunch in the shade of some eucalyptus trees.

When finally the first trickle of juice ran from the tap into a glass, Enrique handed the glass to Christina.

"For good luck," he said.

Christina took the glass. Her friends waited expectantly. She made a big show of properly "tasting" the pale liquid inside. She held it up to the light to see the color and clarity. She sniffed the "bouquet." Finally, she took a sip and swilled it around her mouth as though testing the balance of alcohol and acidity. "Yes," she announced finally. "That definitely tastes like grape juice."

"Hooray!" Marisa led the applause.

While Enrique and the other paid Villa Bacchante staff finished the day's business at the press, Christina led her friends back to the villa. Her housekeeper had already laid a long table with a white tablecloth and set out plates and silverware. There were big bowls of crusty bread and, for once, it seemed that no one was counting their carbs.

Just far enough away that the smoke wouldn't get into anyone's hair, a barbecue was ready to go. Christina took up the tongs herself, taking the role that once was Bill's. She placed the marinated chicken and steaks on the grill and flipped them expertly, all the while chatting to her guests and sipping a lovely pinot noir from a winery down the valley. The owner had harvested his grapes a few days earlier and was only too happy to help Christina with her own first harvest.

"Helping a fellow farmer," he told her.

"Wanting to inveigle himself into the social circle of a supermodel, more like," Marisa muttered. "You know he asked me whether I carry my agency's book in the car?"

Whatever his motivations, the guy from the farm next door looked very happy as he chatted to Paulina, a Polish model Christina had met back in New York when they were both just starting out. Paulina's career hadn't taken off in quite the same way as Christina's, but she had garnered two *Sports Illustrated* swimsuit editions before she married the hedge-fund manager who was now her ex-husband.

Paulina was very much in demand. When Christina's winemaking neighbor skipped off to find her a drink, Ronald Ginsburg, who had flown in that day to offer Christina his support, took his place.

"I'm here to keep an eye on my investment," Ronald explained to Paulina. "I have to make sure Christina's wine is tip-top. I'm backing her in a wager and my reputation is at stake."

"Your reputation?" Paulina was confused.

"Yes," said Ronald.

Paulina looked at him blankly.

"As a wine critic," said Ronald, realizing with a sinking feeling that she didn't know who he was. Neither did she look that impressed.

"That's nice," she said, as she accepted her drink from Christina's neighbor.

Ronald got up and went in search of easier prey.

Another model manqué, Michelle, an English girl who had married a Hollywood producer, was helping Christina with the barbecue.

"Do you remember that interview in the *New York Times* where you said that modeling is hard work?" Michelle asked. Christina cringed at the memory. That throwaway comment had followed her around like Linda Evangelista's infamous assertion that she didn't get out of bed for less than $10,000 a day.

"Well," Michelle continued. "I used to agree with you until today. We had no idea!" she added with a laugh. "Felt good though."

Everyone seemed very pleased with the way the day had gone. When Enrique returned, Christina proposed a toast.

"To the man who really knows what he's doing!"

Enrique accepted his employer's praise shyly and was persuaded to stay for a glass of wine and a steak. Three hours later, Enrique was still there and leading the dancing.

One of the guys had retrieved an acoustic guitar from

the back of his Porsche and was making a pretty good job of a Gypsy Kings cover. When he got tired of playing, Marisa put some dance tunes on the garden stereo. Christina took off her apron and joined Enrique for a turn around the courtyard. Soon everybody was on their feet, suddenly finding new energy.

"I am having the best time of my life," was the frequent refrain.

"May I have this dance?"

Christina found herself passed from Enrique into the open arms of Greg Stroud.

"Greg." Christina smiled up at her old friend. "I'm so glad you're still here. I can't believe I haven't had a chance to talk to you all day."

"You've been busy," Greg acknowledged. "But I have you now."

He whirled her around dramatically. Christina gave a little shriek, though she knew, somehow, that Greg was not the kind of guy who would drop her.

Regaining her balance, Christina wrapped her arms around Greg's neck and they continued to sway to the music.

"I haven't seen you in..."

"Five years," said Greg.

"Is it that long?"

Christina was surprised and slightly embarrassed, wondering if the long gap was somehow her fault. There had been a time in her life when she saw Greg Stroud just about every day. They'd both been living in New York at the time. She was just starting out as a model, he in TV.

Greg was dating Christina's roommate, Angelica, a model from the Czech Republic. Greg had married the girl but—green card in hand—she'd moved on to an investment banker. In his grief, Greg had left New York for

Los Angeles, buried himself in work and rocketed to the top of a cable network.

They'd been good friends back in the day, though. When Greg heard that Angelica was sleeping with someone else, it was Christina he came to for consolation.

Over a decade later Christina remembered that night in her apartment very well. She remembered Greg's face, drawn and tired. He hadn't slept for a couple of days. Angelica had confirmed the rumor via telephone. She was in Milan. Greg was in Helsinki. Greg had offered to fly to Italy to talk things through. Angelica said there was no point. She was flying directly to St. Tropez to join her new lover. So Greg flew back to New York and drove straight from the airport to Christina's apartment.

Christina tried hard to be sympathetic, but what she really wanted to do was dance around the apartment. The thought of Greg without Angelica was too wonderful.

Greg got his divorce. But a month after it came through, he was dating another Czech model. Christina decided that she simply wasn't Greg's type and started dating Rocky Neel instead.

Still, she couldn't help feeling a girlish flicker of pleasure when Greg told her she was looking great.

They danced to three songs before Greg said, "I've got to go. It's way past my bedtime and I have to fly to LA first thing."

Christina planted a kiss on his cheek before she let her arms drop from around his neck.

"Promise you won't leave it so long next time," she said.

"Just try and keep me away," said Greg. He departed with a wink.

Eventually the flames in the fire pit began to die down. Somewhere in the distance, a coyote yipped, as if to say

"Shut up." Enrique retrieved his hat and muttered something about another early start. Those guests who had homes to go to did. Those that were staying at the villa retired to their rooms.

And so the longest working day in Christina Morgan's life was over. She smiled to herself as she remembered the conversation by the barbecue that night. Had she really said that modeling was hard work? She'd had no idea. Getting up before dawn, harvesting a vineyard and getting the grapes into the press before nightfall—that was hard work. And boy could she feel it in her muscles. But what a great day. She hadn't realized quite how many good friends she had.

With her guests safely in their bedrooms, Christina went upstairs to her own suite. She hadn't had any involvement in the design of the Villa Bacchante; Bill's PA, Teak, had overseen the renovations. By the time Christina arrived on the scene, the place was almost finished. Including the bathroom off the master bedroom suite. It was fabulous. Every time she walked in Christina offered her silent thanks to the young PA who had irritated her so much during her short-lived marriage.

It was more like a miniature spa than a bathroom. The enormous tub could fit six ("supermodels," as Bill had bragged) but to Christina there was no greater luxury than having the place to herself.

She turned on the water while she took off her makeup at the double basin. Not that there was much makeup left: more smudges of earth and smears of dried grape. But Christina wasn't as bothered as she might have been once upon a time. The face looking back at her was tired but radiant. Happy. She picked a few stray fragments of leaf and twig from her hair and pinned it up out of the way.

The bath filled quickly. The scent of Christina's

favorite bath oil rose up from the steaming water. She shrugged off her clothes, leaving them in a pile where they fell, and stepped into the tub.

This is true luxury, Christina thought as she slid down so that the water covered her shoulders. The bath oil that shimmered on the water's surface coated her tanned skin with a glitter. She tipped her head back against a folded towel and closed her eyes. Naturally, Bill had fitted the bathroom with a fabulous stereo. The soft sound of a jazz band Christina had seen in New Orleans drifted from eight carefully positioned speakers.

For a while, she just lay there, remembering the harvest with tired pleasure. Feeling so good that she began to worry she might actually fall asleep in the water, she reached for the washcloth on the side of the tub. With long gliding strokes she began to clean away the day. She smoothed the washcloth over her shoulders, down her elegant arms, across her toned, flat stomach and strong tanned legs.

Then, unbidden, a memory of another bathtub entered her mind. Several years earlier. Maybe even more than fifteen. This bathtub was in London. In a flashy hotel. She was just starting out as a model. She was dating Rocky Neel. He'd picked her out of her modeling agency's look book and asked for her number. He had an album at the top of the charts. Christina was only too happy to go for dinner.

A week or so later, he invited her to join him on a gig. The band was playing as part of some big benefit at the Albert Hall. Did she want to go to London?

Of course she did. Christina had never been to London. Rocky flew her there first class. And while he practiced for the benefit, she saw the sights. And made the most of his suite in a Park Lane hotel.

The bath in that hotel was almost as big as this one. A

rarity, apparently, for England. With an hour alone to kill before the rock star took her out to dinner, Christina ran herself a bath. And discovered the Jacuzzi jets.

The soundtrack to that bath wasn't soft jazz. It was the hard rock that had taken her lover from obscurity in the west of England to international fame. But even at full volume the thumping bass and screaming guitars were drowned out by the sound of the Jacuzzi jets.

They were ridiculously powerful. As Christina tried to lay back and relax in the bath, the jets pummeled her body like a dozen tiny fists. She shifted her position to spare a small bruise on one of her thighs—she'd walked into the edge of a table after one too many Southern Comforts. And it was in this new position, with her knees slightly drawn up and to one side, that she found an altogether more pleasurable way to be massaged.

"Oh!" she gasped involuntarily. The jet that had been pounding on her bruise was now playing right between her legs. Christina felt a small furtive shiver as she shifted once more so that the jet was suddenly right against her clitoris. The results were instantaneous. Christina felt such a rush of blood to that part of her body, she thought she might faint. She reached out for the handles on the side of the tub and forced herself to remain in the same position though the intensity of sensation could drive her insane.

"Oh...my...God..."

Christina was just about ready to pass out when the jets stopped.

"Shit."

Disappointed, she sat up. The water eddied to calm. Christina looked down at her body. Her breastbone was flushed. But not just with the heat. Her nipples were hard and pink. Christina pressed the Jacuzzi button again.

This time, there was no messing around. Christina got herself straight into position. She gasped as the jet massaged her closer to ecstasy. She reached down and parted her labia so that her clitoris was totally exposed. She closed her eyes and thought about her rock star lover. Though even his legendary tongue couldn't work this fast, this firmly.

She slipped a couple of fingers inside herself. And soon she felt the first harbingers of an orgasm as the muscles of her vagina contracted around her fingers. A pulsating rhythm. Gentle at first but gathering speed and strength. Meanwhile Christina's legs began to shake. Stars danced behind her eyelids. The sound of hot blood pumping filled her head as her heart beat faster.

Finally her orgasm overtook her. She was drowning in her own excitement. Shuddering and moaning as sensations rushed from one end of her body to the other. Finally, she let out a peal of exultant laughter.

Then she opened her eyes.

Her lover was standing at the bathroom door. He leaned against the frame. Arms folded.

"Having fun?" he asked.

Christina sat up as quickly as she could. But there was no disguising what she had been up to. There were bubbles all over the bathroom floor. The entire room was soaked.

"I've ruined the bathroom," said Christina.

Rocky just laughed. "Beats throwing the television out the window." He unzipped his trousers to reveal an impressive hard-on. "Can I join you in there?"

Over fifteen years later, in her bathtub at Villa Bacchante, Christina emerged from the bubbles feeling slightly shy but very, very refreshed. Was it the harvest that had transformed her? Regardless of the cause, for the first time since she found out about Bill's indiscretion with that call girl, Christina had felt aroused. And happy. And it was good. Maybe it was time to get out there again.

CHAPTER 33

Froggy Bottom had never looked lovelier. The vines had full leaf coverage now and the grapes were growing fat. Set against the blue of the sky, the green of the vines was like the green in a child's drawing. Vibrant. As if each leaf were lit from the inside. But all was not well. As the date of the harvest approached, so too did the date of Kelly's rave.

It got out of control quickly. By the time Guy was able to convince Hilarian that Kelly was serious, news of the planned event was already out on the Internet.

"You've got to stop her," Guy told Hilarian. "Surely the trustees can kick her out."

Hilarian had no doubt that they would, given half a chance. Just that week he'd traveled to Slough for a meeting with Reginald and Georgina at the offices of Reginald's accountancy firm. The legitimate Mollison children were squabbling over the will, and somehow Reginald had heard about Kelly's drunken debacle at the wine fair. He wanted to cut Kelly's allowance to teach her a lesson. Hilarian had argued long and hard to give the girl some leeway.

"If we treat her like a child, she'll act like one," said Hilarian.

"Surely the point is that she's already acting like one," said Georgina smugly.

Hilarian didn't fancy seeing that smug look again.

It was quite a feat he'd pulled off that afternoon, making sure that Kelly got her whole allowance that month. And now he had to deal with Guy's anguish too. He tried to calm him down. Hilarian still hoped that Kelly would lose interest in her plans before they came to fruition.

"I'm sure there is some way we can come to a compromise—" he began.

"Compromise!" Guy wailed. "I can't compromise with my grapes. If Kelly's rave goes ahead, everything will be ruined. Froggy Bottom will be finished."

Hilarian crossed the courtyard in a grim mood. He found Kelly lounging in the sitting room with some of her friends. A fire was blazing in the inglenook. Hilarian thought he recognized one of Dougal's eighteenth-century dining chairs among the kindling.

"A word?" He beckoned Kelly into the kitchen. She rolled her eyes at her friends but followed him all the same.

Half an hour later, Hilarian let himself out of the farmhouse and stood in the courtyard looking pensive. Watching from the window Guy assumed the worst. Indeed, Hilarian didn't have any good news.

"It seems we're too late," said Hilarian. "Five hundred people have already registered their interest on the website."

"So? That doesn't mean anything. It still can't go ahead. What did you say to her?"

"There wasn't much I could say," said Hilarian. "She was feeling rather belligerent."

Guy punched the sofa. "So you're letting her go ahead with it? You've got to tell the other trustees and get her written out of the will. Get her out of here, Hilarian. She's ruining this vineyard. It's either her or me."

Hilarian just shook his head. "Calm down, Guy. I said I would come up with something and I will but I'm not going to tell the other trustees. We don't want them to come down here and start interfering. It won't just be Kelly they try to get rid of, believe me. They'd love an excuse to take this place out of my care, and if they take over the administration of Froggy Bottom, you won't find them anywhere near so understanding and accommodating of your plans."

"What does it matter?" Guy said dramatically. "If the alternative is that all my hard work is ruined anyway."

"Get your wallet," said Hilarian. "We're going into Little Bottom, to the Dragon's Head."

"I don't need a drink," said Guy.

"I know. But there's someone I think you should meet. Bring a case of the 2007."

A month later, the morning of the rave arrived.

Hearing a car horn, Kelly stirred beneath the duvet. Wiping her sleep-crusted eyes, she knelt up on her bed and looked out through her window at the farmyard below. She saw Gina getting out of a van. Gina's brother, Antony, and another three girls (he always traveled with a harem) climbed out after her. Kelly assumed the van was full of Antony's DJ equipment. So far so good. But then Guy appeared. He was wearing those hideous dungarees and carrying a big pair of secateurs. Hilarian followed.

"Oh God," thought Kelly, imagining a row that ended with somebody getting their nuts cut off. She saw Guy stride across to Antony and mouth something at him. Kelly couldn't hear what was being said but she felt certain from the way Guy had his chest puffed out that it was aggressive. Antony was bigger than Guy by a good five inches but he was nodding warily. Guy carried on talking, waving his arms and the secateurs about. He was getting in Antony's face. Hilarian stepped forward and put his hand on Guy's shoulder. Kelly's only champion looked serious as he too addressed Antony. Kelly felt her heart beat faster as the adrenaline began to rush.

"Shit."

Kelly forced herself to get up. She quickly swapped her pajama bottoms for jeans. She had to get downstairs and tell Guy and Hilarian to back off. This was her place and if she wanted to have a party she would. The bloody grapes could rot for all she cared.

"For fuck's sake, Guy," she started loudly as she stormed out of the house in her fluffy slippers, stepping in a puddle en route. "Who the fuck do you think you are? We're having a party, whether you like it or not. You can come if you want to. But if you don't want to, you can just fuck off back to your shed. This is my sodding vineyard."

Guy, Gina, Antony and the three girls all stared.

"Calm down, Kelly," said Hilarian.

"Yeah, babe," said Antony. "Chill out."

Kelly briefly glanced at Antony in confusion but soon she was back on her rant. "You're on my back all the fucking time," she shouted at Guy. "And you," she rounded on Hilarian, "you're not much better. Always treating me like I'm some kind of kid. I'm a grown adult and I do what I want. What I want to do is have a party. I don't give a shit about the grapes."

"We do," said one of the girls suddenly. "We're going to help pick them. It'll be great."

"Good girl," said Hilarian.

"Yeah. It's, like, something I've always wanted to do," said another one. "I've seen it on TV loads of times."

"If we all pitch in," said Hilarian, "we could get it done in a couple of days. And it will be fun, I promise you. I'm glad you young people are seeing sense."

The girls nodded.

"I want to jump up and down on the grapes in my bare feet!" said the third girl. Kelly guessed she was already stoned.

"I'm afraid I'll have to disappoint you there," said Guy. "We've got machinery to do the pressing nowadays."

"Have you gone mad?" Kelly stared at Antony's girlfriends. "Come on. Let's start unloading the stuff."

"The all-nighter's not happening, Kelly," said Hilarian.

"It's for the best," Antony agreed. "Seriously." Antony looked nervously toward the track into Froggy Bottom. Kelly followed his gaze and saw a police car making slow progress down toward the farm.

"What's happening? What are you talking about?" said Kelly.

"Get your boots on," said Gina, who was looking at Guy with something approaching love. "We're harvesting grapes."

What Kelly didn't know at that point was that Hilarian's friend and fellow drinker at the Dragon's Head was the local chief constable. A case of wine and a little negotiation and a police blockade had been set up to turn all prospective ravers back toward Brighton, but only after a couple of crucial carloads had been allowed through. Gina, Antony and his harem had been allowed to evade arrest under the Criminal Justice and Public Order Act on the condition that they, and the next twenty people to arrive would hand themselves over to Guy to form part of a harvesting crew instead.

It was an easy choice. Antony would have agreed to

just about anything to stop the police searching his van, which was carrying not only his speakers but a considerable amount of ecstasy and cocaine that he had intended to sell that night. Antony already had a criminal record. One more arrest and he was going inside.

"You made the right decision," Hilarian assured him. "A boy as pretty as you does *not* want to end up in jail."

"OK, everybody." Guy surveyed his team. While Kelly was getting ready for a day outside—it still involved full makeup—another two carloads of people had arrived. Altogether there were fifteen in Guy's makeshift work-gang now. Everyone was surprisingly eager. "This is how we're going to do it," Guy told them. "I want you to split yourselves into teams of three. Each team will work a row. Now, we're not going to pick every single bunch of grapes you find out there today. We're making quality wine here, not plonk."

His team laughed politely.

"So, before you remove a bunch from the vine, I want you to examine it. We want only the grapes that are properly ripened. No green bunches. But no moldy grapes either. Leave those on the ground for the birds. Come and look at this."

Guy had them gather round and look at the bunch of perfect grapes he held in his hand. "This is what we're looking for."

The teams divided up. Gina and Antony joined Guy. Eventually Kelly came out of the house. She was wearing hot pants. Antony gave a low whistle.

"Fantastic," he said.

Guy just shook his head. "You might want to put your jeans back on," he told her. "You'll get scratched to death by the baskets."

Kelly stomped back into the house.

When she emerged, half an hour later, Guy was the only person left in the courtyard. Everyone else was already up in the vines.

"I guess this means you're on my team," said Guy. "No slacking."

It was hard work and halfway through the day, Guy's happy harvesting team started to wonder whether a day in the cells might have been preferable to a day in the vineyards, but they kept at it. Considering Guy's poor opinion of Kelly's friends, he was impressed to see how well they worked together. The smaller members of each team removed the grapes from the vine while the big lads, many of whom worked as roadies, made easy work of bringing the loaded buckets down to the winery, where they went through another check before they were tipped into the press.

Supplemented by the pickers Guy always used, the new team brought in the harvest in record time.

At sunset, the picking gang retired but it was still a beautiful evening and no one wanted to go home.

While Guy finished supervising the pressing of that day's grapes, Hilarian organized some of the helpers to build a bonfire with a pile of debris Guy had been collecting all summer. Antony set up a couple of his decks in Kelly's sitting room and opened the French doors so that the music could be heard in the little garden that backed onto the vineyard itself.

It was a mellow sort of night. Antony chose music to reflect that mood, no thumping beats but the kind of ambient music they played in chill-out rooms. The perfect soundtrack for a setting sun.

Meanwhile, Gina and a couple of other girls set up the barbecue. There was more than enough food, since they had been planning to cater for so many more. One of the guys also had a carload of beer to go with the burgers, but, interestingly, not one of the pickers wanted beer that night. Everyone wanted to drink Froggy Bottom.

When Guy finally emerged from the winery, Hilarian led a cheer.

"I have had one of the best days of my life," said Gina, throwing her arms around Guy's neck and giving him a kiss. It was a sentiment that was repeated all over Froggy Bottom. Except for Kelly...

Hilarian caught up with Kelly while Guy led the rest of the crew in a South African drinking game. She was sitting a little way off from the others, nursing a plastic cup of white wine and a half-eaten burger.

"We need to talk," said Hilarian.

Kelly blushed automatically in expectation of a telling-off.

"Shall we take a walk?"

Kelly followed Hilarian out of the kitchen garden. They walked up through the vineyard to a rickety old bench that had a view across the vines to the farmhouse. They sat and looked down on the partygoers, silhouetted by the light of the bonfire as they danced like pagans involved in some ancient ritual. Kelly wrapped her arms around her body, partly because she was cold and partly, subconsciously, because she felt very small all of a sudden. Stupid too. Ashamed. Kelly and Hilarian sat in silence for a moment or two while Kelly lit a cigarette and took a few anxious puffs. Hilarian spoke first.

"Today very nearly ended in disaster. I think you know how serious things could have got if you and your friends had insisted on having your rave."

Kelly nodded.

"As it is, they avoided arrest and the grapes are all safely harvested. Disaster averted. But I don't want to have to call in favors again like I did today. Have you got any idea how much I had to fork out to get the police to set up that road-block to turn your punters away? It could have got nasty. Thank God you hadn't already taken their money."

"I'm sorry."

"I can't keep bailing you out."

"You didn't have to—" Kelly began.

Hilarian shook his head. "It's not just today. I've been doing all I can to keep you on the right side of the trustees until now. Every time I turn up in Slough for a meeting, they've got some new reason to stop your allowance. There's no way around it, Kelly. Together with me, those two old duffers are in charge of what happens here for the next four and a half years. Now, you can turn the next four and a half years into a struggle—a battle at every turn—or you can humor the trustees. The more you show that you can take responsibility for what goes on here, the less reason they will have to interfere."

Kelly squirmed.

"I for one want you to be able to take over the reins here at Froggy Bottom as soon as you're able. I think you've got the ability and I think you're interested in what goes on here, but for some reason you're resisting. It's as if you don't think it's cool to want to take the vineyards seriously. Well, if you're worried about what your mates might think, I hope today has shown you that they think making wine is great fun."

Kelly gazed down at the people dancing around the fire. She'd spent much of the day worrying that Gina, her brother and all their mates would be furious with her for the cancellation of the all-nighter, but they certainly seemed to be having a good time right then.

"You could have something truly wonderful here," Hilarian concluded. "But you have to make an effort. What's keeping you from mucking in?"

"What's the point? It just doesn't feel like it's mine. What with the trustees always interfering and the Mollisons still going over the will and trying to get me kicked out. They're going to get it back before my five years are up anyway."

"No, they're not. Your father named you as his child before he died. I can't see any way they can get their hands on this place. The Mollisons will just have to get used to it."

"It's not just that. How do you think it feels that they want to get rid of me so badly? They're supposed to be my brother and sister and they won't even see me."

"You're not missing much," Hilarian assured her.

"All I ever wanted was a proper family but it's like someone up there decided I don't deserve one. Mum wanted to get rid of me. The Mollisons want me gone. I don't belong here. I feel like I don't belong anywhere," she added in a sudden burst of angst.

"Oh, Kelly!" Hilarian wrapped his arm around her. "Of course you belong here. Your father wanted you to have this land."

"I didn't even know him."

"Well, this is how you can know him. By being here. By giving your inheritance a chance to change your life for the better. We all want that for you. Me, Guy, even the crusty old trustees."

Kelly laid her head on Hilarian's shoulder.

"Just think," said Hilarian, squeezing her tight. "In less than five years' time, you could be drinking your own wine, made from the grapes we picked here today. It'll be fantastic wine and it will win the *Vinifera* wager."

"Do you really believe that?"

"I really do. But only if you start believing that this is where you belong and act accordingly. Take this place seriously. A hundred thousand pound's worth of seriously." He winked.

"OK," said Kelly: "I will."

The following Sunday, while Kelly accompanied Guy and Hilarian to the harvest festival at the local church of St. Jude's, Madeleine Arsenault felt a sudden urge to go into the cathedral at Reims. She crossed herself automatically as she stepped into the cool austere darkness of the building, rebuilt by Rockefeller after the devastation of World War II exactly as it had been in Norman times.

Without quite knowing why, Madeleine went to the chapel of St. Teresa and lit two candles. One for herself and one for her brother, Georges.

"I wish you could be here, bro," she murmured over his candle, then she muttered a little prayer of thanks for a harvest successfully completed.

Outside, a group of tourists gathered in the doorway, taking souvenir snaps of the most famous of all the cathedral's statues: the smiling angel of Reims. Madeleine looked up at the angel as she passed on her way out. It was as though the angel were smiling down upon Madeleine alone.

In California, Christina walked to the top of her vineyards and remembered her own harvest weekend. The valley before her was balmy, warm and peaceful. If there is a God, Christina thought, then he probably lives out here.

PART TWO

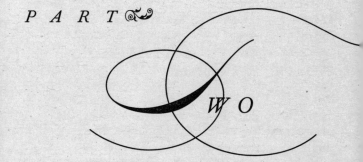

CHAPTER 34

March. All over Champagne, the producers eagerly awaited the moment when the first of the previous year's still wine could be taken from barrel, blended and bottled, wherein the real magic would start.

Mathieu Randon and Odile Levert drove from Domaine Randon's head office in Paris to the winery near Épernay in Randon's sleek black Mercedes Benz. Odile could tell Randon was tense. Nervous almost. She couldn't help but admire that he took his wine so seriously considering that Maison Randon represented such a small part of his luxury goods empire these days.

"Maison Randon will always be the most important part of my business. It's about family pride," he explained when she commented as such.

Odile nodded. She knew the Randons had been in Champagne for generations but it was hard to imagine that Mathieu Randon was ever part of anyone's family. He was one of those men who seemed to have appeared like a toadstool, popping up in the boardroom overnight fully formed and already white-haired. She could not picture him as a tousle-haired toddler, chasing the family dog up and down the rows of vines while his father and mother set about pruning. Or as a seven-year-old helping with the picking. Or even as a surly teen tipping grapes into the press. She couldn't even imagine Randon without a tie on.

"Your opinion is very important to me, Odile," he told her. "I want you to know that I trust your judgment on champagne above anyone else's. Except my own," he added with a half smile.

"Of course," said Odile. "But I don't know why you are so concerned. I don't anticipate any problems. Axel Delaflote is a very competent man and your cellar master, Jean-Christophe, is one of the finest I've ever encountered."

"He should be," said Randon. Randon had paid a small fortune to tempt him away from one of the other big houses, at Axel's recommendation.

When they arrived at Maison Randon, Axel Delaflote was already waiting on the steps of the large house that had once been the Randon family home but which now housed the company's offices and Axel's own apartment.

"Are they ready for us?" Randon asked.

"Of course," said Axel. He had been waiting for Randon and Odile's arrival all morning.

"I'm sorry we're a little late," said Odile. "I'm afraid it's my fault. I had to finish my column for *Vinifera*."

Axel smiled tightly. Odile Levert was one of the few people for whom Randon would wait. Axel wasn't sure he trusted her. He knew she didn't like him. Whenever they were in the same room, they circled each other like a pair of cats. Axel knew that Odile had spent a lot of time with Madeleine Arsenault, as her champion for the *Vinifera* competition. He wondered if Madeleine ever talked about him.

The trio walked to the winery. It was intoxicating to be in Randon's presence. Who could not be impressed by the way his staff reacted whenever he was around? They stopped their chattering and practically genuflected as the master strode by. The winery was spotless. The stainless-steel vats were perfectly burnished. The concrete floor was remarkably dry.

Jean-Christophe was waiting for them by the enormous barrels that held the still wine from Randon's grand cru vineyards at Verzenay and Avize. A long table had been laid with a pure white tablecloth. The glasses—Riedel's own special design for Maison Randon—were polished and ready. Sitting next to them was a plate of white bread for the purpose of cleansing the palate.

It's often said that the magic of champagne comes at the blending stage, when wine from previous vintages is mixed with the new wine to create the house style. However, the still wines they were to taste that day would not be blended before they were bottled. Each of the vats contained juice from the grapes of a single vineyard. The delight of the champagne they became would be in the unique expression of each of those vineyards. Ultimate terroir.

As Randon watched, Jean-Christophe opened the tap at the bottom of the vat marked "Verzenay" and allowed a trickle to flow into his glass. He made a great show of holding the resulting liquid up to the pale spring sunshine. The great doors to the winery had been thrown open to allow in as much light as possible for the purpose of examining the color and clarity of the wine.

Then Jean-Christophe took a sniff and a slurp. He held the wine in the cup of his tongue, aerating it. Then he paused, as though waiting for a chemical reaction to take place in his mouth. At last, he spat into the silver spittoon and nodded. He was pleased with what he'd tasted.

With much theatricality, he filled three more glasses. One each for Randon, Axel and Odile.

"I think you'll find this acceptable," said Jean-

Christophe with the air of a man who knows that he's making an understatement.

They all nosed their glasses. Odile took the first sip. She tried hard not to react at once. She wanted a moment to get the words exactly right. But Randon was watching her closely, studying her for micro-expressions that might reveal her true first impression. And he caught one.

"It's not right," said Randon. Without even bothering to taste his own, he threw his wineglass on to the floor. It shattered on the concrete, splattering wine and shards of glass all over Jean-Christophe. The cellar master jumped back against the barrel as though Randon had swung a punch at him. Odile felt something—possibly glass—hit her stockinged leg, but she tried to remain still. She didn't even look down to see if she was bleeding.

Axel stepped forward. He tried to calm the situation down. He held his own glass out to Randon.

"I think this is pretty good."

"You've been in this business five minutes, Delaflote. Five minutes. I don't want to know what you think. Odile, I'll give you a ride back to town."

Randon turned and walked out of the winery.

On the drive back to Paris, Randon made arrangements for the termination of Jean-Christophe's employment. Odile heard every word of his conversation with Axel Delaflote. She looked out the window. There was no point trying to reason with him. The only way to stay within Randon's charmed inner circle was to stay quiet. And it was very important to Odile that she didn't lose her place in the sun. Not yet.

CHAPTER 35

❧

A day later, having spent yet another hour unsuccessfully arguing with Randon for Jean-Christophe's retention as the cellar master at Maison Randon, Axel sat alone in his office with his head in his hands. The red lights on the telephone in front of him flickered on and off with the regularity of brake lights in a traffic jam as his assistant, Sabine, tried to connect him to various callers, but Axel didn't pick up. Eventually, Sabine poked her head around the door.

"You OK?" she dared to ask.

"Of course I'm OK," Axel snapped.

"It's just that you're not picking up. Is your phone working?"

"Just hold my calls for an hour."

So far, Axel's promotion to the head of Maison Randon had been the very definition of a mixed blessing. On the one hand, it was everything he had ever wanted. He was heading up one of the most famous champagne houses in the world. There were some fabulous perks. People took him seriously now. He could get reservations in any restaurant in Paris, London, New York. Anywhere. As he had promised that night in the car, Randon had installed Axel in a wonderful apartment near the Domaine Randon headquarters in Paris, complete with antique furniture and the kind of paintings that museums clamored to get on loan. There was also the apartment in the house in Champagne, of course, overlooking the vineyards, with a live-in housekeeper and chef, so that Axel could entertain company guests in style.

The downside was that Axel knew he had become the definition of a company man. He was expected to be available to his boss at all times. Most people at Axel's level expect to have to take their work home on occasion, but Randon really took advantage of the concept of 24/7 availability. There were frequent calls in the middle of the night. Axel sometimes wondered if Randon ever slept or if he was, as some of his less reverent employees suggested, a vampire.

And now this. Randon's explosive rage in the winery had unnerved Axel far more than he dared reveal. Axel had expected that Randon would calm down overnight and agree with Axel's position that the still wine from the Verzenay vineyards was perfectly good and Jean-Christophe should be kept on. But Randon was implacable. He refused to revise his opinion that Jean-Christophe had embarrassed Maison Randon by presenting mediocre wine to such an esteemed guest as Odile Levert. Jean-Christophe had to go. Axel had to swing the hatchet.

"But his contract—" Axel tried one last time.

"Will be terminated," said Randon simply before he put down the phone.

Eventually, Axel could stand to be in his office no longer. Informing Sabine that she should tell callers he was down in the *crayères* and thus could not be contacted on his mobile, he headed out.

But Axel didn't go down into the caves. He walked out of the Maison Randon compound and kept walking, hoping that some exercise might clear his head. An hour later, he found himself up on the hill, standing right by the Arsenault vineyards. There was no one up there. Neither in Madeleine's vineyards nor as far as Axel could see in either direction. The rows of vines didn't look like anything much at this time of year, just gray sticks, so harshly pruned one might fear they would never bud and blossom again. But Axel was remembering a time when the vines looked very different. He remembered Madeleine in her cut off shorts, a smudge of dirt on her face somehow adding to her sexiness. Axel felt a familiar twitch in his groin at the thought of Madeleine beneath the tree after their picnic.

If only he could walk down into Le Vezy, knock on the door of Madeleine's house and have her take him in. What he wanted most of all right then was the distraction of her arms around him. Her soft white skin naked against his. Of course, that wasn't going to happen. Madeleine hadn't spoken a word to Axel since the London wine fair. Axel shoved his hands in his pockets and sighed as he began the walk back to his office.

But the desire that had been aroused by thoughts of Madeleine was still with him when he got to Maison Randon and discovered, thankfully, that everyone else had already gone home for the night and there was nothing he could do before morning. Axel still needed some kind of stress relief.

There was certainly, as Randon had joked that first night they dined together, no time for love in Axel's life anymore and that was frustrating. Axel was used to spending time in the company of women. Women drifted across his path far more frequently now, but there was never time to take them out and these weren't the kind of girls who would be happy to read in bed while Axel tinkered with a spreadsheet on his laptop. Still, he craved the touch of a woman's hands.

He had always understood the appeal of prostitutes. The bliss of human interaction without the complications of a relationship. Lately the idea crossed his mind more frequently. There didn't seem to be any reason why not.

So Axel got into his car and drove to Reims. He found himself by the old market by the Pont De Mars. There were a couple of girls there, smoking cigarettes and chatting. They were too cold to make much effort to display their wares that night. Axel had to wind his window down and lean out before either girl even noticed he was looking for some company.

The blond one got up first. She sauntered across, her hands thrust deep in her pockets against the cold, though she was wearing a mini-skirt and no tights. Axel shook his head and motioned with his chin toward the other girl, a brunette. The blonde shrugged and headed back to the wall.

The brunette took a long drag on her cigarette and exhaled as she leaned in through the car window to discuss terms. The smoke made Axel feel a little nauseous but the girl was pretty, in a cheap sort of way. Axel stretched across to open the passenger door and the girl climbed in.

"My name is Claire," she said.

Axel nodded. He didn't need to tell her his name.

"I know somewhere we can go. Take a left past Le Boulingrin."

As they passed, Axel glanced at the brasserie where he had spent many a happy evening, back when life was much less complicated. The warmth of the light spilling out onto the pavement and the laughter of the people sitting in the window seats contrasted starkly with how he felt right then.

Claire had him turn the car into a dark street with a big industrial unit on one side and some abandoned buildings on the other.

"The cops never come down here," she explained. "No residents to make a complaint. Just oral, yes?"

Axel nodded again. He pushed his seat back to give her room and reclined it for his own pleasure. While Claire dipped her head to his lap, Axel let his head loll to one side and gazed sightlessly out the window, trying to think of nothing but Claire's mouth, warm and wet, around his cock. But the stress that had dogged him all day kept pulling him back to a harsher reality. And soon he was looking at the faded words painted below the first-floor windows of the abandoned building he had pulled up beside. "Champagne Arnaud Bernard." Axel had never heard of the marque. What had become of it? What had become of Arnaud Bernard himself? Did anyone remember him? Would anyone remember Axel after he was dead? He had no wife. He had no family. No real friends. He had nothing but his work.

Was this what Stefan Urban meant when he cleared out his desk and announced to Axel as they passed in the corridor, "It's you that I feel sorry for. I feel like Atlas handing over the heavens."

Claire raised her head and looked at Axel with an expression of annoyance. She clearly hadn't expected to have to work quite so hard for her money.

"I'm sorry," said Axel, pushing her away from his softening penis. "I'll drive you back to where I picked you up. This hasn't happened to me before."

"That's what they all say," said Claire.

Axel dropped Claire off at the deserted market. Her friend, the other girl, was still there, along with a guy who Axel could only assume was their pimp. He'd seen him around Reims before. A big guy with a shaved head and a scar that ran right down the side of his face, leaving his left eye permanently closed.

As Axel's car drew near, the pimp stepped forward. Axel couldn't get away quickly enough. He drove back to

Maison Randon. The house was empty. The housekeeper was spending the night with her boyfriend in Épernay. Axel was glad to be alone. He poured himself a glass of red wine and slumped into a chair, but before he could take a sip, his telephone rang. It was Randon.

"Come straight to Paris," he said. "Meet me at Eponine. Eleven o'clock."

Axel knew he didn't have a choice. He headed for the train station.

Axel and Randon talked business over dinner but as Randon didn't mention the termination of Jean-Christophe's job again, Axel allowed himself to think he'd got away with it. Perhaps Jean-Christophe had a reprieve.

There were moments, however, when Axel felt a twinge of panic. Such as when Randon asked him how he was enjoying living at the Randon apartment in the sixteenth arrondissement.

"Be a shame to have to leave it," Randon said.

Axel could only nod. "I like being there very much."

Axel was relieved when the waiters brought coffee and the end of dinner loomed. He couldn't wait to get out of the restaurant and back to the relative safety of his Paris flat.

"It's been a lovely evening," said Axel, after Randon settled the bill.

"What are you talking about, Delaflote? It's far from over."

Axel felt cold.

"We're going to a party," said Randon.

They climbed into Randon's black limousine and glided through the streets of Paris toward an area that Axel didn't know.

"What are your vices, Axel?" Randon asked him as they traveled through the dark. "And you can't say champagne," he added, with an almost avuncular wag of the finger. "In our world, champagne is not a vice."

"Of course."

"Then?"

Axel shrugged. "I don't know."

"Drugs? Girls?"

Axel shook his head.

"Boys?" Randon ventured.

"No. I mean . . . no. Of course not."

"Come on, Axel. There must be something. You can tell me. And it will be strictly between us. We're out of the office now. I'm not going to pass on your answer to the human resources department."

Axel laughed nervously.

"Axel, if you can't express your vices, what chance do you have of them ever being fulfilled? If you tell me that you like fat girls with big muffs, I may well be able to find one for you. If you don't tell me, you'll never know what I can do. And one thing I like to do for my friends is cater to their needs."

"Really," said Axel. "I can't think of anything I need. You've been very kind. The chance to head up Maison Randon. The apartment. The house in Champagne is magnificent."

"Boring," said Randon, waving Axel's praise away.

And suddenly Axel found himself wondering how he could appear more interesting. Which was exactly Randon's plan, he knew. Still he resisted being drawn.

"You know," said Randon. "The main reason I wanted you at the head of Maison Randon is that you remind me of myself at your age. You're a clever guy. Ambitious. I thought to myself that Axel Delaflote is a man who sees things differently. He's not constrained by the usual social mores. Because trying to be a good man is directly incompatible with being a great man."

"I think I understand."

"You know also that the real secret of champagne is dirt."

Axel nodded. He'd heard this speech before. First the dirt in the vineyard and finally the dirt in the glass...

"Our flaws are what make us sparkle," Randon mused.

They were passing through a red-light district now.

Randon's car stopped at a set of traffic lights and Axel found himself looking into the face of a working girl leaning against a wall as though he might know her.

"Remind you of the girls by the market in Reims?" asked Randon.

Axel's head spun as he turned back to face his boss. He felt instantly guilty, though there was no way that Randon could know where he'd been earlier that evening. Was there?

"You should be more careful," said Randon. "You don't know where they've been."

But how did Randon know where he'd been? Axel said nothing.

"And they're not renowned for their discretion."

He did know.

"Our little secret," Randon said.

At last the car pulled up outside a large house. It had the air of a place long deserted. Some of its windows were actually boarded up. It certainly didn't look like there was a party going on.

Randon patted his young protégé on the knee.

"This will cheer you up. Let's go inside."

Axel knew he was stuck. He followed Randon up the dark path and into the house. Behind the tatty-looking door lay a different world entirely. Inside, the house was like a jewel case, all gilding and velvet and mirrors reflecting candlelight. A woman dressed in nothing but a suspender belt and high heels greeted Axel and his boss. Randon tucked a bank note into the top of one of her stockings. She took Axel by the hand and led him farther inside.

"I'll take care of you," she said.

Randon, meanwhile, turned and left.

CHAPTER 36

The harvest at Froggy Bottom was a turning point for Kelly. Chastened by her heart-to-heart with Hilarian and encouraged by the reaction of her friends, who had been so thrilled to take part in the *vendange*, she began to consider that winemaking might not be such a boring occupation after all.

Kelly realized that Hilarian had done her an enormous favor by keeping the whole rave incident from the trustees. She was grateful for that. But she wasn't surprised to learn a few months later that he expected a return on his investment of belief.

One Sunday afternoon, while Kelly was helping him to wash up after lunch, Hilarian broached a difficult subject.

"When did you leave school?" he asked.

Kelly immediately bristled. "Sixteen, why?"

"Did you take your exams before you left?"

"Some of them," Kelly lied.

"Kelly," said Hilarian. "The trustees and I have decided that you would benefit from some more formal education."

"What?"

"Just that. Some more education."

"You want me to go back to school?" said Kelly.

"Not school," said Hilarian. "College. Winemaking isn't just about squashing the grapes and letting them stew, as I'm sure Guy will tell you. There's chemistry involved."

Kelly blanched. "I failed chemistry."

"Well, here's your chance to pass. I've brought you something to look at." While Kelly dried her hands, Hilarian went to his briefcase. He pulled out a leaflet about distance learning with the Viticulture and Enology Department at UC Davis. "This would be the ideal place for you to start."

Kelly gave the leaflet a cursory glance while Hilarian made a cup of tea. Then she put it back down on the table.

"I'm not clever enough to do that," she said.

"Kelly, I know that's not the truth."

"You don't know that. I was the thickest girl in my class. Everyone said so."

"Everyone?"

Kelly nodded. She wasn't being unduly modest.

Kelly had no positive memories whatsoever of her brief years in education. From her first day in school—aged five—when she was sent to stand in a corner for asking a question without putting her hand up, to the very last, when she walked out halfway through her maths GCSE, she could not remember a single moment of praise. The expectation that she would be a failure had been set at the very beginning and repeated to her so often over the years that it naturally became a fact. The thought of setting foot in a classroom again had never occurred to her, and now that Hilarian brought it up, she could only assume he was trying to make a fool of her in some subtle way.

"I haven't got any qualifications at all," said Kelly. "I won't even be able to get on this course you want me to take. Why can't you and Guy just tell me what to do?"

"Because we can only take you so far. And I think you have great potential. If you do this course, you'll be able to tell Guy and me what to do. You'll be able to shape the future of Froggy Bottom on your own. All I'm asking is for you to make a little bit more effort."

Effort. The very word made Kelly tense. *Not enough effort. Needs to make more effort.* In that word she could hear the voices of every teacher she'd ever had the misfortune to meet joining together in a grand chorus inside her head. But they never seemed to notice when she *did* make an effort. Nothing would ever be good enough.

"Just drop it, will you?" Kelly snapped. "I don't want to go back to school."

She left Hilarian sitting at the kitchen table and fled upstairs. When she came back down again a couple of hours later, he was gone. The leaflet was still on the table. Kelly dropped it in the trash bin.

After that scene, Kelly thought that she had heard the last of Hilarian's scheme to get her back into education. She certainly didn't bring it up. Having to think about her school days had really upset her. Her teachers had often accused her of not giving a damn. The reality was very different. She had cared enormously. It hurt so much. So her first assumption, when the parcel of books from Amazon arrived, was that Hilarian was being cruel.

Kelly called Gina to moan.

"They just won't let it drop. Guy and Hilarian bring it up every bloody day. I don't know how many times I have to tell them I was never any good at exams. It's not going to be any different now."

She expected her best friend to sympathize and agree with her. But Gina didn't. Instead, Gina said, "I think they're right. You should do it."

"You don't understand."

"What don't I understand?"

"Why should I line myself up to look a fool all over again?"

"Do you think you're getting back at the people who called you stupid at school by refusing ever to learn anything new? If I were in your position, I would jump at the chance. I will jump at the chance as soon as I get together enough money."

Kelly felt slightly ashamed as she thought of how Gina was still trying to get together her college fees.

"Are you really not interested? Or are you just being chicken?"

"Gina . . ."

"You are," said Gina. "You'd rather definitely remain ignorant than risk looking a fool in front of a teacher. You're a chicken."

Nobody called Kelly Elson "chicken." As soon as she put the phone down, Kelly crossed the courtyard and got Guy out of bed to tell him that she wanted to sign up for the week long course. She made him file her application via the Internet, there and then, so that she wouldn't have a chance to back out.

"I'm really glad you're going to do this," said Guy.

"Me too," said Kelly.

She lay awake for ages that night, wondering what on earth she had let herself in for.

CHAPTER 37

With her first vendange safely undergoing its second fermentation in bottle in the dark chalk caves beneath the house, and the dormant vineyards in Henri's capable hands, Madeleine decided it was time to go back to London.

Apart from her disastrous trip to the wine fair at ExCeL, she had not been to London since the weekend after her father's funeral. In the meantime, Lizzy had been looking after Madeleine's apartment for her. Lizzy's unfortunate split with the physics teacher had been, in one way, a godsend. It meant that Lizzy had needed somewhere new to live and quickly. Madeleine had an empty apartment and needed a house sitter. Everyone was happy(ish). But a year later, Lizzy had met someone wonderful—"*really* wonderful this time"—and wanted to move out of the flat and into his house in Surrey. The flat was empty again. Madeleine needed to clear out her things and make the place fit for a proper tenant. Someone who wouldn't want to be surrounded by her stuff.

Madeleine approached the business of emptying the flat with her usual professionalism. She consulted with a leasing agent, who advised her which pieces of furniture would appeal to a corporate renter and which should be removed. With that knowledge in mind, Madeleine went around the flat with a wodge of Post-it notes, marking those pieces that would remain, those that would be shipped to Champagne and those that would be taken straight to the dump. It didn't take long. Madeleine was not particularly sentimental about the furniture in her London home, all of which had been chosen by an interior designer.

She was similarly unsentimental about her more personal belongings. She decided that almost all the clothes in her wardrobe would have to go. If she hadn't missed them in the best part of a year, she wouldn't miss them now. In fact, Madeleine was so keen to declutter her life that she even brought with her a case full of clothes from the house in Champagne, designer duds that might raise a few quid through one of those genteel dress agencies. Madeleine was ruthless. She needed cash for her champagne house, not Chanel.

It was as she was packing her belongings that she found the old shoe box. It had been stuffed to the back of her wardrobe, at the bottom of a pile of other shoe boxes. The difference was, this one didn't contain Manolos or Louboutins.

Madeleine hadn't looked inside it for ten years. She sat down on the bed and stared at the string that tied the box shut. She could leave it shut, if she wanted. She almost didn't need to open it, so clearly could she picture what she'd find.

Inside the box were the few things she hadn't been able to leave behind when she left Le Vezy to move to London permanently, seven years earlier.

There were letters from her mother, written to Madeleine while she was studying at Oxford. Madeleine's mother had beautiful handwriting and an equally elegant turn of phrase. There were birthday cards. Again written in Madeleine's mother's hand. *Des Maman et Papa.* Constant Arsenault never signed the cards himself.

And here was a photograph of Madeleine with her brother and Axel Delaflote. They were standing in the Clos. Axel and Georges had an arm around each other's shoulders. Madeleine, a couple of years younger and much shorter, stood in front of them. They were all smiling at the camera. The best of friends.

She couldn't help wondering where Axel was right then. She hadn't seen him in Champagne since that morning after the harvest when she ignored him. She knew no one who could pass on any gossip.

Forget him, Madeleine told herself. There was no point being sentimental about their childhood friendship. He'd shown his true colors. She put the photo back in the box and retied the string around it.

Madeleine worked on into the night until the apartment was completely packed away. As she looked at her London life, reduced to so many boxes, she couldn't help but feel a little sad. But she was Champagne Arsenault now. And even on this trip she was representing her champagne house. There was no time for tears. Wouldn't do to have puffy eyes when she began her rounds of the wine importers the following morning.

When morning came, Madeleine dressed carefully in one of the few suits she had kept. It was a soft gray Armani skirt suit, bought off the rack but carefully taken in at the waist by Madeleine's trusty seamstress so that it looked as though it had been made for her. She teamed the suit with a pair of vertiginously high heels. They weren't the most sensible choice, given the amount of running around she would be doing that day, but Madeleine knew that most of the people she would be meeting with were men in their fifties and sixties. They appreciated a nice pair of heels and, as she had always done in the banking world, Madeleine was determined to use every advantage she had to get what she needed. If pandering to a stereotypically male fantasy was what it would take, Madeleine would do it. She got out her red lipstick and painted herself a Monroe mouth.

The Arsenault name still opened doors. The wine crowd in London seemed happy to see her. They remembered her father, if not exactly fondly, then with amusement. They knew that Constant had let the house fall apart in recent years. But they were generally impressed by the results of his final vintage.

Madeleine had prepared a rousing sales pitch, full of talk of history and family pride. Combined with her killer shoes and a shirt unbuttoned ever so slightly too low, it seemed to work. At least, Madeleine found herself on the receiving end of several invitations to lunch at private clubs, if not orders... Unfortunately for the gentlemen of St. James's, Madeleine already had a lunch appointment.

Of the calls she had made before leaving for London, Madeleine felt most optimistic about her conversation with Piers Mackesy, proprietor of Mackesy & Co., the wine merchant. For a start, he had taken her call personally. While most of the other big players had Madeleine arrange things with their assistants, Piers had come straight on the line himself.

"How wonderful to hear from you," he said. "I was wondering how long it would take. I was so relieved when I heard you'd decided to stay on in France and run the house yourself. I had a terrible thought you might sell to that bugger Mathieu Randon."

Madeleine liked Piers Mackesy at once. She told him she would be delighted to join him for lunch after their meeting.

As she sat in the waiting room at Mackesy & Co., Madeleine wondered what Piers would be like. She had met his father, Philip, founder of the company, several times in the early 1980s, when she was just a kid. Philip Mackesy must have been in his late forties then. Madeleine remembered him as a dapper sort of chap. Always beautifully dressed, he drove a fire-engine red Aston Martin DB4. He was the epitome of a young French girl's image of an Englishman.

Philip Mackesy would often stay in the Arsenault family home on his visits to Champagne to see suppliers. Madeleine and Georges loved to see his car pull in through the gates of Champagne Arsenault. Georges, obsessed with James Bond, was absolutely in love with the DB4. Madeleine was quietly keen to get her hands on the gifts that Philip Mackesy always had for her: toys that weren't available in France, English chocolate.

Madeleine's father and Philip were good friends as well as business associates. Once business was concluded, Constant and Philip would sit up for hours, drinking and playing cards, which was how Constant Arsenault actually came to own the DB4 for approximately six months, until Philip Mackesy won it back in another game. Constant Arsenault's beloved Facel Vega HK500 made its own cross-channel trip shortly afterward, but Philip refused to let Constant try to secure its return in another game. Constant was devastated. Madeleine assumed that was why the two men drifted apart. Which was a terrible pity for Madeleine, who had quite a crush on Philip Mackesy's old-fashioned movie star looks...

Philip Mackesy's son didn't disappoint.

Tall and slim with plenty of wavy dark hair, Piers Mackesy was dressed like a City gent in a navy blue pin-striped suit. He wore a crisp white shirt beneath and a silk tie that was printed with teddy bears.

"Oh, hello," he said. "It's *you.*"

He extended a hand toward her.

Madeleine blushed crimson, remembering when she and Piers Mackesy had collided. Her nose in his chest as she exited ExCeL at high speed.

"Creed," she nodded.

"What?" asked Mackesy.

"Your aftershave. Creed Royal Water."

"Spot on," he said, ushering Madeleine into his office. "I should have known that Constant Arsenault's daughter would have a very fine nose."

They lunched in the café at Ludbrooks, the auction house on Old Bond Street. As luck would have it, a wine sale was in progress that day. Mackesy quizzed a few of his friends on the prices that were being achieved. Madeleine goggled at the figures.

Mackesy listened attentively while Madeleine trotted out her speech about the future of Champagne Arsenault. He nodded approvingly when she told him about that year's Clos Des Larmes. He promised that he would give very careful consideration indeed to taking some of her father's last non-vintage Brut off her hands.

Business over, they moved on to more general matters. Madeleine recalled her fondness for Mackesy's father.

"Pushing up daisies since 1997, I'm afraid," he informed her. "But the DB4 is still in fine shape. I'm driving it myself. Perhaps I should come to Champagne and take you for a spin."

Madeleine looked into Mackesy's dark blue eyes, set off so attractively by the crinkles of forty-five years' worth of smiling and saw trouble. Then she glanced down at his wedding ring and saw even more.

"Perhaps," she said, shaking her head at the same time.

The following morning, while Madeleine was lounging in her hotel room, flicking through the TV channels, Piers Mackesy called.

Madeleine swallowed nervously at the sound of the wine importer's voice. "Hi, Piers," she said. "I didn't expect to hear from you again so quickly."

It had to be bad news, Madeleine decided. If Mackesy wanted to take Champagne Arsenault he would not have got back to her so soon. He would have been working out figures, percentages, that sort of thing.

"Is this a good time to talk?" he asked.

Definitely bad news, thought Madeleine.

"Fire away," she said.

"Since you're in London until tomorrow, I was wondering whether you might be available to come out with me this evening? It'd be a busman's holiday for you, I'm afraid."

"Busman's holiday?"

"I'd like to invite you to join me for a wine tasting at Berry Bros. We'd be going incognito. Checking out the competition. I'm thinking of setting up some tastings in my own cellars next year."

"Oh." Madeleine was surprised.

"So, what do you say? It's wine and chocolate. Isn't that what you girls like?"

"I think I could force myself," Madeleine replied. "Though I thought it was the wine producer who had to give the importer bribes. Not the other way around."

Mackesy laughed. "I'll let you make it up to me."

At half past six Madeleine arrived at the St. James's Street premises of Berry Bros. & Rudd. She was familiar with the place, of course. On her very first visit to London, aged eight, her father had taken her to visit the Queen's wine merchants.

Madeleine was ushered through the courtyard to the cellar where the tasting would be taking place. She was early. A waitress took her coat and pressed a glass of champagne into her hand. It was Berry's own label. Not bad. She sipped it slowly as she studied the artworks around the room.

Mackesy arrived a little later. Madeleine slyly watched him as he handed his coat and briefcase to the girls by the door. He was wearing a dark gray suit; well cut, it skimmed his slim body perfectly. Beneath the suit, he wore a white shirt with blue stripes and a tie patterned with small bunny rabbits and Easter eggs, though Easter had long since passed.

Catching sight of her across the room, he smiled broadly and headed over. He went to kiss her on the cheek but at the same time a waitress tried to offer him a glass of champagne. Flustered, he accidentally kissed Madeleine on the lips instead. She stepped back, laughing.

"Good to see you too," she said.

"I did that deliberately." He winked.

"Just as I feared."

He joined her on a tour of the room, reading the framed cartoons. For the most part, they weren't that funny, but it gave them something to do. Though it was beginning to fill up, the room was horribly quiet, as though it were the crypt of a church rather than a wine cellar. Some of the other guests looked terribly serious. It was a relief when the Berry Bros. representative clinked a couple of glasses together and asked everyone to take their seats.

"Let's get this party started," said Mackesy.

Mackesy and Madeleine were right at the front.

"No chance of misbehaving," Mackesy observed.

"Have they put you here based on past behavior?" Madeleine asked.

The woman from Berry Bros. introduced that evening's special guest, Monsieur Radanne from Château de Cacao. Madeleine was pleased to see that his company would be providing the chocolate for that evening's tasting. A box of chocolates from the Château de Cacao was one of her favorite indulgences.

Monsieur Radanne spoke very little English, the woman from Berry Bros. explained, and thus she would be translating.

"You'll have to tell me what she misses out," Mackesy whispered.

A group of uniformed waitresses began to distribute the first of the chocolates.

"This is the first thing I've eaten all day," said Mackesy, sticking his chocolate straight in his mouth and reaching for another one.

"You're going to taste champagne on an empty stomach?" Madeleine raised her eyebrows. "I do hope you're not going to embarrass yourself."

Mackesy gave her his best schoolboy grin.

Madeleine pretended to ignore him and examined the list of wines.

"A Krug rosé," she observed. "They're spoiling us."

"I wouldn't say that," said Mackesy as he poked at the chocolate on his plate with the knife and fork that had been provided. "Is this all the bloody chocolate we're allowed?"

"Ssssh."

Monsieur Radanne was explaining, at great length, how the process of tasting should proceed.

"A sip of champagne," said his translator. "Just enough to coat the mouth. Then a bite of the chocolate. Not more than a third."

"I am going to faint from hunger," Mackesy muttered.

"Pay attention." Madeleine sniffed at her first glass of champagne and took a dainty sip.

"What do you think?" Mackesy asked as Madeleine took a little of the chocolate.

"Not bad. Though the texture is a little oily."

Madeleine wrote her observation down on the forms that had been provided.

"Swot," said Mackesy.

Before Madeleine had a chance to protest, Monsieur Radanne was rattling on again, elaborating, this time, on why the second of his chocolates was called "Takhrai."

"Monsieur Radanne created this chocolate after a research trip to Southeast Asia," began the translator.

"It's the Thai word for 'lady-boy,' " said Mackesy with authority.

"It's Thai for 'lemongrass,' " Madeleine corrected him.

"Not half so exciting. What do you think?"

"Seems a shame to mix anything at all with this Krug."

"I agree."

Mackesy and Madeleine both discarded Monsieur Radanne's lemongrass-infused chocolate truffle. Madeleine made another note.

"You need to work harder," said Mackesy.

"What?" Madeleine looked up from her clipboard.

Mackesy gestured at her tasting glasses. They were all

considerably fuller than his. Madeleine gamely took another swig of the Krug.

After the next combination, an Australian Shiraz and a ginger-infused chocolate ganache, Madeleine scribbled "fascinating." Mackesy leaned across and added his own note next to hers. "Like you."

Madeleine turned to look at him. He held her gaze with the cheeky blue eyes that belied his age. She couldn't help blushing.

Monsieur Radanne held forth about the next combination.

"A twenty-year-old port," said the translator.

"Twenty," Madeleine wrote in her notes.

"Like you make me feel," Mackesy added in his erratic handwriting.

Madeleine felt even younger. They were passing notes like a couple of schoolchildren.

"Are you flirting with me?" she wrote.

"I thought you'd never notice," Mackesy replied. "Should I stop?" he added a moment later.

Perhaps it was something in the air. While a junior chef from Château de Cacao embarked on a live demonstration of the making of a chocolate ganache, Monsieur Radanne took the opportunity to slip his arm around his young translator's slim waist. The guests who had looked so dull as they piled into the cellar straight from work were beginning to warm up too, shouting out questions and comments. Of course, the melted chocolate invited the usual English smattering of double entendres.

A waitress handed Mackesy and Madeleine two small cups of still warm ganache to try with a ginger liquer. Madeleine dipped a finger into the cup daintily.

"I can think of better ways to eat this," said Mackesy.

"*Don't* tell me," Madeleine said quickly.

"Of course not. I'd rather show you," he replied. "You've got a smudge of chocolate on the end of your nose," he continued. "Shall I lick it off?"

He held her gaze. Madeleine swallowed nervously. It was an invitation to go to bed with him. No doubt about it.

This was a disaster. She wanted a business relationship with Mackesy, nothing else. The rose-gold ring on his wedding finger seemed to be shining right in her eyes. Madeleine sensed the end of a beautiful friendship looming.

"Mackesy," she said. "You have no integrity. I should go."

"I could give you a lift in the DB4," he suggested hopefully.

Gathering her coat, she allowed him to walk her to a taxi and no farther.

Back at the hotel, Madeleine threw herself down onto the bed with a groan of disappointment. She'd blown it. She'd known when Mackesy invited her to the tasting it was because he fancied her. Of course he was going to make a pass. And of course she would have to rebuff it. He'd never stock her champagne now. Was she stupid to have let her morality get in the way of business? And, frankly, of her own desires. He was quite ridiculously fanciable.

Madeleine's mobile phone chirruped. She had a text.

"Piers Mackesy Wines would be delighted to stock Champagne Arsenault."

Madeleine bounced on her hotel bed like a five-year-old.

CHAPTER 38

Gina's life had definitely changed since she took Kelly's advice and raised her standards. She'd given up working at the Gloria Hotel altogether. Her chambermaid's wages were nothing compared to the kind of sums she could command by the hour now. Five hundred pounds a night was just the start of it.

It was a curious thing but Gina felt she might have accidentally found her vocation. She was good at being a high-class call girl. Not just the sex part but also the companionship. That was after all what so many of her clients really wanted. They weren't paying to see Gina because their wives had stopped sleeping with them. It was because their wives had stopped *talking* to them.

That was what the guy Gina was lunching with that day complained about most of all. Dennis was a fifty-something businessman from Texas, who visited the UK a couple of times a month. The first time he spent the night with Gina, after picking her up in a smart hotel bar in Mayfair, was a disaster. The poor guy just couldn't get it up. But Gina handled the situation with aplomb and, more importantly, with kindness, and these days she and Dennis didn't bother with sex at all. Gina would just meet him for lunch or dinner whenever he was in London and nod patiently while he talked about the stress of being a mere multi-millionaire in a billionaire's world.

The money was incredible. But Gina was being careful. She really didn't intend to get used to the lifestyle.

After achieving her career aims, she hoped one day to have a husband of her own and some children. Hooking was hardly compatible with that. And so she salted the cash away. But like all small businesses, some investment was required. Gina needed to look the part. She needed to be able to walk into any restaurant or hotel in Mayfair or Chelsea and look as though she belonged there. That meant dressing perfectly. And expensively.

She didn't shop on Sloane Street, however. She shopped in the charity shops and designer resale places nearby. If you were lucky, you could find the most amazing stuff in the Knightsbridge and Kensington branches of Oxfam; designer gear cast off by the kind of women who could not be seen dead in something "last season." Likewise, you could get some great bargains in the resale places, with the advantage that they didn't smell quite so much of the charity shop. These days Gina's wardrobe contained Armani, Versace and Prada, but all of it she bought secondhand. The guys she saw didn't care whether Gina's dress was last season. The concept meant nothing to them. Shame it meant something to their credit-card-toting wives, Gina thought, smiling.

Gina had built up quite a friendship with an elderly woman named Janet who worked part-time in her friend's resale shop in Notting Hill.

"You remind me of my granddaughter," Janet told her. "She's into her clothes just like you are."

Soon Janet started to put aside things she thought Gina might like. Gina gave Janet her phone number and asked her to call whenever something good came in. Janet was under the impression that Gina was an impoverished fashion student. It was sort of true, Gina told herself. She had recently decided that a degree in fashion design might be up her alley.

Janet was getting ready to close up the shop when Gina arrived.

"The minute I saw this woman walk in I thought, she'll have something for our Gina. She was exactly your height. She even looked a bit like you. Nice dark hair. She brought in loads of stuff. Says she's relocating. Lucky it's just me in today so none of it has gone out on the floor. I saved it all for you."

"Thanks, Janet." Gina gave the older woman a hug. "You are a star."

"I'll make us a nice cup of tea while you look through it," said Janet. Then she turned the sign on the shop door to "closed." Gina took off her denim jacket and opened the first box.

"Oh my God, Janet!" Gina exclaimed as she picked out a small black bag. "I have to have this. This is real Chanel!"

CHAPTER 39

One of the people Christina had been most pleased to see during her first harvest at the Villa Bacchante was her old New York friend Greg Stroud, who was now the head of a lifestyle cable channel headquartered in Los Angeles.

It was in his capacity as head of the Good Life Channel that Greg found himself in San Francisco one weekend in April. Christina was delighted to get the call asking whether she'd mind if he dropped by her place before heading home to So-Cal.

Greg drove up to Napa as soon as his last meeting ended. He arrived just in time for the sunset. And a night cap.

"This place is so great," Greg said as he shrugged off his jacket and laid it over the back of one of the patio chairs. "I feel like the city is a million miles away."

Christina handed him a vodka tonic, mixed how he'd always liked it. She'd been surprised by how much she'd looked forward to seeing him this weekend.

"I'm really glad to have you here again," she said. "I hope you're not expecting to be entertained in too much style, however. Everything's pretty casual."

Casual? Christina laughed at herself. Hardly. She had spent much of the day getting ready for Greg's visit. She'd asked Ernestina to stay a little later than usual to help put together a deceptively simple-looking meal. Meanwhile, Christina arranged the flowers that the gardener had cut that morning. She was pretty good at arranging flowers. When she thought she might marry the finance guy and thus spend a lot of time entertaining snotty New York socialites she'd actually done a course in "hostess skills." She also spent a good hour arranging the framed photographs on top of the piano. Would Greg be impressed by a picture of Christina with Governor Arnold Schwarzenegger? she wondered. She couldn't remember Greg's politics.

After the, Christina had to prepare herself. When Greg arrived she was wearing a multi-colored chiffon maxi-dress by Cavalli, accessorized with a pair of simple flat gold Jimmy Choos. Around her neck she wore a couple of heavy bead necklaces. She looked as though she had just walked in from the beach—Nikki Beach, St. Tropez, that is, rather than the wilder reaches of Malibu. Her ensemble was simple. Casual. Beautiful. Greg had no idea that she had tried on eleven different outfits before settling on this chic "at home" style.

Greg admired the dress. He admired the flowers. He praised the food. He went into raptures over the wine.

"Is this really Villa Bacchante's own?" he asked his hostess.

"It is."

"It's fantastic. I bet you're glad you got this place in your divorce settlement."

Christina nodded. "I can't accept any of your praise, though," she admitted. "This bottle is five years old. Made long before I turned up."

"But imagine what your own wine will taste like in five years' time," Greg said to her.

"It better be good." Christina told Greg about the *Vinifera* competition. "Ronald Ginsburg was up here earlier this week tasting the still wine we've just transferred into the bottle."

"Ronald Ginsburg? I'm impressed. I bet half the wine-makers in this valley would kill to have Ginsburg as a mentor."

"I think he gets just as much out of it as I do," said Christina, recalling that whenever Ginsburg went to kiss her good-bye he somehow always managed to miss her cheek and plant a smacker on her mouth.

Greg and Christina hadn't spoken to each other since the harvest so there was plenty to catch up about—weddings, divorces, comings and goings, comings-out. Christina's jaw dropped at the news that a mutual friend was leaving his wife for the pool boy.

"Isn't it meant to be the other way around?" she laughed.

And then they were on to their own news. Greg claimed not to have much, before he revealed that he had been headhunted by a rival cable channel for a vast amount of money, stayed put at the Good Life Channel for even more money and was remodeling his house in Bel Air around the Hockney painting to which he'd treated himself with the resulting golden-handcuff cash.

"And how about you?" he asked Christina. "How come we don't see you in LA anymore?"

"I've been taking time out to reflect," Christina admitted. "Rethinking life. Before I did the ISACL campaign, I felt like my career was on an upswing. And then Bill got caught with that slut in Paris, and you know the rest."

"Go on," said Greg.

Christina took a sip of wine. She hadn't really spoken about her disappointment with the way life had gone with anyone but Marisa, but there was something about Greg that made her feel like unburdening herself. They'd shared a lot of secrets when they were younger. "I got dropped by Guilty Secrets for being out of shape." It was the first time Christina had admitted that. Marisa had persuaded Guilty Secrets to present Christina's departure as her decision. "After that Marisa assured me that something else would come up but nothing has. My diary is looking somewhat empty these days. I really think that my career as a model is finally over. I'm unemployed and unemployable."

"What are you talking about? You're a winemaker. Maybe you should concentrate on making wine."

"You mean making a huge loss? I had no idea how expensive this business is. When I first got here to Napa, someone said to me that the best way to make a small fortune in wine is to start with a big one. They weren't kidding."

"But you make great wine here in Carneros."

"So does everybody else. The Villa Bacchante is just another boutique winery in a valley of boutique wineries.

Why should anyone choose my wine over Schramsberg or Domaine Randon?"

"You need to make this place stand out. It's just a matter of marketing. Capitalize on your celebrity."

"Easier said than done. I swear there's a big reverse snobbery that makes wine buffs automatically dismiss a wine made by anyone faintly famous."

Greg shook his head. Christina brought the subject to a close by asking him to help her carry the dishes back into the kitchen. Though it had been a beautiful day, it was starting to get chilly. They finished supper at the kitchen counter.

But as they drank their coffee, Greg looked pensive. Christina was about to ask him what was on his mind, expecting to hear about some infighting at work or some girl who was tugging on his heartstrings, when Greg said, "The ISACL campaign showed me a side of you I didn't know."

"What do you mean?"

"I mean, you're not just a pretty face. You came over as well as any of those actors and presenters. Have you ever thought about presenting?"

"What? Some fashion TV show?"

"No. Something different."

"What else would I be qualified to present?"

"Luckily for you, it's just come to me. We could make a show. You and me together. Like a cross between a reality show and a food show, based here at the villa. We could film what's going on in the vineyard at any time of the year then come back into the house for a cooking segment. Right here."

"In my kitchen?"

"Sure. It's a great kitchen. This Tuscan style. I love it. Everybody loves it."

"But I can't cook," Christina laughed.

Greg indicated the remains of the beautiful spread on the counter before them.

"Wish I could take the credit, but it was all Ernestina's work," she admitted.

"Ah well. You don't have to be able to cook," said Greg. "It'll be like a house party. Each week a different chef will come in and cook his speciality. You'll choose the wine to go with it."

"I don't know enough about wine either!" Christina exclaimed.

"Do you think any of the guys you see on TV really do? We'll have someone research that, of course. How about your friend Ronald Ginsburg? Now, that would be a coup. He's America's most respected wine critic and you have him wrapped around your little finger."

Christina rolled her eyes.

"I bet he'd come on board. All you'll have to do is look ... lovely ... which shouldn't be hard."

For some reason, the way Greg delivered that last line made Christina blush quite deeply. Perhaps it was the way he had looked right into her eyes as he said it. She felt as though a spark had flown straight from his eyes into hers and traveled all the way to her stomach. She was suddenly quite deliciously nervous.

"Well," said Christina in an attempt to cover up how flustered he'd made her. "Perhaps you should get your people to talk to my people."

Greg grinned. "Get your people to talk to my people" was something they'd said to each other in jest back in New York all those years ago, when they most definitely didn't have "people" to talk for them.

"I'm really excited about this," said Greg.

"Are you?"

"Yes," he said. "Most of all because it means I'll get to spend more time with you."

But not that night. Greg had booked himself into a hotel in Yountville and at eleven o'clock he left.

"I'm bushed," he said. "You have no idea how exhausting it is pretending you know what you're talking about for three days straight."

"You could come for lunch tomorrow," Christina suggested, surprising herself with her directness.

"Wish I could. Got to get back to LA," he said.

"I understand."

Christina walked Greg to the door. As they said goodbye he wrapped his arms around her tightly.

"It's so good to see you," he said.

Christina went to kiss him on the cheek, but, like Ginsburg, somehow missed as Greg turned. She didn't kiss Greg on the mouth; however, she caught him on the side of the neck. Stubbly and delicious. And erotic. Greg loosened his hold and kissed her chastely on the end of the nose in response.

Alone again in her kitchen, Christina balled a fist against her forehead as she relived the kiss and her subsequent embarrassment. She felt sure she wouldn't be hearing from him again in a hurry.

CHAPTER 40

Since he was the head of the channel, Greg didn't have to jump through the usual hoops when it came to setting up a new show. He announced his idea at the following Monday's catch-up meeting and by Friday, Christina and Marisa were in Greg's office, discussing the terms under which Christina would open her beautiful home for the amusement of the American public and hopefully—eventually—the rest of the world. The idea had definitely grown on Christina during the course of the week. Ronald Ginsburg said he would be delighted to be the show's wine expert and Greg quickly pulled together a dream list of top chefs he hoped would be willing to participate—it was a veritable galaxy of Michelin stars!

Just a couple of days later, Greg flew up to Napa to have dinner with Christina and the first chef on his list: Roddy Smith, an Englishman who had left the shadow of Gordon Ramsay to set up a restaurant in Napa Valley that made Thomas Keller's French Laundry look like KFC. The restaurant was so ridiculously hot it had instituted a rather old-fashioned booking policy. You couldn't call to book, you had to write. You had to dine when the restaurant had a space for you, not when you wanted to arrive. And everyone who applied for a table was treated the same. It didn't matter whether you were a supermodel or you worked in a supermarket. There was nothing you could do to get yourself pushed to the top of the waiting list. That didn't stop people trying, though. Just that week, someone had enclosed ten crisp new hundred-dollar bills with his application.

But of course, hoping one day for a TV series of his own, Roddy Smith managed to find a little table near the kitchen door for Greg and Christina at very short notice indeed.

Dinner was wonderful. Though when Christina scanned the menu she wondered whether there really would be anything she could eat. The combinations didn't sound all that appetizing. Like Heston Blumenthal, Roddy Smith approached cooking like chemistry. His workplace looked more like the laboratory of a mad scientist than a kitchen.

Still, Christina was surprised to discover that she quite enjoyed frozen mashed potatoes. And arrangements were made for Roddy to visit Christina's house later in the week to take a look at her own kitchen and decide what equipment he needed in order to bring his unique culinary experience to the masses via her show.

"This show really is happening, isn't it?" Christina said to Greg when Roddy disappeared back into the kitchen to attend to a flambé gone wild.

"It's really happening," said Greg.

He offered Christina his arm as they walked from the restaurant to the valet. She linked her arm through his happily and let it stay there as they waited for the valet to retrieve Greg's Porsche. It took a little while, as it always did when you had a car like a Porsche 911 GT3, Greg observed. "I think the valets have put more miles on that car than I have."

The car arrived. The valet hopped out. Greg crossed to the passenger door to open Christina's himself before the valet could get there.

It was a romantic gesture. But Christina told herself it was just that Greg had impeccable manners. Despite the chemistry Christina thought she'd felt last time Greg visited, nothing had happened between them that night. Likewise when she visited the offices of his company in LA—a meeting followed by dinner *à deux*. Christina decided that she'd misread the signals in Greg's eyes. She had to conclude that he wasn't interested in her romantically. He was all business.

And yet, there was the expression on his face as they waited at a stop sign. He looked across at her and smiled. Warmly, uncertainly, as if searching for her approval.

When they reached Christina's driveway, they got out

of the car and stood in front of the house. Greg started to bid her good night.

"Do you have to drive back to San Francisco tonight?" she asked him.

"I had all my meetings moved from tomorrow morning till the afternoon."

Christina felt a small bubble of hope rise in her chest.

"Where are you staying?" she asked.

"My assistant booked me a room at the Villagio in Yountville."

"You know, you don't have to stay in a hotel when you come up here. My guest room is always at your disposal," said Christina.

"I thought perhaps you'd seen enough of me."

"Not quite," said Christina.

They both smiled at the delicate double entendre:

"Well, it's a pretty long drive from here to Yountville in the dark," Greg demurred.

"I'll show you upstairs," said Christina.

Christina led the way. She pushed open the door to the first-floor guest suite. Perhaps subconsciously expecting Greg to stay, she'd had the maid fix the room up just that morning. The linen was always clean of course. A pile of fresh towels was folded on top of the blanket box at the end of the bed. But that morning, Christina also had the maid put a vase of flowers on the lamp table and a bottle of mineral water on the nightstand.

"I think you'll find everything you need in here," she told Greg.

"Not quite," he said, echoing her earlier sentiment.

He took both her hands in his and pulled her against his chest. Christina closed her eyes as Greg's face drew nearer. Her lips softened and parted beneath his gentle kiss.

Without saying a word, Christina led Greg toward the

bed. He lay her down upon it, somehow pushing the fancy pillows out of the way and onto the floor without pausing in his kiss for even a second. Soon they were stripping each other's clothes off. Christina ran her hands over Greg's smooth muscled chest, perfected by hours in the gym. He dipped his head and circled each of her roseate nipples with his tongue.

"You are so perfect," he said.

As a model, it was a phrase she was quite used to hearing, but coming from Greg it sounded different, more special than ever before. Christina had the strange sensation that she was actually blossoming beneath Greg's touch. Each kiss he laid upon her skin made her glow a little brighter, become more beautiful still.

Naked at last, Christina pressed her body hard against Greg's. Her hands moved frantically over his body, as though trying to make a sensory map of him. She kissed his face, his neck, his shoulders. She softly bit his earlobe, making him laugh out loud at the unexpected pleasure. She felt his penis grow hard against her. She wrapped her legs around him so that there was nowhere for him to go but inside.

"Greg!" she called out his name as he made his first thrust into her. He buried his face in her neck as he too relished the moment. Then he lifted himself above her, so that their eyes locked as he moved again and again. The intimacy of their gaze increased the power of the sensation a thousand times.

The following morning seemed more beautiful than ever at Villa Bacchante. Christina wrapped herself in a fluffy white dressing gown and wandered out onto the terrace with her coffee. The terra-cotta tiles beneath her feet were already warm. She raised her face to the sun.

Greg joined her, wearing nothing but a towel around

his waist. Christina placed a hand in the center of his broad, tan chest and a kiss on his smile.

Making love to Greg—her first lover since the divorce—felt like the end of something. The end of her attachment to her perfect Hollywood marriage perhaps? But it felt like a beginning too.

CHAPTER 41

It was September, and Kelly Elson's second harvest at Froggy Bottom was a rather different affair than her first. This time the friends who turned up for the Froggy Bottom Fandango, as it had become known, were well briefed in the duties they would be expected to perform before the party started. Tents were set up in the bottom field, equipped with proper camp beds so that, when they were able to sleep, the workers would be able to sleep properly. A Portaloo was placed in the vineyard. Kelly and Hilarian drove to the nearest cash-and-carry and loaded Hilarian's Land Rover with enough food and tea bags to keep an army going.

This time the harvest went like clockwork and the after-party was all the better since it felt as though everyone involved really deserved to cut loose.

As she busied herself around the farm, making sure that everyone was comfortable, well fed and, most importantly, pulling his or her weight, Kelly reflected on a year that had changed her life. She certainly looked different. The hairdo was long gone. As were the clubbing clothes.

Kelly had given up the war paint and the acrylic nails. She had given up on the hair-straighteners too. Her hair had lightened naturally after a summer spent working in the vineyards. It fell to her shoulders in loose waves.

It wasn't just the way Kelly looked that had changed. Ironically, the thing that had frightened her most, the thought of going back to school to learn about winemaking, had given her the most enormous confidence boost. Those frightening-looking books that Hilarian had ordered from Amazon turned out to contain whole chapters that Kelly could understand already based on her experiences at Froggy Bottom. The residential course at UC Davis itself added a whole new dimension, not least because it was Kelly's first-ever trip overseas.

The idea of flying to the States alone was terrifying. Guy drove Kelly to Heathrow and practically marched her to the check-in desk. For eleven long transatlantic hours Kelly gripped the armrest of her seat. And then there was the prospect of the university itself...

Even as she finally found herself standing outside the classroom, she considered that she might have made a big mistake.

Her class was a real mix. Many of the people in the lecture were quite a bit older. "Second-lifers" as they referred to themselves, they had given up lucrative jobs in the financial or media industries to become boutique farmers.

At the first session the tutor asked everyone to introduce themselves and talk a little about their vineyards. They weren't all local to California. There were winemakers from Oregon, the East Coast, wealthy retirees planning estates in Italy or South Africa.

"Think we've just about covered the world," said the tutor. "Anybody who hasn't introduced themselves yet?"

"I'm Kelly from Froggy Bottom, England," raised a laugh and several eyebrows.

"Can you grow grapes in England?" someone asked archly.

"Doesn't it always rain there?"

"Actually," Kelly piped up, "we grow very good grapes. At Froggy Bottom we have pinot noir and small plantings of chardonnay and pinot meunier." She said it perfectly this time. "The terroir is similar to that of the champagne region in France."

"Exactly," said the tutor. "Which is why all the big French houses are buying up land in the south of England. Welcome to the United States, Kelly."

It was an odd feeling. There was no sense whatsoever that anyone on the course thought that Kelly shouldn't be there alongside them. She could follow everything the tutor said and as the week progressed, she surprised herself by asking a question that prompted the tutor to say, "That's a very good point, Kelly. I'm glad you brought it up." Kelly was almost too shocked to hear his answer. She was so used to teachers barking, "If you'd been listening you wouldn't have to ask."

By the time the course was over, Kelly's confidence had grown so much that she might have flown home on her own wings.

Back in England, Kelly continued to take her wine studies very seriously indeed. She gave up smoking weed. Or smoking anything at all, for that matter.

"My sense of taste is much too important to me," she explained to Gina.

Hilarian approved. Kelly had all but decimated Dougal's cellar and so he was determined that what remained would be properly appreciated. He insisted that Kelly attend every tasting he hosted, and Kelly was surprised to discover that she really could tell her sauvignon blanc from her chardonnay. Not only that, she could pin down not only the varietal but also the vintage and the vineyard almost as often as Hilarian could.

Her palate had become so refined that Hilarian decided that this year Kelly would be allowed to give her opinion on the blending of Froggy Bottom's latest vintage. Guy agreed without hesitation.

And so the three of them sat down around a portable picnic table in the winery one afternoon and tasted still wine straight from the barrels and when Kelly spoke, everybody listened.

Kelly had also come to appreciate the place where she lived in a very different way. Sunday afternoons that would have been spent lolling around the house in semi-darkness, smoking weed and listening to the kind of music that defied the word were long gone. Now Kelly was just as likely to be found taking a walk through the fields. And, in her very own pair of Hunter wellies (a birthday present from Guy), it no longer mattered to her if it was raining or the fields were full of mud.

Hilarian came out to the farm as often as he could. One Sunday afternoon, while Guy was up in London visiting a South African friend in the UK on holiday, Hilarian turned up to take Kelly for lunch at the pub. And after lunch, a walk.

"Need to watch my waistline," said Hilarian, patting his ample stomach. It was a long time since Hilarian had seen his own feet.

Kelly was in a good mood. She was much better company than she had been. She talked knowledgeably about Hilarian's latest column in *Vinifera*.

"That Odile Levert, though." Kelly whistled through her teeth. "Such a snob."

Hilarian smiled. "She has her opinions but she's a very fine woman."

After that, they talked a bit about how Kelly was getting on with her studies. She had lots of questions for Hilarian regarding the subject of her dissertation. Faced with a barrage of technical terms, Hilarian had to admit defeat.

"In my day, people didn't do all these exams. I got into wine the old-fashioned way."

"By getting drunk every night?"

Hilarian shrugged. "It takes a long time to develop a palate like mine. I took my studies very seriously indeed."

"Ha-ha. I never quite know whether you're joking or not," Kelly observed. "In fact, I don't know a lot about you, full stop."

Hilarian shook his head. "Not a lot to know," he said.

"I don't believe it. Come on, Hilarian. Spill the beans. I know you were married once. What was the story? I want you to tell me everything."

Hilarian's story? It wasn't a happy one.

It had been once. He'd had a wife and a child. They'd been the center of his world. His beautiful wife, Jenny, and their daughter, Helena. And then he lost them.

Hilarian knew that people thought he was a happy-go-lucky kind of guy. He was, luckily, an affable drunk and not a maudlin one. And fortunately, most people didn't ask about his past anymore. For perhaps two years after the crash, he caught the pitying glances. People asked if he was OK and watched closely when he was tasting to see how much he swallowed. But after that, things went back to normal. Old rivalries were resumed. It was because he had married again. People thought that had fixed it. Little did they know.

His second wife, Amanda, had been a receptionist at

Mackesy's, the wine merchants. She was the archetypal Sloane Ranger. At twenty-seven, she dressed just like her mother. A velvet Alice band held her medium-brown hair off her face. She wore pearls during the day, discreet diamond studs at night. They were from the same stock, Amanda and Hilarian. Her people knew his people. In the eyes of everyone else, she was a worthy successor to Jenny and when she bore him a son and then another, Hilarian knew he was supposed to be fully healed. But he wasn't.

And eventually Amanda realized that despite what she saw as her heroic efforts to make his life better, Hilarian wasn't getting any happier.

His daughter, Helena, would have been thirty this year. Perhaps she would even have been a mother herself by now. Hilarian often wondered what she would have been like. His two sons were so much like Amanda and so little like himself that occasionally he wondered whether they were his at all. But if Helena had turned out like her mother, that would have been just fine.

From time to time, he also asked himself whether he would have been a good father to a girl. That afternoon, with Kelly, he thought perhaps he might not have been so bad after all.

"So," Kelly pressed him, "are you going to tell me all about your misspent youth or not?"

Not, Hilarian decided. At least, not yet. Kelly would get the abridged version for now. Hilarian had her in stitches while describing Estranged Amanda.

"I am so happy here," Kelly confided in him when they got back to the farmhouse. "I feel like everything in my life is going right."

CHAPTER 42

Life felt pretty good for Madeleine too. Having made a definite decision to throw herself into life in Champagne, Madeleine felt strangely relieved and relaxed. Her promotional trip to London had paid off in a fantastic way. Waitrose markets were stocking her father's last non-vintage Brut. The best of Britain's wine merchants were eagerly awaiting Madeleine's own first Clos Des Larmes.

Meanwhile, Madeleine was finding other ways to make money from the mess her father had left to her. She decided to open the maison to private parties. She made useful contacts in the best of the local hotels. They sent their guests in her direction and before long she found she was entertaining a couple of groups a week, taking them on an exclusive tour of the house and the chalk caves beneath, explaining every step of the champagne production process as they went.

The processes that she took for granted fascinated Madeleine's guests. Riddling or "remuage" is the process by which sediment is removed from bottles of champagne. It's said to have been perfected by la Veuve Clicquot herself. The champagne bottles are placed into holes in a wooden frame that holds dozens at a time. Over the course of weeks, the bottles are taken from the horizontal to the vertical, upside down, in a series of tiny adjustments. Slowly, slowly, so that all the sediment gathers in the neck of the bottle, forming a plug, which is carefully removed before the cork is put in. Like most of the houses in Champagne, Arsenault had been using mechanized riddling pallets for years, but a couple of old riddling frames remained in the *crayères* and now Madeleine pressed them into service.

She had been taught how to riddle the bottles by her grandmother. It didn't take much practice before the technique came back to her. Her guests were amazed by the speed with which she worked.

"You should have seen my grandmother," Madeleine told them. "She could turn ten thousand bottles in a day."

The crowd was suitably awed.

"But that was nothing compared to some of the top riddlers in the big houses. Sixty thousand bottles a day is the fastest I've ever heard of."

After that, she allowed the guests to have a go at it themselves. It resulted in the odd broken bottle when someone tried to show off and ended up knocking the frame over, but it was worth it. Almost every guest left with a crate of Champagne Arsenault's non-vintage Brut.

Madeleine's second harvest was another good one. Once again, she sold the bulk of her grapes to a bigger house but kept the fruit of the Clos Des Larmes for herself. She made the most of the friends from London who came out to help (the same girls as before plus a couple more), guessing that she could rely on their enthusiasm for just one more year at the most. Then all of them would know that there's nothing romantic about spending seven days without sleep in order to get the harvest done.

Still, the second harvest was a more cheerful affair than the last. Lizzy was still living with the new man, who treated her like a princess.

"It's taking some getting used to!" she said. They were even talking marriage.

Likewise the other girls' circumstances all seemed to have taken a turn for the better and the Clos rang with their laughter.

"This year we'll make a Clos Des Rires," said Madeleine.

Meanwhile, the first series of *The Villa* garnered rave reviews. Unlike many of the so-called supermodels, with their exotic backgrounds, and frankly outlandish looks, Christina Morgan was a model that most people in the United States could relate to. Her looks were all-American. She played the part up by dressing for the show in pure classic American sportswear: Ralph Lauren chinos and crisp pink and white shirts. She wore her long blond hair in a swishy ponytail. Her makeup was kept natural. The makeup girl even added a couple of artfully placed freckles to the bridge of Christina's nose for that "just come in from the fields" look. At Greg's suggestion, Christina played up her background too. When she spoke about her childhood in Iowa on the show and in press interviews, her words conjured up wide-open fields, farm animals, good wholesome fun. They said nothing of the reality of her childhood. How boring it had been. The desperate longing to escape.

The public loved it. Christina was soon getting fan mail by the ton. She had to take on an assistant to wade through it, sending out signed photographs to those who included a self-addressed envelope and, of course, making sure that none of them were the kind of letters that might signify a future stalking problem.

Christina's newly raised profile also had the effect of reviving her modeling career. Guilty Secrets tried to woo her back to their catalog. Marisa vetoed that. "Lingerie isn't the kind of work we're looking for anymore," she explained. Marisa did however advise Christina to jump at the chance to be the face of Aspire, a big international cosmetics line. The media made much of the fact that Christina was replacing a model ten years her junior.

"Beauty is ageless," gushed the director of Aspire Cosmetics, as though Christina were sixty-three rather than thirty-six. "Women all over the world can relate to Christina Morgan. Her experiences have only made her more beautiful."

There were changes at the Villa itself too. Prior to the series, the Villa Bacchante had not been open to the public. It was Greg who suggested that it was time to change that. There was a small area of land near the gate that wasn't suitable for growing vines. With Greg's help, Christina applied for permission to build a tasting room with a picnic area. The design of the building echoed the faux Tuscan architecture of the main house. It was surrounded by a garden planted with fresh herbs, like rosemary and lemon verbena, which filled the air with a fabulous scent, mingling with the roses that were a vineyard tradition. From the tasting room she sold Villa Bacchante's wine and other local produce that had been featured on the show.

It was wonderful. Christina had to admit that she got a kick out of the tasting room. Far from being "the great unwashed," most of the people who visited her property in Napa were interesting folk, eager to know about wine rather than coming just to gawp at her home. From time to time, Christina even helped out with pouring glasses. She enjoyed chatting with the wine aficionados and felt exceptionally proud when even the biggest snobs grudgingly admitted that the Villa Bacchante made good wine. Sales went through the roof.

Meanwhile, Christina kept up her involvement with ISACL. Rocky persuaded her to hold a fund-raising dinner for the charity at the Villa Bacchante. It was sponsored by Greg's cable company, who were only too pleased to pay for the catering in return for some footage of Christina's glittering guests. The theme was Bacchanalia, of course. Fancy dress. All the staff (handpicked by a Hollywood casting agent for their suitably gorgeous Roman looks) were dressed in short white tunics. Christina wore a costume originally made for Saffron Burrows in her role as Andromache in *Troy*. It seemed suitably goddesslike.

Greg wore a simple tunic and a wreath of vine leaves. He was a little self-conscious until he'd had a couple of glasses of wine. It wasn't just because he was wearing a skirt, it was also because it was the first time Christina and Greg had gone public with their relationship. As they danced to a slow song at the end of the evening, Christina didn't care who saw them together. She just lay her head on Greg's shoulder and let him waltz her around the room. She was completely, perfectly, happy.

Her happiness continued the next day as she filmed the first segment in her winery for season two. Bottles filled with wine from her very own first harvest were about to get their corks. Christina donned protective specs and stood in front of the production line as the necks of her bottles were dipped in liquid nitrogen, freezing the sediment that had been shaken down by the gyropalettes so that it expanded and popped out.

"This process is known as 'disgorgement,'" Christina told her viewers.

The bottling machines had rattled into life again in Sussex too. And there were changes afoot. Hilarian suggested that a new look was needed to persuade potential customers that Froggy Bottom had moved on from the days when Dougal might as well have been making sparkling vinegar.

Kelly was delighted to take up the challenge of designing a new label.

Everyone agreed that you can't be called "Froggy Bottom" and not have an amphibian somewhere on your bottle. Kelly spent half a day on the Internet looking for a book her mother had read to her when she was a child. Those bedtime stories formed some of her happiest memories. She ordered the book in secret, then, when it arrived, she proudly presented the book and her idea for a label image to Guy and Hilarian.

The book was *The Wind in the Willows*. The illustration that she wanted to copy was a tiny picture of an open-topped classic car sailing over the brow of a hill. At the wheel...

"Mr. Toad," said Hilarian.

"Great idea, eh?" said Kelly.

"Kelly," said Hilarian. "There's a clue in the name here. Mr. *Toad*?"

"And..." Kelly looked confused. "You wanted a picture of a frog. Same thing, isn't it?"

Hilarian sighed but relented when he saw the disappointment creep into Kelly's expression. "Close enough," he told her.

And so the Froggy Bottom label went to press with a picture of Mr. Toad. What did it matter really? It was a funny, humorous little image that would hopefully catch the eye of the wine buyers and their customers in turn. Kelly, at least, was very pleased with it.

Guy wrote the blurb for the back of the label, making much of the "young team" eager to "shake up" the world of winemaking.

"We don't advise you to go shaking up this bottle, however," Guy's blurb concluded. "Acting like a racing driver could leave you with nothing to drink."

When the first bottle bearing the new label rolled off the production line, Kelly snatched it up and cradled it in her arms like a newborn child.

"We made this," she said to Guy proudly.

She finally felt like part of the team.

The post always arrived late at Froggy Bottom. Guy and Kelly were out in the vineyard long before the postman skidded into the courtyard in his red and yellow van and so it wasn't until lunchtime that they found out what had been delivered.

Guy handed Kelly the big envelope. She held it. Her face dropped.

"What is it?"

"I think it's my results from UC Davis," she said. She peered at the American stamp and the postmark that covered it. "It's definitely my results."

"Go on, then. Open it."

"I can't."

"Why not?"

"What if I've failed?"

"You won't have failed."

"I might have."

"Well, if you have failed, not opening the envelope isn't going to change things, is it?"

Kelly knew that but right then, with the envelope still sealed, all her dreams were still intact. Once she opened the envelope and saw that capital letter "F," it would all be over. The good feeling taking the course had given her would evaporate. She would be officially thick again.

"For heaven's sake." Guy snatched the envelope from her. Kelly made a desperate lunge to grab it back but Guy held it high above his head and well out of her reach.

"Sit over there," he commanded, pointing toward the

kitchen table. "And don't move until I say so. I'm going to open this damn envelope for you."

Kelly sat at the table. She leaned forward on her elbows, closed her eyes and covered her ears. Guy ripped the envelope open, pulled out the letter and scanned it quickly.

After what seemed like an age, Kelly opened her eyes and looked up at him. He was frowning.

"I knew it. I knew I'd bloody failed!" Kelly cried. She pushed her chair back from the table and got ready to run upstairs and sob.

Guy merely laughed at her distress. He grabbed her arm as she tried to get past him.

"You passed, you silly sausage. What's more, you passed with distinction."

He handed her the letter. She wiped her eyes and began to read.

"Which makes you even more highly qualified than I am," he went on to say.

Kelly's smile returned as she saw that he really wasn't joking.

"I passed with distinction! I've never passed anything with distinction before!"

"Congratulations," said Guy. "You really deserve this."

He gave her a hug. She continued to snuffle her disbelief into his shoulder.

"How are we going to celebrate?" Guy asked.

"Well," said Kelly. "Now that I am officially the most highly qualified winemaker at Froggy Bottom, I'm going to start bossing you about!"

The one person Kelly really wanted to tell about her success on the wine course was Gina. Before she would allow herself to celebrate, she had to tell her best friend. She called a couple of times but went straight through to voicemail. Guy started getting impatient to open a bottle of Froggy Bottom's finest and toast Kelly's new qualifications. So they went ahead.

Gina finally phoned the next morning.

"Where have you been?" Kelly asked. "I've got big news. I passed that exam."

"I knew you would," said Gina.

"This will be you soon. Celebrating passing your first-year exams at uni."

"I don't know if I'm going to go," said Gina.

"What?"

"I'm not sure what the point is anymore. I'm making really good money. I couldn't earn the same in any ordinary job."

"Come and see me again," said Kelly, thinking that maybe it was time to have a serious talk about where Gina's life was headed. "How about this weekend?"

"I can't," said Gina. "I've got a job. I'm going to St. Tropez. Staying on a yacht."

Kelly could understand why Gina was finding it so hard to break away from the world she'd become involved in. Who wouldn't want to spend their weekends on a luxury yacht? "But it's not as if this guy is your boyfriend," she said.

"You know what?" said Gina. "I sometimes wonder if there isn't a little part of you that is actually jealous of what I'm doing with my life. You're stuck out in Sussex not getting laid and I'm traveling all over the world, getting paid to have better sex than I've ever had."

Kelly was shocked by the force of Gina's accusation. Not least because she wondered in part if it wasn't true. Perhaps she was jealous. Gina was certainly right that Kelly hadn't had much sex since she moved to Froggy

Bottom. Now that she wasn't into hanging out and smoking weed all day, the guys she used to sleep with seemed to find her less interesting. They certainly interested her far less. A few weeks earlier she had been to a party in London and got off with a bloke in the kitchen but it was nothing more than a kiss really. Perhaps Gina's love life was making her envious. But it wasn't a "love life," was it? Gina was having sex for cold hard cash.

"Don't go making the mistake of thinking that one of them is going to fall in love with you, Gina. That only happens in *Pretty Woman.*"

Kelly suddenly found herself talking to dead air. She replaced her own receiver thoughtfully. She didn't feel so much like celebrating anymore.

CHAPTER 43

Axel Delaflote drove through the night from Champagne to the center of Paris. Randon had summoned him at ten o'clock that evening to discuss the ongoing plans for the expansion of Maison Randon. The meeting could not wait until the following morning. Randon was flying out to Napa via London the next day.

Tired and slightly angry, Axel looked at the table as he explained to Randon once more that none of the owners of the vineyards the great man had earmarked for domination were amenable to becoming part of the Domaine Randon empire.

"They don't want our money. They're all doing very well."

"Then we must set about weakening their position," said Randon.

"I don't know how we do that," said Axel. "This year's harvest was excellent. They're all about to release excellent vintages."

"Use your imagination," said Randon. "That is what I pay you for. I want Madeleine Arsenault's vineyard or your head."

"I can't get anywhere near her," said Axel in exasperation.

"Then perhaps you should hand over some of your responsibilities. There's someone I'd like you to work with."

Randon walked across his office to the door that led on to a small private library. Someone was waiting in there.

"I'd like you to meet Monsieur Tremblant," said Randon.

"Jesus," Axel said under his breath as he took in the man's horrible and horribly familiar face.

Axel left Randon's office with a headache but he didn't go straight home. Right then, he wanted to be away from everything to do with Domaine Randon and that meant staying out of his apartment, with the portraits of his employer's cold-eyed ancestors hanging on the walls, as though they were Randon's spies, watching his every move.

Neither did Axel want to go somewhere too familiar. His usual haunt was likely to be full of people he knew, who would ask too many questions about life as Mathieu Randon's sidekick, and he wasn't sure that he would be able to refrain from punching anyone who referred to him as Randon's "poodle" that night. Axel went instead to the bar of a hotel about a mile away from where he lived. It was one of those corporate places, recently refurbished to bring it into line with the rest of the chain to which it belonged, with identical fixtures and fittings so that the traveling businessman could feel at home whether he was in Paris, France, or Paris, Texas. If you didn't step outside you wouldn't know the difference.

Axel took a stool at the long, highly polished bar in the lobby. It was meant to evoke thoughts of Paris in its decadent heyday but there was something just a little too clean about the place. Antiseptic. Right down to the smell. Not that there weren't a few dubious characters there.

Axel ordered two vodka martinis in quick succession and felt the violent energy within him subside just a little. He caught the eye of a woman at the other end of the bar. She was exactly his type. Slender. Dark. She'd painted her eyes with great sweeps of eyeliner that gave her the air of an Ancient Egyptian princess. She reminded Axel of a girl he'd seen in London a couple of times. She had the same narrow shoulders. Slender arms. Tiny waist. The way she flicked her cigarette ash into the ashtray. That same calculated languidity. The girl slowly smiled at Axel with the self-assurance that made him confident she wasn't a tourist, nor was she there on any ordinarily respectable sort of business.

Axel slid a fifty-Euro note across to the barman. He stood up, keeping eye contact with the woman the whole time. She knew what he wanted. As he left the hotel, she followed him. This is becoming a habit, thought Axel.

CHAPTER 44

For a girl with a past like Kelly Elson's, the appearance of a police car always spelled trouble. It put a shiver down her spine. She couldn't help feeling guilty when she saw that blue and yellow livery. And so her first thought, when she saw the squad car pull into the courtyard at Froggy Bottom, was that they were coming for her.

Perhaps someone had complained about the noise from the last Froggy Bottom Fandango, even though the nearest house was a mile away. Or perhaps they were going to arrest her and Guy for making illegal hooch—was there some kind of special license she needed to be a winemaker, she wondered. She hoped Guy was on the case. The last thing Kelly expected was that the two police officers getting out of the car would ask whether she had time to see them. As she stood at her front door, Kelly almost had her wrists out for the handcuffs.

She said she did have time.

"Then perhaps we better come inside," said the female officer. "Put the kettle on, eh?" she added with a sorry sort of smile.

"What's the matter? Is it my mum?" Kelly asked, feeling panic rise. Did Marina need bailing out?

"No. It's not your mum. But it is bad news, I'm afraid."

Kelly sat down. She couldn't think whom the bad news might pertain to. Apart from her mother, she had no family that she knew of. Guy was fine. He was in the winery. Hilarian had called just that morning with news of his post-*Vinifera* party hangover.

"I believe that you knew Ms. Gina Busiri."

Knew? In that single, past-tense word, Kelly heard the full story.

"Is she dead?"

The male officer nodded. "I'm sorry. I know she was your friend."

"She was my best friend," said Kelly.

"We know," said the female officer. "That's why we're here. We need to know who you think she might have been with when she died."

"Where did you find her?"

The female officer insisted on making Kelly a cup of tea before she gave her the blow by blow. At the same time, her colleague went out to the winery and asked Guy if he would mind coming and sitting in the kitchen while Kelly heard the worst. Guy downed tools at once.

"Her body was found about four weeks ago. In the Marne. That's a river in France."

"I know," said Kelly. "It runs through Champagne."

"She'd been dead for a couple of days, we think. The French police guessed that she was English from her Marks & Spencer's tights. She was identified from police records. Fingerprints."

Kelly nodded. She remembered the day that she and Gina had been arrested for shoplifting.

"Her brother confirmed the identification. He put us on to you. We need to know why you think she might have been in France. Who she might have been seeing."

"We fell out. I haven't spoken to her for a while."

"Was she visiting a friend, do you think? Or a client? Was she on the game, Kelly?" the female detective asked. "It's important that we know."

Kelly bit her lip. It was strange. She still felt as though, in trying to help the police piece Gina's last moments together, she would be betraying her.

"I don't think she was meeting a boyfriend," Kelly admitted at last. "I think she was meeting a client."

It was a harrowing afternoon. Guy, Kelly and the police officers sat at the kitchen table and went through the details of Gina's life as Kelly knew them. Kelly covered her eyes with her hands as she recalled the early days of her friendship with Gina. She described their first meeting with an older girl at the hotel who told them exactly how she managed to buy Gucci shoes on a chambermaid's wages and encouraged them to follow suit.

"So, you worked as a prostitute too," said the female detective.

Kelly kept her eyes firmly on the table as she confirmed the worst. She didn't dare meet Guy's eye after that.

The male detective then brought out an envelope full of photographs. He handed them to Kelly one by one and asked her to say when she saw one she recognized. They were mostly police mug shots. Men who looked as though they would kill their own grandmothers for a fiver. Kelly didn't recognize any of them. In some small way, she was relieved she didn't, though she knew it wouldn't help Gina.

"I'm sorry. I don't know any of them."

"Don't worry," said the female detective, squeezing Kelly's hand. "We will find out who killed your friend."

After the police left, Kelly and Guy went back to the kitchen table. Guy put the kettle on at once. He'd become almost English in his reaction to disaster. Kelly gratefully accepted another cup of tea, though she couldn't face the biscuits he also put in front of her—the remains of a packet of Hob Nobs, Gina's favorite.

"I can't believe she's dead," said Kelly. "It doesn't feel right. I mean, I feel like I'd know if she wasn't alive anymore. Perhaps they got the wrong girl."

Guy squeezed Kelly's shoulder but she knew he couldn't offer her any reassurance on that count. Gina's brother had identified the body. The fingerprints and dental records also matched up.

"I encouraged her to go on the game," said Kelly. "It's my fault."

"She made her own choices," said Guy.

"It wasn't just for the money. She wanted to make something of herself. She was saving up so she could go to college."

"I know."

"She could have got a loan instead. I should have encouraged her to do that."

"Yeah," said Guy. "But that was up to her. Do you want more tea?"

"Open a bottle of wine."

Guy frowned.

"Please. Just one between the two of us. I'm not going to drown my sorrows. I just want to make them shut up a bit."

"What do you want? Red or white."

"Petrus," said Kelly. "Gina liked that."

Guy went into the cellar and brought out a bottle from 1982. Having decided that Kelly could be trusted, Hilarian had returned some of Dougal's bottles to the cellar to make room in his own, though this particular Petrus was the one bottle that Hilarian had told them should be drunk in his absence only if nuclear war had been declared.

Kelly sobbed when she saw the label.

"I told Gina we would open this when we both got our degrees," she said.

"Shall we open something else?"

"No," said Kelly.

Guy got two glasses out of the cupboard and made sure they were properly clean before he poured out the first sip.

"To Gina," said Guy.

"To Gina," Kelly choked.

That evening, Kelly told Guy more about herself than she had ever done before. She told him about growing up with her mother. She told him her hazy memories of Dougal and of living in the cottage tied to the big house in Norfolk. She remembered playing on the grass and walking on the fabulous beaches, but then she was uprooted and moved with her mother to South London, where, if you could find any at all, the grass was full of broken glass and dog shit.

She told him about the men who had drifted through her mother's life. None of them were what you would call "gentlemen." A couple of them used to smack Kelly's mother about. One of them even put her in hospital. He smashed her cheekbone. It was hard for Kelly to concentrate on doing well at school when there was so much to worry about at home.

"I didn't know what to do. I tried to protect Mum but she kept going back to them."

"There wasn't anything you could do," said Guy. "She was supposed to be protecting you."

"Perhaps she just couldn't."

Kelly hadn't told anyone but Gina the full story of her life. And now Gina was gone. She hadn't spoken to her mother since she had arrived to stay at Froggy Bottom. She had never felt so alone. Especially now she was sure that she was going to lose Guy too. How could he not see her differently after that day's revelations?

"Can I sleep with you?" Kelly asked suddenly.

Guy was taken aback. "With me?"

"Just tonight. In your flat. I don't think I can be here on my own. Everywhere I look I keep thinking of Gina and the times she was here too."

"OK," said Guy. "Fetch what you need. Let's go across the courtyard."

They lay down on the bed fully clothed. Kelly rolled into the side of Guy's body and laid her head on his chest. Guy kissed the top of her head. Moments later, she was fast asleep.

Guy lay awake for a few more hours, holding Kelly in his arms. That day's revelation about her past had, as she suspected, been a huge shock to him. And he hated himself for the way he'd felt himself begin to react. So bourgeois. His first instinct was disgust. But it was so fleeting. Kelly had come to mean so much to him. She'd been young and unsupported. Her early life sounded like a nightmare. Kelly's life was the result of generations of pain. But she was trying to be different. She was different. She was his Kelly. And he loved her.

PART

THREE

CHAPTER 45

Madeleine, it's Piers Mackesy."

The sound of his perfectly modulated English voice never failed to make Madeleine smile. Almost two years after she turned down his advances in London, Mackesy still continued to prove a particularly helpful contact, putting Madeleine in touch with many hotels and restaurants across France that she might not otherwise have thought of approaching with her champagne. It seemed there wasn't anyone he didn't know.

"I'm coming to France," he said now. "And I'd like to visit Champagne Arsenault and see how Clos Des Larmes is coming on."

Madeleine could think of nothing she would like better.

Piers Mackesy drove to Champagne in the red Aston Martin DB4 that Madeleine remembered from her childhood. When it drew up to the gates of Champagne Arsenault, she was taken right back to the days when she and Georges would race into the courtyard at the sound of the engine's growl. Piers climbed out looking even more like James Bond than his father. Madeleine felt her heart do a little flip at the sight of him but quickly quashed it before she reached him and allowed him a very chaste kiss on the cheek.

Although the nature of their relationship was still flirtatious and the strength of her attraction to him as he stepped out of the car was surprising to her, Madeleine would not let it go further than lighthearted banter. Wine industry gossip was that Mrs. Mackesy was more than happy to spend most of her time in a different country than her husband. They had no children and she'd recently accepted a consultancy position in the fine art department of an auction house in New York. Meanwhile, Mackesy cut a swathe through London. But he had never hinted at marital discord and the ring remained. Perhaps he was just too classy to use the "wife doesn't understand me" line. Perhaps he was happy with the status quo.

They lunched beneath the rose arbor in the garden. Mackesy was entertaining as ever, full of wine world scandal that made Madeleine alternately laugh and sigh. After lunch, she showed him around the winery, and then they climbed down into the caves, where she proudly showed him her Clos Des Larmes, lying in the silent, chilly chalk cellars like a thousand green glass pupae waiting to become butterflies.

"I'm very pleased with it so far," Madeleine confided.

"So you should be. I know it's going to be excellent."

Madeleine tucked her hand through his arm and gave him a little squeeze.

"I've got something else to show you," she told him then.

"Steady . . ."

"Don't get too excited. It's more wine."

She led him through another dark, damp corridor to that part of the *crayères* where her father had kept his own wine.

"Papa's personal collection," Madeleine explained. "I decided it was about time I went through it properly and tried to match up what's in here with the bottles listed in his inventory. I'm about halfway through."

"Perhaps I should come and help you. Though it would be a terrible hardship to have to spend a great deal of time down here in this dark, cold place."

He took a step closer to Madeleine.

"I should have warned you to bring a sweater," she said.

"You know the best way to get warm is by taking your clothes off and snuggling up to another naked person."

"Is it really?" asked Madeleine drily. "I'll bear that in mind."

She handed Mackesy the inventory. Fifty pages in her father's spidery handwriting dating back to the sixties. Mackesy flicked through the little book and nodded approvingly at some of the names.

"Where you see a little pencil star," said Madeleine. "That's a bottle that I've already accounted for."

"Looks like some interesting stuff," said Mackesy. "There's certainly plenty of it."

The rack containing Constant Arsenault's personal collection was ten bottles deep and twenty bottles high.

"Let's see what we have here."

Placing the inventory list on the floor, Mackesy carefully slid a bottle of red wine—a magnum—from the bottom of the rack, making sure not to disturb the settled sediment as he did so. He blew a cloud of dust from the label. A smile tweaked at the corners of Madeleine's mouth as she anticipated the moment when Mackesy realized exactly what he was holding. His eyebrows indicated his surprise. Madeleine confirmed with a nod and a grin.

"I couldn't believe it either," she said. "Château Mouton Rothschild 1945. And there are six of them!"

"Wow," said Mackesy.

"The crate too. Though that's in bits. Could easily be put back together though."

"Incredible."

Mackesy peered closely at the label.

"It's worth, what, thirty thousand pounds a bottle."

"If it's real."

"Of course." Madeleine nodded.

Mackesy got out his glasses.

As Mackesy continued to study the bottle, Madeleine started to get twitchy. She paced the little chalk-walled room. Eventually, she could stand it no longer.

"It is the real thing, isn't it?"

"Hmmm." Mackesy took off his glasses. "I have to say I'm not sure. Perhaps we should take this up into the day-light."

"OK."

Madeleine led Mackesy back to the metal ladder that ascended to the winery.

"You go first," he said. "I'll bring up the rear."

"I'm sure you'd love to," said Madeleine. "But my concern, as patron of Champagne Arsenault, for the safety of my guests dictates that I make sure you leave the *crayères* ahead of me."

Mackesy did as he was told.

They sat down on a bench in the courtyard and Mackesy got out his glasses a second time, for another look at the Mouton.

"Nope." He shook his head.

"What do you mean by 'nope'?"

"This is my speciality," said Mackesy. "I've seen hundreds of bottles and there's something not quite right about this one."

"In what way?"

"It's just an instinct. It's hard to explain. But when you've handled as many bottles of Mouton as I have, you simply get a feel for the real thing. It's like when an art historian looks at a counterfeit painting. A good one. All the details are right but somehow it doesn't quite add up."

"You're telling me that my father bought fake Mouton?"

Mackesy nodded.

"I'm ninety-nine percent certain this isn't the real McCoy."

"But he wouldn't have been so stupid. My father lived wine."

"Indeed he did. But it's a very convincing fake. All sorts of people would have been fooled. I suspect this particular bottle dates from the seventies."

"Rats," said Madeleine. "I thought I was sitting on a fortune."

"There's a one percent chance that you are."

"That's not really what I was after."

"I'm sorry. Let me take you to dinner in Paris to commiserate."

Madeleine hesitated, but only for a moment. There was no harm in going for dinner, was there? She had to go into Paris to run some errands, in any case, and a trip in the DB4 would be infinitely more interesting than the TGV. She could get the last train home.

"I'll just get changed," she told him.

Mackesy made a reservation at Macéo, on the Rue Des Petits Champs. Mackesy knew Mark Williamson, the quietly charming owner, well.

"He's guaranteed us a corner table," Mackesy told Madeleine.

"Not that we need one," she reminded him.

Madeleine liked Macéo. The main room was quietly elegant with a beautiful view of the gardens of the Palais Royal. The maitre d' led them to a table tucked away in the corner, in the Bibliothèque Salace, where a preserved melon belonging to the author Colette had pride of place beneath shelves groaning with erotic literature.

"I've read them all," said Mackesy. He ordered champagne.

"What are we celebrating?"

"There's always something."

Madeleine bit her lip and looked up, as though she were trying to think what that day's celebration might be in aid of.

Axel Delaflote, she thought suddenly. Why on earth had he popped up in her mind again?

Probably for the simple reason that he was standing not twelve feet away from her.

Madeleine sat bolt upright.

"What is it?" Mackesy asked, as he turned in the direction of Madeleine's gaze.

The maitre d' was leading Delaflote and his date to the table right next to theirs. The woman, who was walking ahead of the men, clocked Madeleine immediately and gave her the once-over, as women are prone to do. Madeleine couldn't help staring in return. Delaflote's date was stunning. And familiar. At least six feet tall in her high heels. Straight blond hair that hung almost to her waist. Her dress—vintage Hervé Leger, Madeleine recognized at once—revealed dangerous curves. She could be a model.

The girl sat down and surveyed the room with the peculiar grace of a giraffe looking out over the savannah. Delaflote was about to sit down himself when he noticed Madeleine.

"Madeleine!" He went to kiss her. She subtly avoided his approach. "What a pleasure. This is Viviane Caine," Axel introduced his date to Piers.

"Piers Mackesy. I think we've met somewhere before," he said to Viviane.

"I doubt it," she drawled in a Texan accent. "You probably just recognize me from the new Guilty Secrets campaign. Most guys do."

"Ah. Perhaps," said Mackesy, looking slightly crushed.

"Well, I hope you enjoy your meal," said Madeleine, getting up suddenly. "May I recommend the quail? Always good here. Though watch out for the small bones, Axel. I wouldn't want you to choke. Come on, Piers."

Mackesy looked confused. "But . . ."

"We should get to that party you were talking about before the hostess is too drunk to notice we turned up."

"Ah, yes," said Mackesy. "The party."

He reluctantly left his gazpacho.

"Good-bye, Axel. Viviane."

Viviane managed a lazy smile before turning back to her menu.

"Good-bye, Madeleine," said Axel. "You'll be ready to talk to me soon, I hope. You have my number."

"Oh yes," said Madeleine. "I've got your number."

"What was that all about?" Mackesy asked when they got outside.

"Can we just go for a walk?" Madeleine asked.

"Of course. That was Randon's man, wasn't it?"

Madeleine nodded tightly.

"You cut him dead. What did he ever do to you?"

"You mean, apart from tell me I don't know how to run a champagne house?"

"Which you clearly do," Mackesy said quickly.

"I don't want to talk about it."

"Then I won't make you."

But she couldn't not think about it.

She and Mackesy strolled through the dark streets around the Church of the Madeleine. It was starting to rain. Mackesy tried to lighten the moment with gossip about wine world acquaintances.

"Ah, Casanova's street," he said as they turned into Rue Danielle Casanova.

"Oh for goodness" sake. Danielle Casanova," said Madeleine. "The *resistance fighter* not the roué."

Mackesy shrugged. "I was just trying to make you smile."

"I'm sorry."

"Maybe I should try something different."

Without asking for permission, he pulled Madeleine toward him and planted his lips firmly upon hers.

Madeleine rewarded him with a thump.

"Shit. I forgot. Must have more integrity." Mackesy rolled his eyes as Madeleine stormed off in the direction of L'Opéra.

He caught up with her.

"I'm sorry," he said.

"It's OK. I'm sorry I thumped you. Which hotel are you staying in?"

Mackesy looked at her quizzically.

"Which hotel?"

"The Hyatt Madeleine," he said. "I liked the name."

"Isn't that in this direction?" Madeleine jerked her thumb toward the Rue Malesherbes.

"Yes, but... The station is in this direction... I should get you back to Champagne."

"Let's go to your place," Madeleine said.

"What? You want to? For a nightcap?"

"Sure," she said. "Why not?"

She stuck out her arm and hailed a taxi.

In the back of the car, Madeleine took Mackesy by the collar and pulled him toward her. They started kissing.

"Are you sure?" Mackesy murmured into her mouth.

"I am."

Madeleine let Mackesy press his body hard against hers as the cab crawled through the glittering wet streets. The rain was slowing the traffic down but the lovers couldn't wait.

The taxi driver kept his eyes on the road as Madeleine unzipped Mackesy's fly and slipped her hand inside his trousers. Just a few minutes of kissing but he already had an enormous erection. Meanwhile, Mackesy lifted the hem of Madeleine's skirt and slid his hand up her smooth stocking-clad leg to the red silk knickers she had bought just that afternoon in Galeries Lafayette in an emergency shopping trip. Red knickers for good luck, the girl at the counter had said. They certainly seemed to be working.

By the time the taxi journey ended, Mackesy was just about ready to fuck Madeleine right there in the back of the car. But she tucked his penis back into his trousers and he managed to look presentable as he dealt with paying the fare, hopping from one foot to the other impatiently while the driver counted out change. Meanwhile, Madeleine dashed across the pavement to the safety of Mackesy's hotel. All the buttons on the front of her new black dress were undone, exposing the red slip that matched her knickers.

Mackesy opened the door to the lobby and ushered Madeleine inside with his hands on her buttocks. She laughed at his cheek.

They continued to kiss in the mirrored elevator to the seventh floor where Mackesy had his room. While he was busy kissing every bare inch of her skin he could find, Madeleine caught a glimpse of herself over his shoulder. She was surprised at the wild woman looking back at her. Her hair had come loose. Her lips were red and swollen from kissing. Her cheeks were flushed. She felt so turned on that she ground her pelvis against Mackesy's thigh like a stripper in some cheap nightclub.

The elevator doors opened and the couple stumbled out onto the landing, still kissing as Mackesy fumbled in his pocket for his key.

They half danced into his suite, shedding more clothes as they went. Mackesy pulled off his shoes without untying the laces. Madeleine meanwhile unfastened his belt and pulled his trousers down to his knees.

With buttons all the way down the front from collar to hem, Madeleine's dress was extremely easy to wriggle out of. It wasn't long before she stood before Mackesy in just her red slip. Tiny knickers. Stockings. Black. Seamed. And her brand-new black Louboutin pumps with their red soles that matched her underwear.

Mackesy looked as though he was about to say something but settled instead for growling into the side of Madeleine's neck. He wrapped his arms around her and squeezed until she could barely breathe. Then he smothered her neck and breastbone with yet more kisses. Madeleine let herself melt beneath Mackesy's ardent attentions. She felt as light as the dress she had just discarded when he scooped her up and carried her into the bedroom.

Once there, Madeleine kicked off her shoes and stretched out luxuriously on the chocolate-colored satin bedspread. Mackesy was completely naked by now. His erection stood out so proudly in front of him that Madeleine couldn't resist draping her knickers from it, like a flag. He modeled them for her while Madeleine took in the body that had been hinted at by those lovely suits: his broad chest with its tidy smattering of dark hair, his strong legs, his big shoulders. His stomach was impressively muscled for a man in his forties. Sexy as hell.

She wondered whether he was appraising her in the

same way as his gaze wandered from her face to her breast-bone and lower, to the tops of her thighs. Subconsciously she brushed her hand across her breasts, outlining their perfectly rounded contours. Advertising their soft warm perfection. Did he find her as attractive as she found him?

His body gave him away. Mackesy tossed Madeleine's knickers into the corner of the room. His erection was still enormous.

"My turn to tease you," Mackesy growled, kneeling on the floor beside the bed. He pulled Madeleine so that her bottom rested on the edge of the mattress. Her feet were on the floor. He parted her knees and positioned himself between them. He pushed the red silk slip out of the way, exposing Madeleine's pelvis and the neat little triangle of her pubic hair. Placing his hands on either side of that triangle, Mackesy carefully spread Madeleine's labia to expose her rosebud clitoris and bent his head toward it.

"Oh God."

Madeleine began to shiver with delight before Mackesy got anywhere near her. She grabbed up handfuls of the satin counterpane in deliciously nervous anticipation as she felt his hot breath on her pubis.

Mackesy was soon using his skillful tongue to flick Madeleine's clitoris from side to side. The tiny bud was already engorged and each movement of Mackesy's tongue against it sent a little jolt of power throughout Madeleine's entire body.

The sensation was almost too intense. Madeleine tried to sit up. To stop him. But Mackesy wouldn't let her. He pushed Madeleine back down onto the bed almost roughly and continued to work at her vagina with his warm, wet mouth. While his tongue massaged her clitoris, he slipped a finger into her and sought out her G-spot. The combination of the two actions—his tongue flickering against her clit and his finger stroking her deep inside—increased her pleasure immeasurably.

Madeleine gasped as Mackesy worked faster. She reached for his head, wanting to pull his mouth away from her before she exploded, but he still would not stop. He was determined to take her all the way no matter how much she protested. Eventually, Madeleine didn't want to protest anymore. Some animal part of her psyche took over and suddenly every nerve in her body was starting to sing. Like a roller coaster reaching the top of a loop, there was only one way to go.

Madeleine felt the muscles in her thighs grow tense as she braced her feet against the floor and Mackesy continued to lick her. She closed her eyes and gave in to Mackesy's insistent ministrations. Her vagina tightened around his finger with the first hint of the orgasm to come. This time it was Madeleine who said, "Don't stop," when Mackesy seemed to be slowing down. She was so close. She could feel it.

"Keep going," she demanded throatily. Mackesy did as he was told until he felt Madeleine's vagina begin to pulse and her hips start to buck up toward his mouth. Her breath came out in a series of excited little yelps. Her limbs tensed and twisted on the chocolate satin sheets. She seemed unable to stop her body from arching toward the sky. She cried out, "Piers!" She was lost. Then she collapsed back, with her arm across her eyes. Excited, exhausted, and ever so slightly embarrassed.

The following morning, Madeleine was out of bed before Mackesy awoke. She almost managed to get out of the room without waking him. But not quite.

Madeleine sat down at the bottom of the bed.

"About last night—" she began.

"Well, I think we were pretty well behaved, all things considered," Mackesy interrupted.

"Gold stars all round," Madeleine agreed.

There was nothing else to say. Mackesy suggested breakfast but Madeleine said she had to be out of there and on the train back to Champagne.

"Meeting with a guy from the CIVC," she lied.

So they said good-bye. It was an awkward sort of farewell. Madeleine half wanted to evaporate into thin air to avoid the moment. She half wanted him to wrap her in his arms again and force her to stay. He kissed her on the cheek. Madeleine closed her eyes to feel the kiss once more as she descended in the lift to the lobby, but she felt sure she would never see him again.

CHAPTER 46

Mathieu Randon was very pleased to have Viviane Caine front his flagship brand. She was arguably the hippest model in the world right then, having stolen Kate Moss's latest boyfriend. Such associations mattered when you were trying to get into the heads of the faceless scumbags they called the "general public." Not that the general public would be able to afford even a single glass of Éclat, of course.

Domaine Randon was working to a plan that the fashion world knew well. None of the big fashion houses made money on their haute couture, but the glamorous association shifted their mass-produced diffusion lines and brand-name perfume by the ton. Likewise, a fabulous new image for Éclat would, eventually, shift a European wine lake's worth of Domaine Randon's cheaper brands.

It was a pity Viviane Caine's beauty was only skin deep. Both men and women loved her. Her face gave the impression of a lively intelligence combined with warmth and compassion. Alas, it was just an impression. One didn't have to spend long in Viviane's company to discover that her only topic of interest was herself. Thankfully, she had borrowed not only Kate Moss's boyfriend but also the supermodel's zip-lipped attitude to the media, and so, for the most part, the illusion remained unbroken. She was a blank canvas and an empty vessel. There was no risk that Viviane Caine would suddenly get morality and bite the hand that was feeding her cocaine habit as Christina Morgan had done.

Still, Randon didn't want to spend a lot of time in Viviane's company. That was why he asked Axel Delaflote to take her out to dinner and joined them only at the end of the evening for coffee.

But just because he didn't want to spend three hours listening to her talk about herself didn't mean Randon had no use for Viviane at all.

Axel left them in the restaurant. Randon took Viviane back to his place. If she had seemed a little put out that her new employer had skipped dinner, the lines of coke Randon arranged on a silver tray on the coffee table helped her get over it. She fell upon them like an asthmatic grabbing for an inhaler.

"You're a mysterious guy," she said as, lines snorted, she settled herself on one of Randon's enormous leather sofas. "But that's OK because I'm mysterious too."

It was Randon who snorted this time. Viviane Caine was no mystery to him. She'd been reading too much of her own press. She'd realize one day that there was nothing to her at all. She was merely the sum of freakily good bone structure enhanced by a makeup artist's skill and a photographer's art. Painted and lit well she was a goddess. Stripped bare, a nobody. Just like the rest of them.

"Did you like the pictures?" Viviane nodded toward the contact sheet that lay on the glass-topped coffee table.

"They were OK," said Randon, picking the sheet up and tossing it back down again with some disdain. He had been very pleased indeed but there was no need for her to know that now.

As a young man, Randon had quickly learned that every woman wanted the opposite of what she got the most of. Plain Janes like his former secretary, Bertille, needed to be complimented into bed. A woman like Viviane Caine, whose entire life was praise and compliments, needed to be made insecure before she took her clothes off.

But she took Randon's lack of enthusiasm in her stride.

"Perhaps you need to pay for a better photographer," she said.

"Maybe," said Randon.

There was a moment of silence as they simply looked at each other. They were sizing each other up, trying to work out who was in charge here.

"So," Viviane swirled her glass so that the ice cubes tinkled against the crystal. "Are you keeping me from my beauty sleep for any particular reason?"

"I thought you might like to sleep with me," said Randon bluntly.

A slow smile spread across Viviane's famously wide mouth. It might have been interpreted as a smile of disdain, but Randon knew otherwise. He could tell in the way she suddenly angled her body toward him that he had her. No mystery to Miss Caine...

"What on earth gave you that impression?" she began. He knew she wanted him to praise her body and catalog the ways she turned him on but Randon wasn't going to oblige. He didn't want to get into some long drawn-out flirtation. That didn't interest him at all.

Instead, Randon got up and walked across to the sofa where Viviane was lounging. He grabbed her roughly by the wrist and yanked her onto her feet.

"Hey!" she said, stumbling a little in her high heels. "What's up with you?"

"But you like it like that, don't you," said Randon.

It was a statement, not a question.

And it was true that Viviane didn't protest as he squeezed her wrist tighter and pulled her closer. When she was close enough, Randon tucked his fingers into the neckline of her red dress and, in a single, horribly effective motion, ripped the garment from collar to hem.

"For fuck's sake!" said Viviane. "This is vintage fucking Leger."

"I'll buy you a new one," said Randon quite calmly.

"It was a one-off, you fucker."

"Language," said Randon.

He crushed Viviane's mouth beneath his own. That kept her quiet. While he kissed her, he made short work of the rest of her clothing. Her La Perla bra fell apart as easily as a cobweb and she wasn't wearing any knickers. No mystery there either. Randon smiled to himself. Viviane Caine was exactly the kind of girl who thought going commando was *le dernier cri* in libertine sophistication. So daring. Yet so commonplace these days.

Randon stuck a finger straight inside her. She gasped in surprise. Her brow wrinkled. But again her protests were short-lived. Soon she was moaning hungrily and leaning into Randon as he worked at her warm wet cunt.

"Where I come from they call this finger-banging," she said almost wistfully.

"I don't care what they call anything where you come from," said Randon. "Shut up or I'll have to silence you again."

"Are you always so..."

She didn't shut up. And so soon she was on her knees in front of him, taking his penis in her mouth.

It gave him a little kick, seeing her kneeling on the floor. His very own supermodel whore. But not as big a kick as it would have been to see Christina Morgan there.

"Does this feel good?" Viviane somehow managed to ask without taking her mouth from his cock.

Randon answered her by putting his hand on the back of her head and pulling her closer so that his penis slid farther down her throat. Her eyes widened with annoyance but he didn't take any notice. He just held her there. She soon settled back into giving him what he wanted.

And meanwhile Randon concentrated on what he wanted. Christina Morgan where she deserved to be. *Her* lips wrapped around his cock. Or Madeleine Arsenault. The stuck-up bitch. *Her* face looking up at him for approval. He was going to finish that girl off in more ways than one. Viviane had no idea that she was being used as a blank canvas again. To Randon right then she was merely a screen for the projection of another dream, just as she was every time she stepped into a photographer's studio.

But Viviane was not just a classically pretty face. She fellated Randon with such skill that he was soon on the point of coming. The speed with which he got there surprised him. He glanced down at her. She looked pleased with herself. She winked.

That wouldn't do.

Randon pushed her away from him. Viviane fell backwards onto her arse.

"Hey!"

"Get up," he said, grabbing her roughly by the wrist again.

Viviane struggled to get up from the floor. She was still wearing her Manolos and they made her as unsteady as a foal trying to walk for the first time. Randon quickly grew impatient and bodily lifted her back onto her feet. She followed him into the bedroom.

"You are one crazy man," she said.

"I'm just getting started."

Randon's bedroom was like a hotel room. There was nothing to betray the man who slept there. No personal pictures. Not a thing out of place. Not even a stray pair of cuff links on the simple ebony nightstand. The bed was made to military standards of precision. Plain white sheets. A gray cashmere blanket for those colder nights. Anyone who hoped to get a glimpse into the real man behind Domaine Randon would be very disappointed.

Still Randon wasn't concerned whether his infrequent guests thought the austerity of his official home strange.

He discarded his robe as he shoved Viviane down onto the bed and climbed on top of her. He pulled her legs apart and pushed straight into her. She gasped. He was quite a big man. But soon she had her legs wrapped around his back.

Viviane was quite the theatrical lover. Each thrust from Randon elicited some vocal response. She threw her head back and periodically raked her fingers through her hair as though she were feeling transported. From time to time she changed the routine and raked her fingers down Randon's back instead. Her beautifully manicured fingers, painted in Chanel polish so dark red it was almost black, left dramatic pink welts on Randon's skin.

"Are you going to come?" she asked him. It was half-enticing, half-impatient. It stopped Randon's arousal in its tracks.

"Keep quiet," he said, pulling out of her and flipping her over so that she lay facedown in the pillows.

He entered her from behind, trying to find his rhythm again. The pillows at least muffled Viviane's squeaks and moans.

But it wasn't enough. As he pumped, Randon reached into a drawer in his nightstand and took out a bottle of lube. He squeezed some into his hand and massaged it into Viviane's anus. In an almost seamless movement, he pulled his penis out of her vagina and stuck it into her arsehole.

Viviane shouted out in protest but Randon took no notice. His big, strong body pinned hers to the bed. There was nothing she could do but try to bat him away with her hands. It made no difference. In fact, he liked it more when she struggled. It made him harder. She felt it.

He came as he always did. Silently. In an eerily controlled fashion. He pulled out at once and fell back onto the bed, breathing heavily. As he stared up at the ceiling, waiting for his breath to calm down, Viviane slithered across the mattress to be closer to him. She rolled into his side. She slung an arm across his chest. She rested her head on his shoulder and closed her eyes.

"The guest bedroom is on the other side of the apartment," he said.

CHAPTER 47

Back in Champagne after her night with Piers Mackesy, Madeleine found herself feeling pretty down. She knew that what they had done was wrong, but at the same time, she found herself wishing she could see him again. She knew that Mackesy would be in Champagne again that afternoon, visiting some houses near Ay. Perhaps, she allowed herself to dream, he would drop by. At least they could try to repair their friendship.

And so Madeleine jumped to attention when she heard a car crunch on the gravel in front of the house. She abandoned her laptop and looked out of her office window hopefully. But it wasn't the DB4. It wasn't a car she recognized at all.

Madeleine was alone in the house that day. Henri, who could normally be relied upon to drift in and out several times, had taken the day off to visit his daughter in Normandy. Still Madeleine felt fairly safe as she opened the door to the stranger.

"Madeleine Arsenault," said the man, as he grabbed for Madeleine's hand and kissed it roughly. "What a pleasure."

"Who are you?" asked Madeleine, suddenly wishing she had been a little less trusting and not opened the door so wide. Though she battled against the part of her that made such primeval judgments, wanting so much to believe that you couldn't judge anyone by the way they looked, her every instinct was to get rid of the man now stepping inside. Everything about his face spoke of violence, from his twisted little mouth to the scar that closed his eye.

"You don't mind if I come in," he said. Madeleine did mind but it was a statement, not a question.

She looked out into the street in desperation, hoping that someone would be passing by. But there was no one else to be seen except her visitor's driver, who looked no less menacing.

"My vineyard manager will be back in ten minutes," said Madeleine, hoping that would be enough to scare the men off.

"Ten minutes is all we need," said the man. "My name is Michel Tremblant, but you can call me Mick. I was a friend of your father's."

"He never mentioned you."

"I dare say he didn't. We didn't see much of each other in his last couple of years. I was inside, you see."

Madeleine felt her insides begin to liquefy. This was getting worse.

"But we were great friends once, your father and I. He liked to play cards."

"I didn't know that," Madeleine lied.

"But he wasn't very good at it. And when I went inside, he still owed me two hundred thousand Euros."

"What?"

"A lot of money, isn't it? I expect he thought I'd write it off when I went into prison. Or that I might forget about it while I was doing time. But I got out earlier than I expected to, thanks to a very generous friend of mine. And now I need the money back. You've inherited Champagne Arsenault. You've inherited the debt."

"Why should I even believe there is a debt?" asked Madeleine.

"Just because you don't believe there's a debt doesn't mean I won't get upset if you can't pay it," said Mick.

"I can't pay it."

"I'm a reasonable man," said Mick. "I didn't expect you to have the cash to hand. But I do need it soon. Christmas, shall we say? I need to buy presents for my kids. *Au revoir,* sweet Madeleine." He kissed her hand again and was gone.

Closing the door firmly behind him, Madeleine sank onto the bottom stair. Two hundred thousand Euros was a ridiculous amount of money to lose in a bet and yet...she remembered the day that Philip Mackesy sent a truck to pick up her father's Facel Vega and take it back to England after their last card game. Constant Arsenault had never been a cautious man. Which had made it all the harder after Georges's death.

"You must have encouraged him to climb too high," Constant berated Madeleine after Georges fell from the apple tree in the Clos and broke his neck. That Georges might just take after his father and live for the thrill of the high climb or the big bet didn't seem to occur to him.

"Oh, Papa," Madeleine cried into her hands. "What am I supposed to do now?"

CHAPTER 48

Christina Morgan felt a small twinge of something approaching annoyance when she saw Viviane Caine in the new Randon Éclat advertising campaign. But it was just a small twinge. Really, there was no reason for Christina to envy Viviane anymore. She didn't need the Éclat campaign or the Guilty Secrets advertising deal. Christina had something far better.

Like the first, the second season of *The Villa* was a huge success. It was no surprise whatsoever when Greg announced that the channel was going to commission a third. Getting high-profile guests was no problem at all. Top chefs flew in from all over the world to take part and winemakers clamored for the exposure *The Villa* could bring them. Having Ronald Ginsburg as the show's resident critic definitely gave *The Villa* kudos among the wine fraternity. Meanwhile, the show had been extended to include a "dinner party" segment, wherein assorted celebrities who had no direct link to the world of food and drink would sit around a table and discuss their latest projects.

As the show never failed to mention, the Villa Bacchante was a proper, working vineyard, but Christina no longer had to worry about how she would distribute her wine and persuade people to buy it. In fact, she had the opposite problem. The wholesalers couldn't get enough of her. It was difficult to meet the demand. It meant that Christina faced an interesting dilemma.

She had hoped to age her wine in the bottle for at least two years before it was degorged and the fermentation process stopped. But her management team tried to persuade her to bottle far earlier than she wanted to in order to get it into the shops.

"Strike while the iron is hot," said Karl, who worked with Marisa on maximizing Christina's exposure. "In two years' time, the public will be going crazy over some boy-band star's cider instead. Then you can keep your wine in barrels for ten years. Twenty. You'll have made your fortune."

Christina was almost ready to agree. But Ronald Ginsburg stopped her.

"There's no way you're going to rush out your first vintage," he said firmly. "I've got money riding on you, remember."

"That's not a persuasive argument," said Christina.

"OK. Forget me. Forget the money. *You* have a reputation riding on it. I believe that if we do this right, we can win that wager at the *Vinifera* awards and the Villa Bacchante will be established as a winery to be reckoned with. A good reputation will long outlast the show."

Christina wavered. She had definitely enjoyed the serious attention the villa had been getting in the pages of *Vinifera* as pundits discussed the progress of her wine in anticipation of Ronald's silly competition.

"You want to be taken seriously, I hope," said Ronald.

Christina did. "OK," she said. "We'll stick to the plan."

"Good girl."

It wasn't as though Christina needed the money. Her bank account was looking very healthy indeed. Especially since the launch of the magazine to accompany the show. Within two months of hitting the newsstand, *Villa Living* was rivaling Oprah's O. Like Oprah, Christina appeared on every cover of her magazine. She had just shot the Thanksgiving cover, for which she dressed in suitably autumnal shades of orange and brown.

She was doing far better than she ever imagined possible. Suddenly, the question of what she would do when the modeling came to an end was no longer an issue. She barely had time to breathe. She did however find time for her continuing involvement with ISACL. Following the success of the "I Don't Buy It" campaign, ISACL had become the Hollywood charity of choice, inundated with requests from all the big agents, keen that their clients should be associated with such a popular cause. Christina went from being a minor player in the charity to being the star around which it revolved. She was fronting the latest campaign, standing right in the middle for the group photograph that would appear in *Vanity Fair*. Rocky stood to the side of her: Midge Ure to her Bob Geldof. People soon forgot that ISACL was Rocky's baby.

Christina was interviewed in the *New York Times* Sunday magazine.

"The 'I Don't Buy It' campaign is still an important initiative for ISACL," she told the interviewer. "Consumer pressure works. Many of the brands we named and shamed in that first infomercial investigated the working practices of their suppliers as a result." She discussed a high-profile case in which an American designer had moved her production back to the United States after discovering that child labor had been used to produce some of her designs. The designer had raised her prices to cover the increased costs but had found, to everyone's surprise, that the public were only too happy to pay extra for a clean conscience.

"Her business is booming," Christina confirmed. "And as a gesture of gratefulness, I wore one of her dresses to the *Vanity Fair* Oscars party."

The journalist continued, "You famously lost the Maison Randon advertising campaign as a result of your involvement with ISACL and it's been rumored that was part of the reason for your divorce from Bill Tarrant, who was dropped from the campaign at the same time. Do you ever think that the personal cost of your principles might have been too high?"

"Not at all," said Christina in a heartfelt way. "In fact, I can look back on the Maison Randon episode and say that it freed me from a lot of things that were wrong in my life." She talked about the series of events that had led her to the place in which she found herself now. She brimmed with happiness as she talked about how Greg had come back into her life and the domesticity they now shared between Los Angeles and the Napa Valley.

"No," she concluded. "I have no regrets at all. I can't imagine any sum of money that would be worth more than my spiritual enlightenment, the freedom I gained from it and the way my life has turned out as a result."

"Spiritual enlightenment," Randon spat when he read the piece. That stupid American woman was still spouting her yoga speak. And libel! Following the "I Don't Buy It" campaign, Christina had entered into an agreement that she would never mention the name of Champagne Randon in an interview ever again. She had just fucked up in a big way. Randon picked up his mobile and flicked through the contacts until he found the number for his lawyer. They had every reason to slap a writ on her that afternoon.

But then Randon thought better of it.

He closed his phone. Perhaps the best course of action was to appear to ignore this latest indiscretion. To go after her with writs might have the opposite effect to that which Randon wanted. His beloved brand name had appeared just once in an interview that would be old news by Monday morning. Taking Christina to court would put Maison Randon on the front pages again in a bad way. Who goes to such lengths to protect their innocence unless they're guilty, was what Randon thought every time he saw that someone had initiated a libel action. And yet, Christina could not be allowed to get away with it. Something had to be done to bring that stupid woman back down to earth. It was time to get creative.

Randon spent a few moments sitting at his desk, just

looking into space as he ran a few pleasant scenarios—pleasant for him, that is—through his head. Then, with his humor partially restored, he picked his phone up again and scrolled through the numbers therein until he found Odile Levert's.

PART Four

CHAPTER 49

That year Gerry Paine threw the *Vinifera* Christmas party at Macéo. It took place two weeks before Christmas. The guest list was comprised of the usual suspects. Hilarian caught the Eurostar over on the morning of the party and met up with Odile and Ronald for a quick sharpener in Willi's Bar before they put on their best professional faces for the official engagement next door.

Hilarian noticed at once that Ronald was wearing a new Rolex. Gold. It was impossible not to notice. Ronald was waving his arms around like a Muppet.

"Don't let it catch the light like that," Hilarian told him. "You might blind me."

"Nice watch," said Odile. "If you like that kind of thing."

"A little gift to myself. From my television fee."

Hilarian shook his head. Bloody Ginsburg. To think he had been so angry when Gerry Paine insisted he champion Christina Morgan and her Villa Bacchante for their wager. The old git had lucked out big-time with his segment on her TV show.

"They've commissioned another season," said Ronald, as he adjusted the time on his watch by a couple of minutes.

"Perhaps you might like to share the wealth," said Hilarian. "Must be exhausting for you week after week. You should take a holiday. I can think of a couple of people who might be suitable stand-ins."

"Christina and I have a great rapport," said Ronald, ignoring Hilarian's hints. "She's a true professional. And a fantastic winemaker, to boot."

"You still think she's got a chance against my Arsenault Clos Des Larmes?"

"Clos Des Larmes?" Hilarian said the name with reverence.

"First vintage in a decade."

"You really think it was such a good year in Champagne?" said Ronald.

"I do," said Odile. "I look forward to taking your money. Trust that I will buy myself an altogether more tasteful souvenir than your piece of bling, dear Ronnie."

"You're forgetting about Froggy Bottom," said Hilarian.

"Yes," said Ronald. "We're all forgetting about Froggy Bottom."

Hilarian took a thoughtful sip of his drink. Ronald wanted to get a rise out of him, he knew, but he wasn't about to give in to the goading.

"Look out," he said instead. "Here comes Gerry."

"What are you three doing in here?" Gerry asked. "The party's started next door."

Of course, no wine magazine's Christmas party could really be expected to be a sober sort of affair. By five o'clock, the guests who had begun the afternoon talking about that year's *en primeur* prices were confessing their darkest desires. Ronald Ginsburg in particular took great advantage of Gerry Paine's hospitality. So it was hardly surprising that the old guy was a little unsteady on his feet as he stepped out of the restaurant onto the icy street. The leather soles of his handmade shoes offered very little grip and he was soon "arse over tit" as Hilarian put it. When Hilarian, Odile and Ronald himself had finished laughing at the sight of Ronald on his bottom in the gutter, they realized that Ronald couldn't get back up. Hilarian and Odile did their best to help him, tucking their arms beneath his armpits, but the pain was too much.

An ambulance was called at once. Ronald had broken a hip.

Hilarian and Odile accompanied Ronald in the ambulance. Ronald had almost begged Odile to come along, fearing that his schoolboy French would not be enough to keep the Parisian doctors from sawing off his leg. All the cockiness he had shown in Willi's Bar was gone. He looked every one of his seventy years as he lay on the gurney beneath a gray blanket.

An X-ray revealed that the break was a bad one, which would require a complicated operation and a long period of recuperation afterward. Ronald would not be going home for Christmas. That was for sure.

He definitely would not be fit to film a segment on Champagne for *The Villa*'s special New Year's edition. He'd been planning to drive out to the country from Paris that very evening. The film crew had arrived at Charles De Gaulle from Los Angeles that afternoon and was probably even now settling in at the Château Les Crayères.

"Well, you're not going anywhere," said the surgeon. As it was, because Ronald had been drinking all afternoon—and drinking heavily—the operation he needed would have to be put off until the morning at the very earliest. He was facing a night of agony.

"This is a disaster," said Ronald. "Worst of all, I was supposed to be having dinner in Paris with Christina the night after the shoot finished. Just her and me. In her hotel suite so we could taste her wine."

"Oh dear," said Odile. "But probably for the best, Ronald dearest. You know she would have been all over you like a rash."

Hilarian sniggered into his handkerchief but managed to disguise it as a sneeze.

Hilarian had to leave to catch his train back to London. Odile stayed a little longer, translating the forms that Ronald had to fill out before the operation could take place. She stepped outside for a moment to check her messages on her mobile and found one from Randon.

"I have a small favor to ask of you," he said.

She called him back and told him about Ronald's accident. When Randon replied, "It's an ill wind," she knew exactly what he meant.

At the Château Les Crayères in Reims, *The Villa*'s traveling production crew was recovering from their long-haul flight to Paris. Rather than eat in the dining room, Christina and Greg had ordered room service. Christina laughed with delight when it arrived. She had stayed in plenty of top hotels but she had never seen a TV dinner presented quite so beautifully. The sommelier even took a moment out from the restaurant to come and pour their wine.

Christina and Greg were just about to start eating when the telephone rang. Greg took the call. It was Ronald. She could tell by the look on Greg's face that the news was not good.

"Shall I have my office arrange for your wife to be flown over?" Greg asked. "No? Well, if you're sure that a visit from her definitely *won't* make you feel better . . . But of course you mustn't worry about the Champagne segment. We'll think of something. Unless you can suggest anyone who might be a good stand-in."

Greg wrote the words "Odile Levert" on a notepad.

CHAPTER 50

Odile Levert hesitated for just a couple of seconds when Greg Stroud called and asked—nay, practically begged her—to take over from Ronald for *The Villa*'s special report from France.

Greg ran through the list of champagne houses that would be taking part in the following day's shoot. They were all pretty obvious: Bollinger, Moët, Veuve Clicquot.

"May I make a suggestion of my own?" asked Odile. "Something a little more boutique. Champagne Arsenault?"

"We'll check it out. We need you here really early, I'm afraid. Like before breakfast. Can I send a car for you now? I'm sure we can find you a room here at Les Crayères."

"That won't be necessary," said Odile. "Just tell me where you'd like me to appear in the morning and I will be there."

Odile was actually already on her way to Champagne. She had taken Greg's call on the platform at the Gare De L'Est, from whence she took a train to Épernay. She was met at the station by Mathieu Randon's driver, who took her straight to the Maison Randon house, where she would join Randon himself for dinner.

Randon, alerted to Odile's arrival by the gatehouse, was already standing on the front step when she arrived. He opened her car door for her. The perfect gentleman as always.

"I'm very glad you could make it at such short notice," he said, kissing her on both cheeks. He led Odile into the house, where a uniformed servant was ready with a silver tray and two glasses.

"Champagne?" Randon suggested.

"Of course."

Odile followed Randon into the dining room.

"No Axel this evening."

Randon was unable to disguise an irritated intake of breath.

"He's in Montpellier."

"Ah. And how are his efforts to buy that extra land you want coming along?"

"Taking rather longer than I hoped. I'm not sure he's got what it takes. Certainly Madeleine Arsenault seems to be immune to his charms."

"She has more tenacity than I imagined," Odile agreed. "I can't think of anything that will part her from her birthright, save a real calamity."

"Calamities can always be arranged," said Randon. "Tell me more about her father's gambling debts."

"That would be indiscreet." Odile smiled.

But then the conversation moved on to the other reason for Odile's presence in Champagne that night.

"So, you're ready for your television appearance?"

"I have to admit I'm looking forward to it," said Odile. "I'm especially looking forward to properly meeting Christina Morgan. Poor Ronald is distraught."

Randon laughed.

"But of course you've met her many times," Odile continued.

"Unfortunately for me," said Randon.

Odile snorted. "Then you still haven't forgiven her for giving you that ticking off about those poor children. I thought you might hold it against me that I agreed to appear on her show."

"When it dovetailed so neatly with my desire to have you here in Champagne tonight? Not at all. On the contrary, I would say that your invitation to appear on the show was the perfect win-win situation for me."

One of the house staff trotted over to the table with two white plates. In the middle of each plate was a small tower of thinly sliced vegetables, topped off with a little pastry lattice. While the girl, who was on a sabbatical from Domaine Randon in Napa, explained what she was serving in awkward French, Odile studied Randon closely. Randon was too busy studying the girl to notice that he himself was being observed. His desires might as well have been printed on his forehead, thought Odile. The girl certainly seemed to notice. She was blushing crimson by the time she had finished describing the dish.

Randon sent her away with a nod.

"Bonne dégustation," he said.

Odile had often seen that look in Randon's eyes. The women he turned it on seemed to respond to it. Odile never had. It had never come up. From the moment she met Randon it was as though he knew where Odile Levert's extra-curricular interests lay. Once that was out of the way, Randon could address her as an equal rather than as a woman—he clearly didn't think that women were naturally his equals. She wondered whether she would have been allowed so close to him otherwise.

"Tell me what you're going to be talking about on this *Villa* show," said Randon. "Plugging any particular house?"

"You know I can't do that," said Odile. "I have my reputation for impartiality to think of."

"Indeed you have. To your impartiality," toasted Randon.

At midnight, Randon decided that it was time to wind the evening down. Odile knew that he would. She wondered if he would be going to bed alone.

"I hope you enjoy the rest of your stay in Champagne, Odile."

"Thank you."

"I'm afraid I will have left to go back to Paris before you get up in the morning but I look forward to hearing exactly how you get along. Don't spare me any details, will you?"

Odile promised. "You'll hear absolutely everything, I promise."

That night Odile was staying at Maison Randon. After bidding Mathieu good night she climbed the huge stone staircase to the first floor and the most prestigious of the house's eight guest suites. It was as luxuriously appointed as any top hotel. The sheets had been turned back. A pair of toweling slippers with the Randon crest had been placed on the floor next to the bed. The crested slippers faintly amused Odile. Somehow she didn't think they had been Randon's idea. Still, they were a nice touch, she thought as she slipped off her heels.

Odile climbed into bed and picked up the reading material on her nightstand. She had asked one of Randon's many staff to go out and find her as many different issues of *Villa Living* as she could. The girl had done quite well.

Odile picked up an Easter issue.

Christina Morgan was dressed in pink. She was holding a huge round cake decorated with small chocolate eggs and chocolate bunnies. She grinned at the camera. It was easy to see why America had taken her to their hearts:

Odile couldn't help smiling at the picture. This was going to be a very easy assignment.

Odile replaced the magazines on the nightstand and picked up the newspaper she had bought for her train ride. It wasn't that she was such an avid reader of this particular rag but there was a story she was very interested in following. The rest of the nationals didn't seem to be quite so bothered. It was a small story, Odile supposed, in the scheme of things. Still, it had captured the imagination of one writer at least.

"A life ruined. A good start with a loving family didn't protect her from what fate had in store. 'She was a good student,' a former teacher from her high school commented. 'Not outstanding but certainly never a child who would dream of causing any trouble. I'm so shocked to discover that she ended up working as a prostitute. She wanted to be a veterinary nurse.'

"The case has similarities with three unsolved murders from the 1980s," the piece continued.

Their photographs were laid out in chronological order of their deaths. Three beautiful girls. All brunettes.

Odile ran her finger over the girl in the final picture. Forever youthful and forever smiling—the only advantage of dying before your time was up. Live fast, die young. She'd probably even said that was how she wanted to go, thought Odile. Most teenagers do at some point.

It was too sad. She let the newspaper drop to the floor and turned out the light.

The following morning, Odile woke bright and early for the shoot.

She liked to think celebrity didn't impress her but as the driver pulled off the main road through Ay onto the side street that led up to the Bollinger compound itself, she couldn't resist getting her mirrored compact out of her purse. She powdered away a little shine on her forehead and reapplied her signature red lipstick. She thought of it as putting on her armor. How many women were brave enough to meet a supermodel barefaced?

Meanwhile, Christina was preparing for the meeting in her own way, catering to her own insecurities. The production assistant, Sammy, had spent half the night online and printed out a little pile of articles on Odile Levert. If Odile was intimidated by the idea of Christina's beauty, Christina was equally intimidated by the thought of having to make conversation with a super-brain like Odile.

With five minutes to go before Odile was due at the house, Christina was cramming in some last-minute study, reading the most recent of the articles Sammy had found. Christina knew that women were her harshest critics. She didn't want to give Odile any ammunition if she was hoping to write an article suggesting that Christina was just a pretty face.

On her arrival at Bollinger, Odile was swept straight through the courtyard to meet Christina and Edward, the show's director. Odile was surprised to see that Christina was wearing a cocktail dress. It was six o'clock in the morning.

"We thought it would be nice to shoot your segment as if you ladies were talking at the end of a dinner party," Edward explained. "You're about the same size as Christina. Wardrobe has some great dresses for you to choose from."

"I have my own dresses in my bag," Odile responded, in a way that made Edward feel just a little ticked off.

"She hates the idea of pretending it's the evening," Christina muttered as Odile went away to change. "She's going to hate the whole program."

Edward tried not to show that he suspected Christina might be right.

They waited nervously for Odile to be ready. Half an hour later, she emerged from makeup. She looked stunning in a short black dress with her hair scraped back from her face. Christina suddenly felt unsophisticated.

But despite Odile's initial frostiness, exacerbated no doubt by the fact that Christina had vetoed the idea of filming anything at Champagne Arsenault (she remembered the beautiful Madeleine too well) the segment shoot went smoothly. Edward was very pleased. As was Greg, who watched it all.

"You know," he said. "We should get Odile on again. She's nothing like I expected. There's a kind of easy chemistry between you two. Like you know each other really well."

Christina nodded. The rapport she seemed to have with Odile once the cameras were rolling had surprised her too.

"Well, I have to go," Greg announced. "I'm flying to Frankfurt tonight. Boring meeting."

"What a shame," said Odile.

"Yeah. I'd rather be in Paris, that's for sure. Hey, Christina's at a loose end tonight now that Ronald's laid up. Maybe you girls should have dinner instead."

Odile cocked her head to one side.

"Christina and Ronald were going to taste Christina's new wine together so he could tell her how it's coming on. But I'm sure your opinion is just as valuable."

"You forget that I'm backing Champagne Arsenault against Villa Bacchante at next year's *Vinifera* awards," said Odile.

"Exactly," said Christina.

"Then this will be a chance for Christina to show you what you're up against."

Odile laughed.

"We don't have to drink Villa Bacchante," said Christina.

"No, really," said Odile. "I would love to."

"Perfect," said Greg. "Then it's all set. I'm glad. I hate the idea of you being in Paris alone." Greg kissed Christina on the forehead.

"I'll look forward to it," said Odile.

CHAPTER· 51

After the film crew had packed up and Greg left for Frankfurt, Christina took a private car back to Paris. She was staying at the Hotel Plaza Arc De Triomphe. Greg had booked the Terrace Eiffel Suite on the eighth floor, thinking that it would be the perfect place for him and Christina to have a little pre-Christmas celebration. His meeting had squashed that, but still Christina was very pleased to have such luxurious accommodations. She'd visited the Terrace Eiffel Suite many years before, during Paris Fashion Week when a much more important model was using it as her pied-à-terre.

The original plan had been for Ronald to come to the suite for an early supper with Christina and Greg, to discuss the new season of *The Villa* and to taste a bottle of Christina's sparkling pinot noir. So, the chef at the Plaza Arc De Triomphe had been put on stand-by to prepare a lovely little meal to complement the Villa Bacchante Blanc de Noirs. It seemed a shame to waste it. But would allowing Odile to taste her sparking pinot give Champagne Arsenault an unfair advantage in next year's competition?

"I doubt it," said Greg. "The wine is in the bottle now. What's she going to do? Open all the bottles and stick some sugar in?"

Besides, he continued, it would be a good idea for Christina to get to know Odile better. Ronald was getting old. It might be wise to have his replacement lined up.

Odile was just a couple of minutes late. She was wearing a black dress that Christina recognized as Alexander McQueen. It gave Odile an air of austerity and authority that was softened by a quirky collar and big cuffs. Christina wished she had dressed up a little more. Treating the suite as a "home away from home" she'd gone for a big cashmere sweater and jeans. She hoped that dinner would distract from her outfit.

Within seconds of Odile's arrival, a young waiter arrived in the suite with a chilled bottle of Villa Bacchante's Blanc de Noirs.

"The moment of truth," said Christina as the waiter twisted the cork from the bottle.

"Looks good," said Odile, observing the wine as it was poured into the glass. It gave a beautiful fine mousse and the color—thank goodness, thought Christina—was a perfect pale rose-gold.

"Shall we?" Christina lifted her glass toward her nose.

"This is the first bottle you've opened?"

"In company," said Christina.

"Then I'm honored."

They were silent as they appreciated the bouquet. Christina's shoulders softened as she confirmed that it wasn't corked, that is, tainted and moldy-smelling, at least. Odile raised her spirits further when she announced,

"This has a lovely forward bouquet of peaches and apricot. The autolytic notes are very subtle."

Odile took a sip and cast her eyes downward as she searched for words to describe the taste.

"Very crisp. Lovely finish."

Christina exhaled with relief.

By now dinner was ready to be served. Christina and Odile seated themselves at the dining table, which had a fabulous view of the Eiffel Tower.

"I never get tired of seeing it," said Christina. "I grew up in Iowa. Sometimes when I'm in Paris, I can't quite believe I'm here. I have to pinch myself."

"I have the same feeling in California," said Odile. "Every time I'm in San Francisco on my way to Napa, driving over the Golden Gate Bridge. As a girl, I never thought I'd get out of France."

Christina was surprised. Odile didn't seem like the kind of woman who had ever doubted her potential.

The waiter laid in front of them an appetizer of foie gras that was the perfect compliment to the Blanc de Noirs. The entire menu had been designed so that the diners could drink the same wine throughout, from the lobster main course to the chocolates at the end.

All the same, as each course arrived, Christina took a sip of wine nervously, praying that there would be no clash of flavors. There wasn't. At least, none that she could detect. And though she watched Odile very closely, Christina didn't see anything on her guest's face that betrayed disappointment with the matching of the food and wine. Perhaps Villa Bacchante could include "good with most foods" in its next press release.

"You must be very excited about your first vintage," said Odile.

"I am," said Christina.

"Well done," Odile toasted her. "I think Champagne Arsenault has some serious competition."

While the waiting staff was clearing the dining table, Odile suggested that she and Christina take their coffee out onto the terrace. It was cold out there though crisp and dry. The two women cradled their coffee cups to keep their hands warm.

On the hour, the lights on the Eiffel Tower flickered so that the world-famous landmark seemed to glitter like a Christmas decoration.

"I still get a kick out of that," Christina admitted. "Though you must find it boring, living here, seeing it all the time."

"Not at all," said Odile. "From time to time, when I look up and see La Tour Eiffel, I think about the other people who are looking up at it at the same time. Think of how many people have been proposed to at the top of it, or in its shadow. It's a wonderful romantic symbol in this city of lovers. Think of how many people are kissing as they gaze on it right now."

Christina saw Odile's eyes flicker toward her lips. Christina glanced through the terrace doors into the suite. The table had been cleared. The staff was gone. When she looked back at Odile, the Frenchwoman was still focused on her mouth. Christina felt heat flood her cheeks.

"There's a view of the Eiffel Tower from every single room in this suite," Christina said as breezily as she could. "Even the bathroom. There's a special kind of glass in the windows. It looks opaque, but you flick a switch and suddenly it's clear."

"I'd like to see that."

Christina would ordinarily have been happy to show anyone the view from the bathroom, but it felt quite important right then to keep Odile in the public areas of the suite.

"Show me," Odile persisted. She began to walk inside.

"OK," said Christina. "It's in here. Through the master bedroom."

They walked into the master en suite, which was as big as the average sitting room. The bathroom was decked out in white marble with gold accents. Over the bath hung what looked like an enormous gilt mirror.

"Watch this."

Christina pressed a button on a handset inside a waterproof sheath. The mirror was suddenly a window. The Eiffel Tower twinkled at them again.

"That is amazing. It would be wonderful to have a bath and look at that view." Odile stroked the edge of the marble tub. "It has a Jacuzzi," she observed.

"Yes," said Christina.

"Can we use it?"

Christina's expression was unsure.

"I always think it's such a pity to stay in a place like this and not make the most of it. Live like a rock star. Let's open another bottle of your Blanc de Noirs and see how it tastes in a truly decadent setting."

Odile had already turned on the taps. She took a bottle of bubble bath from the counter and squeezed it all into the running water. Soon the bath was full of tiny bubbles, creamy and thick, like whipped cream.

"I'll find you a bathing suit to wear," said Christina. "I brought a couple on this trip."

"I don't need one." Odile smiled. "Unless there's a strict house policy that bathing suits must be worn."

Christina's mouth dropped open. "No," she said eventually. "Of course not. I just thought . . . I thought you might be more comfortable."

"Covered up? I'm a Frenchwoman, my dear. We're not quite so shy about our bodies as you Americans are. Not that you personally have any reason to be so shy."

"I'm not shy," Christina spluttered.

"Of course not."

Odile slipped off her shoes then pulled her dress off over her head in one fluid motion. Beneath it, she wore only a pair of plain black panties. Silk. Well cut. No bra. She had small breasts that didn't really need the support.

Her limbs were surprisingly long and tight and tanned. The muscles in her arms and legs were elegant, like a ballerina's. Christina's first thought was that if Odile had been just a couple of inches taller, she could have made it as a catwalk model. She had the perfect, slender figure that the fashion masters loved to design for—no bumps to ruin the line. Christina had always been too curvy for the haute couture shows. She had never really found herself in great demand in Paris. You did fashion or you did *Sports Illustrated*. Very few girls crossed over.

"Do you think the water is ready?" Odile asked.

Christina realized that she had been staring at Odile's body.

"Try it out."

Odile stepped out of her panties. She kicked them in the direction of her dress and shoes. Then, wearing nothing but a smile, she stepped into the bath and lowered herself down into the soft white foam. She did it very slowly, like a siren disappearing beneath the waves. Christina couldn't help staring again. She had never met anyone quite so content in her own skin.

"Is it hot enough?" Christina asked eventually.

"It's perfect," said Odile. "Come on in."

Christina hesitated. "I'll go and grab us some more wine first."

Seconds later, she found herself in the suite's sitting room and in a quandary. Should she nip into her bedroom and change into a swimsuit and robe? She ordinarily wore a swimsuit in the hot tub back in California. And this was a similar kind of situation, right? But if Christina went back in there in a one-piece, or even in her bikini bottoms, it would look prudish. Worse, it might look as though she was making some kind of negative comment on Odile's manners.

Christina remembered what her grandmother used to say. "Manners are for the purpose of making other people feel comfortable." That was what mattered. If Odile felt most comfortable in the nude...

Taking a big swig of wine, Christina made her decision. She took off her cashmere sweater and jeans and replaced them with a long Japanese robe. Nothing underneath. Then she headed back into the bathroom.

Odile was relaxing. She had her eyes closed, her head tipped back against the side of the tub.

"I thought you'd run away," she said, without opening her eyes.

"Just talking to the chef," Christina lied.

"He did a wonderful job tonight," said Odile. "Everything was delicious."

Christina undid the belt of her robe and climbed the steps to the tub, intending to discard her cover-up at the very last minute. She hoped that Odile would keep her eyes shut until she too was submerged. She didn't. Odile opened her eyes right as Christina was casting the robe away, in a gesture that seemed altogether too dramatic for having been witnessed. Christina blushed to the roots of her hair.

"Is that what they call a Brazilian?" Odile asked.

After that opening gambit, the conversation could

only get less embarrassing, Christina decided. She settled into the bubbles opposite Odile and did her best to relax. Being covered to the neck with warm water helped, as did more of Villa Bacchante's Blanc de Noirs. But eventually there was another lull in the conversation. The timer on the Jacuzzi jets clicked back to zero and the water was still.

Christina looked toward the two fluffy towels that were draped over a chair nearby. Not near enough. While she was wondering how she could get out of the tub and to the towels without provoking any more cringe-making observations about her body, Christina was ambushed.

Odile moved from her side of the tub to Christina's and planted a kiss right on her lips.

Christina didn't protest. Indeed, eventually it was she who led Odile by the hand out of the bathroom and into the master bedroom. They headed straight for the enormous bed. Christina pulled back the champagne-colored satin counterpane while Odile threw the surplus pillows onto the floor.

Odile lay back first and pulled Christina down on top of her. The tension that had been growing between them all evening exploded in their kisses. Christina grabbed at Odile's body hungrily. She threw her head back and gasped as Odile bit her shoulder in a moment of uncontrolled passion.

They tumbled over and over, exploring each other's bodies as though there might not be another chance. Christina sucked at Odile's tiny pink nipples. Odile returned the favor, making Christina sigh with delight. Odile was the first to venture lower. She cupped Christina's warm pubis in her hand.

At that moment, they locked eyes. Odile searched Christina's green eyes for permission and found it there in the crinkles of a smile. Permission granted, Odile parted Christina's labia with her fingers. Christina was already wet. She arched upward as Odile stroked the smooth pink skin of her vulva.

"Lay back." Odile pushed Christina down onto the mattress again.

With well-practiced fingers, Odile found Christina's clitoris. She moistened the clit with Christina's own wetness and set to work massaging the tiny nub into life. She could tell how well she was doing from the sound of Christina's breathing and from the way Christina held the top of Odile's arm. The faster and firmer Odile worked, the harder Christina's fingers gripped her.

"Stop, stop!" Christina moaned but Odile could tell that it wasn't an order. Instead, she pressed her mouth against Christina's swollen red lips and silenced her with kisses.

Christina's eyes flickered as she fell into a sort of pre-orgasmic trance. All her inhibitions had finally deserted her, forced out by the stronger sensations that were taking over every fiber of her body. She felt entirely physical. Animal. This was what her body was for. Pure enjoyment.

Blood filled her clitoris, amplifying the shock waves that started there and reverberated throughout her being. The ecstasy was intensified still further when Odile sucked on her nipples, flicking them from side to side with a tongue that promised much more joy later on. Meanwhile, Odile dipped her finger inside Christina's vagina again and lubricated her clitoris for the final stretch.

This time Christina begged Odile not to stop. She closed her eyes tightly and gripped Odile's arm so hard that she would leave red marks. Her orgasm built inside her. It started like a small electric charge. Pins and needles.

This was the point at which all might not be lost. While Odile was busy with her clitoris, Christina twisted her own left nipple between her fingertips, trying to regain the sensation of Odile sucking there. Odile took the hint. She sucked and stroked and sucked until Christina started gasping as though she could no longer breathe. Now there was no going back.

Christina's cries rose in volume until she was almost shouting.

"Oh God!" she cried as her orgasm cascaded through her body. "Odile! Oh God!" She clamped her hand around Odile's wrist to stop her from carrying on. It was all too much. Christina collapsed back onto the pillows. When she looked up at the chandelier above them, she was amused to see that it was jangling.

Odile stayed the night. The following morning they drank coffee together on the terrace where it had all started. It was a beautiful day. The sky was clear and blue. Odile pointed out more landmarks for Christina.

"My house is just over there."

Her mobile phone beeped. Odile had a text. She sent one back, smiling as she texted.

"I should go," she said. "Just one more kiss."

Christina leaned into Odile's embrace. They kissed passionately. Odile slipped her hand inside Christina's cashmere sweater and pushed it up to reveal her breasts. She placed another kiss on Christina's nipple before she let her go.

"I'll see you soon," she said. *"Au revoir, ma chérie."*

CHAPTER 52

Hilarian arrived in Slough for the last quarterly meeting of the Froggy Bottom trustees that year with a spring in his step. Not even the fact that he had to be in Slough could dent his mood. He carried with him a bottle of Froggy Bottom's new release for each of his fellow board members and looked forward to telling them that Kelly herself had designed the wonderful label. That should shut old Reginald up for a little while.

But Hilarian sensed that something was afoot the moment Reginald's secretary swung open the door to the wood-paneled boardroom where the trustees always sat. Reginald was smiling. That wasn't usual or especially comforting, though perhaps it could be explained by a sudden attack of Christmas spirit. However, Georgina's tight little mouth was also twisted into an approximation of a happy face. Definitely bad news.

"Good afternoon, Hilarian," said Reginald, ostentatiously looking at his watch. Hilarian was five minutes late.

"Traffic," said Hilarian.

"That's why I always set off fifteen minutes sooner than I think I ought to," said Georgina. "Prior planning..."

"Christmas presents from Kelly," said Hilarian, ignoring Georgina's dig as he arranged the bottles of Froggy Bottom's first sparkling wine—a blend of pinot noir with just a little chardonnay—on the polished wood table.

Reginald immediately picked up the nearest bottle and set it back down again on top of a pile of papers, so as not to mark the French polish. "Ideal for pre-Christmas lunch aperitifs. Kelly's very own vintage," Hilarian continued.

"Her vintage," echoed Georgina with a little snort. "We're afraid not."

Hilarian listened with growing horror as Reginald launched into his speech. After four years of looking for a way to part Kelly from Froggy Bottom, it seemed that the Mollisons had at last found their legal loophole. They'd employed a new lawyer who went through the wording of Dougal's will like a forensic scientist, taking each and every letter and full stop and turning them inside out and upside down in his search for the tiniest crack that would let him insert a scalpel to cut Kelly off.

Now Reginald explained the position. Certain phrases jumped out. "Exact words of the will." Reginald shook his head. "*His* child," "Quite specific in that regard," "Kelly named as his child in an entirely separate document." "Good reason to believe that Kelly Elson is not the illegitimate daughter of Dougal at all . . ."

"Reginald, you know I'm no fan of legalese. What exactly does this mean?" Hilarian asked.

"It means that, as trustees, Georgina and I will be voting to suspend maintenance payments to Kelly until the matter of her parentage has been properly investigated."

"What?" said Hilarian. "You can't."

"I'm afraid we can. It is absolutely within our discretion. We'd advise you to follow suit."

"And then . . ."

"If it is revealed that Kelly has been benefiting from the proceeds of Dougal's estate under erroneous circumstances, then ownership of Froggy Bottom will be transferred to Dougal's legitimate heirs at once."

"We need to appoint a lawyer to investigate this on Kelly's behalf," said Hilarian.

"I don't believe we need to do *anything* on Kelly Elson's behalf until we know exactly who she is," said Georgina.

"She's Dougal's daughter," Hilarian said simply. But even as he said it, the first fingers of doubt began to inveigle themselves into his mind.

"That's what he was told. But whose word do we have except that of Kelly's mother? A woman, who, according to reports from the housekeeper at the time, was not entirely to be trusted. A DNA test should prove it," Georgina concluded.

"We don't have Dougal's DNA," Hilarian pointed out.

"Ah, but we don't need it," said Reginald.

Hilarian was confused.

"Because we have the DNA of his legitimate children," Reginald continued. "If a test shows that Kelly isn't related to them, we have the answer."

"You're not serious."

"We are deadly serious. As should you be," said Reginald. "Dougal entrusted us with ensuring that his estate was properly managed."

"As it is. Under Kelly. And she needs ten thousand pounds for new rootstock and maintenance. The rootstock is urgent. If we're going to expand the vineyard this year, it needs to go into the ground in the next few weeks. I want her to have the money now."

"We disagree. I think that concludes our business for today," said Reginald. "Thank you for coming along, Hilarian."

"What? You think that's it?"

Reginald nodded. Georgina was carefully packing her papers back into her briefcase. Along with the bottle of wine.

"You're so bloody pleased with yourself, aren't you?

You bloody smug little shit. And you." Hilarian pointed at Georgina. "You're going to withhold Kelly's money."

"We don't know that it's her money—" Reginald began.

"You're going to withhold Kelly's money," Hilarian persisted. "And still go home and drink the wine that she worked so hard to produce?"

Georgina took the bottle out of her briefcase and put it back on the table, as if to make a point.

"You're a pair of bastards. What does it matter to you whether Kelly gets ten thousand pounds this month? It's not like it comes out of your pockets. Dougal's other kids don't need the cash. And they don't need the vineyard. They don't even want it. They never went anywhere near there while Dougal was alive! That vineyard was Dougal's pride and joy and neither of them gave a fig about it. They didn't even bother to go to the funeral."

"That has nothing to do with it. It's not up to us to decide whether or not Dougal's heirs *deserve* their inheritance, Hilarian—though I have to say that his son, Damien, is very interested indeed in making wine. He'd be delighted to take Froggy Bottom on."

"Now that it's properly up and running, I'm sure he would. Now that Guy and Kelly have done all the hard work and it's a viable prospect rather than an enormous money pit. I can't help thinking he's been waiting for exactly this moment."

"At the end of the day it's a simple matter of the law," said Reginald. "The trust refers to a vintage made by Dougal's *child*. If Kelly Elson is not Dougal's child then the vineyard cannot be transferred to her. She isn't mentioned by name."

"I'm going to hire the best lawyer in the land to make sure Kelly keeps Froggy Bottom."

"That's up to you," said Reginald. "The trust will not

be able to release any money in that regard, of course. It'll have to come out of your own pocket."

"Then it shall."

"Hilarian," Georgina sighed. "I really don't know why you're getting so worked up about the little trollop. If you ask me, she's pulled the wool over your eyes for much too long. Do you seriously think she cares about that vineyard? The second she gets her hands on the deed to Froggy Bottom, she'll sell it and use all the money to buy drugs. I know her type. I see them in front of me at the Magistrates' Court every day of the week. Shoplifters, drunk drivers, glue sniffers. They come back again and again. They can't help themselves. You can't change the essential nature of someone from that kind of stock."

"You met her only the one time," Hilarian spat. "And so you wouldn't know how much she's changed already. Besides which, she's from the exact same stock as those other bloody idiots you seem to revere so highly."

"Hilarian," said Reginald sharply. "Miss Nuttall and I do not need to listen to that kind of language."

"Then listen to this." Hilarian pulled himself up to his full height. "Kelly *is* Dougal's daughter and had he had the chance to properly meet her before he died, I'm sure he would have left her *every* penny he had. She's a good girl. She's bright, she's hardworking, she's kind. She has proven herself to be dedicated to the future of Dougal's vineyard. Whatever you and his loser offspring try to do to her by trawling through Dougal's will, looking to rob her of Froggy Bottom with your sneaky semantics, she has already inherited Dougal's passion and talent for wine. I know that Dougal would have been delighted to call Kelly Elson his heir. If she were my daughter, I would feel very proud indeed."

Georgina and Reginald shared a look. Reginald gave Hilarian a slow hand-clap.

"A very pretty speech," he said. "Come on, Georgina. I want to show you that new print in my office."

They exited, leaving Hilarian alone in the wood-paneled room.

Hilarian drove straight from Slough to Sussex. He got there just before seven. Kelly and Guy were in the kitchen of the main farmhouse, poring over a diagram of the new vineyard they were planning on a field they had recently leased from the farmer next door.

"Did you get our money?" Kelly asked excitedly. "Look." She showed Hilarian the diagram. "I've finished the diagram. It's going to be amazing."

Hilarian shook his head. "I'm afraid we have a little problem with the other trustees."

He told them the full story. Guy slumped forward onto his folded arms in despair. Kelly tried not to show she was bothered.

"But it'll be OK, won't it?" she said when Hilarian had finished. "Because I am Dougal's daughter. You said I was like him."

Hilarian nodded sadly.

"You are like him. I'm sure it will be OK," he said.

"Then we won't let it worry us. I'll have the test done as soon as possible and we'll buy the new rootstock after Christmas. Hilarian, cheer up!" she demanded. "When the test comes back positive, we'll invite Reginald and Georgina up here and properly show them our plans. We'll win them over. Especially if we come back from the *Vinifera* show in San Francisco with a medal."

Guy frowned. "I don't know if we can afford the tickets," he said. "If we're not getting any money this month..."

"You don't need to buy tickets," said Hilarian. "*Vinifera* will cough up. Gerry Paine wants his own Judgment of

Paris. You're not going to miss that show, Guy. No matter what happens, the wine in this bottle"—he waved the bottle that Georgina had given back—"is your wine. You've both worked so hard for this. No one can take that away."

"Too right," said Kelly.

But Kelly's bravado didn't last. Alone in her bedroom, she sat in front of the mirror and looked at the face reflected there. She picked up the framed photograph of Dougal that stood on her dressing table and peered closely at the man she could barely remember. Did she have his nose? His eyes? His mouth? She couldn't tell. All Kelly could see was her mother's chin. Her mother's hair. Her mother's frown. And all she could think about was her mother's unreliability. The dozens of men who had drifted through Marina's life. Even Kelly herself had defamed her mother as a slut who would sleep with anyone for a packet of fags.

Kelly climbed into bed and pulled the covers right up to her neck.

"Please let me be Dougal's daughter," she prayed. The alternative was just too awful. To lose Froggy Bottom would be to lose everything. She didn't have anywhere to go back to. She hadn't spoken to her mother in years. If Dougal wasn't her father then she didn't know who was. She had no grandparents. No siblings. No cousins. Her best friend was dead, murdered by someone who had yet to be caught. Froggy Bottom was all she had.

CHAPTER 53

The day after Christina's encounter with Odile, Greg returned to Paris from Frankfurt.

"Did you miss me?" he asked her.

Christina confirmed she had with a nod.

"Did you have an OK time without me?"

"OK," she said.

"What did you and Odile talk about?"

"Girl stuff," Christina said breezily. "Tell me about Frankfurt, I'd much rather hear about that."

As far as Christina was concerned, her moment with Odile was just a slip in reality. It wouldn't happen again. There was certainly no need for Greg to know about it. Especially if Odile did not take Ronald's place on the show. On the flight back to Los Angeles, Christina encouraged Greg to look for a young American replacement for the venerable old critic.

"Another guy," said Christina. "I think the balance works better."

"Sure. If you really think so," said Greg.

"I do."

And so Christina slipped back into happily-not-quite-married-life with Greg as though Paris had never happened. There was plenty to occupy them both with the upcoming holidays. Greg's parents were flying up to Napa for Christmas. The Villa Bacchante itself was a hive of activity as the staff tried to fulfill last-minute orders for Christmas fizz.

Christina was at the beauty salon, having her fingernails painted a poinsettia red, when her lawyer called.

"Todd." She smiled into the phone. "I got your gift basket this morning. Thank you so much. It's beautiful. I was about to call and wish you a happy Christmas."

"That's very kind," said Todd.

"So, what are your plans for the holidays? Are you going—?"

"Christina," Todd interrupted her. "Are you at home? I need to fax something through to you. I'm afraid it's bad news."

Christina covered her mouth with her hand as she read the letter from Bill's lawyer. After the divorce settlement was finalized, she had thought she would never see that dreaded letterhead again.

Having read only halfway through the unexpected and deeply unwelcome missive, Christina called Todd to discuss it.

"He can't be serious. I mean, he really can't do what he's proposing, right?"

She heard Todd draw breath on the other end of the line.

"I have to be honest with you; I have never dealt with anything like this before. I don't know of anyone who has, but I think there's a strong possibility that some judge somewhere might consider that your ex-husband has a point."

"Oh my God." Christina put her free hand to her face. "Am I going to lose my home?"

It was unbelievable. The letter from Bill's lawyers said he wanted to renegotiate the divorce settlement. Christina was stunned. At the time of the divorce, Christina's friends considered that Bill got off lightly. Some of them had suggested that Christina should go back for more. But she took the villa and a tiny amount of cash and limped away quietly, exhausted from the very public nature of the fight. And now it was Bill who wanted a bigger slice of the pie, because, as the writ said: "We consider that the value of the Villa Bacchante at the time of the divorce was greater than the estimate given by Miss Morgan's lawyers..."

If it was decided that the valuation of Villa Bacchante was fraudulent, explained Todd, then Bill could indeed ask for a recount. What's more, on the basis that the valuation was wrong, Bill was claiming a substantial portion of the wealth Christina had generated since the divorce thanks to the television series about the Villa Bacchante. He wanted a share of the profits from the TV program, from the magazine and from the resulting wine sales.

"But how on earth can he be entitled to anything? He was unfaithful to me!" Christina exclaimed. "He left me. He filed for divorce."

"Doesn't matter," said Todd. "Bill is claiming that were it not for him, you would not have had the house in Napa in the first place. Without the house you would not have made the decision to become a winemaker and you would not have an award-winning television series and associated merchandising rights under your belt. He is claiming that your success with this series is due in large part to his hard work in finding you the perfect vineyard in the first place. I'm surprised he doesn't want credit on the series too," Todd added in an attempt to inject some levity. It didn't work.

"But any court in the land would throw a claim like that out, surely? You know what I was like after the split, Todd. Bill almost destroyed me. He didn't want the villa then. It wasn't worth anything. He was happy to get rid of it. I made it what it is today. I've worked so hard."

Christina began to cry.

"I know that," said Todd. "And that's what we'll rely on when this goes to court. But I'm afraid I'm ninety-nine percent certain this will go to court. And it'll be a landmark case. There are a lot of divorcees out there who will be going back for a second bite at the cherry if we don't win."

That was no consolation for Christina. Much as she liked Todd, there were times when she wasn't completely sure that he wouldn't sell her down the river. She began to wonder if this was something Todd could keep out of court but would choose not to because he thought the resulting case would make his name.

She pulled out the old copy of *Hello!* That article would prove that the villa was a gift and, as such, surely Bill had forfeited all rights to it the moment he handed it over. She faxed the article through to Todd, who came back to her with the unwelcome news that the article did not constitute the evidence they needed.

"Though he may have said that the villa was a gift," Todd explained, "the original deed was in both your names."

Trust Bill to give a gift with strings attached.

"It's ridiculous," Christina complained to Greg that night. "I divorced him to get him out of my life. Am I going to have to pay for him until he's dead? Am I going to lose the villa?"

Greg cradled her against his chest.

"Sweetheart, you won't lose the villa," he promised. "I'm going to do everything I can to make sure that doesn't happen."

"Because you don't want to lose the set of your most successful show," snapped Christina, directing her frustration at Greg now too.

"Because I love you," said Greg. "That's the only reason."

She looked up at him. His eyes softened as he gazed down on her.

"And I love you," she said, burying her face in his chest again. She meant it too. As she said it, she wished to God she hadn't betrayed him with Odile. Even if Greg never found out, she knew she'd tainted something wonderful.

CHAPTER 54

There was little pre-Christmas jolliness going on at Champagne Arsenault. The last of the Christmas orders had gone out, along with their accompanying invoices, but Madeleine had a bigger debt to worry about.

After Mick Tremblant's first visit, Madeleine had quizzed Henri about the man and his connection with her father. Henri knew of Mick Tremblant. Most people in town did. He knew that he'd gone to prison after being arrested for drug dealing, but he didn't know if Mick had ever played cards with Constant Arsenault. Henri advised Madeleine to go to the police. But there was technically no offense, they said. Mick had asked for the return of a debt. He'd made no threat. The only thing she could do was alert them if he actually broke a law.

Since then, Madeleine had seen the man just once more. It was Halloween. Several neighborhood parents had given in to pester power and allowed their children to go trick-or-treating. Madeleine opened the door expecting some neighborhood kids and found instead Mick and his henchman on the doorstep, with those vile "Scream" masks covering their equally scary real faces.

"By Christmas," was all he said.

Madeleine tried to ignore him. If Mick Tremblant did turn up for his money and she didn't have it, what could he do? He was well known to the local police. He wouldn't risk doing anything stupid, surely. Madeleine decided that if he showed his face again, she would call his bluff.

The day he turned up was a sad and gray sort of day. Madeleine found a Christmas card from Mackesy in the mail. She hadn't seen him since that morning in Paris. Their fond flirtatious relationship had degraded into something more business-like, conducted entirely by e-mail. She looked at the kiss below his signature and wondered whether he had scribbled it there deliberately or absentmindedly. Did he really think about her at all? He was probably looking forward to a Christmas *en famille*. Madeleine put his Christmas card with all the others on the mantelpiece in her office.

The doorbell rang.

Before she got to the door, Madeleine knew who would be there. She heard two gruff voices singing a traditional carol, but altering the words to something altogether more blasphemous. She kept the chain, fitted after Tremblant's first visit, on the door as she opened it just a couple of inches.

"*Félicitations,* Mademoiselle Arsenault," said Mick Tremblant, removing his Santa hat with a flourish. "I have come to collect your Christmas donation to the poor."

"I don't have your money," Madeleine said simply.

"Now, that's not what I wanted to hear," he said. "My

children will have no Christmas presents unless you've got what I've come for."

"Then I'm very sorry but they'll have to go without. I'm afraid, Monsieur Tremblant, that I've decided I won't be responsible for my father's debt to you. I have no reason to believe that my father ever knew you at all, let alone played cards with you. You should know that I have informed the police that you have been bothering me and I won't hesitate to get them involved if I feel threatened in any way. In fact," she bluffed, "I've had an alarm installed since you were last here. If I press the button my finger is resting on right now, I will be instantly connected to the local police station."

Mick Tremblant took a step back as though he was the one who felt threatened.

"Wow. That's fighting talk," he said.

"Find someone else to pick on," said Madeleine. "There's nothing for you here."

Mick Tremblant raised his hands. "If you say so, my dear. We're terribly sorry for having disturbed you. *Bon Noël.*"

Then, to Madeleine's surprise, he merely turned and walked away, his enormous henchman shuffling after.

Could it be that easy? Madeleine asked herself as she climbed into bed. Perhaps it was. From talking to Henri, it seemed that Mick Tremblant was really quite a small-time crook. In all probability the debt he claimed her father owed him didn't exist. Tremblant had just been trying it on. And now that he thought Madeleine had a direct line to the police station, it wasn't worth the bother.

She pulled the sheets up to her chin. On nights like these she truly wished she had someone with her. Someone to hold her tight and reassure her that she had indeed seen the baddies off. It took quite some time before she was able to fall asleep.

It was about three o'clock in the morning when Madeleine stirred awake again. Like an animal sensing the presence of a predator, she knew at once that something was not quite right. Her eyes looked out blindly into the darkness of her room with its small windows and heavy velvet drapes. She could see nothing. But she could hear something very strange indeed.

It was a creaking sound, like the mast of a great sailing vessel groaning in the wind. The creaking was punctuated by a high-pitched whine, like the sound wet logs make when you throw them onto a bonfire. Madeleine's mental image was, alas, almost spot-on. Still it took a while before she connected the noise with its source: the ancient beams in the ceiling of the room below groaning and spitting as they started to burn.

By the time she opened the door of her bedroom, smoke was curling its way up the stairwell. There was no time to strategize. She had to act on animal instinct. Darting back into the bedroom, Madeleine snatched up just one thing—the shoe box full of her mother's letters and the old photographs, from its place in the bottom of the wardrobe. Then she raced from the house, using the stairwell at the opposite end of the corridor to the one that was on fire. At the top of that stairwell, she turned and paused just long enough to see a flash of yellow flame chase her.

Madeleine called the fire brigade from her mobile phone as she ran.

When she got outside the front of the house, she found a crowd had already gathered.

"We've called the *pompiers*," said Monsieur Mulfort.

"My son saw the smoke when he was coming back from the bar."

"Thank you," said Madeleine.

"They'll be here any second," Monsieur Mulfort assured her. "But you look terrified. Let me hold you."

Madeleine refused his kindness. But the fire brigade wasn't there in seconds. Or even minutes. It was at least another half an hour before the fire engine roared up to Champagne Arsenault, and by that time, it was much too late. The fire had spread from the hall into the upper floors. The old wooden beams merely acted as fuses for the fire to race along. Sparks shot up into the sky like fireworks as the roof began to cave in.

Though they worked on the blaze until dawn broke, the fire brigade could save nothing of Champagne Arsenault but the walls around the courtyard. Madeleine could only watch as the once grand house burned. Her family history, going up in flames.

CHAPTER 55

"Clearly it was arson," Madeleine insisted to the local police chief, Inspector Delahey. "Mick Tremblant came to my house that afternoon. He asked for the money. I told him I didn't have it and the very same night my house catches fire. You really think that's a coincidence?"

"Mademoiselle Arsenault," Delahey sighed. "I understand that you must be feeling very tired and upset. But don't let the shock of the fire trick you into making false accusations. The preliminary report from the fire department suggests that the fire was probably started by a candle left unattended when you went to bed."

"What? I didn't leave a candle burning."

"I'm sure you didn't mean to. I know how you girls love scented candles," said Delahey. "My wife fills the place with them. I told her when I heard about your fire: that could happen to us, dear, if you're not careful."

"I did not leave a candle burning," Madeleine reiterated. "You know that's rubbish."

"Then perhaps it was an electrical fault," said Delahey. "It was an old house. When did you last have the electrics checked? In either case, I'm happy to wait for the fire department's full report. I'm not about to go out and arrest someone just because you don't like the look of him... Now, where are you staying at the moment? Do you have people you can spend Christmas with? I don't like the thought of you spending Christmas alone, Mademoiselle Arsenault."

"I will be fine," said Madeleine, "if I think that you're doing your job. At least try to find out where Mick Tremblant was last night. Him and his henchman."

"That's easy," said Inspector Delahey. "They were playing cards at Maison Randon with me and Axel Delaflote."

Axel could hardly bear to look at the gates of Champagne Arsenault. Split and warped by the heat of the fire, they hung from their hinges like a pair of broken wings. Mathieu Randon was not quite so squeamish. He wound down the window on his side of the car and leaned out for a better view.

"Must have been quite some blaze," he said. "Thank goodness Mademoiselle Arsenault was not hurt. The caves remain untouched, yes?"

"As I understand it," said Axel.

"And the Clos Des Larmes?"

"Covered in ash, but that shouldn't be a problem. The vines are dormant right now, of course."

"Of course. And where is Mademoiselle Arsenault staying?"

"Delahey said she's at the hotel by the bank."

"I think we should pay her a visit," said Randon.

Axel could think of nothing he wanted to do less than go to Madeleine's hotel with Randon. But Randon wasn't about to let up. And Axel wasn't in the position to refuse his boss's orders anymore.

Though Randon never mentioned it directly, the events of that night at the party in Paris sat between them like a grenade without a pin whenever they met. Axel berated himself on a daily basis for having been taken in. Randon had made him feel like a friend and an equal. He'd encouraged Axel to reveal his darkest desires, and now that he knew them Randon used them like invisible handcuffs. There was certainly no way that Axel could leave Maison Randon unless Randon decided it was time for him to go. And so he turned the car in the direction of Madeleine's temporary home.

Madeleine was in her room, going through a pile of papers retrieved from her father's strong box, which thankfully had survived the fire, when the hotel receptionist called to say she had a visitor. Her heart sank as she reached the lobby and saw the back of Mathieu Randon. When he turned and smiled at her, she felt positively queasy.

"Come to gloat," she said.

"Not at all," he assured her. "I've come to offer you my assistance."

"I don't need your assistance."

"I thought you might say that. You modern girls have

made a rod for your own backs, refusing to allow yourselves to be looked after from time to time. So, knowing that you would be too proud to accept my help, even though you need it, I took the liberty of putting in place a scheme that will lift a great weight from your mind anyway."

"What do you mean?"

"I understand that your father died owing rather a lot of money, thanks to his penchant for the card tables."

"It's not true," said Madeleine.

"That's not what Mick Tremblant said. I'm very sorry you had the misfortune to have to meet him, Madeleine. He's not a very pleasant man. He has, as I think you might have guessed, some very ugly connections and he's not afraid to use them. The last thing you need, after such a tragedy as this fire, is to have to worry about someone like him. And so, because I admired your father and his champagne house so much, I decided to neutralize your little problem with Tremblant for you."

Madeleine shook her head uncomprehendingly.

"You're familiar, from your years in banking, with the concept of selling debt. Well, Mick Tremblant has sold your debt to me. He won't be bothering you again. I've paid him off. From this day forward, you need deal only with me."

"What?"

"I think you'll find me a very flexible lender, Madeleine. I understand that you're not in a position to pay me back right now and so I'm going to give you time to come up with the cash."

Madeleine snorted. "I don't have to listen to your crap. If you really gave Mick Tremblant two hundred thousand Euros on my behalf, then I'm sorry. He pulled the wool over your eyes. My father had no gambling debts."

"Now you're lying to me. This must all be very stressful for a dear sweet girl like you. No family. All alone in the world. How it must haunt you to think about what might have happened had you not woken in time to escape the fire. And though the fire was an accident, who would blame you for feeling jumpy when it came so close after your run-in with that pimp? There are nasty people out there, Madeleine. You have until April to pay back the money you owe me. I'll accept cash. Or, if you prefer, I'll accept property. I'm ready to renegotiate my offer for Champagne Arsenault whenever you are—though, of course, now that the house has burned down, my offer will be considerably lower than it was."

"I'm never selling to you, Randon. And if you continue to threaten me, I will file a complaint with the police."

"With my friend Inspector Delahey? A good idea. Good afternoon, Madeleine."

Randon left.

Outside, Axel was waiting for him in the car, reading that day's newspaper.

Randon climbed into the passenger seat. "Still standing firm. Brave little woman. I can see what you liked about her. Let's go back to the house."

Axel folded the paper. Randon took it from him.

"Another whore found dead," he read. "She looks familiar. Wasn't she one of Tremblant's girls? Really, I can't believe the police haven't made any progress. Makes me think they know exactly who they're looking for but for some reason they don't want to take him in. Don't you agree, Delaflote?"

Axel didn't answer.

·　　·　　·

Inside the hotel, Madeleine retired to her room and tried to put Randon's visit out of her mind as she plowed on through the paperwork rescued from her father's strong box. The very next day, she met with a man from the company who insured Champagne Arsenault.

"A payout of this size is never straightforward," he warned her as they stood outside the burned-out house. "There will be investigations. It could be months before you get the money to start rebuilding."

Odile Levert was equally gloomy about Madeleine's prospects of quickly getting her hands on any cash. Odile invited Madeleine to join her for Christmas at her Paris apartment.

"Perhaps you should sell to Randon," she said. "Not everything. Just the vineyards on the hill."

"He doesn't want those. He wants the house and the Clos Des Larmes."

Odile and Madeleine both looked at the bottle on the table between them. Three days after the fire, Odile had visited Champagne Arsenault to lend Madeleine her support. With Odile at her side, Madeleine dared for the first time to inspect the state of the caves. They were untouched. They'd endured thousands of years. Two world wars. Of course they could protect their precious contents from a house fire. Madeleine's Clos Des Larmes slept on beneath the ground like Snow White in her glass coffin.

"If we win the *Vinifera* wager," said Odile, "that will be a start to getting you back on track."

"Do you think we have a chance?"

Odile opened the bottle. The wisp of vapor that escaped was like a genie that could grant just one wish.

"I think so."

"I will rebuild Arsenault, Odile. I will."

Odile nodded. "I know."

Later, while Madeleine dozed on the sofa, Odile returned Mathieu Randon's call.

"Season's greetings," he said. "I hope you are enjoying your Christmas holidays. How is my little investment?"

CHAPTER 56

Kelly celebrated Christmas at Froggy Bottom with Guy and Hilarian. On Christmas Day, they opened a bottle of Kelly's first vintage: Froggy Bottom's Blanc de Noirs, Cuvée Kelly.

"I think you should do this," said Guy, handing her the bottle.

Kelly removed the cork with a pop.

"At least we know it's fizzy," said Hilarian, as he mopped some spray from his tie.

Kelly filled three glasses and sat down. Together with Hilarian and Guy, she took a moment for quiet contemplation of the wine in her glass. It looked perfect. Everything she had hoped for. She watched the tiny bubbles busily rising to the surface in neat regular strings. The color was just as it should be: like glossy wet straw. The faint scent of fresh baked bread drifted to Kelly's nose. A hint of apple too.

"Merry Christmas," she chinked her glass against Hilarian's and took her first mouthful. Guy and Hilarian watched as Kelly closed her eyes and let the flavors explode in her mouth.

"Like apple crumble," she said. "It's heaven on earth."

The men agreed. Guy was giddy with relief as he described the complex flavors that came to him. Hilarian was quietly pleased. He felt like a father witnessing his child's triumph in a school game.

"What do you think?" Kelly asked him. "Are we going to win your bet?"

"I'd put money on it," said Hilarian.

But first there was the hurdle of Dougal's legitimate children and the paternity suit. As soon as he'd told Kelly what was going on, Hilarian had swung into action. He'd called an old family friend who knew the perfect lawyer to fight in Kelly's corner. Though the lawyer wasn't able to dismiss the Mollisons' case for removing Kelly from Froggy Bottom out of hand, he was able to stall for time. He discouraged Kelly from taking a DNA test until the last possible moment, explaining that there may not be a need to take it at all. He demanded all sorts of paperwork, which would take the Mollisons and their lawyers months to assemble, giving them precious time.

As Kelly sipped her very own wine over the Christmas table, Hilarian looked at her fondly. But lately he knew he had been looking at her differently, searching for something in her smile. Over the past four years, he had told Kelly many times that she reminded him of Dougal but now he had to admit that he couldn't really see it. There were no features in Kelly's face that were obviously Mollison attributes. Her eyes were hazel where Dougal's had been blue. Her lips were much more generous. Her nose, thank goodness, was nowhere near as big as those of her supposed half siblings. In objective terms, Kelly was lucky not to have any of the Mollison features, but now Hilarian worried what that might mean.

He was no longer sure that Kelly was his friend's daughter. That was the bottom line. And that was why it was so important that Kelly got to represent Froggy Bottom at the *Vinifera* awards before the DNA test took place. Hilarian wanted Kelly to have something that could never be taken away from her. He wanted her to have the sense of achievement that would come from knowing that, whatever happened, she had made an award-winning wine.

"Give me some more of that," said Hilarian, holding out his glass. "This is world-beating stuff, I tell you."

In California, Christina and Greg's Christmas was greatly overshadowed by Bill's attempt to wring more money out of the divorce. Todd had not managed to persuade Bill's lawyer that his demands were groundless. Bill's lawyer had suggested a "compromise" settlement to the tune of several million dollars. Todd had declined to settle on Christina's behalf, hoping that his continued indignation would eventually encourage Bill's lawyer to give up. Bill's lawyer was not giving up. They were going to court. It was a disaster for the television series.

"There's a possibility that you may have to stop filming on location at the villa until this is sorted out," Todd explained.

Greg did his best to cheer Christina but it was difficult. The media had picked up on the lawsuit of course and every day *The Villa*'s press officer turned up with another envelope full of cuttings that Christina didn't want to see. At first, many of the journalists who wrote about the case claimed to be horrified that Bill could make such ridiculous demands on his ex-wife, but, as usual, it wasn't long before other pundits stepped out in Bill's favor. A large part of the general public's interest in Christina was due to her former marriage to Bill Tarrant. There was no doubt that being married to him had enabled her to move in circles she might not otherwise have had access to. Of course he should be able to benefit from her success.

"I can't stand it," said Christina, as she read yet another nasty article written by a bitter ex-husband who'd had to give too much away in his own divorce. "It's like getting divorced all over again."

Greg held her close. "But it's different now. You're not on your own. Whatever happens," he said, "I'm by your side. You've got us."

On Christmas Day he pulled out his trump card.

"I know that you're kind of preoccupied with the lawsuit and all but there's something I've been meaning to ask you. I had meant to ask you in Paris but I got called to Frankfurt. Damn shame because the terrace of that suite at the Plaza Arc de Triomphe would have been the perfect place."

"Greg, will you just ask me?"

He got down on one knee and pulled a box out of his jacket pocket.

"Christina, will you marry me?"

She could only say "Yes."

CHAPTER 57

It was the first day back at work for most people after the Christmas and New Year's holidays. Sitting in the best hotel room the insurance would fork out for her while her case was still under investigation (which was far from being nice), Madeleine's hand hovered over the telephone. The clock on the bedside table seemed to be marking the passing minutes even more slowly than usual. At two minutes past eleven she picked up the phone. It would be two minutes past ten in London. Surely he must be in his office by now.

Even as she dialed his number, the screen on her mobile flickered to life. He was calling her.

"I just heard about the fire," said Piers Mackesy. "Why on earth didn't you call me?"

"It's time to sell my father's collection," Madeleine told him.

Less than a week later, Mackesy drove over from London to help Madeleine inspect her father's private collection for damage.

Before he took over the running of his father's wine import company, Mackesy had traveled all over the world advising the fabulously wealthy on what they should have in their collections and how it should be kept. He still advised Ludbrooks, the auction house, on some of the wine they presented at auction. The way a wine had been kept was of great importance when it came to its value at resale.

On his second trip into the Champagne Arsenault *crayères*, Mackesy was much more subdued than he had been before. Purely professional.

The best of the maison's wine was kept two levels deep. Like Odile, Mackesy was satisfied that the Clos Des Larmes would have suffered no damage due to the fire. Likewise, Constant Arsenault's collection.

"This should keep for another ten years," he said, pulling out a bottle of Petrus.

"I don't want to keep it," said Madeleine. "I want to sell it. Now. I'd like you to tell me how much you think Papa's wine is worth."

Mackesy exhaled.

He looked up and down the racks, as though counting.

"You could get a couple of hundred for one of these, so multiplying by the number here...There's a good few thousand. But by the time you've paid the auction house...and it's a lot of hassle. Wouldn't you rather keep it? Drink it yourself?"

"The insurance may not pay out for months. I can't wait that long. I need all the money I can get. Besides, some of it is worth more than a few hundred a bottle. I want you to look at these again."

Madeleine crouched down and carefully pulled out one of the bottles of Mouton '45. Piers shook his head.

"You said that you were ninety-nine percent certain this is a fake," said Madeleine. "Which means that there's still a one percent chance it isn't. I need a second opinion."

She handed Mackesy the bottle. He moved so that he was standing directly underneath one of the dim, bare lightbulbs that lit the tunnel. He got out his glasses once more and held the bottle close to his face.

"I'm sorry," he said, taking his glasses off and pinching the bridge of his nose. "I can't vouch for this wine, Madeleine. I can't authenticate its provenance. Looking at it again right now, I'm afraid I do have to revise my opinion to say that I'm ninety-nine point nine percent certain this bottle is worthless."

"But..." Madeleine couldn't help herself. Her eyes began to glisten.

Mackesy's mouth twitched. He hated to see a woman cry. Particularly if he was responsible. However obliquely.

"I'm sorry," said Madeleine, accepting his handkerchief to dab at her eyes. "It's just that I was rather relying on the money."

"Well, there's some other good stuff down there. We should be able to realize about twenty thousand pounds."

"That won't even replace the windows," Madeleine sighed. "Oh God."

She slumped against the cold chalk wall of the cave. Mackesy had the urge to put his arm around her but resisted. He handed her the bottle instead.

"I'm very sorry," he said.

"It's OK," said Madeleine, wiping her eyes rather more vigorously. "It was a long shot. Thank you for coming over here. Thank you for looking at this." She put the bottle on the ground, handling it rather less reverently than she had done. Then she leaned over toward Mackesy and kissed him on the cheek. It was the first time she had kissed him since that night in Paris.

Driving his Aston Martin DB4 back to the Eurotunnel later that evening, Piers Mackesy could still feel the touch of Madeleine Arsenault's lips on his face. The light fresh fragrance of her scent filled his lungs when he took out the handkerchief she had borrowed. Sitting at a set of traffic lights, he drifted off into a reverie about the beautiful Frenchwoman, picturing her wet blue eyes as she took in the bad news about her father's cellar. It was too sad.

Mackesy pulled his car over into a lay-by and flipped open his Motorola.

Madeleine was sitting in her badly decorated hotel room when she got Piers's call.

"Had to call you before I go into the tunnel," he said.

They exchanged pleasantries, though Madeleine didn't feel much like chatting to anyone. The thought of God knows how much longer in this shitty hotel was not terribly uplifting.

"Madeleine," he said at last. "I wanted to tell you that I've been thinking about those bottles."

"And..."

"I think I may have been too hasty in my verdict. Having given it some serious thought, I'm ninety-nine point nine percent certain that the wine you showed me today is a genuine 1945 Mouton."

Madeleine blinked in surprise.

"Really?"

Piers took a deep breath. "Yes," he said firmly. "Yes, it is."

"What made you change your mind?"

"Just a feeling," he said.

"So you think I can sell it?"

"Yes. And I would be more than willing to put my name to any letter of authenticity you require. I'm sure that Harry Brown will agree with me and be delighted to put your father's entire collection in his next fine wine auction at Ludbrooks."

"You're serious?"

"I'm going to call him the moment I get off the phone to you. I'm sure he'll bite your hand off for the chance to have it in his catalog. The Chinese and the Russians have been paying crazy prices for Mouton. So, if you're certain you're ready to part with a whole case of it, then we'll get you enough money to rebuild Champagne Arsenault. Are you certain?"

"Am I ever! Thank you, Piers. Thank you. Thank you. Thank you! If you were here with me right now I would smother you in kisses."

"Can I collect next time I see you?" he asked.

"Piers Mackesy," Madeleine scolded playfully. "You have no integrity!"

Harry Brown, head of fine wine at Ludbrooks, practically wet himself with glee when he took Mackesy's call. Brown envisaged an entire auction dedicated to Constant Arsenault's collection. A glossy catalog with a bottle of Mouton '45 on the cover. He pictured the boys and girls at

Sotheby's and Bonhams turning green. But Mackesy persuaded him otherwise.

"I don't think we have time for all that," he told his former colleague. "Madeleine Arsenault is keen to get her hands on the money ASAP. You've heard about the fire, of course. She wants to start rebuilding. So she needs the cash. I'm afraid if we wait too long, we'll lose out to one of the other houses. Possibly even Tajan."

Mackesy paused significantly. He knew that the mere mention of the French auction house would drive Brown insane.

"My suggestion is that you add this case of Mouton on to the end of your next fine wine sale."

"But that's in March. The catalog has already gone out..."

"Call all your big boys and let them know it's coming up. Six weeks or so is plenty of time for any serious collector. They're just waiting for something like this."

"Mackesy, I don't think we'll get the best price if we try to rush it."

"If you don't rush it," Mackesy concluded, "someone else will."

And so Constant Arsenault's case of twelve bottles of 1945 Mouton found its way into an appendix to the list of fine wines to be sold at Ludbrooks in March.

The crowd that attended the fine wine auctions at Ludbrooks had changed somewhat over recent years. When he first started out in the wine trade, Piers Mackesy knew most of the old buffers who shuffled into the wood-paneled room for the sales. And, truth be told, most of them were more interested in trying to work out how much their cellars were worth than buying anything new.

But one by one, these contemporaries of Mackesy's father had passed away (their own collections auctioned in the very room where once they had watched proceedings). Now the auction crowd was altogether different. More cosmopolitan, for a start. To Mackesy's left an elegant woman talked Russian into her mobile phone. In front of him, two men bantered in Mandarin. They all looked so much slicker than the old crowd. No ruddy-faced bon viveurs. In fact, most of them looked as though they never touched a drop. They were collecting wines like small boys collected football cards. Because it was the thing to do. They didn't care what was inside the bottle. It made Mackesy feel a little less guilty about what he hoped would come to pass.

Harry Brown strode into the room like a man who thinks he is about to make history.

"Ladies and gentlemen," he said. "It is my pleasure to present to you today some of the finest wine I have ever had the pleasure to auction during my long and illustraious career at Ludbrooks."

"Get on with it, Harry," Mackesy muttered under his breath.

An hour later, the hammer fell on Madeleine's case of Mouton '45 at five hundred thousand pounds.

"A new record for that wine," the Russian woman observed.

"Yes," said Mackesy. "I believe it is."

"It went to Mathieu Randon," the woman continued. "I recognize his man. I only hope it's the real thing."

Mackesy suddenly felt very hot.

"Would you excuse me," he said, slipping out of the row during a lull in proceedings. He called Madeleine from the lobby at once. Having driven the wine over, she was staying at Claridge's. She couldn't bear to attend the auction herself. Too nervous, she claimed. When Mackesy told her the figure, she whooped. When he told her who had paid it, Madeleine punched the air.

"Yes! I would just love to see his face when he realizes that he's just helped me resist his kind offer to take Champagne Arsenault off my hands! Piers, I owe you a drink," she said.

"A very large one," said Mackesy.

Madeleine's heart was full of joy as she prepared to meet Piers Mackesy for dinner that evening. She'd chosen Petrus at the Berkeley Hotel. A suitably extravagant venue to celebrate such a wonderful result. Five hundred thousand pounds was more money than she had dared to dream the Mouton '45 would raise. Added to that another fifty thousand pounds or so from the rest of her father's collection. Madeleine was well on the way to having enough money to start to rebuild the house, no matter what the insurance company concluded.

Mackesy was waiting for her at the table. He looked handsome as ever, in a gray suit. And smelled delicious.

"Creed."

"Of course."

Madeleine couldn't pretend that she hadn't thought about what it would be like to make love to Mackesy again a thousand times since that evening in Paris. Sitting opposite him now as he told her in comic detail about the characters who had bid for her father's wine, Madeleine felt the temptation more than ever. But tonight he looked slightly tense.

"Are you all right, Piers?" she asked him.

"It's been quite a nerve-racking twenty-four hours," he admitted.

"What do you mean?" Madeleine asked him.

"I mean, if those bottles were '45 Mouton, then I am a Chinaman."

Madeleine narrowed her eyes.

"Your father was an extremely talented winemaker," said Mackesy. "And he was also extremely talented at making wine labels."

"What are you accusing—"

"Madeleine," Mackesy quickly put paid to her outrage, "I have to tell you now. Your father was in league with my old man. They had quite the cottage industry in fake plonk until they fell out over the Facel Vega. Unless I am much mistaken, your Monsieur Randon just paid half a million pounds for twelve bottles I would pass over in Sainsbury's."

"But . . . Piers," Madeleine was simultaneously shocked and delighted. "Why would you do this for me?" she asked.

"Because I have no integrity." Mackesy smiled.

Madeleine had plenty to toast that night. The thought of paying Randon off with money that she had effectively conned out of him was too delicious. It called for a lot of champagne.

At the end of the evening, Mackesy took her hand across the table.

Madeleine shook her head. Mackesy withdrew his hand at once.

"You're right," he said. "We must never be more than friends."

"We should call it an evening," said Madeleine. "I'll see you at the *Vinifera* awards in San Francisco."

"Wouldn't miss it for the world. It's going to be your night."

PART Five

CHAPTER 58

Gerry Paine of *Vinifera* was very excited about the up-coming sparkling wine competition. With two months to go, the contest featured heavily in the magazine, with articles by Odile, Ronald and Hilarian on why they thought that each of their chosen vineyards had the potential to carry the day. Gerry's dream of a "three goddesses in bikinis" cover shot had not come to pass, but there were plenty of great photographs to illustrate the coverage. Kelly was pictured up to her knees in mud at Froggy Bottom. Madeleine posed in the ashes of Champagne Arsenault, holding a photograph of her great-grandmother, making it clear that she had inherited her forebear's tenacity. Christina allowed Gerry to use a photograph of her pretending to press grapes with her feet that had been originally shot for *Villa Living* magazine.

Since he was bankrolling the big prize, Gerry had final say on how it would be judged but he agreed with the three critics that it was important that their peers judge the three wines. From a short list of other critics and wine experts who would be in attendance at the festival, Odile, Hilarian and Ronald were each allowed to choose one judge. Three seemed to be the magic number. Three wines, three sponsors and three judges. Still, even with so few judges to choose, the process of picking the panel took as long as picking a jury, as each critic tried to work out which of his or her peers would be most likely to share his or her taste.

Eventually, however, the panel was chosen. The competition itself would take place on the last day of the three-day festival and the announcement of the result would be the highlight of the grand finale dinner.

Kelly had Hilarian buy her ten copies of the issue of *Vinifera* in which the competition details appeared. She was looking forward to the festival like a small child looking forward to Christmas. Her airline ticket had pride of place on the shelf above the Aga, along with her invitation to the gala dinner with her name written upon it in beautiful calligraphy. She found herself looking at it several times a day, hardly able to believe that in such a short time she would be there in San Francisco, presenting her wine for the judgment of the world.

She had a childish hope that if Froggy Bottom could win the competition, her half siblings would give up their quest to shake the vineyard from her hands. As it was, the lawyer that Hilarian had found seemed to be keeping them at bay, arguing that their reasons for demanding the test were spurious at best.

The only thing to do in the meantime was keep going. Kelly and Guy worked in the vineyard as though they would be there forever. While Hilarian's fellow trustees insisted on holding back funds pending a conclusion to the legal matters, Kelly and Guy were unable to continue with their plans to buy more rootstock, but those vines they already had were flourishing. Guy predicted another harvest as good as Kelly's first.

The four harvests that had taken place since Kelly arrived at Froggy Bottom had been good enough to give rise to four distinct vintages. The first had been called "Cuvée Kelly." The second "Cuvée Guy." The third "Cuvée Hilarian." The fourth was awaiting a name.

"I think we should call it Cuvée Gina," said Guy one afternoon.

Kelly agreed. Thoughts of Gina were with her constantly. The detectives investigating her death had come up with no new leads since they first visited the farm. Lately Kelly had the awful sense that they were about to give up altogether and Gina's murder (for that was what it had to be) would never be solved.

"I miss her so much. I wish she could be coming to San Francisco with us," Kelly said.

"She'll be with us in our hearts," said Guy. "And you're going to bring home the *Vinifera* trophy for her."

CHAPTER 59

Christina's lawyer, Todd, had not managed to keep her out of court. After all the to-ing and fro-ing, Bill's petition had been accepted and a date was set for the two parties to meet and discuss his claims in front of a judge.

This court appearance would be the first time Christina had seen Bill in the flesh since they last went to court for the finalization of their divorce settlement. Though she would have said that she was over Bill (indeed, Marisa would have argued that she was never really into him), there was still something horribly sad about the idea of seeing him on the other side of the courtroom. If only she could have known at that first dinner party that just five years later they would be facing each other like this.

She dressed carefully. Todd suggested that she try to project an air of vulnerable femininity.

"Do you want me to cry?" Christina asked.

"Might not be a bad idea," said Todd.

And so she chose a pale peach-colored suit with beige accessories. She piled her hair on top of her head in a neat and demure chignon.

Greg was with her that morning. He gave her ensemble the nod of approval.

"You look beautiful," he said.

Christina fell into his arms.

"I don't know what I'd do without you," she said.

"I promised you I'd be there every step of the way," he assured her. "Now, because I know in my heart that the judge will say you're going to keep the villa, I'd like to take a couple of moments away from thinking about your loser ex to talk about the show. We're going to do a segment on the *Vinifera* awards, of course. I was thinking it might be nice to have an interview with Odile Levert..."

Christina turned away. "Do you mind if I think about this later, sweetheart? I need to compose myself for seeing Bill in court."

As it happened, Christina didn't have to wait until she got to the courtroom to see her ex-husband. His limousine driver somehow transpired to pull up right next to Christina's own driver in the car park.

"Shit," said Christina when she saw him.

Realizing the problem, Christina's driver asked whether he should move the car to the other side of the lot.

"Yes," said Christina tightly. "And if you could run

over my ex-husband while you're at it, I'd be most appreciative."

Christina was slightly irritated to see that Bill looked as good as he had the first time they met. Recently, three months in rehab had all but repaired the damage done by the hard living he'd indulged in immediately after their split. He looked slim, tanned, relaxed. As he stood on the steps of the courthouse, talking to his lawyer, he was joined by a young girl who Christina recognized as one of the minor players from that movie he made in New Mexico. Wasn't she one of twins? She weaved her arm through Bill's and clung on to him territorially as Christina and Todd walked past. Christina wished that Greg were with her but he had a conference call to make and would be coming later.

Bill and Christina didn't even say hello to each other. Todd made a weak joke. Christina laughed ostentatiously, though she felt far from happy inside.

"What is the worst-case scenario?" Christina asked Todd one more time.

"The very worst case? The judge could award the villa to Bill. But that is the very worst case. It won't happen. Be brave."

Brave? Facing a top Hollywood actor in court was not for the fainthearted. Bill gave an Oscar-worthy performance as he talked about the "spiritual contract" he felt he had entered into when he married Christina and the ambition (hers not his) that had eventually driven them apart. By the time he had finished speaking about his life post-divorce—the depression that had sent him hurtling toward expensive addictions and the costly months in rehab to get him back out again—even Christina felt like she should write him a check. Bill's lawyer summed things up by quoting a huge figure to represent Christina's earnings from *The Villa* and suggested that fifty percent of that total might be a good place to start.

"Imagine the pain suffered by my client every time he sees *Villa Living* on the magazine racks as he waits in line at a drugstore for his prescription medication. The Villa Bacchante was the house in which my client hoped to raise his children."

"Oh, please," Todd groaned.

On the other side of the court, Bill's companion squeezed his arm and looked lovingly into his eyes.

Then Todd stood up.

Once again he reprised the character sketch he had put forward at the original divorce hearings. It was Christina who limped away from that battle, he reminded everybody present. While the divorce proceedings raged, she had spent months living as a hermit. *The Villa* had saved her. She had worked hard to rebuild a career destroyed by Bill's infidelity. Far from being worth more than the figure presented at the divorce proceedings four years ago, the Villa Bacchante was worth far less than Bill had paid for it. He'd been ripped off. It was only worth something now because of Christina's determination. Her hard work. Christina had succeeded in spite of Bill Tarrant. And since Bill had robbed her of the best of her years, the villa was probably all she would ever have.

As he sat down, Todd gave Christina a wink.

"Very best of my years?" she mouthed back at him. "Thanks a lot."

The morning progressed like an episode of *Judge Judy*, with each side claiming the other had inflicted outrageous psychological damage during the course of their single year as Mr. and Mrs. Christina's head was set spinning as she listened to herself being described variously as a saint or a gorgon. She was brave, intelligent and courageous. She was grasping and mean. She wanted to block her ears. She certainly didn't want anyone else to hear the accusations. She hoped that Greg knew every word that came out of Bill's lawyer's mouth was a lie.

Christina turned and looked behind her to see where Greg was sitting, but she couldn't see him. He had promised that he would race to the court as soon as he finished that morning's conference call. Perhaps he'd arrived just too late and the court officials had refused to let him in. Perhaps they decided that there was no space. The back four rows of the court were full of people that Christina recognized as journalists.

At around lunchtime, the judge announced that she had heard enough. It was time for her to retire and consider her verdict.

The deliberations took just over an hour but it was the longest hour of Christina's life. She retired to a small room with Todd. It was hot. The air-conditioning wasn't working properly. There was a fabulous California day beyond the walls and Christina longed to be enjoying it but she knew that was an impossibility. Other, more anonymous visitors to the court sat on benches in the beautiful gardens. Christina and Bill couldn't do that. Her one consolation was that, Todd assured her, Bill's room was worse than this one.

"Like practice for prison," he said. "Which is where your lying ex deserves to be."

Still Greg hadn't showed up. Christina called his mobile. No answer. She left a message asking him to call back as soon as he could. She wanted to speak to him before she had to face the judge again. Just to hear his voice would give her the strength to get through the worst.

At last, the clerk of the court rapped on the door and informed Christina and Todd that the judge would be ready for them in five minutes. They filed back into the courtroom. The public gallery was still full of reporters. Bill and his party took their seats. The urge to look across at him was incredible but somehow Christina managed to keep her eyes straight ahead.

The judge walked back into the room. She was an elegant woman. African-American. In her fifties, Christina guessed from her professional status and her confident and dignified bearing, though with her shining, plump face, she could have passed for a woman twenty years younger.

When Christina had first seen the judge that morning, her heart sank. She had been hoping for a man. Indeed, when she heard Todd say that Judge Tony Henderson would be sitting on their case, she'd assumed she'd got her wish. A male judge would have been easy. Christina could have batted her eyelashes or turned on the waterworks and been guaranteed a sympathetic response (it had always worked for speeding citations) but a woman . . . women always judged one another more harshly. As Judge Toni Henderson walked back to her place on the bench, Christina thought she saw her smile at Bill's attorney.

Had Judge Toni, as Todd had warned in his summing up, mistaken Bill Tarrant for the fine, upstanding hero he'd played in a dozen movies?

"Please be seated," said Judge Toni. "Except for you two, Miss Morgan and Mr. Tarrant."

"I'm going to lose the villa," said Christina to Todd. "I can feel it."

She clenched her fists, feeling her nails digging into her palms. Her legs were shaking as she waited to hear the verdict.

It went in their favor.

"I find for the defendant," said the judge. "The terms

of the original divorce settlement remain in place. It seems to me that Miss Morgan gave Mr. Tarrant two of the best years of her life between their courtship and their marriage. I don't believe she owes him anything more."

A good portion of the people seated in the gallery burst into applause. Still so racked with nerves, it took a moment or two before Christina realized what had been said. In fact, even as Todd high-fived his assistant, Christina wasn't sure she'd won.

"It's yours," said Todd. "The villa's still yours."

"Oh! Oh!" Christina's face crumpled and she started to cry.

On the other side of the courtroom, Bill's face crumpled too. The starlet beside him also looked dismayed.

"She probably hoped she'd be leaving court with a richer man on her arm," Todd observed as Bill pushed his way out of the courtroom with the starlet trotting behind.

Christina posed on the steps of the courthouse for a few pictures, acknowledging wearily that if she didn't stop and pose then, they would take the pictures anyway and they wouldn't necessarily get her best side. Or even try to.

Todd gave a short statement on her behalf.

"My client is quite exhausted after today's proceedings but she is very happy with the judge's decision. Now, if you'll excuse us, Miss Morgan would like to get back to the villa. Running a vineyard is a full-time job that doesn't stop just because you have to go to court."

Todd gave his favorite client a squeeze.

On the other side of the car park Bill Tarrant gave his own interview, which Christina saw on the TV in the back of the limo as she was driven home.

"I didn't know when I bought the Villa Bacchante that it would become such an important part of Christina's life. In fact," he laughed, "I have to say she seemed rather underwhelmed. But listening to my ex-wife in court to-day, I realized just how much the villa and the vines surrounding it have come to mean to her. I underestimated her dedication to the craft of winemaking. Just as I underestimated her in so many ways during our short but wonderful marriage. There's nothing left for me to do but wish her well."

It was so gracious that Christina almost fell in love with him all over again.

"That man is being advised by a real professional," Todd said in admiration.

Christina was subdued. She would never have believed that the Villa Bacchante could be worth so much money, or, more importantly, that it would have become worth so much to her. It was more than a house. It was her life. She closed her eyes and imagined the green of the vines. She would have her wedding there, she decided. Now that this nightmare was over, she and Greg could plan their future for real.

There was much celebrating to be done. Christina invited the entire legal team back to the villa. She called Greg en route. Still no answer.

They got to the villa. She thought she might find him there but his car was gone. Strange.

The celebrating continued until one of Todd's juniors threw up on the patio. After that, Todd decided it was time for everyone to go home. Christina was glad. It had been a very long day. Still she looked forward to raising one more toast to her good fortune when Greg got home.

About half an hour after everyone else had gone, she heard his car crunch into the driveway. Greg walked in, looking considerably less happy than Christina felt.

"Where have you been?" she asked.

"Driving. Needed to clear my head."

"It was my day in court. You said you'd be there. We won, in case you wondered."

Christina got up and walked across to him. She put her arms around his neck.

"I forgive you for not being there. You're here now, that's all that matters."

Greg unwound Christina's arms.

"I don't think I'm stopping," he said.

"Greg," Christina was getting angry now. "What's going on?"

"These arrived by courier today. From Jeremy Fraser. The English tabloid guy. He wouldn't say how he got hold of them but he did say he could keep them out of the papers."

Greg handed Christina the brown envelope. She pulled out the prints contained inside.

"What is this?"

"You tell me. That's Odile Levert, isn't it?"

Christina's mouth dropped open as she looked at the photograph of her and Odile standing on the balcony of her Parisian suite. Christina's sweater was pushed up. Odile had her mouth on Christina's breast.

"Don't worry," said Greg. "This is as far as they're going to go. I've made sure of that. Can't have Middle America thinking their favorite daughter likes girls."

"But—"

"I don't know what else to say. I love you, Christina. But this is too much for me. I wish I were the kind of guy who could get off on pictures of his girlfriend kissing another woman, but I'm not. It just looks like infidelity to me. And in Paris. In the very place I had hoped to propose."

"Greg, I can—"

Greg simply put his hand up to silence her excuses. "I need some time to think about this."

"Not too much time," Christina pleaded.

Greg shook his head. "Maybe it's for the best if we call this done."

CHAPTER 60

The Thirty-fifth Annual *Vinifera* Magazine Wine Awards ceremony was to be the first big event ever held at San Francisco's newest hotel, the Gloria. Situated on the edge of the city's financial district, the fifty-story, seven-hundred-room building, which dwarfed the nearby Transamerica Pyramid, was the jewel in the Gloria Hotel chain's crown.

Like its sister hotel in London, the San Francisco Gloria had a spectacular restaurant on the very top floor, which was called, just like its British counterpart, Montrachet—to capitalize on the good reputation of its Michelin-starred namesake rather than to save on the cost of printing new menus, of course. Meanwhile, the hotel's ballroom was the perfect location for the *Vinifera* awards. The room on the forty-ninth floor was elegant and well thought out. The 360-degree view—from the Bay Bridge to the Golden Gate—was stunning. It was quickly booked out for months in advance.

Vinifera magazine already had a long and fruitful relationship with the Gloria Hotel chain. Elsa Miller, the events manager at the San Francisco Gloria, rolled out the red carpet for Gerry Paine and his team. She was only too delighted to offer a special room rate for the magazine's devoted readers, anticipating a hotel full of discerning guests who definitely wouldn't stint in the bar. Once the deal had been struck, Elsa briefed the head sommelier at Montrachet, who had been imported from London to give the San Francisco restaurant a kick-start. He went into ecstasy as he remembered the sheer volume of wine they had shifted at the dinner following *Vinifera*'s last UK event. All of it top-notch stuff.

The event was duly advertised in the magazine and *Vinifera*'s readers snapped up the chance to spend three nights in San Francisco with the world's best winemakers. The hotel was soon booked out in its entirety. Elsa Miller anticipated a triumph.

Kelly and Guy arrived in San Francisco the day before the *Vinifera* festival started. Six bottles of Froggy Bottom's Cuvée Kelly had already been flown out to California with Hilarian earlier that week to ensure that the wine would have time to recover from the journey before the all-important grand tasting.

As she settled into her thirtieth-floor room, Kelly couldn't help but think how far she'd come since she'd been a mere employee of the Gloria Hotel chain. What a joy it was to be able to lie back on one of the hotel's famously comfortable beds legitimately, though it still made her feel a little naughty. If Kelly didn't look out the window, she might have been in the Gloria on Park Lane. The satin bedspreads, the faux-suede upholstery on the headboard and chairs, even the "limited edition" prints on the walls were all exactly the same.

Guy had the room next door, which was a mirror image of Kelly's. The same fixtures and fittings, arranged on the opposite side of the room.

Guy was determined to make the most of his first visit to San Francisco. Kelly, of course, had been through the city before on her way to the residential part of her viticulture course at UC Davis. But she hadn't had time back then to see any of the sights. Now she wanted to make up for it.

Having unpacked, Guy and Kelly took a walk along the Embarcadero to the famous Fisherman's Wharf. From there they took a ferry to Alcatraz. The legendary San Francisco weather wasn't on their side. Even though it was May, it was as foggy and cold as a November day back home. But Kelly began to cheer up as they crossed the icy water toward the island where so many famous prisoners had been incarcerated. She couldn't help but grin as the Golden Gate loomed into view, like a magical castle appearing from the clouds.

Though why do they call it the Golden Gate if it's always been painted red? she wondered.

Kelly and Guy wandered around lonely Alcatraz in silence, with the other visitors, following the instructions of a recorded tour guide on their headsets. But they shared glances, and when they took off their headphones Kelly found that she was pleased to be able to talk to Guy again. She'd almost missed him for that hour.

Guy had missed her too. It had struck him quite recently that wherever he was, whatever he was doing, his first choice of partner-in-crime was Kelly. He felt calm and happy in her presence. She made him laugh. She seemed to find him funny too. He found her beautiful. More than ever on that boat ride back from Alcatraz as the sea-breeze reddened her cheeks. If kissing her wouldn't have made things so very complicated, with Kelly effectively about to become his boss when Froggy Bottom came out of trust, he might have taken the chance.

They walked back to the hotel from the quay arm in arm. By the time they met Hilarian for tea in the hotel's small city garden, the fog had lifted and the sun was shining. They were in a holiday mood.

"Our wine," Hilarian assured them, "is ready to kick ass."

The first item on the festival schedule was the welcome dinner, but before then, Kelly and Hilarian had an appointment in the hotel ballroom. Gerry Paine had requested that the three women representing the three vineyards take part in a small photo shoot. Though she knew that it was inevitable, Kelly was a little nervous. She hadn't seen Christina Morgan and Madeleine Arsenault in the flesh since the wine fair in London, when the bet was first announced. She had an image of Christina of course. There wasn't anyone in the world who didn't know her face. However, she had no recollection of Madeleine at all but the sight of her shoes covered in bright green puke.

To her credit, Madeleine didn't mention the incident at all when she walked into the ballroom. On the contrary, she was very friendly. She kissed Kelly on both cheeks and complimented her dress.

"This is very exciting, *non?*" Madeleine said.

Kelly nodded. "I've tasted some of your wine before," she said. "Five years ago."

"Then you tasted my father's wine," Madeleine explained.

"I liked it."

"He was a very talented man."

Madeleine had arrived in San Francisco just a couple of hours before the photo shoot, most of which time she spent trying to track down someone who could confirm that her wine, also sent on ahead, had arrived safely and in one piece. After that, she had just half an hour to change out of her jeans and into one of three dresses she had brought with her.

She'd shopped for something to wear in a tearing hurry. She dashed into Galeries Lafayette while she was in Paris visiting the lawyers who were working on the Champagne Arsenault insurance case. She didn't feel in the mood to shop that day. The insurance company was still being sticky. Their investigators agreed that it was possible that the fire had been caused by arson but the local police and fire department said that the case was closed. They weren't looking for any suspects.

And so the insurance payout was still a long way off. And because of that, the hundred thousand prize that Gerry Paine was offering looked more and more appealing. If Champagne Arsenault won, it would mean that Madeleine could continue with her plans to rebuild the house without having to wait for the insurance. It also meant, more importantly, that she could continue to pay Henri and the boys to work the Clos Des Larmes. Madeleine was determined that she would not miss out on a harvest that year.

Though the opening dinner was still a couple of hours off, the lobby of the Gloria Hotel was thronged with photographers. Over the past couple of years, the *Vinifera* Wine Awards had become the kind of event that attracted the paparazzi. It was the latest craze among film stars. You made your money doing movies, and then you became a farmer. In the eighties, the trend had been toward cattle ranching in Montana. These days the fashion was to buy a vineyard and make your own wine. Organic, of course.

The concierge had helpfully provided his favored paparazzi with a list of the stars who would be staying at the Gloria that weekend. Christina Morgan was top of everyone's list. Post–court case triumph, she was still very much in the news.

Christina didn't disappoint. At half past six, her limousine pulled into the circular drive in front of the hotel. Ronald Ginsburg accompanied her, still on crutches. Christina realized what a mistake that was as she found herself marooned on the red carpet for what seemed like an age while the driver hauled Ronald out of the car and he limped around it to join her.

"I'm here as a winemaker," she said to the paparazzo who asked her for her opinion on her ex-husband's attempt to part her from the villa. "I don't want to comment on my private life. Neither do I have any opinion on Bill's engagement to his co-star."

She did however answer a couple of questions about that year's grapes.

"We're going to make a fabulous vintage this year."

Then she posed for some photographs. Christina was wearing a beautiful dress. Zac Posen, hazarded one of the girls at the reception desk. "You can tell by the cut." It clung closely to the contours of her body before flipping out at the knees in a signature Posen fishtail. The pale peach fabric was lent a subtle glitter by the occasional gold thread, which was echoed by the gold buttons down the back. Christina's long blond hair was piled on top of her head in a neat chignon, held in place by a pin decorated with a bunch of gold grapes.

Though she smiled brightly, anyone looking closely would have noticed the shadow of sadness in her eyes. Never before in her life had she felt so keenly the horror of always being at the end of someone's lens. Though she'd burned those Paris photographs, the images would not leave her. And the damage they'd caused seemed to be permanent. She tried to call Greg just before she left for the hotel. He hadn't picked up. He hadn't picked up a single one of the hundred calls Christina had made since he walked out of her house. He'd given her no chance to explain or even to apologize.

Christina could not wait to get her hands on Odile Levert.

But Odile wasn't there.

Of the French team, only Madeleine Arsenault was present. Christina took in the woman's dress. Her shoes. Her hair.

Gerry stepped forward to introduce them.

"Christina, you remember Madeleine."

Madeleine smiled and offered her hand. Christina didn't take it. Instead, her eyes narrowed as she looked Madeleine up and down, slowly, like a girls' school bully. She interpreted Madeleine's smile as having a slight smirk to it. It was a knowing look, Christina decided. Madeleine was Odile's little protégée. There was no doubt she knew all about that night in Paris. In all probability, Odile and Madeleine had timed the arrival of those pictures on the tabloid editor's desk in an attempt to force Christina out of the competition.

Madeleine must be livid that the pictures hadn't made it to publication, thought Christina. Well, she was going to show that French bitch what she was made of.

"Despite everything, I'm here," Christina said out loud.

"Yes," said Madeleine. "Of course you are."

Christina glared at her.

"Ladies," Gerry called. "I need all three of you over here."

He waved his arm in the direction of the set he'd commissioned for the photograph. An archway of vines.

"I wonder if you might consider putting these on. Just a bit of fun."

A stylist appeared with three toga-like garments.

"Not that you need any help to look like goddesses," he said.

"No," said Christina curtly. "That wasn't part of the deal."

"I'd rather not," said Madeleine.

"It'll look a bit silly if I'm the only one," said Kelly.

Gerry was crushed. But the women were not to be persuaded. Instead they arranged themselves in the faux bower in the clothes they had arrived in. Christina made sure that Kelly separated her from Madeleine. Kelly, finding herself in the middle of two such glamorous women, appeared in every frame looking slightly stunned.

Madeleine was a little perturbed by Christina Morgan's odd behavior. She knew that they were competing against each other in the wine challenge but that didn't explain the extent of her froideur, which had basically tipped over into rudeness. Refusing to shake Madeleine's hand. Refusing to stand next to her in the photographs. Even making snippy comments about Madeleine's dress. Christina had been a complete bitch. Thank God Madeleine wouldn't have to see her again until the final night of the festival.

Madeleine retired to her room. The telephone on the bedside table was illuminated to say she had a message. She was expecting something from Mackesy. He had promised to call when he got into San Francisco so that they could catch up over drinks before the opening night dinner. Madeleine did not expect to hear Axel's voice.

"I have to see you as soon as possible," he said.

Madeleine pressed "delete."

The next couple of days were very busy. Madeleine had made arrangements to meet several American wine importers to discuss the possibility of sending part of her first Clos Des Larmes vintage to the States. Mackesy made personal introductions for her in many cases. He, meanwhile, spent much of the weekend in Napa, visiting producers who wanted a distributor in the UK.

At the Gloria Hotel, Guy and Kelly joined the *Vinifera* readers at several grand tastings. They were determined to have fun. There was nothing they could do to change the outcome of the competition now. They might as well enjoy the two days they had to wait for the results.

Hilarian didn't have much time to play. He was on the panel for several blind tastings that weekend. Prizes were to be awarded in every conceivable category of wine: from sherry to Shiraz. Hilarian lent his expertise to the judging of dessert wines in particular. He was after all the Noble Rotter.

Ronald and Odile were similarly occupied. Though Odile had spent part of Saturday in Napa, as a guest of Domaine Randon, she certainly wasn't welcome at the Villa Bacchante.

After the photo shoot and opening dinner, Christina decided it would be best to bow out of the festival until the grand awards ceremony on the closing night. Greg dropped in over the weekend, but it wasn't, as Christina hoped, to tell her that he'd changed his mind. Instead he came with a rented van to take those possessions of his that had been at the villa back to Los Angeles.

Christina attempted to persuade him to stay.

"We need to talk about this," she said.

"I can't," he told her. "Not now. All I keep thinking is that when you accepted my marriage proposal, you did it having slept with someone else just a week before."

And then he left.

Christina threw herself down onto the bed they once shared. She understood now that Marisa had been right about her marriage to Bill. That marriage clearly hadn't been for real. She knew because as she lay on the bed now she could hardly breathe. It was as though one by one her ribs were turning to stone, creating a tomb for a heart that would soon be dead. Her heart was properly broken. That was how she knew she really loved Greg.

CHAPTER 61

The last day of the *Vinifera* Wine Festival arrived. A hundred readers crammed into one of the Gloria Hotel's smaller conference rooms to watch the judging of the extraordinary sparkling wine competition that had been dubbed (annoyingly) the Gloria Cup in honor of a deal Gerry Paine had struck with the hotel chain earlier that month.

The contestants and their sponsors sat in the front row and watched closely as a white-jacketed waiter opened the first bottle and poured out three glasses for the judges, who were seated at a table onstage. The table was covered with a pure white cloth and held nothing but the tasting glasses, some water and a plate of plain white bread.

"Do you think that's ours?" Kelly asked Hilarian. In the glass, the variation in color between the three wines was almost indiscernible. Kelly listened hard as the judges described the bouquet and taste of each wine, but the wines shared many notes in common. It was impossible to tell which wine was which.

While the *Vinifera* readers enjoyed the judges' banter, Madeleine sat on her hands so that she wouldn't worry her cuticles as she listened. Beside her, Odile Levert made notes of her own for an article Gerry wanted describing the atmosphere of the competition. From time to time Odile glanced at Christina Morgan, who had not looked at her at all since they filed into the room.

Christina kept her eyes on the judging panel. Her recent court appearance had given her plenty of practice in ignoring the people around her and she was determined not to acknowledge Odile Levert yet. The moment would come.

The judges indicated to Gerry Paine that they had come to their conclusion.

"Thank you. Well, that's it for now, ladies and gentlemen. You'll find out their verdict tonight when we present the grand prize to the first ever winner of *Vinifera* magazine's Gloria cup."

Hilarian squeezed Kelly's hand reassuringly.

"It's us," said Odile to Madeleine.

"We've got it," said Ronald to Christina.

Christina got to her feet. "I hope so."

"Can you give me a hand?" asked Ronald. Christina asked the chap to her left whether he wouldn't mind helping Ronald up. She was starting to wonder whether Ronald was just using this hip thing as an excuse to grab hold of her.

The Froggy Bottom crew hung back as the other spectators filed out of the room.

"How do you think that went?" Kelly asked anxiously.

Guy was already sniffing at the half-empty glasses the judges had left behind.

"I still can't tell which is which," he said. "Damn, I was convinced that we were wine number one. Now I'm not so sure."

"We were number two," said Hilarian.

"No," said Kelly, picking up glass number three. "It's this one."

"This really isn't getting us anywhere, is it?" Hilarian sighed. "Come on, kids. Time to get ready for dinner."

Alone in her room, Kelly laid her two favorite party dresses on the bed with the intention of deciding between them while she was in the shower. But moments later, she found herself looking out of the window at San Francisco. There had been no fog that day. She could see as far as the Golden Gate. And while she was looking at the view, Kelly remembered a book her mother had read to her as a child. One of the pictures was of this exact vista.

Kelly pulled her mobile out of her bag. Using the phone's camera she took a picture of the view from her window and sent it as a text message to her mum.

CHAPTER 62

The dress that Madeleine Arsenault wore for that evening's *Vinifera* award ceremony was a gift from Odile Levert. Genuine vintage Dior from his New Look collection. Madeleine balked at the tiny waist of the full-skirted black taffeta ballgown but Odile was adamant that it would fit her and she was right.

"I'll try to get it back to you in perfect condition," said Madeleine.

"It's a gift," said Odile. "I think of you as a little sister. I want you to have something to remember me by."

"Remember you by." Madeleine shivered. "That sounds

final. Though perhaps you will never speak to me again if we don't win tonight."

Odile kissed Madeleine on the forehead.

"I should get ready myself," she said.

Madeleine met Mackesy in the hotel bar for a couple of drinks before dinner.

"You look simply stunning," he said.

To complement Odile's gift of a dress, Madeleine had kept the rest of her ensemble understated. She had piled her hair on top of her head. She wore no jewelry except for a pair of small diamond studs that had been a gift from her mother. The lack of a necklace only served to emphasize the elegance of her long neck and delicate shoulders.

Madeleine walked into the ballroom on Mackesy's arm, fantasizing for just a moment that they could walk out of the dinner and back to one room together too. He looked quite unbearably handsome in his black tie.

The atmosphere in the ballroom was full of excitement. It had been decorated to look like the set of a painting by Caravaggio. Each of the round tables was set with an enormous still life of fruit and flowers (lots of grapes, of course) that had been sprayed with gold paint to reflect the fact that *Vinifera* would be awarding its "golden grape" awards that night.

The volume of chatter as old friends and enemies greeted one another drowned out the carefully chosen classical music. Mackesy soon saw a couple of Napa Valley producers he wanted to pay his respects to. Madeleine reluctantly let go of his arm and spent a moment talking to Kelly and Guy from Froggy Bottom. Unlike Christina, Kelly seemed happy to fraternize with her fellow competitor.

"That's an amazing dress," Kelly commented.

"You look very lovely yourself," Madeleine replied. "Both of you."

Guy pulled at the collar of his rented shirt. Kelly was dressed in green. Her lucky color, she explained to Madeleine.

"It really emphasizes her eyes," said Guy.

Madeleine felt warmed by the obvious affection Guy had for his colleague and Kelly's resulting blush.

But it was as though the temperature dropped when the Domaine Randon crowd walked in. Madeleine found herself turning to look for Axel as if he'd sent her some telepathic call. Her eyes lit on Randon paused in the doorway. Axel stood to his right. They made such a dramatic picture, two tall elegant men in tuxedos, that the entire room was a little quieter for a moment.

"Wow, he's good-looking," said Kelly, nudging Madeleine. "The one with the black hair. Do you know who he is?"

"Oh yes," Madeleine nodded curtly. The pose in the doorway convinced her that Axel's transformation into Randon's heir was all but complete. "Actually, I need to have a word with him," she said. "Will you excuse me?"

There was no point waiting. Madeleine walked right up to the Domaine Randon party. Axel's expression was surprised. Mathieu Randon, however, greeted Madeleine with a wide grin. Like they were the best of friends. He opened his arms. "Madeleine Arsenault, how lovely to see you here. Representing your little champagne house for the very last time."

"Monsieur Randon," said Madeleine. "You're a bit premature. I think I have a few good years in me yet."

"If you'd like to stay on at Champagne Arsenault after it changes hands, then I'm sure we can consider the possibility. But I should tell you I employ only the best for Domaine Randon. I'll have to ask Monsieur Delaflote here to give me his opinion on your talents as a wine-maker."

"Well, as you know," said Madeleine, "Monsieur Delaflote is of the opinion that I am no vigneronne."

She met Axel's gaze directly. He gave the slightest shake of his head.

"But that's beside the point," Madeleine continued. "I do believe you and I have some business to conclude, Monsieur Randon."

"Ah yes. I can take the money you owe me from the price I'll give you for your burned-out champagne house, if you like."

"Actually," said Madeleine, "I was going to ask you whether you would prefer cash or check?"

"You've got the money?"

"You seem surprised. I had a windfall. I sold some of my father's cherished wine collection at auction earlier in the spring. Mouton '45. I believe you have a penchant for that vintage."

Randon's face remained almost expressionless but Madeleine saw his pupils contract before he turned and began to talk to someone else as though she had never been there.

Madeleine shrugged. She turned to look for Mackesy. Axel caught her by the arm.

"I need to speak to you," he said.

"I don't need to speak to you. Don't you see I deal directly with your boss these days? I talk to the organ-grinder, not the monkey."

"Do you really think he's going to leave you alone if you give him that money, Madeleine? He means to have Clos Des Larmes whatever he has to do to get it. Trying to humiliate him like that? You just put your head in the noose."

Madeleine snorted.

"Look, I know what he can do. We need to talk about this more, but not here. I'm going to slip out after the entrées have been served. You do likewise. We'll meet in your room. I can't risk going back to mine. What is your room number?"

"My room? Why would I tell you?"

"Because you need me now. You need to hear what I've got to say."

"You work for Randon, Axel. Why should I trust you?"

"Because I love you."

"I love you."

Madeleine just stared at him as he repeated the words that she had longed to hear when they lay side by side in bed five years before. Now she could only assume that he was dropping those words out as some sort of trick. He had treated her with such disdain. For the past five years he had worked for a man whose only source of pleasure seemed to be to threaten Champagne Arsenault. And yet . . .

"I mean it," Axel said. He took both her hands in his and squeezed. And as he did so there was seriousness in his eyes. Something that couldn't be faked. "Go back to Mackesy now," he said. "But meet me in your room later. I need to get out of this, Madeleine. We need each other."

"It's 3709," she told him.

"Thank you."

The guests had been instructed to take their places. Mackesy looked at Madeleine quizzically as she took her seat beside him.

"Your friend Delaflote looked a bit agitated," he said. "I expect he's desperate because I have you and he doesn't."

"You don't have me," Madeleine reminded him. "You have a wife."

"Sometimes you're such a pedant." Mackesy smiled.

As the waiting staff began to swirl around the room setting amuse-bouches on the plates of every guest, Madeleine glanced behind her to the Domaine Randon table. Axel was sitting two places from Mathieu Randon. He had a woman on each side. He didn't look terribly desperate about anything right now. Madeleine decided that when Axel left the ballroom to meet her, she would remain exactly where she was.

CHAPTER 63

Kelly found herself sitting next to Gerry Paine. Like Madeleine Arsenault and Ronald Ginsburg, he had been kind enough not to mention the circumstances of their first meeting at the London wine fair. Until now.

A waiter accidentally dropped a couple of peas in Gerry's lap as he placed a serving dish on the table.

"It's nothing," Gerry insisted as he flicked the peas onto the floor. "No need to worry. On the other hand," he turned to Kelly, "I think you still owe me some money for a dry-cleaning bill."

Gerry let Kelly go pale before he made it clear it was just a joke.

Hilarian watched Kelly and Gerry Paine from a few tables away. He'd winced on her behalf when he saw her sit down next to the silly man, but after a few minutes Kelly seemed to have recovered herself and she and Gerry were chatting amiably.

"Your little girl has really grown up these past few years," said Ronald Ginsburg as he squeezed himself into the seat next to Hilarian. "I'm looking forward to seeing if you've made a winemaker of her."

"I think you'll be pleasantly surprised," said Hilarian.

"I hope not," said Odile as she sat down on Hilarian's other side. "I still intend to collect on this bet we made. Anyone want to raise the stakes while we still can? One hundred thousand sterling each?"

Hilarian and Ronald gawped at Odile.

"Have you gone insane?" Hilarian asked.

"No. I wouldn't suggest it if I didn't know who was going to win."

"You think you're going to win?" Ronald was aghast. "Oh, Odile. You are a very silly girl."

"If you think I'm so silly, Ronald, you'll be happy to raise your stake. Or are you just blustering to cover up the fact that you're scared I know exactly what I'm doing?"

"Er, guys," Hilarian interrupted them. "We're not really going to raise the stakes, are we? I mean, as it stands, whoever wins tonight will walk away with one hundred and fifty grand, including Gerry's prize."

"Hilarian," said Odile. "You look nervous. Do you want out?"

Odile pulled her checkbook out of her bag. She filled in a check for a hundred thousand pounds but left the payee blank.

"The money is in my account," she said. "Come on, boys, double or quits."

Their conversation was cut short when Gerry Paine popped his head between Hilarian and Odile.

"Looking forward to hearing the results, boys and girl?"

"I am ready to wet myself," said Hilarian.

Christina's guest for the evening was Marisa. Their table was full of people who had made big donations to ISACL for the chance to sit near Christina Morgan, but she wasn't interested in making small talk with anybody. Instead, she huddled close to Marisa and argued with her about the best way to confront Odile that night.

"Just a second," said Marisa. "What was the name of the guy who sent Greg the pictures again?"

"Fraser. It was Jeremy Fraser."

Marisa pouted her bottom lip as she considered the name.

"Wasn't it Fraser who handled that French girl who fucked Bill?" Marisa mused.

"Yes," said Christina. "It was."

"And who set that up?"

Christina's eyes automatically flickered toward the Domaine Randon table.

"Have you considered that maybe Odile doesn't know that the photographs were even taken?" Marisa asked.

"They're friends," said Christina. "They set me up together. Jesus, I thought that Randon might have given up on getting his revenge on me by now."

"What do you want to do?" asked Marisa. "I can have someone look into it tomorrow and find out for sure whether Randon's involved."

"Oh, he's involved," said Christina. "I've never been more sure of anything."

Axel hardly touched his entrée. Instead, he moved the food around his plate while he waited for the perfect moment to make his exit. From time to time he glanced over at Madeleine, hoping to catch her eye. But he didn't. He hoped it was because she understood the importance of being subtle and was doing a very good job of watching Axel's movements without alerting anyone to the fact.

"Excuse me." While Randon was deep in conversation with a senior guy from Galaxy, the world's largest wine and spirit company, Axel slipped away. He practically ran to the elevator and headed straight for the thirty-seventh floor. He found an alcove with a view of the door to Madeleine's room and waited there.

But she didn't come. Fifteen minutes later and Axel was still alone. He worried now that Randon would have noticed his absence from the table. How much longer would Madeleine make him wait? This was taking subtlety too far. Twenty minutes. Twenty-five...

Axel waited thirty minutes before he gave up on her. It didn't matter anyway. He didn't have to tell her what he knew before he did what was right. Axel knew exactly who had torched Champagne Arsenault. He'd transferred the money to Mick Tremblant's offshore account. Axel knew Randon thought he had him over a barrel. Randon knew about the prostitutes. Hell, Randon had set some of the meetings up. But what did Axel care if the whole world found out what kind of guy he was? Only the opinion of one woman had ever mattered to him anyway. He'd loved Madeleine Arsenault since he was a child.

He knew that going to the police was a dangerous move. He was as guilty of arson as the sidekick of Mick's who lit the match. There were other things too that would have to come out. Stefan Urban, he hoped, would vouch for Axel's good character and explain the difficulties of working for a man with a talent for intimidation like Mathieu Randon. Jean-Christophe, the winemaker, could attest to the threatening atmosphere at the champagne house. And even if a court didn't excuse Axel for his weakness in the face of Randon's bullying, and chose to send him down, still it would be worth it to see Randon destroyed.

It started now.

Axel opened his Motorola and dialed France. He called the office of the serious fraud squad in Paris and began the tale.

"Where are you now, Monsieur Delaflote?" asked the woman who took his call.

He gave her his exact whereabouts.

"Thank you for your call. I'd advise you to stay where you are. We will be in touch with you very shortly."

Axel closed his phone and exhaled in relief. He took the memory stick containing a backup of his computer files from Maison Arsenault and slipped it under the door to Madeleine's room.

CHAPTER 64

Axel Delaflote rejoined the Domaine Randon table just as Gerry Paine announced that it was time to present *Vinifera*'s "Wine of the Year Awards." A ripple of excitement spread through the diners, both those who had submitted wines for judging and those who had taken part in the judging panels.

Odile, Hilarian and Ronald alternately nodded their

approval or bitched as the winners in each category were read out. Ronald had been on the judging panel for Bordeaux-style reds.

"Are you going senile?" Odile hissed at him when the winner in that category was read out.

"Got your period again?" Ronald asked when he heard the winners in Odile's speciality.

But both Odile and Ronald were quietly impressed by Hilarian's choices in the "stickies," as the ultra-sweet wines were called.

"At last," said Gerry. "The moment we have all been waiting for. At least, the moment that I have been waiting for. As you know, almost five years ago, I came up with the idea of a contest for three of my favorite wine critics..."

"Here we go," said Ronald.

"I forgot it was all Gerry's idea," said Odile.

"...I challenged them each to find and champion a sparkling wine from that year's vintage. Odile Levert championed Champagne Arsenault of France."

"Of course it's of France," said Odile testily. "It's champagne."

"Ronald Ginsburg chose the Villa Bacchante of California's own Napa Valley."

"Are you going to split your winnings with Gerry if you come out on top?" Hilarian asked Ronald as he remembered how Ronald's sponsorship of Bacchante had really come about.

"Hilarian Jackson of England chose Froggy Bottom."

Hilarian looked over to Guy and Kelly, who were now sitting side by side. He gave them the thumbs-up.

"And so, five years later, each of the vineyards has released its vintage and today, in *Vinifera*'s first ever Gloria Cup competition, they were compared side by side in a blind tasting by some of the wine world's most distinguished palates. The results are in." Gerry waved three envelopes. One bronze. One silver. One gold. "And I'd like to invite *Vinifera* columnist Odile Levert onto the stage to make the presentation of this year's bronze medal."

Odile got to her feet. "The moment of truth draws ever closer."

She strode across the stage to a very satisfying round of applause and took the bronze-colored envelope that Gerry held out to her.

"Here goes," she said. "This year's bronze medal in the Gloria Cup goes to ..."

She ripped the top of the envelope and pulled out the slip of paper inside.

"The Villa Bacchante for its Carneros Blanc de Noirs!"

Odile led the applause as Christina Morgan rose from her seat and walked up to the stage, weaving through the tables with all the elegance and assurance her years on the catwalk afforded her. The sequins on her platinum-colored dress caught the light and gave the appearance of a curious kind of aura. She looked like a goddess. Half a dozen men jumped up to help Christina climb the stairs.

"Congratulations," said Odile as she handed Christina the trophy and leaned in to kiss her cheek. "Well deserved."

"As is this," said Christina, stepping back from Odile's embrace and landing a stinging slap right across her face.

The crowd gasped.

"What was that for?" Odile managed.

"Ask your friend Monsieur Randon," said Christina into the microphone. "Hey, Randon. How many kids have died in your factories since I saw you last?"

CHAPTER 65

"Delaflote," said Randon, talking over his shoulder. "Get my lawyer on the phone."

"Get him yourself," said Axel.

"What?"

Randon swiveled in his chair to face Axel head-on.

"I just resigned," Axel said.

Up onstage, Marisa tried to persuade Christina to give up the microphone. Shaking uncontrollably, Odile returned to her seat.

"You must have given her a terrible rating," said Hilarian.

"I have no idea what her problem is," said Odile.

Ronald squeezed Odile's hand. "Time of the month, I expect." For once, Odile didn't upbraid him for suggesting as much.

Onstage, Marisa finally wrested the mic from Christina's hand and pushed her behind the curtains at the side of the stage.

"I smell a writ," said Marisa. "We'll deal with this later."

In the glare of the spotlights, Gerry Paine swiftly moved proceedings along.

"The silver award will be presented by Hilarian Jackson," he said.

Madeleine was so busy watching the commotion Christina Morgan's outburst had caused at the Domaine Randon table that she didn't hear her name being called.

"Champagne Arsenault's Clos Des Larmes."

"It's your moment, darling," Mackesy kissed her. "Get up there."

"Thank you," said Madeleine, as she accepted the congratulations of a hundred people on her way to the stage. "Thank you."

"Bloody hell," said Kelly. They were the first words that came to her when she realized that since Christina and Madeleine had already been ranked, there was only one possible winner left.

"My God," said Odile to Hilarian. "I owe you a hundred thousand pounds."

Hilarian didn't argue as Odile wrote his name on the check, though he wasn't certain they had actually officially raised their stakes.

"I've got to go now," she said. She planted a kiss on his cheek and one on Ronald's too. "Make sure you pay up, Ronald. I love you both."

"Is she all right?" Ronald asked. "Now, Hilarian, I think you'll find I didn't actually agree to a hundred thousand."

"Forget it," said Hilarian. "You're needed up there."

Onstage, Madeleine tipped the champagne glass–shaped trophy toward the crowd as though proposing a toast. Mackesy tipped his glass back at her. Then she looked out into the crowd for Axel. She had a sudden urge to receive his congratulations too. But she couldn't see him. Everyone at the Domaine Randon table was on their feet, but not to give Champagne Arsenault a standing ovation.

"Mathieu Randon?" asked the first detective, recognizing Randon from an old interview in *Vinifera*. If he hadn't been on duty that night, Detective Madden would have loved to have been at the festival as a guest.

Axel felt his heart leap. He couldn't believe his call to the fraud squad had been acted upon so quickly.

Randon confirmed his identity.

"We need a word," said Detective Madden.

Finally, Ronald Ginsburg made it up onto the stage. He opened the gold envelope with the best sense of ceremony he could muster, given that he already knew what the note inside said and its implications for his bank account.

Kelly and Guy leaped up together. Kelly threw her arms around Guy's neck.

"This is for us," she said. "You and me."

On her way to collect the trophy she danced in the aisle with Hilarian. She planted a big kiss on Gerry Paine's cheek. She had another for Ronald. And a final one for the check.

"Thank you." She waved the trophy and her check in the air. "I can't begin to tell you how much this means to me. Froggy Bottom saved my life."

The guests at the Domaine Randon table missed Kelly's impassioned speech.

"Mr. Randon," said Detective Madden. "We're very sorry to have to interrupt your celebrations tonight. I have here a warrant for the arrest of Axel Delaflote. I understand he's one of your employees."

Axel got to his feet automatically but there was nowhere to run.

CHAPTER 66

And so to the real highlight of the winemakers' year. The business was over. The results were in. The climax of *Vinifera*'s wine weekend, for the professionals, was the private party in Montrachet at the top of the Gloria Hotel. Downstairs in the ballroom, the paying punters danced and played air guitar to Bon Jovi, unaware that some of their fellow dinner guests were headed upstairs for Ronald Ginsburg's exclusive little shindig. It was the wine world's equivalent of the *Vanity Fair* Oscar bash.

When she reached the hotel's fiftieth-floor restaurant, Madeleine Arsenault was delighted to discover that one of the best tables by the windows had been reserved for the Champagne Arsenault team. Not that she had a team in tow. Odile had disappeared. Madeleine guessed she must have been gathering herself after that awful moment with Christina Morgan. Mackesy too had made his excuses. An important call from Europe, he claimed. Madeleine guessed it must be his wife.

Madeleine searched the room for someone she might sit down with but found no one she felt like talking to then. She was confused about what had happened to Axel. As far as she could tell, the entire Domaine Randon party had left the hotel.

Looking out over the glittering lights of San Francisco, for the first time that day Madeleine's thoughts turned to home. Champagne was home, she knew now. As much as it had been when she was just a small girl and Georges was alive and everyone was happy. Georges would have loved this—the triumph of being named one of the best wines in the world. She wished they could be sharing this moment. She wished, more to her surprise, that she could be sharing it with Constant. Her father.

It was almost two o'clock in the morning. The band was playing all the old favorites. Kelly Elson and Hilarian Jackson took to the floor for "Putting On the Ritz." They wheeled around in a comic approximation of the foxtrot like the father and daughter they had become to each other. Kelly squealed as Hilarian threw her into a spin.

Christina Morgan held court on the other side of the dance floor. No matter how good or bad they thought her wine was, every man and woman in the room wanted to talk to the supermodel.

Madeleine suddenly found she was content to be alone. She watched a sailing boat pass beneath the Golden Gate Bridge. She lifted her glass toward the ghostly lights on the boat's mast and silently toasted her father.

"We did it, Papa," she said.

CHAPTER 67

While the rest of the wine world was living it up at Ronald Ginsburg's party, Mathieu Randon was in his limousine, being driven back to the Domaine Randon château in Napa Valley. He didn't feel like partying. Delaflote's arrest had been quite an embarrassment, even if Randon was sure that it would soon prove to be a blessing. Lately, Delaflote had shown himself to be a touch too sensitive for the job of Randon's right-hand man.

When Randon arrived at around one o'clock, the château was empty. The staff had been sent away for the weekend. There were times, like this one, when Randon didn't feel the need to have half a dozen people at his beck and call. Times when he wanted to be completely private.

But he wasn't going to be able to be alone that night. Shortly after the limousine left, another car pulled up to the back of the house. Randon saw the headlights sweep across the garden as he was undressing in his bedroom. This was unusual. The gate at the back of the house was left open during the day for deliveries but with no staff on the premises, it should have been locked shut. Perhaps it was a member of the staff coming back to retrieve something he or she had forgotten. Or to play house. Randon once had a butler pretend that the house was his in order to impress a girl. He'd brought her back, not knowing that Randon was in residence. Randon had sacked the butler and slept with his girlfriend.

But this wasn't a member of the staff, though it was someone Randon recognized. He pulled his shirt back on and went downstairs to play the magnanimous host.

"Odile," said Randon. "What a pleasant surprise."

"I'm very sorry to turn up uninvited," said Odile.

"No, no. I'm glad you're here," said Randon. "Come out to the winery with me. I've been meaning to show you some Mouton '45 I bought at auction in London back in March."

"I heard about it," said Odile, as she followed him across the dark yard. "From the collection of Constant Arsenault."

"Ludbrooks didn't exactly make that clear," said Randon.

"I saw that wine in Arsenault's caves last year."

"Then I'd be grateful if you could confirm its authenticity," said Randon as they entered the winery and he switched on the light.

"I can confirm its *in*authenticity," said Odile. "You must know you were ripped off."

Randon paused. "Really?"

"Oh yes. Piers Mackesy's evaluation of its provenance was guided more by love than his usual good judgment. I have no idea how he got Harry Brown at Ludbrooks to sign off on it. I guess passion makes people persuasive. But you must feel a fool, Randon. Having bought fake wine."

"Well, well, well. I don't like to feel a fool. Young Mademoiselle Arsenault has some explaining to do. The ensuing lawsuit could cost her dearly."

"Cost her Champagne Arsenault, you mean."

Randon grinned. "Of course that's what I mean. I'll have to sue Mackesy and Ludbrooks too, I suppose. But I don't understand why you want to tell me this. Madeleine is your little pet."

"It's just that I would hate for you to go to your grave thinking you'd owned a real Mouton '45."

Randon narrowed his eyes.

"Why are you really here, Odile?"

It went right back to the very first time Odile and Randon met. In Bibliotek. After Randon bawled her out for offering Bollinger, Odile sat in the kitchen shaking. Odette was unsympathetic. Earlier that day, the sisters had argued about something insignificant. Odile was far better at arguing and Odette was still punishing her for having won.

"He seemed like a nice enough guy to me," said Odette.

He certainly seemed to like Odette. Each time she passed the table he patted her on the bottom.

At the end of the evening, Randon left an enormous tip. Odette couldn't keep from crowing about it all the way back to the tiny flat she and Odile shared in St.-Germain-des-Pres.

"And what's more," she said, "he's invited me to a party tomorrow night. Out in Champagne."

"He's a sleazebag. You shouldn't go," said Odile.

"Why the hell not? It'll be full of people worth meeting. I might find someone who can get me a job somewhere interesting. Or become my lover so I don't have to work anymore! You don't think I intend to work as a waitress for the rest of my life?"

"You'll meet other people, Odette. I don't like that man. I hated the way he kept grabbing you by the ass. There's something about him. Something violent. I saw it as soon as he walked in. Like Dad."

"Dad never touched me," Odette reminded her. The subtext was that she didn't believe her father had ever touched Odile either. "But this isn't even about him. You're just jealous that I might have the chance of going up in the world."

"Or getting fucked by an old man who won't remember your name in the morning. Please don't go."

"Odile," said Odette. "Sometimes your jealousy is a real bore. When I have my rich famous lover and my enormous apartment, I shall remind you that you told me not to go for it."

"I'm *begging* you not to go for it," Odile replied. "Not with him."

Odette threw her coat around her shoulders.

"I'm on my way up."

In reality, Odette was on her way out. Had they known it at the time, would they have parted differently, Odile wondered. Would she have told Odette she loved her, despite the way they fought? Would Odette have returned the sentiment?

Her body was found four days later. The dress she had taken from Odile's wardrobe without permission was tattered and torn. Odile identified Odette's body in the hospital. Her beautiful face was ruined. Cut and bruised. Swollen from having been in the water for so long. From that moment on, whenever Odile thought of her sister, she thought of that Halloween mask. White and puffy as a maggot. She hated Odette's murderer for that more than anything.

They couldn't pin anything on Mathieu Randon. Sure, forensic evidence proved that he'd had sex with Odette in a hotel in Reims but he claimed it was consensual and she left straight afterward. The police took his word for it that Odette did leave. The guy on the hotel's front desk said he had a stomach bug that night and spent quite a bit of time in the staff bathroom when he should have been on duty. The CCTV camera that watched the front door was on the fritz. There was footage of Odette walking into the hotel—skipping across the marble floor of the lobby in borrowed shoes—but nothing more after that.

The police concluded they had no reason to hold Randon, a successful businessman. It wasn't even as though he was committing adultery. His wife had died six months earlier. Suicide.

Soon they started to suggest that Odette's death was suicide too. The cuts and bruises were the result of being tumbled in the river after her death. Her stomach contained enough drugs to kill someone susceptible.

"But she had everything to live for!" Odile had protested.

The police psychologist explained that the family of a

suicide victim quite often had no real idea of their loved one's state of mind.

It seemed so obvious to Odile. The hotel where Randon "entertained" her sister that night was owned by his company. Odile had seen the kind of henchmen who passed for staff at Domaine Randon. It wouldn't have taken much to persuade men of that ilk to cover up for him.

But Mathieu Randon walked away with his reputation intact. Still Odile was certain she knew the truth and that one day she would confront him with it.

She knew her revenge would not come soon. She knew that she would have to wait. As far as Randon was concerned, the case was closed and Odile had given up. She left her job at the Bibliotek and moved to London. There she got a job in another restaurant and continued her rise as a sommelier. After that she moved to the buying team of a wine merchant. She got a column in a free newspaper, which was followed by a more prominent column in a regional paper and finally by her column in *Vinifera*.

She changed her surname to her mother's maiden name. There was nothing about her father that she wanted to be reminded of. After Odette's death he acted as though he no longer had any daughters at all. Along with the name change, Odile gradually changed her image. She grew into her features a little. While she knew she would never be as beautiful as Odette, she became what might be called "handsome." She dyed her dark brown hair jet-black. She dressed only in black or cream. She affected an air of mystery. She told no one about her background and didn't correct them when they assumed she must have grand origins.

Five years after Odette's death, Odile's father was knocked down and killed by a car while weaving home from a bar. After that, Odile felt free to visit her mother again. One afternoon, when Odile was walking through the square of her hometown, a good friend from school walked by without even acknowledging her.

"No way! Is it really you?" the friend asked when Odile caught her by the arm. "I wouldn't have recognized you in a million years. You look...fantastic!"

At last, Odile felt confident that Mathieu Randon would not recognize her either.

"Tell me what you want, Odile."

Randon's eyes narrowed.

Odile looked up at the barrels of that year's pinot noir, stacked ten high on the other side of the cellar, while she considered her opening sentence.

"You killed my sister," she said at last.

"Ah yes," Randon sneered. "The Dying Swan. Pity she didn't know how to swim."

Odile realized in that moment that Randon had known who she was all along.

"So maybe I was with your sister when she died. You're an unstable woman, Odile. You drink too much. All you critics do. Who's going to believe an alcoholic fantasist? And you've spent the last ten years as my lapdog. I've got plenty of dirt on you. But how are you going to make this accusation stick? Where's *your* evidence?"

"I don't want to see you in court, Randon."

"Then what do you want? Money? Filthy cash for a clean conscience? That's very nice, I must say. Pretending to be all concerned about your poor sister's memory when all you really want is to buy more shoes. That's what all women want, isn't it? Even the likes of you."

Odile fingered the blade in her pocket.

"You should ask for forgiveness," she said.

"Of you?"

"Of God."

"I didn't know you were a Christian, Odile."

"Not a good one," she told him. "I'm about to break one of the commandments."

Randon cocked his head to one side in bemusement. His biblical knowledge was sadly lacking. He was thinking about adultery when Odile plunged the knife into his chest.

But her aim was not as true as she would have liked. The shock that registered on Randon's face quickly transmogrified into anger as he realized he wasn't dying yet. The knife had been hindered by the thick brocade of the waistcoat he had thrown over his shirt, so that by the time it reached Randon's flesh, it barely had the force to scratch him.

Odile reeled back with the knife in her hand, ready to attack again. With frightening speed, Randon snatched for her wrist and caught it. He twisted that wrist until Odile could not hold on to her weapon anymore.

The knife clattered to the ground. Odile bent to reach for it but Randon jerked her arm up and backwards, causing her to squeal in pain. He yanked her upright and continued to twist her arm. Odile was sure it was breaking. The pain was so bad. So intense.

"You thought you would kill me?" Randon said in faux disbelief. "Really, Odile. That isn't very friendly. After all I've done for you."

Still holding Odile's arm up behind her back, Randon wrapped his other arm around her neck. He pulled her close to him and whispered in her ear, using the tone she imagined he had used with her sister. Soft, almost loving.

"I always liked you. I liked the way you didn't seem to be controlled by your emotions like other women. You were always more like a man. Now I see that you're just like the rest. So highly strung. So prone to outbursts of irrationality. All those years wasted by holding a silly grudge."

He squeezed tighter. Odile tried to keep him from crushing her windpipe with her free hand, but soon the blackness was starting to creep in at the corners of her sight. She knew that she was dying.

"Such a shame," Randon cooed. "Such a shame."

CHAPTER 68

At three in the morning, the *Vinifera* party was still in full swing. Almost everyone was on the dance floor now. Someone had initiated a conga. Kelly and Hilarian joined in immediately. Guy, shy as he was, took a little persuading but at last even he was singing along and kicking up his heels with the rest of them. Soon the partygoers were spinning around the room like a runaway train, with the people at the end of the train suffering whiplash as they weaved in and out of the tables at high speed.

Eventually, Hilarian decided he could no longer keep up. He let go of Kelly's waist and spun off in his own direction, ending up by sitting down rather heavily in Ronald Ginsburg's lap.

"Get up, you ridiculous old drunk," said Ronald, who had been sitting down precisely because he could no longer stand up himself.

"Pot calling kettle," said Hilarian.

He lurched to his feet and tottered dramatically from side to side.

"Goodness," he said. "Clearly I haven't had enough to drink. I have the most terrible case of delirium tremens."

Then the music stopped and so did the conga. Now that she was standing still Kelly also began to get the shakes.

"Whoah!" she said, leaning on a table for support. "I feel really weird."

Weirder still was the fact that when she looked around the room, Kelly saw that several other people were suddenly finding it impossible to keep their balance. Kelly leaned against a wall, only to find that it too was shimmering and shifting. The floor was actually undulating. Like ripples in a pond. Tiny waves. Getting bigger.

"Oh man," she said, half to herself as she sank down on to the floor. "What have I been drinking?"

"Kelly." Guy grabbed her hand and yanked her up again. "It's an earthquake."

Soon the car park was full of bewildered-looking tourists. There was screaming. Car alarms set off by the quake rent the air. The hotel manager, who had run straight outside, kept shouting "Stay calm" though it was clear he had no idea what else to do. Few people had the sense or the nerve to follow official earthquake survival advice, which was to stay put indoors, beneath a door frame or under a table to better avoid falling debris. Guy and Kelly had practically carried Hilarian down twenty flights of stairs.

The evacuation of the Gloria Hotel started quite calmly, but as the earthquake continued to rock the building like a monstrous child trying to shake coins out of a piggy bank, the panicking began. Somebody unhelpfully shouted, "We're all going to die!" which made everyone not yet outside the building quicken their step until some people were running and what had been an orderly walk soon became a stampede.

Christina Morgan's status as a supermodel held no currency in a natural disaster. Pushed along by the sheer weight of people behind her, still in her Rupert Sanderson wedges, she stumbled and fell to the floor. As she fell, she was sure she actually heard her ankle snap. Whatever happened, she found she couldn't get back up.

"Hey! Hey! Somebody help me!" she yelled as the people continued to surge past her, but another tremor shook the altruism right out of her fellow escapees and Christina was left on the floor.

"You have got to be fucking kidding me!" Christina shouted as the building's sprinkler system kicked in and simultaneously shorted the emergency lighting system, plunging the Gloria Hotel into darkness. "Somebody help!"

Madeleine was sitting at the desk in her room, about to see what was on the memory stick pushed under her door, when she felt the first tremor. She wasn't sure what to do. Stay put? She had a vague recollection that you were supposed to stand in a doorway. Or perhaps you were supposed to get into the bath? As a result, she dithered. She was one of the last to leave her room and try to get outside. She was on the thirtieth floor when the lights went out, leaving her to feel her way downstairs in the dark.

"Help!"

She heard the weak call as she got to the seventeenth floor and almost kicked Christina Morgan in the side.

Madeleine crouched down.

"Are you hurt?" she asked the other woman.

"Do you think I'd be sitting here on the floor if I wasn't?"

"Is that Christina Morgan?" Madeleine asked. "It's Madeleine. Madeleine Arsenault."

"Oh great. I suppose you're going to leave me here now that you know it's me."

"Are you crazy?" said Madeleine. "Besides, I beat you in the competition. Give me your hand."

Slowly, slowly, Madeleine helped Christina get to her feet.

"Lean on me," she instructed. "I'm stronger than I look."

Madeleine felt Christina put her weight onto her shoulder. Though she still couldn't see her properly, Madeleine guessed that Christina must be three inches taller than she was and commensurately heavier too.

"Oh, this is ridiculous," said Christina. "You can't hold my weight. You go on down and tell them I'm up here."

Christina's suggestion coincided with another roar from the earth which shook the Gloria Hotel like a baby's rattle. A light fitting fell from the wall behind them.

"I'm not leaving you here," said Madeleine.

This time Christina didn't demur.

"Let's go."

Outside in the car park, those guests who had already made it out huddled together and watched anxiously as the emergency services swung into action. There was a very real danger that the Gloria Hotel would collapse. Guy would have liked to be able to take Kelly and Hilarian farther away from the quivering building but there was really nowhere to go. Behind them, a freeway overpass flipped up and down like a skipping rope. Everywhere was dangerous.

"Do you think there are still people inside?" Kelly asked.

"Alas, almost certainly," said Hilarian.

Ronald Ginsburg was sitting a few feet away from them, taking greedy gulps of oxygen. He'd sobered up fast. Hilarian wandered across.

"Have you see Odile?" Ronald asked.

"I thought she left to drive up to Napa."

"Then hopefully she got out of the city before this started," said Ronald. He wiped at his eyes, which were watery but not just from old age this time. Hilarian realized for the first time that Ronald actually cared about the woman he'd always called the "Frigid Frog."

"I'm sure she'll be fine," said Hilarian. "Hope so."

Piers Mackesy lurched up to Hilarian. "Have you seen Madeleine Arsenault?" he asked.

Hilarian shrugged. Guy and Kelly had no better answer.

"She left the ballroom ages before the earthquake started," said Kelly. "She congratulated me on her way out."

Mackesy was wide-eyed with worry. "I'm going back in there."

"Are you nuts?" said Ginsburg. "Guy, Hilarian. Hold that man down."

"She'll be out," said Kelly. "She'll be out of there any minute. She got out of the fire at her house, didn't she? She knows how to survive."

"We're going to die!" Christina shouted as an aftershock rent the building and another chunk of masonry smashed onto the stairs just ahead of them.

"Don't panic," said Madeleine though now she could smell smoke. She looked back and saw the glow of flames in the stairwell above them. Her thoughts immediately took her back to Champagne Arsenault and the flames that chased her out of her home. The important thing was just to keep going. To keep Christina going.

"Leave me here. You can get out faster. Send the firefighters back in for me."

Madeleine wouldn't do that. She had seen how quickly a fire could take hold. There was no time to fetch reinforcements.

"You've just got to keep walking," she said firmly. "We're on the thirteenth floor now. In a minute we'll be on the twelfth floor. In ten minutes we'll be outside."

"But there's nothing to go on for," Christina said suddenly. "There's nobody waiting for me out there, you know. My fiancé left me because I slept with Odile Levert."

"What?" Madeleine couldn't help but chuckle at the incongruous nature of the confession, given they were fighting for their lives.

"You didn't know?" said Christina.

"Of course not. French people don't talk about their private lives. I didn't even know she liked girls that way."

"Jesus," said Christina. "I can't believe I'm going to my death having just outed someone as a lesbian."

"I won't tell anyone."

"You won't have a chance to tell anyone. We're going to die in here. We're going to fucking well die."

"Will you please shut up and keep walking? There is someone I want to see when I get outside."

Madeleine and Christina were on the seventh floor when the emergency services got to them. An enormous fireman quickly relieved Madeleine of her burden. He threw Christina over his shoulder and effortlessly carried her the rest of the way, emerging from the hotel lobby to give the press *the* photo that would be used to illustrate reports of the earthquake worldwide: the supermodel rescued.

Madeleine was close behind, unharmed but for a couple of scratches.

Mackesy was waiting for her. He enfolded her into his

arms and held her close for a very long time. Madeleine breathed in the familiar scent of him. His had been the face she wanted to see, but now that she knew he was safe, reality was already creeping back in. She pushed him away. It was hopeless. Somehow, realizing how much he meant to her, when she thought she might lose him to the earthquake, only made the fact that she couldn't really have him anyway sting more than ever. She'd been an idiot. He'd never promised her anything because he didn't want to. When the earthquake was forgotten, everything would be the same as before.

"What's the matter?" he asked, pulling her back to his side. "I was so scared when I couldn't find you."

"We can't do this," she said. "We don't have the right to be together. You should let your family know you're all right. I need to make some calls too."

"Where are you going? It isn't safe for you to wander off. You might fall into some crack and break your neck."

"It isn't safe for me to stay here anymore either. I might end up with a broken heart."

"Madeleine!"

Mackesy tried to hold on to her hand but she pulled away.

Madeleine slunk past the journalists, who were already buzzing around, keen to interview her on her part in Christina's rescue. Her thoughts now turned to Axel. Her childhood friend. Her former lover. Where was he? She could see him nowhere in the crowds that huddled in the car park. She found a girl from Maison Randon and asked if she knew anything. The girl shook her head.

"He left before the end of the dinner," she said. "I haven't seen him since then."

It took a while, but at last Madeleine got through to the emergency services hotline.

"Axel Delaflote. D. E. L. A…" she spelled the word out.

"I found him," said the hotline worker, with a faint note of amusement.

"Which hospital?" asked Madeleine.

"None. He's in police custody."

And so "The Big One," the earthquake that California had been expecting for decades, had come at last.

The following morning the sun rose on a very subdued San Francisco as the emergency services continued to search the wreckage for survivors and residents of a city that had been living on borrowed time returned to their damaged homes to salvage what they could. The design flaws that caused the Gloria Hotel to fare so badly would be debated for months and later in court as the residents and partygoers who had suffered injuries as a result sought compensation.

There was damage outside the city too. Tremors had been felt as far north as the Napa Valley. The cellar master at Domaine Randon wept openly when he arrived to inspect the damage there. Three hundred new French oak barrels filled with pinot noir had been shaken free from their "unshakeable" cages. But there was worse to come.

"I think there's somebody under here!" a rescue worker yelled.

CHAPTER 69

Christina had, as she suspected the moment she fell, broken her ankle.

The newspapers all carried the photograph of her being evacuated from the Gloria Hotel. After that she was airlifted to a hospital well outside the earthquake zone. At Marisa's suggestion, Christina issued a statement from her hospital bed saying that she would be making a huge donation to the San Francisco emergency services. She also pledged that she would throw a party at Villa Bacchante for the brave men and women, just as soon as she was well enough to do the catering!

Flowers started to flood into the private hospital where Christina was being cared for. Within an hour there were too many for her room. She authorized the nurses to distribute the excess flowers throughout the hospital and to local seniors' homes. She asked, however, that the cards be delivered to her, so that she might look through the good wishes. She needed cheering up.

And that was how she found out that Greg had sent her flowers.

"I'm sure they were lovely!" Christina said when she called him. "I'm afraid they're probably cheering up the room of some little old lady now."

"That doesn't matter," said Greg. "As long as you're safe. I was so worried. Marisa had to stop me from driving straight up to San Francisco and into all the chaos."

There was a moment of silence.

"Will you come and visit me here in the hospital?" she asked. "I mean, if you're going to be in the area."

"I think I could make a little trip out of my way," said Greg. "I'll see you in half an hour."

"Half an hour?"

She had assumed that Greg was in Los Angeles. In fact, he was waiting by a baggage claim conveyor in the Oakland airport.

Christina was discharged from hospital the very same day but there was no doubt that it would be a long time before she could look after herself properly again. Her housekeeper, Ernestina, said that she was only too pleased to have the extra hours, but Greg said it wouldn't be necessary.

"You think I'm going to miss the opportunity to give you a bed bath?" he joked.

Christina knew that the hard work would begin once she was back home. She and Greg still had plenty to talk about. She'd been unfaithful. Greg was within his rights to be angry with that for a very long time. But now she dared to believe that he would forgive her. She thought she understood what had attracted her to Odile. That horrible need to be validated, to feel that she was beautiful by seeing her worth in someone else's uncontrollable lust for her.

Having lost Greg, she had finally realized that the validation of strangers wasn't worth nearly so much as the steady kind of love he offered. And that Greg saw something more in her than physical charm. Something enduring. Something real.

When Christina told Greg as much, he covered her face with kisses.

"Did you really believe that I wouldn't come back to you?" he said. "I am never leaving you again."

CHAPTER 70

Meanwhile, the Froggy Bottom team returned to England in a strange mood. On the one hand, they were triumphant. They'd beaten the French and the Americans and come home with the cash. On the other hand, their victory at the wine awards had been all but forgotten in the aftermath of the earthquake. And then, of course, there were still tremors to face at home.

Kelly knew she would be flying back to hear whether or not she had to take a DNA test to prove she was Dougal Mollison's daughter.

"It's bad news," said the lawyer.

A week later, a courier arrived at Froggy Bottom with the results of the DNA test. They suggested, with ninety-nine point nine percent certainty, that Kelly was not in any way related to Dougal's legitimate children, which could mean only one thing: she wasn't related to Dougal either. Dougal's true heirs began proceedings to have Kelly removed from Froggy Bottom at once.

Kelly tried to seem brave. She managed not to cry when she first heard the bad news. Likewise, she kept up a stoic demeanor when she relayed the information to Guy. But inside, her heart was breaking. She walked back into the farmhouse and saw the place that had become her home as though she were seeing it for the very first time. But how different this was from the actual first time she saw Froggy Bottom. The Aga that had looked like a relic from a different age seemed so friendly. She stroked the worn-out kitchen table that she'd once pronounced scruffy. The Welsh dresser with its sticky drawers was a treasure to her now. The kitchen chair with the tattered wicker seat. It was all so precious.

Would Froggy Bottom's new owners ever love this place the way she had grown to?

And what would become of her? She was an entirely different woman from the one who had arrived in the middle of the night wearing boots that were perfect for sticky nightclub floors but useless in the mud. Would she have to go back to working as a chambermaid? She couldn't, could she? She spent the night crying into her pillow.

The following morning, Hilarian arrived. He assured Kelly that he had resigned from the board of trustees and would have nothing more to do with Froggy Bottom either. Not only were the Mollisons taking back the farm, they were claiming the hundred thousand pounds that Kelly had won in San Francisco.

"They're a bunch of shits," said Hilarian. "This place will go to ruin without us here. Dougal's children don't know the first thing about wine. It's an absolute disaster. They have made an enormous mistake."

A chirrup from Kelly's mobile interrupted Hilarian's rant.

"It's from my mum," she said with surprise. "She says she's at the station."

Guy drove to the station to bring Marina back to Froggy Bottom while Kelly waited with Hilarian in the house. Hearing Guy beep his horn to announce their arrival, Kelly put down the spoon she had been polishing absent-mindedly for the best part of twenty minutes. When she walked out into the courtyard, Guy was helping Marina down from the Land Rover. Kelly had forgotten how short her mother was. She must have had a hell of a job getting into the passenger seat of such a high car.

At last mother and daughter stood face-to-face for the first time in five years.

"Hello, Mum," said Kelly.

"Hello, sweetheart."

They remained a couple of feet apart, as though an invisible wall still existed between them, until finally, Marina opened her arms. Kelly rushed forward into them and burst into tears.

Still wiping her eyes, Kelly brought Marina into the farmhouse.

"You've already met Guy," she said. "This is Hilarian…"

"Oh hello, Hilarian," said Marina with a smile. "I remember who you are. Hilarian used to visit your dad, Dougal, out in Norfolk. He used to help me tidy up after everyone else had gone to bed."

"Oh God," said Kelly, observing her mother's grin and Hilarian's sudden violent blushes. "Don't tell me you guys had a fling…"

Setting aside his profound fear of medical procedures, Hilarian submitted to allow a swab to be taken from inside his cheek. Kelly gave another and the results of the resulting DNA test were as Marina had suggested. There was an almost perfect match. A ninety-nine point nine percent certainty that Kelly Elson was related to Hilarian Jackson.

"The funny thing is," said Hilarian, as they popped open a bottle to celebrate, "I think I always knew."

They were sitting at the kitchen table in the farmhouse—Kelly, Hilarian and Marina. A little family reunited.

"I've got another surprise for you," said Hilarian then.

464   *Olivia Darling*

He held out a check for two hundred thousand pounds.

"I got this money in a bet that you helped me to win. It's from Odile and Ronald and Gerry. The Mollisons can't touch this. It's yours to do what you want."

Kelly stared at the check.

"You're my daughter. I wasn't around while you were growing up but I want you to know that I will always be there for you from this moment on."

And Kelly knew that he meant it.

All the same, Kelly had to quit the farm. With the knowledge that Hilarian was her father, Kelly didn't even bother to fight. The remaining trustees kindly gave her a month to find somewhere else. During that time she continued to work with the grapes, as did Guy. But he wasn't as enthusiastic as he had been.

A week before Kelly had to leave, the two friends sat together at the top of the vineyard and looked down on Froggy Bottom. Scene of so much happiness and laughter.

"You could stay," said Kelly. "I'm sure that whoever gets to buy this place will want to keep you on. You're the only one who really knows about the grapes here. You are Froggy Bottom."

Guy shook his head. "It's not the place, Kel. *We're* Froggy Bottom. You, me and Hilarian. I don't want to be here if you guys won't be here too. Anyway," he said, "I should go back to South Africa. I haven't been back in over five years. My mum is beginning to forget what I look like."

"How long will you be away?"

"I don't know. Apart from anything else, if I don't have a job here, I might not be allowed to come back. I won't get the visa."

"Are you serious?"

Guy nodded. "It's not so bad. I'll easily get a job in Stellenbosch. It'd give me a chance to do something different. I've done sparkling wine now. I can make a nice big red. It would be a new challenge for me. A bit of cabernet sauvignon. Some merlot."

"You hate merlot," said Kelly.

"Well, maybe if I find some new way to work with it, I'll create a merlot I can actually drink. We've got to see this as an opportunity."

"We?"

"Slip of the tongue," said Guy.

They were silent for a moment, looking out over the vines.

"Though you could come with me," Guy said at last.

"Do you mean it?" Kelly asked him. "To South Africa?"

Guy nodded. "What do you think? Would you go for it?"

"I'd go for it. We could buy our own vineyard there. With the money Hilarian won in the bet."

"Do you want to do that?"

"Oh yes."

Guy and Kelly turned to face each other. Guy looked at Kelly with pure love. It was impossible for him to remember right then that he had ever looked at this woman before him in any other way. The love he felt for her now had completely wiped from his mind the memory of the angry young girl who had made life so difficult.

Likewise, Kelly had no memories of Guy but happy ones.

Guy took Kelly's face in his hands. She felt her stomach leap at the prospect of what was to come. She closed her eyes, as if to allow him the privacy to make his move. A little piece of her offered up a silent prayer. Please let this go right. After so many months. After five years. It would have been too cruel for this kiss not to be perfect.

With her eyes closed, Kelly could still tell exactly where Guy's mouth was. She could feel the air between them crackle as he drew closer. She felt his breath on her face. Warm and soft. Then, finally, his lips against hers. Bumping tentatively. Tenderly. She let her mouth relax. Her lips parted to receive him.

Afterward, they sat back and stared at each other. Thank goodness it felt right. Thank goodness. But for a moment they couldn't speak. It was as though they were stunned. It was Kelly who broke the tension first. She laughed. Guy knew she wasn't laughing at him. He laughed too. With relief. Then he caught her cheeks between his hands again and peppered her face with yet more kisses, which she returned tenfold and delightedly.

It was half an hour before they came up for air. They were lying on their backs by this time, looking up at the clouds that seemed to be forming love-hearts above them.

"I'm going to come with you to South Africa," said Kelly at last. "And we're going to create a fabulous new vineyard. I can't think of anything I want to do more."

"I'll raise a toast to that," said Guy.

EPILOGUE

CHAPTER 71

The news that Axel Delaflote was to be tried for the murder of two call girls—one French and one English—quickly spread throughout Champagne.

It didn't seem quite right. Despite his transformation from a straightforward country guy to a first-class arsehole under the influence of Mathieu Randon, most people who had met him found it very hard to believe that Axel could be capable of murder. Yet it seemed he was. There was CCTV footage of him with the French girl on the night she died and now evidence had emerged that seemed to link him unequivocally with the English girl too.

A black Chanel evening bag, containing credit cards and a driver's license belonging to Gina Busiri, had washed up on the banks of the Marne just days before the *Vinifera* awards ceremony. It was found by a community-minded citizen who took it straight to the police station. From there it was passed on to the detectives running the investigation into Gina's death, who stripped the bag for anything that might offer them a clue. Tucked inside the lining was a business card belonging to Axel Delaflote.

When she heard about Axel, Madeleine was horrified. She decided it just went to show that it was impossible to really know someone, even if they had been part of your life for years. For a few weeks after she first heard about the arrest, Madeleine would wake in the night, feeling chilled by the knowledge. She wondered if the memory stick pushed under her door in San Francisco had been from Axel. She hadn't got as far as reading any of the documents upon it and of course it had been lost in the earthquake. Perhaps it held his confession.

When she heard Axel had been convicted, she cried for days. Gradually, however, the feelings subsided. Life went on. The seasons changed. Two years after her triumph in San Francisco with her first Clos Des Larmes, Madeleine released a second vintage to great acclaim.

A couple of weeks later, Madeleine was spending an afternoon in the vineyards on the hill.

Pausing in her work, she looked up. The sunlight reflected on the windscreen of a fast-moving car caused a flash that caught her attention. She watched the sleek red sports car winding its way through the vineyards toward the village. Toward Champagne Arsenault. Finding no one there, the driver turned his car around and headed up toward the vineyards on the hill.

As it drew closer, Madeleine recognized the Aston Martin DB4. There could be only one driver.

"Just passing through," said Piers Mackesy.

Madeleine raised an eyebrow. "Really? You should have called ahead."

"OK. Not just passing through," he admitted. "I had to see you."

"I suppose I should be flattered but—"

"I'm divorced," he blurted out. "Papers came through yesterday."

"But—"

"I know. I didn't tell you I was doing it. I should have. But I thought you might think I was just saying it to get you into bed. After the earthquake I knew that I loved you but you made it clear that you weren't to be messed around with. You've clearly never trusted me. Why should you? Never had a reason to. I've been a complete dog in my time. Built up quite a reputation. But the way I felt about you was different. I had to do something about it. I couldn't pretend it didn't matter. So I asked for a divorce and actually went ahead with it. Rather surprised myself."

"What should I say?" Madeleine bit her lip. "Does one say congratulations?"

"You don't have to say anything," said Mackesy. "Just kiss me. Now you're allowed."

Madeleine hesitated.

"I knew it. You don't feel the same. I'll go," he said.

"No." She turned and reached for him. "Stay."

It was all the encouragement he needed. He took her hand and pulled her toward him. Madeleine looked into his eyes. He saw her pupils dilate, her gaze soften.

Madeleine made the next move. She cupped her hands around Mackesy's face and brought him closer, shutting her eyes and opening her mouth ever so slightly as she did so. Mackesy followed her cue. Their lips met. Gentle at first but soon there was nothing tentative about it. They were like two teenage lovers, desperate to get enough of each other before curfew and homework and a whole twenty-four hours until they could see each other once more.

"I have wanted you so much," Madeleine murmured into Mackesy's mouth.

They headed back to the house, remaining lip-locked during the drive. Once inside, Madeleine struggled with the buttons on Mackesy's shirt. She ripped off the last stubborn two. Mackesy pulled Madeleine's T-shirt over her head. She shimmied so that her jeans fell into a puddle of denim around her shoes. She stepped out of them altogether and allowed Mackesy to start dancing her backwards towards the bed.

When she felt the edge of the bed against the back of her calves, Madeleine sat down on the mattress. Mackesy dropped her hands and stood a little way off, admiring his lover in all her glory. Madeleine played up to it, adopting a luxuriant pose. She lay back. Her dark hair fanned out across the white linen. Her pale skin and black lingerie made the perfect graphic picture. Mackesy let his gaze drift down her long legs to her shell-pink toenails.

Playfully, Madeleine pointed one of her feet toward him. Mackesy rushed to hold it. He lifted her leg and pressed his cheek against her instep. Then he placed a kiss on her ankle. Another on the sole of her foot, which tickled and made her squeal.

Her eyes were laughing. Mackesy dove onto the bed beside her. They kissed again and soon Madeleine was easing down Mackesy's underpants and taking his erection in her hand.

Mackesy's hands were all over Madeleine's body. He tucked his fingers into the back of her flimsy lace knickers and followed the crease between her buttocks down to the top of her legs. Between her legs.

"Let's get rid of these, shall we?" Mackesy suggested.

Madeleine willingly complied. She rolled onto her back and lifted her hips so that Mackesy could pull the knickers off. But he had other ideas. He took a flimsy side string in each hand and ripped them.

"We'll go shopping tomorrow," he promised her with a grin. Then he parted her legs and lowered his head toward her neatly shaped pubic hair.

Madeleine groaned appreciatively as his tongue touched her clitoris but she couldn't wait any longer. Mackesy was a master of cunnilingus, but Madeleine didn't want to lie back in the pillows right then. She wanted him inside her.

"Come here," she commanded.

Pushing his fringe away from his eyes, Mackesy raised his head.

"Come here."

He pulled himself back up the bed and balanced above her on his elbows.

"I want you inside me," Madeleine said.

She took hold of his penis again. It was harder than before. He wanted her as much as she wanted him. That confirmation made Madeleine's own pulse throb more urgently in response.

He closed his eyes and pressed his pelvis against hers.

"I want to be on top," she told him.

Mackesy duly lay down on his back. Madeleine sat up astride him and looked down into his face. She studied his eyes as though looking one more time for a reason not to do this. She didn't find one. Her own expression relaxed.

"You look beautiful up there," he said, touching her face again.

She was still wearing her bra.

"Take it off," he said.

With a single, subtle action, she freed herself from the black lace cups that had been holding her so prettily all night. Mackesy smiled at the first sight of those fabulous breasts, shaped like a pair of perfect champagne bowls and topped with nipples like small flowers of pink frosting. They were begging to be licked. Mackesy tried to raise his head toward them but Madeleine held him down by the shoulders. She moved so that she was hovering directly above Mackesy's penis. It pressed upward insistently.

Madeleine took Mackesy's penis in one hand and lowered herself down onto it. Her eyes closed automatically as though to see as well as to feel at that moment might be a sense too much. How easily he slid inside her. All the way, so that her buttocks rested upon his hipbones.

Madeleine eased herself up again, her hands back on Mackesy's shoulders for balance. He held her gently by the waist, encouraging her to keep moving. Gradually, Madeleine's rocking grew faster. Her eyes still tightly closed. She let her head hang forward so that her long hair brushed Mackesy's face and chest. The sweet smell of her fine dark tresses filled his lungs.

"Look at me," he instructed her.

Madeleine opened her eyes and locked onto Mackesy's face as he studied hers. Her cheeks were flushed rose pink with exertion. Her smooth lips seemed bigger. Her eyes darker.

Inside her body, Madeleine could feel Mackesy's penis as though it had become part of her. She could feel the pulse of the blood flow that made him harder as she rode him faster.

"Don't stop!" he begged her. She wasn't about to. Madeleine wanted to feel Mackesy lose control.

Determined that he wouldn't be the only one coming that night, Mackesy licked his fingers and reached for his lover's clitoris. Madeleine shuddered with pleasure as his fingers made contact and drew her closer to a climax.

Mackesy's breathing grew ragged. Each time Madeleine's body moved downward, he thrust up to meet her. He grasped her by the waist again, holding her more firmly.

Madeleine threw back her head, exposing her long white throat. All sensation was centered on the point where Mackesy entered her. All she could hear was the rush of blood through her veins.

The excitement finally overtook them. They couldn't wait. They had wanted each other for far too long. Mackesy pulled her down against him, breaking her rhythm. Down, down, down, down, down. Going impossibly deep inside her. She closed her eyes. She groaned.

Mackesy sighed her name as he came inside her. When she finished bucking with her own orgasm, she fell upon him, laughing softly into his shoulder.

"How long before you're ready to do that again?"

CHAPTER 72

The coroner's office could be excused for being overwhelmed. The earthquake—the biggest the state had seen since 1906, had left an enormous workload for the six-strong coroner's team. And so the body of Odile Levert was processed in a somewhat perfunctory manner. Head injuries, the coroner decided. Commensurate with her having been hit by wine barrels dislodged by the earthquake. If anyone suspected foul play, they didn't have time to investigate it.

A long search for Odile's family found no living relatives (her mother had passed away two years earlier). It was Ginsburg who eventually had her body collected from the morgue and arranged for her cremation. *Vinifera* ran a special memorial pamphlet inside the main magazine. It contained some of Odile's most infamous and inflammatory reviews along with tributes from her former colleagues.

Almost two years after the earthquake and Odile's death, Ronald and Hilarian met in Champagne—at Les Crayères in Reims, Odile's favorite restaurant—and lunched at a table set for three. Afterward, they drove up to the windmill near Verzenay and discreetly scattered Odile's ashes around the vines. They knew she'd like the view from up there.

"She used to bang on about it often enough in her column," said Hilarian fondly.

"Did you bring the wine?"

"Of course."

Hilarian opened the boot of the car and fetched out a chilled bottle of Froggy Bottom, Cuvée Kelly.

"She said it was the best in its year."

Ronald raised the toast to their former colleague.

"That girl knew her wine."

CHAPTER 73

Two and a half years after the San Francisco earthquake, for most of the good people of the city, life was entirely back to normal. The horror of that terrible night had faded. Earthquakes were once again just something you thought about when renewing your insurance.

Just one earthquake casualty remained in the intensive care unit of the hospital.

Mathieu Randon lay in a coma. There was no shortage of visitors to his room. In his absence, control of Domaine Randon had fallen to two men. Both of them visited Randon's bedside as frequently as possible, hoping that their would be the face he saw when he came around.

Such loyalty, they had both decided independently, would be rewarded with greater power.

But, so long after the earthquake, Randon still showed no sign of recovering from his injuries.

"I hear he was a really powerful guy," said one of the nurses charged with rolling Randon over from time to time to make sure he didn't get bedsores.

"Don't think he's going to be chairing any board meetings any time soon," said the other nurse, as she bestowed Randon's bum with a gratuitous slap that set her colleague giggling.

"You can't do that! It's disrespectful."

"Just watch me," said the nurse, giving Randon's bottom another smack.

That was when it happened...

"Dr. Levinson! Dr. Levinson! Come quickly." The nurse who had administered the slap ran down the corridor as though the devil were right behind her.

Dr. Levinson cut short his flirtation with the new girl at the admissions desk and raced to his patient's side. The other nurse was standing with her back against the door, as though the man in her care had returned from the dead, rather than just the nearly dead.

Dr. Levinson leaned over his patient and held his breath as Mathieu Randon slowly but quite deliberately opened his eyes.

"Welcome back, Monsieur Randon," said the doctor. "Is there anything we can do for you?"

"Yes," said Randon in perfect English. "I think I'd like a glass of champagne."

ACKNOWLEDGMENTS

Writing this book has been such fun in great part because of the wonderful people I've met during the process. Special thanks are due to:

Peter Hall of Breaky Bottom in Sussex; Annie Lindo of Camel Valley in Cornwall; top sommelier Guy Harcourt-Wood; Marius Latergan of Morgenster in Stellenbosch, Adam Mason of Klein Constantia in Cape Town; Christian Denis of Bollinger; Remi Brice of Champagne Brice; Michael Mackenzie and Laurent Chiquet of Champagne Jacquesson; Simon Berry of Berry Bros. & Rudd; Michaela Baltasar and Philip Lambert of Clos Du Val in California; Tim Ludbrook; Amy Poon; Jack-Olivier Parisot; Mark Williamson; Steven Spurrier; Marguerite Finnigan; Guy Hazel; Victoria Routledge; Serena Mackesy; my agents, Antony Harwood and James Macdonald Lockhart; and my editors Carolyn Mays and Kate Howard, and in the US, Caitlin Alexander, as well as copy editors Justine Taylor and Pam Feinstein. And last but not least, Nat Wilde—a.k.a. "The Lovely Nat." Dear Nat, thank you. You really are lovelier than "an Aston full of shoes" (copyright: Victoria Routledge).

ABOUT THE AUTHOR

Thirty-two-year-old Olivia Darling was born and raised in Cornwall. At the age of eighteen she met an Italian art student in St. Ives and ran away to Tuscany in hot pursuit of him. The love affair didn't last but Olivia's sojourn in Montepulciano inspired a much more enduring passion for Vino Nobile. She lives in London.

In the high-stakes world of international auction houses, fine art experts vie to get the world's most fabulous and expensive paintings into their salerooms. And amid the glamour and money are those who are willing to do anything to get their hands on something...

PRICELESS

The sizzling new novel by

Olivia Darling

Coming from Dell Books in Summer 2010